D1374622

THE SUMMER HOUSE

THE SUMMER HOUSE

MARY NICHOLS

First published in Great Britain in 2009 by
Allison & Busby Limited
13 Charlotte Mews
London W1T 4EJ
www.allisonandbusby.com

A CIP catalogue record for this book is available from
the British Library.

10 9 8 7 6 5 4 3 2 1

13-ISBN 978-0-7490-7984-0

Typeset in 11.5/15 pt Adobe Garamond Pro by
Allison & Busby Ltd

The paper used for this Allison & Busby publication
has been produced from trees that have been legally sourced
from well-managed and credibly certified forests.

PEFC
PEFC/16-33-111
CATG-PEFC-052
www.pefc.org

Printed and bound in Great Britain by
MPG Books Ltd, Bodmin, Cornwall

Born in Singapore of a Dutch-South African father and an English mother, MARY NICHOLS came to England when she was three and has spent most of her life in different parts of East Anglia. She has been a radiographer, school secretary, editor for one of the John Lewis Partnership house magazines and an information services manager for an open learning company, as well as a writer. From short stories and articles for a variety of newspapers and magazines, she turned to writing novels. Mary writes historical romance for Mills & Boon as well as family sagas. She is also the author of *The Mother of Necton*, a biography of her grandmother, who was a midwife and nurse in a Norfolk village between the wars.

www.marynichols.co.uk

Prologue

February 1918

HELEN SAW THE car snaking its way up the hill from her bedroom window. She had been standing there for several minutes contemplating the bleak hillside. The peaks still had snow on them and even on the lower slopes there were a few pockets where it had drifted, white against the blue-black of the hills in winter. The car disappeared for a minute behind an outcrop and then reappeared a little nearer. She knew it was her father's Humber, even from that distance. Cars were so few and far between in the Highlands of Scotland, the arrival of one was an event. The inhabitants of the village would make a note of it, wonder who it belonged to, where it was going. It had been like that when Papa brought her here. Her great aunt, Martha, had quickly silenced gossip, let it be known that Helen was staying with her to await the birth of her baby while her husband was away fighting in France. Whether they accepted that, Helen neither knew nor cared.

It hadn't been too bad at the beginning. Before her bump began to show, she had been allowed to go for walks, to go shopping, to take tea with the vicar and his wife, to dream that Oliver would come and rescue her and everything would be all right again. But as the weeks went by and no letter came from him, she fell into a kind of lethargy, a feeling that it didn't matter what she did, she could not alter anything. 'There, what did I tell you?' Aunt Martha said, not for the first time. 'He's had his fun and now he's left you with the consequences. That's men all over. You didn't really believe all his lies about being in love, did you?' The trouble was she didn't know what to believe and her tears, so copious at the beginning, had all dried up inside her.

No matter how often she went over what had happened, how often she recalled what they had said to each other, she and Oliver, the promises they had made, how safe, almost invulnerable, she felt when she was in his arms, how often she reiterated that Oliver loved her and would stand by her, she could not convince herself any more, let alone Papa and Mama and Great Aunt Martha. They had won.

The car was chugging up the last steep incline now. It would be outside the house in less than a minute and her father would climb out from behind the wheel and come inside. Now her lethargy turned to apprehension. Would he be any less angry, any less obdurate, any less unforgiving than he had been when he left her there? Her father was one of the old school, steeped in class divisions, used to having servants all around him, of shooting and fishing and hunting; of owning most of the village and dictating to its inhabitants, of dictating to her. She had been educated at a girls' boarding school and a finishing school in Switzerland, then lived at home until a suitable husband could be found for her. Getting a job or doing something useful had not even been considered; daughters of earls did not go out to work and they married young gentleman of their own kind. Looking back, it was strange how she had accepted that so easily.

She turned and looked at the room which had been her prison and her refuge for the last six months. It was a solidly furnished room, matching the solidity of the house: an iron bedstead with brass rails, mahogany wardrobe and chest of drawers, a washstand on which stood a bowl and jug and whose cupboard housed a chamber pot. There was linoleum on the floor and a couple of mats either side of the bed. Compared to the luxury of her room at Beckbridge Hall, with its thick carpet, chintzy covers and bright curtains, it was spartan, but she supposed that was part of her punishment. On the bed lay a packed case. It wasn't large; she hadn't brought much with her, just a couple of dresses, underwear, stockings, nightclothes and toiletries. Her aunt had given her dresses of her own to alter to fit as she grew bigger, black and brown in scratchy wool or stiff taffeta. Apart from the one she was wearing she would not take them away with her.

She heard her father being greeted by her great aunt and decided she had better put in an appearance and left the room. At the top of the stairs she paused and looked down. He was taking off his coat and hat. Handing them to Lisa, her aunt's only indoor servant, he looked up and saw her. Perhaps he had not been prepared for the size of her, but he did nothing to hide the disgust on his face.

She came downstairs slowly, hanging onto the banister and watching her feet, which had almost disappeared beneath the bump of her abdomen. At the bottom she looked up at him. He was tall, his bearing aristocratic, his suit impeccably tailored. His hair was greying at the temples and his moustache was already white. Had it been like that six months before? His grey eyes, she noted, were cold. 'Papa. Did you have a good journey?'

He looked her up and down. 'It was damned tiresome. Are you ready to go?'

'Yes, Papa.' He had driven himself the whole way and she knew why. Having his chauffeur drive him up would have been easier, but servants talk and the whole object of the exercise had been secrecy. No one in Beckbridge, no one among their acquaintances, none of their relatives must ever learn of Helen's shame.

'I've arranged an early lunch,' Great Aunt said, leading the way into the drawing room, where a fire burnt. The drawing room and the dining room were the only rooms allowed a fire, however cold the weather, except the kitchen, of course, which was Lisa's domain. Helen had often woken to find a tracery of frost on the inside of her bedroom window.

'Good. You will forgive me for not staying, but it is a long drive. I want to get as far as Edinburgh tonight, if I can. No sense in dawdling.'

No sense at all, Helen thought, but wondered where he was taking her. Not home, not with that bump in front of her to advertise that she was heavily pregnant.

They went into the dining room and Lisa brought in the dishes. Helen ate for the sake of her baby, but the food had no taste. She was glad when the silent meal was over and it was time to put on her hat and a cloak, which concealed her bulging figure better than a coat. Her father took her case from Lisa and put it in the boot. She turned to her great aunt. 'Goodbye, Aunt Martha. Thank you for having me.'

'Goodbye, child.' She pecked Helen's cheek. 'Now you remember what I said. When it is over, put it behind you and be a dutiful daughter. Think of your poor Mama and your husband. Pray God, this dreadful war will be over soon and we can all go back to life as it used to be.'

'Yes, Aunt.' As she settled herself in the passenger seat, she knew life would never be as it used to be. And she had been a dutiful daughter. That was half the trouble. She had even obediently married the man her parents had chosen for her. It wasn't that she hadn't wanted to marry Richard; she had simply been too ignorant to know any better.

Her father settled himself behind the wheel and they set off southwards. 'Where are we going, Papa?'

'To London.'

'London?' She was astonished.

'Yes. There is a clinic there where you can have your child. They are known to be discreet. Your baby will be looked after and placed—'

'Placed! Oh, Papa!' He hadn't changed. He was still implacable. She must give up her child. At the beginning she had argued strongly against it, but Aunt Martha had worked on her every day, nagging at her that she must think of what her poor mother was going through because of her wickedness. She could have more babies. What was so terrible about giving one away to a good home, to someone who really wanted a child? It went on and on, like a dripping tap. She would not have given in if she had heard from Oliver, but there was nothing, not a word.

'Don't "Papa" me. You may thank your mother you haven't been thrown out, disowned. That a child of mine should... If Brandon had lived...' He stopped and shut his mouth tight. Mentioning her brother always put him in a strange mood. Helen had loved her brother and mourned his death as keenly as her parents, but they had never considered that. Immersed in their own grief, they had no time for hers. But Richard had.

It was Brendan's death that had brought Richard to Beckbridge Hall. He felt he ought to tell her parents of their son's last heroic fight; the official notification that he had been killed in action didn't tell them very much. In spite of the sadness of the occasion Richard had impressed not only Helen but her parents with his confident manner and ready smile. They had invited him to stay. He was charming and sympathetic and Helen had liked him, liked the way he turned to her, drawing her into the conversation when her parents might have excluded her. They went riding and walking and talked about anything except the war.

'Will you write to me?' he had asked before leaving and she had agreed. Their courtship had been conducted by correspondence, until he had returned to England on much-needed leave and they met again and he proposed. Her parents had been keen on him, telling her she would never find a better husband: brave, handsome, wealthy, such a charming man and quite a catch. She had believed them. Somehow he managed to get an extension to his leave and they had been married straight away. He had returned to France after a two-day honeymoon and all they were left with were letters. How could you make love by correspondence? She had accepted that, looked forward to each rather impersonal missive and the time when they would be together again. And in the meantime she had continued to live at home.

She had helped her mother run the house with its depleted number of servants, coped with shortages of everything including food, alcohol and coal, not to mention her father's increasingly irascible temper. It was frustration, she realised; he was an ex-soldier and wanted to be out there in the front line, doing his bit, but he was too old and unfit. He was intensely patriotic and would entertain young officers from all the services, offering them baths and meals and often a bed, which would have been all very well in their affluent days before the war, but like everyone else they were having to pull in their belts and such largesse was a struggle to maintain.

'Louise, I am an earl,' he said, when her mother protested. 'We have standards to maintain. Offering hospitality to our boys in uniform is the least I can do, since they won't let me put one on myself.'

'Thank goodness for that,' her mother said. 'But finding extra food is not exactly easy and finding coal to heat the water for constant baths is a problem.'

'So it may be, but I hope I shall never be accused of meanness.'

And so her mother, under his thumb as she always had been and always expected to be, continued to welcome officers based in the area. They would stand on the thick Axminster carpet of the drawing room, listening to her father holding forth about how he would conduct the war, sipping gin cocktails and marvelling at everything they could see, from silver goblets to delicate porcelain, bronze busts to portraits of Hardingham ancestors going back generations. Helen would be politely friendly to them all, treating them all alike. Until she met Oliver.

Sitting beside her grim and silent father, the only noise the hum of a well-tuned engine, she allowed herself to drift back to the previous spring. The war was already three years old and the casualties had been horrendous. Even in the quiet backwater of a Norfolk village they could not remain untouched. Besides Brandon there had been others, some killed, some wounded so badly they would never work again, and some whose minds had been turned by the horror. But in spite of that the daffodils still bloomed, the apple trees in the orchard were covered in pink blossom as they were every year, the migrating birds returned. Had they seen the hell that was Flanders? Some of the men who called at the Hall talked about it. Some were silent, too silent. Helen tried to be cheerful, to make everything as normal as possible, but sometimes she needed to escape. At such times she retreated to the summer house.

It stood in the grounds facing the lake; a wooden building with windows on three sides and a small veranda at the front. When they were children – she and Brandon and her cousin Kathy – they would use it as a changing room to put on costumes before going swimming. It had a padded bench along the rear wall in which they kept a croquet set, a couple of cricket bats and some stumps and bails. Now, sitting beside her father, whose concentration on the road before him was absolute, her mind went back there.

She saw again the young man seated on the bench, propped against the corner smoking a cigarette. He was in the uniform of a Canadian captain. Seeing her, he scrambled to his feet and pinched out the cigarette. He was exceptionally tall, but not gangly. His hair appeared dark brown at first, until a shaft of sunlight coming through the window revealed the auburn streaks. He had crinkly, humorous eyes and, unlike so many of the officers who came to the house, he had no moustache. His smile revealed even, white teeth. 'Lady Barstairs. Am I trespassing? Perhaps I should not be here.'

'No, it is perfectly all right. Do sit down again.'

Being polite, he would not sit while she stood, so she sat down on the bench and he resumed his seat beside her.

'I assume you are one of Daddy's guests.'

'Yes, I came with a pal, who introduced me to Lord Hardingham. He welcomed me, offered me a cup of tea and a bun.'

'He likes to do that. He calls it "doing his bit".'

'And so he is. Makes us feel at home.'

'I'm glad.'

'It's so peaceful here,' he said, looking out towards the lake. A pair of swans swam majestically in the middle surrounded by half a dozen mallards. 'You would never know there was a war.'

'Have you been out in France?'

'I was in the attack on the Somme last year. Took some shrapnel in the thigh and got shipped back here to recuperate.'

'I'm sorry. Does that mean you'll be sent home?'

'No. The job's not finished yet, is it?'

'You are very brave.'

'Not brave, Lady Barstairs.' He laughed lightly. 'Obstinate perhaps.'

'You think we can win?'

'We have to, don't we?'

'You sound like my husband.'

'He's out there?'

'In the Flying Corps.'

'Now there's a brave man! You wouldn't get me up in one of those machines for a king's ransom.'

'Tell me about yourself,' she prompted.

'What do you want to know?'

'Oh, everything.' Why she said that she did not know. She didn't even know his name, nor what kind of man he was, and her parents would certainly not approve of her sitting alone with a man to whom she had not been introduced. They were sticklers for things like that. 'Start with your name.'

'Oliver Donovan.'

She offered him her hand. 'How do you do, Mr Donovan. I'm Helen Barstairs, but you know that already.'

'Yes. I saw you up at the house, talking to an English officer. My pal said you were the Earl's daughter. Say, what's the difference between an earl and a lord? I've heard him called both.'

She laughed. 'A lord is really a baron, a viscount is one step up from that, and from viscount you go up to earl and marquis and then duke, which is the highest. All except the duke are addressed as "my lord". The duke is "your grace" or "my lord duke".

'Oh, I see. And is your husband a lord or something?'

'No, but as an earl's daughter I am allowed to keep my title, even if my husband doesn't have one. Strictly speaking I am Lady Helen. How did we come to be talking about the British aristocracy? You were telling me about yourself. Donovan is an Irish name, isn't it?'

'Yes. It was once O'Donovan. My great grandfather went to Canada during the famine of 1846 to start a new life with his family and he dropped the O. He found work on a farm near Ontario, where my grandfather was born. Grandpa grew up and married the daughter of an Englishman, and by the time Pa was born he had a farm of his own. Pa inherited it. He married Mom and that's when I came along. My folks worked hard to give me a good education and when I left school, I was apprenticed to a motor engineer. I just got through that and was working at the local garage when the war started, so I volunteered. My company looks after the regiment's vehicles.'

'What will you do when the war is over?'

'Go back to it. One day I plan to set up a business selling and servicing motor cars. Believe me, they are the transport of the future.'

'Are you married?'

'No.'

'But you do have a girlfriend?'

He had looked at her a little sideways at that and she found herself blushing. 'No. That's something for the future.'

'You sound optimistic.'

'Best way to be. Aren't you?'

'Sometimes I wonder. There doesn't seem to be much good news, does there?'

'Not from the front. When did you last see your husband?'

'Nearly a year ago now.'

'You must have been childhood sweethearts.'

'Why do you say that?'

'You look so young. You can't have been married very long.'

'Less than a year. And I'll be twenty-one later this year.'

'A whirlwind romance.'

'I suppose you could say that. We had only known each other a few weeks when he proposed, but Richard's father was known to my father and both families were in favour of the match. I hardly had time to get to know him before he went back to France. Sometimes I can't even remember what he looks like.' This had been an extraordinary admission and she had no idea why she made it to a perfect stranger, except he did not seem like a stranger. Talking to him was like talking to someone she had known all her life, from whom she had no secrets. She felt she could tell him anything and he would not judge her.

'It will come back to you when you see him again.'

'Yes.'

'No doubt you have letters from him.'

'Not as many as I did. And they are so impersonal, as if he is afraid—'

'Everyone out there is afraid.'

'I meant afraid to open his heart.'

'Do you open yours to him?'

'No, I suppose not,' she said, surprising herself. 'I don't think he'd like me being over-sentimental. It's not how he was brought up, nor me come to that. Stiff upper lip and all that.' She laughed a little in embarrassment. 'I don't know why I'm telling you this.'

'I suppose because you need to.'

'Perhaps. Please forgive me.'

'There's nothing to forgive.' He paused. 'Do you often come and sit in here?'

'Yes, it's quiet and I like to look over the lake and dream a little.'

'What do you dream of?'

'A world at peace, contentment, children. I was hoping…' She paused. 'It was not to be.'

'They will come.'

'Do you think so?'

'Yes, or what are we fighting for? Just before you came, I was sitting here thinking of my folks and what would be happening on the farm at this time of year…'

'You must be homesick.'

'I reckon I am, but I've enjoyed my time in England, and with people like you and your parents making me welcome, I can't complain.'

'You are welcome, you know. Come again, come as often as you like.'

That had been the beginning. They met frequently after that, sometimes in the house when he was with comrades and they would chat as friends do, sometimes walking in the grounds, but most often in the summer house. It was as if they gravitated there without having to arrange it. She would stroll down there and shortly afterwards he would arrive, or it might be the other way around. They talked a lot and before long she realised she knew this man a hundred times better than she did her husband, whose letters had become less frequent and more stilted, as if he were writing to a stranger – which in truth she was, someone he had met briefly and then left behind. It came to her slowly but inexorably that her marriage had been a mistake, that if she had met Oliver first she would never have married Richard. It was a terrible discovery, made more shocking when she realised she was falling in love with Oliver. They were so in tune with each other, almost as if they could read each other's minds. If they saw each other across a crowded room, their eyebrows would lift and they would smile; it was as if they were alone, as if no one existed for them but each other. And later they would be alone in the summer house.

She tried to deny it, she really did, but it was undeniable. And when he confessed that he felt the same, they fell into each other's arms. Even then they held back from the brink, but it became harder and harder to deny the physical expression of their love. It grew worse the nearer the time came for him to return to France. She didn't know how it happened, but one day when they were trying

17

not to talk about the fact that he was soon to leave her, she found herself in his arms and they were stripping the clothes off each other in a frenzy. This time she did not hold back, did not try to stop him. It was gloriously fulfilling and though she knew she ought to feel guilty, there was no time for that, no time for anything but each other.

Those last few days were a revelation. Every minute they could manage, they spent together. He could arouse her so completely she was blind and deaf to everything but his murmured words of love, his dear face, his robust, muscular body. She gave herself to him wholeheartedly, roused him as he roused her, and gloried in it. It wasn't just the sex; they loved each other.

'You'll tell Richard?' he had asked her the day before he left for France. 'You'll tell him you want a divorce?'

'Divorce?' Such a thing had never entered her head. She had never given a thought to the future. Now it hit her with the force of a blow to her ribs, taking the wind out of her.

'How else can you marry me? And you will marry me, won't you?'

'I don't know how to tell him.' Now she had been forced to confront it, she was left with the guilt, shot through with misery because she couldn't see a way out. 'I don't know how to tell my parents either. There'll be the most unholy row. And you won't be here.'

'I wish I could be. I'd stand by your side and defy the world, but I can't. I have to go, you understand that, don't you?'

'Yes.' She had cried, oh how she had cried! He had comforted her, held her in his arms and made love to her all over again. She clung to him, not wanting to let him go, but it was getting dark and she knew she had to go back to the house and he to his barracks. In the end she had promised she would tell Richard, but not until he came home. It wasn't fair to spring that on him while he was away fighting. They said their goodbyes in the summer house and she went back to the Hall, dragging her feet with every step. She had not seen him again.

She did everything she had always done: she was gracious towards the servicemen who came to visit; helped her mother when the servants drifted away, one by one, to more lucrative employment; went to church and prayed for victory; prayed that Oliver would come safely back to her; prayed, too, that Richard would understand when she told him she wanted a divorce. No one in her family had ever been divorced; it was unheard of in their circles and she knew there would be an awful row when her parents found out. In the end it hadn't been the prospect of a divorce in the family that caused the uproar, but her confession that she was pregnant.

It was teatime and, for once, the three of them were alone in the drawing room. Her mother was presiding over the silver teapot and the bone china cups and saucers; her father was reading a hunting magazine. She suddenly decided to get it over with and blurted out, 'Mama, Papa, there is something I have to tell you.' She waited until she had their attention. 'I'm pregnant.'

'But you can't be,' her mother said, puzzled. 'Richard has been gone a year.'

'It isn't Richard's.'

'What?' her father roared, flinging his magazine on the floor and getting to his feet.

'I said I'm pregnant.' She had looked up at him defiantly, but it took all her courage.

'You dirty little slut! I never thought…' He stopped because he simply could not get his breath and his face had turned purple. She cringed, half expecting a blow. 'Whose is it? I'll kill him. Did he force himself on you? Were you afraid to tell us?' He was grasping at straws and she could have said she had been raped, but she could not do that, could not deny her love for Oliver.

'No, he did not force me. We love each other.'

'Rubbish! You are a married woman. You love your husband.'

'No. I thought I did, but now I know I don't. I intend to tell him when he comes home and ask for a divorce.'

'You will do no such thing. We'll have to get rid of it.'

Her mother had gasped at that. 'Henry, you don't mean an abortion?'

'Yes. I'll find someone willing to do it.'

'No, you will not!' Helen had screamed at him. 'I want this baby.'

'You can't possibly mean to keep it,' her mother said. 'It's unthinkable. What will you tell Richard? What will everyone say?'

She had become reckless. 'I don't care what people say. I shall explain to Richard and when Oliver comes back, we are going to be married.'

'You can't, you already have a husband.'

'Oliver?' Her father picked up on the name. 'Who is Oliver?'

'Captain Oliver Donovan.'

'Where did you meet him?'

'Here. He's one of your protégés, a Canadian.'

'And that's how he repays my hospitality, is it? I shall go to his commanding officer and have him kicked out...' He was pacing the drawing room floor, so agitated she was afraid he'd have a heart attack.

'Henry, I don't think that's a good idea,' her mother said softly. 'We don't want to draw attention to Helen's plight, do we? Perhaps she should go away, she could stay with my aunt in Scotland. We can always say she has gone to be near Richard.'

'He's in France,' Helen reminded her.

'Then for the purpose of saving your good name, he'll have to come back,' her father snapped.

'If you think I am going to get into bed with him and then pretend the child is his, Papa, then you are mistaken. I will not deceive him.'

'You already have.'

'I'm sorry for that, I never meant to hurt him, and in any case I do not think he will be too upset. I don't think he loves me.'

'And what about Richard's parents? His father is a judge, for goodness sake. Have you thought of anyone else besides yourself? To think a child of mine should behave in such a wanton and depraved manner is more than I can stomach.'

'It wasn't wanton or depraved. Oliver and I love each other. He will accept his child. He'll be pleased.'

That was more than her father could take. He ordered her to her room just as he had when she had been naughty as a child, and her meals were brought to her by the chambermaid. After three days of solitary confinement, her mother came to her. She had been writing to Oliver, but put her pen down and covered the sheet with blotting paper.

'Helen, your father and I have made the arrangements.' She sat down heavily on the bed. 'You are to go and stay with my Aunt Martha in Scotland until it is time for the child to be born, and then you will go into a private clinic. You haven't told anyone about this, have you?'

'No.'

'What about Kathy? Does she know?'

Her cousin Kathy lived with her parents in Beckbridge Rectory. She and Kathy had gone to the same boarding school, and as schoolgirls had giggled over shared secrets and later had laughed together over the different young men who came calling. Until Richard came along. She supposed it was bound to make a difference to their relationship; she was suddenly a married woman and Kathy must have felt left out. They had remained friends, though not so close, but even that had come to an end when Kathy had come upon her and Oliver in the summer house. It had precipitated a terrible quarrel; dreadful things had been said, mostly about the effect it would have on Richard if he found out. Helen had tried explaining, but Kathy wouldn't listen and had gone home in a huff. It was then Helen realised that Kathy was in love with Richard. They hadn't spoken since.

'No, I've told no one.'

'Good. And no one will be told. If you want to correspond with Kathy, you can, but you will do it through us. And you will say nothing of your disgrace, do you hear? I could not bear it to become common knowledge.'

'Great Aunt Martha?'

'She knows, of course. But as far as her friends and neighbours are concerned, you are staying with her to await the birth of your husband's baby.' Mama had smiled grimly. 'Not that you will be expected to do much socialising; Aunt Martha is old-fashioned. In her day, pregnant women were kept hidden away.'

'And I am to be kept hidden.' The prospect was not a happy one, but given the atmosphere at home, she would be glad to get away. She would spend her time knitting and sewing for the baby and writing long letters to Oliver. He might even manage to get leave and come to see her, though she realised that was unlikely until the war ended. She prayed it would be soon; if Oliver came back before Richard it would make it so much easier, if only because she would have an ally. 'But what happens when I return home? You can hardly hide a baby.'

'You won't be bringing it home. It will be adopted.'

'No! I will not agree to that.'

'Helen, do not be obtuse. You know you cannot suddenly produce a baby when everyone knows your husband is away in France and has been there over a year. And what do you think he will say when he comes home?'

'Then I shall stay away. Find somewhere else to live.'

'How? What will you live on? You have never wanted for anything in your life, never done a hand's turn of work, and you certainly would not have the first idea how to go about bringing up a child. I can promise you Papa will not help you and I dare not go against him. When it is all over, you can come back here as if nothing had happened. We will none of us mention it again.'

'And keep it secret from Richard, I suppose,' she said bitterly.

'It would be best.'

She knew she was getting nowhere and was tired of arguing. It would be a few more weeks before she began to show and by that time Oliver would have replied to her letter, might have managed some leave. But she hadn't been given even that respite; she had been packed off to Scotland the very next day.

Her father was drawing into a petrol station. She watched while he got out, spoke to the attendant who came out to serve him, paid the man and returned to the car. Then they were on their way again, without either having spoken. They stopped for lunch at a hotel. The conversation was confined to polite enquiries about what she would like to order. Was it going to be like this the whole way? Could she get through to him if she tried? But what was the use? Aunt Martha had been right; Oliver had deserted her. Either that or he was one of the many casualties of war, and without him she could not hope to bring up a child. It didn't matter; she didn't feel anything for it. It was an uncomfortable lump that wouldn't let her sleep at night, that made her want to go to the lavatory every five minutes. She would be glad to be rid of it. So she told herself.

They stayed in Edinburgh overnight. The hotel was luxurious, the bed far more comfortable than the hard mattress at Great Aunt Martha's, but it did not help her to sleep. They left very early the next morning and the pattern of the previous day was repeated. Helen tried to make conversation, to remark on how much warmer it was as they journeyed southwards. She wondered if they might take a little detour to go to Beckbridge, she would have liked to see her mother. But of course Papa would not do that. She could not go home until her figure was back to normal. It was late at night when they entered the suburbs of London and it was then she began to wonder where this hospital was. It was another half hour before her curiosity was satisfied.

They drew up outside a dingy red-brick building in a part of the city she had never been in before. Her father got out and fetched her case from the boot. 'Come along,' he said. 'I want my bed even if you don't.'

Stiff with sitting for so long, she clambered awkwardly from her seat and followed him up the steps. A plaque on the wall announced it was the St Mary and Martha Clinic. They entered a gloomy hall, lit by gaslight. There was a desk and a bell, which he picked up and rang vigorously. It was answered shortly by a young girl in a grey uniform to whom he gave the name of Lord Warren and told her the matron was expecting him. While she was gone he turned to Helen. 'You are to be known as Mrs Jones, please remember that.'

She nodded, not caring what she was called. She didn't like the smell of the place, nor the strange cries coming from its interior. For the first time she began to be afraid of the ordeal to come. 'Are you going to leave me here, Papa?'

'Yes, of course. What else did you expect? I'll go to my club tonight and then I'm going home. When I hear from Matron that it is all over, I shall return for you.'

If he had been going to say more, he did not, because Matron was hurrying towards them. 'Do not address me as Papa,' he murmured.

Matron was fat. She wore a navy blue dress and a wide belt that seemed to cut her in two. Her hair was scraped back beneath a starched cap. 'My lord, please come this way. Would you like some refreshment before you go?' She ignored Helen, who trailed behind them, weariness in every bone of her body, the fight gone out of her. She longed for her mother.

The matron conducted them to an office where the particulars of her pregnancy were noted. She had been sick early on but otherwise had kept well. The doctor she had seen in Scotland had said there was no reason to expect complications; she was young and well nourished.

'And the expected date is the middle of March, I understand?'
'Yes.'

A servant arrived with a tea tray but Helen was not offered any of it. She was handed over to a nurse to be conducted to her room. She turned back to her father, wanting to say goodbye, had his name on her lips when she remembered his stricture that she should not address him as Papa. He had not said so but she guessed he was pretending she was a servant for whom he felt some responsibility. For a second her spirit returned. She straightened her back. 'Goodbye, my lord. Please remember me to her ladyship.' Then she followed the nurse.

Normally patients would not arrive so far in advance of their due date, but her father had not wanted to risk her giving birth in Scotland or on the way to the clinic. She had her own room and was expected to remain in it and take her meals in solitary splendour. That palled after the first day and she asked to be given something useful to do. She was allowed to help the other patients, those who had already given birth, taking them their meals, fetching glasses of water, talking to them. They were mostly young, unmarried and ill-educated. Some had even been ignorant of what was happening to them until their bodies began to swell. Some had been raped, some abused by male relatives. She was appalled. Not one seemed to have a loving partner and not one expected to take their infants out with them. And the nurses were far from sympathetic. What had her father – the man who had given her life, had nurtured her through childhood, a loving, if strict, disciplinarian – brought her to?

Helen's baby, a lovely dark-haired girl, was born in the early hours of the morning of the fifth of March, ten days earlier than expected, and put into her arms. She fell instantly in love with her. The fact that Oliver had deserted her didn't seem to matter any more. She wanted to keep her. She helped bathe and dress her in the little garments she had made for her and was allowed to give her a feed. The pull of the baby's mouth on her breast set her weeping again and strengthened her resolve. This tiny child was hers and she'd be damned if she would give her up. She would call her Olivia.

It was a resolve she was not allowed to keep. Her parents came the very next day to fetch her home. She was so pleased to see her mother she burst into tears and held out her arms. Her mother hugged her. 'Hush, my child, it's all over now.'

'No, it isn't. Look at her, Mama.' She pointed to the crib beside the bed. 'Just look at her. Tell me you don't feel something. She is your grandchild, for God's sake.' Instead of looking at the baby her mother looked at her father, but he was sternly implacable. Helen reached out and plucked Olivia from her cot and cradled her in her arms. 'Look, Mama. See what huge blue eyes she has. And she has such a strong grip. Look.' Helen lifted her hand to show the baby's hand closed tightly around her little finger. 'She is mine, my flesh and blood. I love her with all my heart. I cannot give her up. Don't ask me to, please.'

'Helen, don't be silly,' her father said, while her mother looked as if she was going to cry. Unable to bear the pain she knew her daughter was experiencing, not daring to share it, she turned away.

The nurse who had helped at the confinement entered the room. 'Everything has been arranged, sir. Doctor Goldsmith would like to see you in Matron's office before you go. There are one or two details he needs to go over with you. I'll take the child.' She went to take the baby from Helen.

'No, you don't!' Helen screamed at her. 'You can't have her. She's mine.'

'Helen,' her mother begged. 'Please...'

'Tell them. Tell them I'm going to keep her. Tell them I withdraw my consent.' She was hanging onto the child so tightly the infant began to wail and the nurse looked helplessly at her father.

He strode over and forcibly prised open Helen's arms so that the nurse could take the child. Helen, blinded by tears, saw the blurred form of the nurse disappearing through the door. Her father followed, leaving Helen sobbing uncontrollably.

'Darling, please don't take on so,' her mother said. 'You know it isn't possible to keep her. What's so terrible about giving her away to a good home, to someone who really wants a child and can't have one of her own? One day you will have children with Richard and they will be welcomed. Now be a good girl and let me help you dress. I've brought one of your favourite dresses, the blue and grey striped wool. It will be nice and warm. We don't want you to catch a chill in the car.'

Helen got out of bed and began to dress like an automaton, then flung her few possessions in her case, strangely empty without the tiny garments which had been taken away with her baby. While they waited for her father to come back, she wandered over to the window and looked down on the busy street. Two storeys below her, a woman came out of the entrance carrying a baby. The infant was wrapped in the shawl Helen had knitted for her; even at that distance she recognised it. She beat her fists on the glass and yelled defiance until she was forcibly restrained and given a strong sedative. Under its influence she stumbled out of the hospital, flanked by her mother and father, and got into the back of the car, but she was not so subdued that she didn't vow that one day, however long it took, she would find her daughter again, and then nothing on earth would part them.

Chapter One

1940

THE YOUNG MAN in the hospital bed opened one eye and quickly shut it again. A half smile played about his features. Nice features, Laura thought, unblemished by the terrible burns that many downed pilots had to suffer, but he could do with a shave. And he was so young. She leant forward and smoothed the blond hair from his brow as his eyes opened and looked straight into hers. She smiled and dropped her hand.

'This must be heaven,' he murmured, grinning at her. 'And you are my guardian angel.'

'No, you are still in the land of the living. And I am certainly no angel.'

'You look angelic enough to me.' Beneath the starched cap, she had dark, not quite black hair, swept back and up from a distinct widow's peak. She had warm amber eyes in an oval face with high cheekbones, a straight nose and a firm mouth. Her figure was as good to look at as her face, cinched into a tiny waist by the wide nurse's belt. Her legs, even in stout, flat-heeled shoes, were long and shapely.

'Have you met many angels?'

'Can't say I have.'

'There you are then; not qualified to judge.'

He looked around him. There were twenty beds in two straight lines, each one containing a patient. A locker beside each held a jug of water and a glass; some had a vase of flowers, others a photograph. Some patients were sitting up reading, some had headphones and were listening to the wireless, others lay still and almost lifeless. A few were restless and being calmed by nurses. The rows of windows were heavily criss-crossed with sticky tape. Outside the sun shone, making the same criss-cross shadows on the beds and across the polished floor.

'Hospital?'

'Yes. The Royal Masonic, Hammersmith. Part of it has been taken over by the RAF. There's a doctor here who knows a bit about burns.'

'Burns?' He lifted a bandaged hand and touched his face.

'No, only your hands and they will heal. You won't need skin grafts or anything like that.'

'Thank God for that. Can't have my boyish good looks ruined.'

'No, you're still the same handsome devil you always were.' She smiled. 'You were lucky.'

He grinned. 'What's your name?'

'Staff Nurse Drummond.' She leant over to help him sit up, then picked up a cup of water and put it to his lips. He drank thirstily before sinking back onto his pillow.

'I meant your Christian name.'

'Laura.'

'Laura,' he murmured. 'I like that, it's pretty.'

'Don't let Matron hear you call me that. I'm Staff Nurse and don't you forget it.'

'Staff Nurse is too starchy for someone as pretty as you are. Are you married?'

'No, but I will be tomorrow.' Tomorrow. She could hardly believe her wedding was only a day away.

'Congratulations! He's a lucky dog. Airman, is he?'

'Yes, a squadron leader.'

In normal times this would be her last day at work; a man like Bob would not expect his wife to work and, in any case, the authorities disapproved of married nurses on the grounds that they could not look after patients properly and run a home at the same time. But these were far from normal times and women with no family ties were expected to work. She would have a week off, the same as Bob, and then return to duty, living at home until they could find a house of their own. It really would make no immediate difference to her working life, except for the gold band on her finger and the allowance she got as Bob's wife. The young airman told the whole ward about the wedding and she went off duty with the good wishes of the patients ringing in her ears.

At the door she was stopped by Matron. 'Staff Nurse, a word if you please. Come with me.'

Mystified, Laura followed her to her office and stood uncertainly as she flung open the door and gestured her inside. The room was packed with her colleagues, who clapped enthusiastically. 'We wanted to wish you good luck,' Matron said, bending down to retrieve a package from behind her desk. 'A little something for your bottom drawer to show our appreciation of your sterling service.'

Laura, surprised and delighted, took the parcel and to cries of, 'Open it!' she undid the ribbon. It contained a pair of sheets and pillowcases.

'Thank you, thank you so much,' she said, overcome by their generosity.

Dr Gibbs produced a bottle of sherry. A strange collection of glasses was found and a toast drunk. By the time she left an hour later, she was surrounded by a warm glow of goodwill, helped on by the sherry. Clutching her parcel, she set off for the Underground and home.

It was a balmy evening; the sun was just going down behind the rooftops, throwing long shadows across the road. It could have been any evening in peacetime, except for the barrage balloons swaying lazily overhead, the sandbags stacked round doors and the taped-up windows. And the uniforms. Almost everyone seemed to be wearing one of some kind: khaki, navy, air force blue or the green of the Women's Voluntary Service. There was even a Boy Scout in a khaki shirt and shorts, cycling down the road, pedalling for all he was worth.

Laura took the Underground to Edgware and walked the rest of the way to her home in Burnt Oak. She let herself in and carefully drew the curtain over the door before switching on the light and hanging up her cloak and gas mask on the coat stand in the corner.

It was a typical three-bedroomed semi-detached house. The stairs went up on the left and there was a narrow passage on the right with two doors. The first led into a sitting room, which contained a three-piece suite, a table with a lace cover, on which stood a vase of flowers, a glass cabinet for displaying ornaments, a bookcase each side of the fireplace and a mirror over the mantelpiece. It had a square of carpet surrounded by lino. The second door led to the dining room. That had a dining table and chairs, a sideboard and a cupboard in the chimney alcove. Beyond that, facing her, a third door led to the kitchen. Here, her mother was putting an iron over her wedding dress.

Unlike Laura, who was tall and slim, Anne Drummond was tiny, a little plump and she had fine blonde hair, very different from Laura's dark locks. 'You've done that once already,' Laura said, kissing her cheek.

'I had to press mine so I thought I'd give it another going-over. Go and hang it on your wardrobe while I make tea.' It had proved almost impossible to buy clothes or even the materials to make them and Anne's dress was a blue silk she had had in her wardrobe for ages and hardly worn. It was outmoded but they had altered it to bring it up to date, something everybody who could use a sewing machine and a needle was doing. Coats were being made into jackets, dresses into blouses, men's trousers into boys' shorts.

'Did you manage to order the flowers?'

'Yes, but they couldn't guarantee what they'd be. They said they'd do their best.'

'That's all right. Just so I have some. They gave me some bed linen at the hospital and the woman who puts the Hammersmith emblem on all the hospital sheets and pillowcases embroidered our initials on them. Wasn't that a lovely thought?'

'Yes. Put them in the front room with the other presents. There's more come today. Everybody in the street seems to have brought something. And our friends at the church.' Anne was a regular churchgoer, though Laura, being so often on shift work, did not attend so often. She had gone the previous Sunday to hear the banns read for the last time.

'Oh, how kind everyone is. I didn't know I had so many friends.'

Her mother had been shocked when Laura told her Bob had proposed, saying she hardly knew him, that he was a pilot and could be shot down at any time, making her a widow before she had had time to be a wife, that he came from a completely different background and she could not see Bob's hoity-toity parents agreeing to it. Laura had countered that she had known Bob for six months but it seemed like forever, and as for the war, everyone had to take risks and seize what happiness they could when they could. And as for Bob's parents, she wasn't marrying them. It was said confidently, though she did wonder how she would fit in with his lifestyle. She had always watched the pennies, made her own clothes and never had a fire in her bedroom; economies like that were second nature to her, and nowadays everyone was being urged to do the same, but did that include a wealthy baronet and his wife? What was the point of worrying about it? 'Bob loves me and I love him,' she had said. 'Please, please be happy for me.'

Her mother had pulled herself together and smiled. 'If you are happy, then I'm happy.'

'That's all I ask. It won't be an elaborate wedding; it wouldn't be right, what with the war and everything. I'll buy some material and make myself a dress.'

'You can have my dress. I kept it for you.'

'Did you? I didn't know that. Will it fit?'

'We can alter it.'

Laura had hugged her impulsively. 'You're the best mother in the world, you know that, don't you?'

'Oh, give over.'

On her way upstairs, she went to look at the gifts. They were small, inexpensive presents for the most part and most were useful things for the home. Besides the sheets and pillowcases she had been given by her colleagues, there was a glass fruit bowl and six little dishes; a set of fruit spoons; a matching teapot, milk jug and sugar bowl; two vases; a tablecloth; more pillowcases; two towels and a framed picture. She was overcome by how generous everyone had been. All carried cards of good wishes, and Laura had made a list so that she could write and thank them all. In contrast, there was a huge punchbowl and glasses from Bob's sister, whom she had yet to meet. It was kind of her, but Laura wondered when she would ever use it. There was nothing from his parents, though they had not gone so far as to boycott the wedding, sending a formal acceptance of the invitation. She supposed they had given their present to Bob.

She went upstairs and hung the dress on the wardrobe door, standing back to admire it. Mum had had to shorten it for her own wedding, but she had kept the spare material. They had joined it back on with a wide band of lace and used more lace to trim the bodice, then narrowed the wide tops of the leg o' mutton sleeves. Laura was thrilled with the result. The veil was spread over the mirror of her dressing table and her shoes were standing side by side beneath it. She smiled, picturing Bob as she walked up the aisle towards him. He would be in uniform, of course, his cap tucked under his arm, smiling at her with love in his eyes. And Steve, as fair as Bob was dark, would be beside him with the wedding ring in his pocket. Already her nerves were beginning to tingle.

Still smiling, she returned to her mother in the kitchen, where a batch of newly baked sausage rolls cooled on a wire tray. Even the butcher had been kind; as well as the sausages, he had found them some ham, sliced very thinly to make it go round. And her mother had managed to get a little dried fruit and a couple of eggs and made a cake. It was only eight inches across and two inches deep but they hid it under an iced cardboard cake borrowed from the local baker.

They had barely sat down to eat when the siren wailed. Anne got up, covered the sausage rolls and put them on a shelf in the larder, then set about gathering up everything they needed for a night in the Anderson shelter: blankets, pillows, a torch, some matches, a packet of sandwiches and a Thermos flask of tea. She also grabbed a little attaché case in which she kept their birth certificates, her marriage licence, the rent book and a few precious snapshots and mementoes. 'If we are bombed out, we'll need to prove this is our house and we are entitled to be re-homed,' she had told Laura, who had never seen the case before the raids started.

In spite of the warmth of the day that had gone before, the shelter struck them as dank and airless. Seven pounds it had cost them for a few sheets of curved corrugated iron and some bolts. They had made a big square hole in the back garden lawn and assembled it, covering it with the turf they had dug out, though it didn't go all the way over the top. After putting a couple of deckchairs and an oil lamp inside, they had left it and there it had stood, unused, mocking them for months when the threatened air raids failed to materialise. Now it was in constant use.

They made sure the door was secure before lighting the lamp and settling down in the chairs. Anne had brought some knitting and Laura a book to read. But far from concentrating on those, their ears were attuned to the noises outside. They could hear the distant hum of aircraft, though whose they were they could not tell, and the sporadic sound of an ack-ack gun, and then, far away, a kind of *crump*. None of it sounded very close, but it was more than they had heard before.

Anne unscrewed the Thermos and poured two cups of tea. 'Might as well have this while we can.'

Laura sipped hers reflectively, wondering if Bob was in the skies above her. She never thought of her own danger, only that of the man she loved. 'Please God, bring him back safely,' she prayed over and over again. Due to the losses, some from sheer exhaustion,

Air Chief Marshal Sir Hugh Dowding had ruled that pilots must have a minimum of eight hours off duty in every twenty-four and a continuous twenty-four hours off every week, which meant they could leave the base. Bob always made for Burnt Oak and Laura. Sometimes they went dancing, sometimes to the pictures if it was an evening or, if it was daytime, they would walk in the park or listen to a lunchtime piano recital, or take a meagre picnic into the country. They had not been able to see each other quite so often lately; he had been in the air almost every day, at night, too, if the weather was clear enough for bombers to see their targets, but he phoned when he could to reassure her he was in one piece and couldn't wait to make her Mrs Rawton. And tomorrow it would happen.

She had asked Bob about his sister being a bridesmaid, but he had said she wouldn't be able to get leave from the WAAF and so Nurse Bradley, one of Laura's colleagues, was going to be bridesmaid instead, and she was providing her own dress. Her mother was going to give her away. Bob's parents thought it was a strange arrangement but Laura would not go searching for male relatives she hardly knew to take on the role. Everything was ready but the nearer the time came, the more nervous she became.

God forbid that Bob was shot down or she was caught in a raid, which would be the ultimate disaster. She would not let herself think of those, but there were minor problems that occupied her mind as well: the flowers not arriving, the ceremony being spoilt by an air raid, or dissension among the guests, who would be a very mixed lot. Her father's mother and sister, who had never got on with Anne, had not even bothered to reply to the invitation Laura had insisted on sending them, which had prompted her mother to say she wasn't at all surprised; they were an unforgiving lot, a statement that puzzled Laura. There would be a few of her mother's friends from the church she attended, some of Laura's schoolfriends, colleagues from the hospital and friends of Bob and his parents. He had taken her to see them the last time they had a whole day off and she had sensed they didn't approve of her.

His father, Sir Peter Rawton, was all right, but Lady Rawton had been so snooty, looking down her nose and asking probing questions, trying to catch her out. She had felt like a naughty schoolgirl and, being uncomfortable, she had behaved like one, too, blushing and stammering and dropping her serviette. When she had bent to pick it up, the crumbs had slid off the plate she had on her lap onto the thick carpet and she had made matters worse by falling to her knees to try and pick them up. 'Please do not bother,' Lady Rawton had said in her cut-glass voice. 'We have servants to do that.' If it hadn't been for Bob, smiling sympathetically at her, she would have left there and then.

Was the gulf so great between her background and Bob's that it could not be bridged? It was stupid, she told herself. Class snobbery went out with the last war, or it should have done. Or was it simply a question of wealth: theirs and her lack of it? Bob had dismissed her fears as nonsense and so she tried to tell herself that was exactly what it was: nonsense. But she dreaded to think what her mother would make of them when she met them at the wedding. Mum could be very outspoken and could give as good as she got when occasion demanded. And she'd have no truck with snobbery. Laura was glad the proposed meeting of parents had not taken place; everyone had been too busy.

She sighed and opened her book just as the all-clear sounded. It was nine-thirty. They gathered up their belongings and trooped back into the house. Everything was as it should be. People were coming from their own shelters and returning indoors or emerging from the brick shelters along the road and hurrying to wherever they had been going when caught out by the siren. There was no damage that they could see and Laura and her mother wondered aloud where the bombs had fallen. They made themselves a cup of cocoa and went to bed.

The squadron had scrambled at four o'clock and climbed high into the sky above the cloud cover. For several consecutive days enemy bombers had come over in larger and larger numbers, determined to wipe out the country's air defences. The weather had been far from ideal, but many had got through and dropped their bombs. It seemed to Bob that they hadn't been at all sure of their targets, because, though many landed on the airfields and did tremendous damage to buildings and aircraft, others landed in the countryside and some on the London suburbs. It was this aspect that worried him most. Laura was in London. He couldn't wait to make her his wife and take her away for a few days – a few days in which, apart from the more pleasurable things associated with a honeymoon, he would persuade her to get out of London.

The cloud was thick and they couldn't find the enemy, even though they knew they weren't far away, and after half an hour they were recalled; the Stukas had dropped their bombs wherever they could and were on their way home. Bob was relieved. He was on standby until ten and then he could leave the base and go home to Maida Vale from where he would go to his wedding. His mother was far from enthusiastic about him marrying Laura, but he had been unshakeable. She would welcome Laura into the family or she would lose her son; it was as simple as that. He had hated doing it to her, but the idea of giving Laura up was so far out of the question he would not even think of it. She was his love, his life, his very existence and without her, he might as well give up and let Jerry shoot him down in flames. Mother had given in and agreed to attend the wedding. She had even promised to smile and try very hard to like the girl with whom he had chosen to share his life. His father, who liked Laura, had simply shrugged his shoulders as if pandering to his wife was the extent of his ambition. It was strange when you considered he was good at his job, a man of decision, a man respected by everyone at the Ministry from Lord Beaverbrook down.

He taxied to a stop, left his Hurricane to his ground crew, who would refuel it, and strolled back to the dispersal hut with Flight Lieutenant Steve Wainright.

'Not long to go now,' Steve said, as they flung down their helmets and shrugged themselves out of their flying jackets. Bob was still doing his job, still leading the squadron, but he was on tenterhooks and Steve supposed it was wedding nerves. Bob was more than his squadron leader; he was his best friend, as close as a brother considering what they went through together day after day.

Bob looked at his watch. It was almost nine o'clock and not yet dark. 'Nineteen hours and I'll be standing at the altar. God, I'm nervous. It's worse than my first solo flight. Have you got your speech ready?'

'Yes, word perfect.'

'Tell me what you're going to say.'

'No fear. You can wait to hear it with everyone else. Have you written yours?'

'Not exactly. I know it begins "My wife and I..." Then after everyone has had their laugh, I just have to thank everyone and sit down. You don't think she'll change her mind, do you?'

Steve laughed. 'Not a chance!'

'Steve, if anything should happen to me—'

'What, between now and two o'clock tomorrow afternoon?'

'No, afterwards. When I come back to ops. You'll look after her, won't you?'

'Don't be daft.'

'I mean it. I'm an old hand now and old hands are few and far between. The odds—'

'Shut up, Bob, for God's sake. You're giving me the creeps.'

'Will you? I don't think she can expect much sympathy from my folks.'

'You don't have to ask, but talking of odds, they're no different for me.'

'Have you got someone?'

'Not at the moment, but who knows?'

'Then I'll reciprocate. There's a letter in my locker addressed to Laura. If anything should happen, give it to her, will you?'

'Yes, but that's no way to talk on the eve of your wedding.'

'How right you are.' He laughed in an embarrassed way. 'I don't reckon we'll have to scramble again tonight, the cloud's too low. I think I'll risk a quick phone call.' Laura had had a telephone installed at the beginning of the war so that she could be summoned if there was an emergency at the hospital and to let her mother know she might be late, and now Bob rang her as often as he could. Unable to use the telephone in dispersal, he disappeared at a sprint towards the mess and was back five minutes later, smiling. 'She hasn't changed her mind.'

Steve laughed. 'Is that all you wanted to ask her?'

'No, but the rest is private.' The words were hardly out of his mouth before the phone rang. He picked it up. 'Scramble,' he said, grabbing his flying jacket and helmet.

Laura woke and reached across to switch on the lamp on her bedside table and peered at the alarm clock that stood beside it. Eight o'clock! How could she have slept so long, today of all days? She switched off the light and hurried to open the blackout curtains. The sun was shining in a cloudless sky. Perfect. And Bob had phoned when he landed to tell her he was safe, so all was well. She turned to look across at her wedding dress. It was not a dream. Today she was to become Mrs Rawton and tonight they would be at a little cottage in the Peak District, which Bob had rented for a week.

Anne put her head round the door. 'I thought I heard you get out of bed. Shall I bring your breakfast up here?'

'No, I'm not hungry. To tell the truth, I feel a bit sick.'

'Nerves, I expect. Come down and have a cup of tea and a bit of toast, then you can have a long soak in the bath.'

'I think I'll go for a walk first. It will clear my head. I've got time, haven't I?'

'All the time in the world. Everything is ready.'

Laura washed and dressed and tried to swallow a mouthful of toast, but found she could not. The cup of tea went down and straight up again. She smiled wanly. 'I must look awful.'

'A bit pale. Perhaps a walk will do you good, put some colour into your cheeks.'

Laura abandoned her breakfast and slipped out of the house. She walked down the street and round the corner towards Edgware Road, lined with shops and thick with traffic in spite of petrol rationing. It was a road she had known since she was eight years old, when her father had been given promotion and was able to afford to move out of that squalid tenement in Stepney. The house in Axholme Avenue was her mother's joy because it had a bathroom and a separate kitchen with a gas cooker, something they had never had before. She had delighted in making it a real home. It was sad that Dad had only lived a couple of years after they moved. It had been a struggle for Mum to continue to pay the rent and bring up her daughter, but Laura had wanted for nothing. And now she was going to be a wife herself, but while Bob was still in the air force, she would continue to live with her mother. She thought that was one reason why Mum had become reconciled to the inevitability of her marriage.

Her sickness had passed, as it had passed each morning for the last week, and though her mother might say it was nerves and she might agree with her, Laura had a feeling that it was nothing to do with nerves. She had missed a period. Only by ten days, but it was enough to give her little pangs of guilt. She had been strictly brought up, the difference between right and wrong hammered home to her all through her adolescence. Her boyfriends had been vetted by her mother and later by the matron at her training hospital, where she had been closely supervised. Giving in to boyfriends was wicked, she had been told, and if they objected when she refused they were not worthy of her. Bob had not been unworthy and giving in to him had not seemed wrong at all. No one need ever know and, in any case, it might come to nothing. The life they were leading nowadays – the hard work, the constant fear, the sleepless nights – were enough to upset anyone's regularity. It did not matter, not now. Smiling to herself at the prospect of having a child that looked like Bob, she turned for home.

The flowers had arrived, a bouquet of white lilies, which would not have been Laura's first choice, and a posy of carnations for her mother to pin to her dress. A tray of buttonholes had been sent to the church for the guests. 'I wish your father were alive to see this day,' her mother said as she helped Laura into the dress. 'He would have been so proud to give you away.'

'Yes, I know. I thought of that too. But we mustn't be sad. Perhaps he's looking down on us and smiling.'

'Perhaps.' Anne picked up a hairbrush and Laura sat at the dressing table so that she could have her hair brushed. 'This reminds me of when you were little,' Anne said, taking the brush down from the crown in long smooth strokes. 'I loved brushing your hair every night, after you had been bathed and had your nightie on ready for bed. Your dad used to sit and watch—'

'And tell me fairy stories. He always added his own bits to them and made them sound a little different.' She paused. 'Do you still miss him?'

'Yes, of course I do. It never goes away, that feeling of loss. But we have to stop grieving sooner or later and get on with things. I had you—'

'You won't lose me, you know. Don't ever think that.'

'I don't. How does the saying go? "A son is a son until he gets him a wife, but a daughter is a daughter the whole of her life".'

'You've never told me how you and Dad met.'

'Haven't I?' Anne paused. There were some things she had never told Laura, was not sure she wanted her to know. Brought up in a Dr Barnardo's orphanage, she didn't remember her own mother, who, so she had been told, had died when she was born. No one mentioned her father. When, at thirteen, the orphanage found her a live-in job as a scullery maid in one of the posh houses in Maida Vale, in the same street as the Rawtons, she had been given her birth certificate with its stark entry, 'base born, father unknown'. Sometimes she wondered if her mother's name really had been Smith.

She had worked at the house in Maida Vale for four years, a skivvy with no life apart from the work she did, the bed she slept in, the food she ate. The other servants hardly spoke to her and when they did it was with contempt, and she realised being illegitimate was a scourge, something of which to be ashamed. She had a half day off each week and she spent it walking the streets of London, strolling in the park listening to the band, reading in the library, anything that didn't cost her more than a penny or two. If she got back too soon, they always found something for her to do, even though she was supposed to be off-duty. So, unless the weather was exceptionally bad, she stayed out. On that particular day she had walked all along Oxford Street, Clerkenwell Road and Hackney Road, all the way to Victoria Park, where she intended to sit on a bench to rest a few minutes before returning.

'I saw him playing football,' she said, just as Laura began to wonder if she had forgotten the question. 'It was the dockers versus the crew of the *Respite*. He was good, even I could see that, and when he scored a goal I clapped and shouted "Bravo!" When the players trooped off, the man who stood next to me called him over.' She smiled a little. 'He said, "Hey, Tom, come over and meet this little lady, she's an admirer of yours." I was terribly embarrassed but Tom didn't seem to mind.'

He had looked her up and down with his head on one side. Because she was provided with a uniform for work, she only had one frock to wear on her half day. It was grey cotton trimmed with a little white broderie anglaise round the collar and in tucks down the front to the waist. The skirt stopped just short of her ankles, revealing black button boots. Her hair was drawn into a severe bun and was topped with a little black hat with a red silk rose on the front. She was acutely aware that she looked shabby, but he must have seen something he liked in her because he smiled.

He wasn't very tall, only a little taller than she was, and he had fair hair and the beginnings of a fluffy pale moustache. But it was his eyes that held her. They were grey with green flecks in them and they were looking at her with an interest no one had shown in her before, except Mrs Colkirk, her employer, when she came to the orphanage to look her over before deciding to take her on. But Tom's look was altogether more benign and she found herself smiling back. 'He asked me if I had enjoyed the game and when I said I didn't know anything about football, he said he'd have to educate me. It went on from there.'

'That doesn't sound much different from the way Bob and I met.'

'No, I suppose not.'

He had gone home to change but as that was not far away, he arranged to meet her an hour later. She had nowhere to go for that hour, so she found a bench and sat down, wondering if she had dreamt that a young, handsome man had arranged to meet her, Annie Smith, orphan and bastard. He probably wouldn't want to know her if he found out about that and it would be better to keep quiet about it. She didn't say anything that day, nor the next time they met, or the next. It was beginning to worry her and when it was evident he was seriously courting her, she had plucked up the courage to tell him. It made not a bit of difference, he told her, he still wanted to marry her.

Life, which had been one grey existence of endless drudgery, became a glorious golden time. It did not matter that he was a docker and subject to the whims of dockmasters whether they gave him a day's work or not. It did not matter that his mother did not take to her; she supposed Tom must have told her why she had no relatives. It did not matter that she could not afford to buy a new dress or a new pair of shoes. Nothing mattered except that they loved each other.

'How long before you knew you wanted to get married?' Laura asked her.

'A few weeks. We had to wait for a house, but when one became vacant near his mother in Prince Albert Lane, he took on the tenancy and asked me to name the day.'

'And you never regretted it?'

'No, of course not.'

'There you are then,' Laura said, watching in the mirror as her mother coiled her hair up on top of her head and pinned it in little swirls ready for the coronet and veil to be fastened on top. 'What's so different now?'

Anne laughed. 'Nothing, I suppose. There, how does that look?'

'Lovely. Thank you, Mum. Not only for doing my hair, but for everything. I couldn't have asked for a better mother.' She turned in her seat to look at her. 'You're crying! Please don't cry.'

Anne attempted a laugh. 'Well, you shouldn't say such soppy things. Now, why don't you go and sit in the front room? It's cool in there. You don't need to put your headdress and shoes on until the last minute.'

When her daughter had gone Anne went to her own room to change into her wedding outfit, but she did not immediately undress. Instead she sat on the bed and picked up the framed photograph of her husband that she kept on the bedside table. The picture had been taken in France, during a lull in the fighting, so he had told her. He was in uniform, standing in front of a cottage door, though he had explained it was not a cottage but a backcloth the photographer had rigged up. Almost everyone in the unit had had his picture taken and they were all posed in front of that fake door. It was in sepia, but she had no difficulty picturing the light brown colour of his centre-parted hair, his slightly darker moustache and the keen blue eyes.

He had joined up right at the beginning, which he needn't have done considering dockers were required to unload vital food and wartime supplies being brought in by the merchant navy. For once in his life he would not have been competing for every job and yet he had given it up to go and fight. She thought she might have driven him to it. He had been fed up with her mooning about, longing for a child, gazing into other people's prams and being depressed every month when she was once more disappointed. She had suggested adoption but he would not hear of it. If they could not have their own child, he'd be damned if he'd bring up someone else's.

In the summer of 1917 he had become ill with dysentery and was sent to a field hospital, but they needed the beds for the wounded, so as soon as he began to recover, he had been sent home on two weeks' leave to recuperate. That leave had been precious. He was weak and he would not talk about the war; he knew, like it or not, he had to go back, so they made the most of it, having what he called a second honeymoon, which was silly because they had never had a first. The result was the miracle she had been praying for.

She remembered how she felt on being given the news. It had been blustery and cold, threatening rain, but she hardly noticed it. The dreadful reports from the front, the daily lists of casualties, the Zeppelin raids all dwindled into insignificance as she walked home to that horrible slum in Prince Albert Lane, treading on air. At last, after years of trying, of thinking she could not have children, she was pregnant. In the middle of the carnage, she was going to bring a new, precious life into the world – all the more precious because she thought it would never happen.

As soon as she got home, she had written to tell him. 'Dearest Tom. Wonderful, wonderful news. After all this time I'm expecting a baby. The doctor confirmed it today. I can't wait to hold my own child in my arms and I do not care if it's a boy or a girl, though it would be nice for you to have a son. So, come home safely, my darling, and share my joy...' The letter had meant so much to him he had kept it. She'd found it among his things after he died, creased from much unfolding and folding. In the thick of the fighting at Ypres, the news that at last she was pregnant had helped him to endure it, he said, and he couldn't wait to come home to be with them both.

He had come home, but he was not the same man she had seen go off to war. Once slow to anger, he had become morose and quick-tempered and sometimes he coughed his heart up. It had been difficult to settle down into civilian life, especially as he was no longer fit for his job as a docker and had to take work as a storekeeper in one of the dockside warehouses. He was always punctual, reliable and polite, and gradually, over the years, he was given more responsible work, somehow hiding the fact that his eyesight was not all it should be, and they had left the slum that was Prince Albert Lane and rented this house. Her dream home. And he had not lived long enough to enjoy it, nor to see Laura grow up into the lovely woman she was. Sighing, Anne put the picture down, put on the blue silk dress, did her hair and went downstairs to the sitting room.

Laura was pacing the room. It was difficult to sit still but there was a good half hour before she needed to finish getting ready and she did not want to crease her dress. Anne had just joined her when the doorbell rang. 'It's never the car already,' she said. 'It's much too early. It must be the postman.' She disappeared into the hall.

Laura heard low voices, then a long pause, which made her wonder what the postman could have brought. Another gift perhaps? Her mother returned. Behind her Laura saw the tall bulk of Steve Wainright. He was twisting his cap in his hands. 'Laura...' Her mother started and then came to a stop.

'Steve, what are you doing here?' Laura jumped to her feet. 'You're supposed to be going to the church with Bob.'

'Laura.' Her mother tried again and moved aside so that Steve could step forward. 'Flight Lieutenant Wainright has something to tell you.'

Laura looked from Anne to Steve, a puzzled look on her face. He gave a little cough to clear his throat. How could he say it? How could he break her heart? She was looking achingly lovely in the white satin gown. It contrasted so sharply with the raven hair and the creaminess of her skin, it made her look almost ethereal. He was silent, struggling with the words.

'What is it? What has happened? Tell me, for God's sake.'

'I don't know how to,' he said. 'It's Bob. He's—'

'No,' she said firmly. 'I spoke to him. He said he was down safe and sound. He said...' She stopped. The rest of what he had said was for her ears alone and centred round the fact that the next night they would be man and wife and they could make love all night if they chose. They would wake up together with nothing to do but walk and eat and do it all again.

'It was cloudy early on and we were recalled, which was when he rang you, but it cleared and the bombers came back in huge numbers. We scrambled again. Every available fighter was in the air.'

'He's hurt, in hospital somewhere?'

'No. I'm sorry, Laura, so very sorry, but I saw him go down. He was harrying one of the Stukas when he saw a Messerschmitt on the tail of one of the new lads and went after it. Another dived out of nowhere and got him. I yelled at him to bail out, but he couldn't hear me.' He hoped she would assume that Bob had died instantly.

It was a full minute before the impact of what he had said suddenly hit her. 'No! No! No!' She screamed and ran towards him, thumping his chest with her fists, as if it was all his fault. He grabbed her wrists and held her until she subsided into noisy sobs, putting her head on his shoulder and soaking his uniform. He put his arms round her and looked helplessly at Anne, who stood like a rock, almost as shaken as Laura. She caught his eye and went to her daughter.

'Hush, Laura, hush.' She took her from Steve's arms and led her to the sofa, where she drew her down and sat rocking her. She did not know what to say to comfort her, could not tell her not to cry, that life must go on, that she would get over it. Laura would not even hear her, much less listen. She simply sat with her, holding her tight.

Steve looked on, saw the weeping girl in her beautiful white dress, the bouquet of white lilies lying on the table beside a pile of gifts, and was near to tears himself. He pulled Bob's letter from his pocket and put it on the arm of the sofa, meeting Anne's eyes as he did so. She nodded and he backed away quietly until he was in the hall again. He had lost his friend, shattered the dreams of a lovely woman and he could do nothing. Now was not the time to go into the details of how Bob came to be shot down. It was a moment's inattention, something so alien to the man who had led the squadron so ably. Steve could only assume he had been thinking of his wedding and not what he should have been doing. He had shouted a warning, but it had been too late. Bob's aircraft went spiralling out of control, smoke pouring from one wing. 'Bob, get out!' he had yelled.

There had been no answer, but he knew Bob was still conscious because the Hurricane seemed to straighten out and head for the coast, though still trailing smoke. They had been over Canterbury at the time and the foolish brave idiot was trying to avoid coming down on houses. Steve had followed him, while keeping an eye out for more trouble, hoping against hope that Bob would bail out and he could pinpoint the spot for a rescue. But then they were over the sea and the Hurricane had burst into flames and gone down like a spent firework. Bob was gone and only an oily stain on the water showed where he had gone in. There was no time to mourn even for a second; he had turned in a fury to hunt down the doer of the deed and was soon involved in a battle of attrition which only ended when he shot down one of the enemy fighters. Whether it was the same one, he could not tell. His anger and his fuel spent, he had returned to base and a debriefing. It was only after that, when he went back to their room, that the full impact of what had happened hit him.

There was Bob's best uniform pressed and ready to put on, his shoes polished until you could see your face in them, his bag half-packed, ready to go on leave. His locker was still littered, but a photograph of Laura that he had had framed and which had been standing on it, had been popped into the open top of his bag. That would be sent to Bob's parents along with all his other belongings. Steve picked it up and sat on the bed with it, running his fingers over the smiling face. He knew Laura would be dressing for her wedding. She would be happy at the prospect, laughing with her mother, putting the finishing touches to the food for the reception, which was to be held at her home. It was then that tears pricked his eyes. He had lost many friends and colleagues since this war started and though he was always sorry, there was never time to grieve, no time to dwell on the young lives lost. Indeed, it would be considered unhealthy and unhelpful. But Bob had been special and Laura was special. He knew he would have to be the one to tell her.

Now, in the room behind him, the sobs continued as if they were never going to stop, and Anne's voice soothed ineffectually. He had never witnessed such grief, never felt so futile. Ought he to go? But supposing they wanted him to do something to help? He turned to go back, hesitated, then made his way to the kitchen. He put the kettle on and searched around for the teapot and tea caddy. He found milk on the floor in the larder, standing in a bowl of cold water to keep it fresh. There were cups and saucers already set out on the sideboard and he fetched two of these to the table. There wasn't a lot of room to put them down; the table was laden with food covered with clean tea cloths. Friends and relatives and Laura herself would have had to contribute their rations to provide it.

The doorbell rang and, after a moment's hesitation, he went to answer it. A car stood at the curb, white ribbons tied on its bonnet.

'I'm afraid the car won't be needed,' he told the uniformed man on the step. 'There's been a bereavement. How much are you owed?'

'Serviceman, was he?'

'Yes, a pilot.'

'Then there'll be nothing to pay. And offer the lady my condolences.' He touched his cap and turned away. Steve shut the door and returned to the task of making tea. Practical considerations like what was to happen to the feast could be left until later, though the arrival of the car had reminded him that someone would have to go to the church and tell the vicar and the congregation. He could offer to do that for them. He poured two cups of tea, added a good dash of brandy from a bottle he found in the sideboard, and took them into the front room. Laura had stopped crying from sheer exhaustion, but she lay in her mother's arms, looking like a ghost. She was clutching Bob's letter in her hand.

'Bless you,' Anne said, seeing the tray in his hand. 'Was that the car?'

'Yes. I sent him away. He said there'd be no charge.'

Anne touched Laura's wet cheek. 'Sweetheart, the flight lieutenant has made us a cup of tea. Sit up and drink it, there's a good girl.'

Dutifully, she sat up and took the cup and saucer from him, but she was not really there; she was in a land and a time of her own. He handed the second cup to Anne. 'Is there anything I can do to help?'

'I don't know.' She looked round vaguely. 'I can't think of anything but Laura.'

'I understand. You know, someone should go to the church. Would you like me to go?'

'Oh, would you? I would appreciate it. Tell them… I'm sure you'll know what to say. But don't let anyone come back here, not today. Tomorrow perhaps.'

'I understand.' He picked up his cap.

'Can you come back though? Tell me what everyone said. In a little while we'll have to sort things out.'

'Yes, of course.' He left them to their grief.

'Mum, what am I to do?' Laura sobbed. 'I can't think straight. All I can think of is Bob and I won't ever see him again. I can't believe it. I don't want to believe it. I keep hoping it's someone's idea of a sick joke and he'll walk through the door and laugh at me.'

'No one would joke about that, Laura, and certainly not Steven. You could see he was in a state himself.'

'I know. I was clutching at straws.' She paused to sip her tea, it was hot and strong and tasted of brandy. 'But there are things to be done, aren't there? I'll have to cancel the wedding and tell our friends. And the cottage. I don't have the address. Do you think his parents would know it?' Her voice broke on a sob but she gallantly pulled herself together. 'I'll have to send the presents back.'

'Steve has gone to the church for us and there's time enough to see to everything else tomorrow. Why don't you go and lie down? You're exhausted.'

'Perhaps I will.' The brandy in the tea, together with her natural exhaustion, was having its effect. She climbed the stairs like an old woman, hanging on to the rail and pulling herself wearily from step to step. Anne followed, helped her out of her dress, then settled her onto her new bed and pulled the eiderdown over her.

'Call if you want me,' she said, bending over to kiss her daughter's paper-white cheek. 'I shan't be far away.'

Her heart was heavy for Laura's grief; she felt the pain of it herself, reliving the day Tom had died. But he had been ill a long time and died in his bed. In some ways it had been a merciful release. Would Laura ever feel that this was a release? Somewhere, hidden in places where she kept all her dark secrets, Anne felt a frisson of relief that she had her daughter back. It was wicked but she had never felt this marriage was right. In that she agreed with that dreadful snob, Lady Rawton. 'Forgive me,' she whispered as she went back downstairs and began wrapping up the sandwiches, the sausage rolls and the canapés in little greaseproof paper packets. She would give them to anyone who had contributed to the food, and return their presents. By the time Laura came downstairs again, all trace of the wedding must have disappeared.

Steve came back while she was doing it. 'How is she?' he whispered, when she had let him in and gestured for him to take a seat.

'Trying to rest. She's worn out, poor dear.' She put the kettle on. 'Did you see everyone?'

'Yes.' He hesitated. 'Except Bob's parents weren't there, none of his family that I could see. Of course, they are his next of kin and would have been informed officially by the wingco, who was going as a guest in any case. They would have known not to go.'

'They might have had the courtesy to let us know.'

'I expect they assumed someone would tell Laura.'

'Then I am doubly glad you came. It would have been ten times worse if the poor dear had got as far as the church.'

'I would not have let that happen.' He paused. 'Everyone was milling about the churchyard, wondering what to do. They were on the point of sending someone to find out when I arrived.'

'Thank you. I don't think either of us could have coped with a deputation.' The kettle whistled and she poured water on the tea leaves. 'When do you have to go back?'

'Tonight, but I've a late pass. Is there anything else I can do?'

'It's an imposition, I know, but could you ask Bob's parents if they know the address of the cottage he and Laura were meant to be going to tonight? Laura's worrying about it. Someone will have to ring or write and explain why they haven't turned up.'

'I'll do it. Put it from your mind.' He paused as she resumed wrapping up parcels of food. 'What are you going to do with those?'

'Give them to the people who gave me the stuff to make them.'

'Don't you think that might offend them?'

'We can't eat it and I can't let it go to waste, can I? Food is precious. That's understood.'

'Yes, I suppose so.'

'They nearly all live in this neighbourhood. If I gave you a list, would you take it to them?'

'Of course.' Steve sipped his tea, a little surprised at her coldness, as if she could not get rid of the evidence of the wedding fast enough. But everything would dry up and spoil if left on the table, so perhaps she was right.

She turned on him as if she had read his thoughts. 'What do you expect me to do? Crumple in a heap like my daughter? Sit and howl and let everything moulder away like that woman in Dickens' book?'

'*Great Expectations*,' he prompted.

'Yes, well… If she comes downstairs and sees all this food and those presents, it'll set her off again. Better they should be gone. And if that sounds hard and unfeeling, then I'm sorry—'

'I don't think you are unfeeling, Mrs Drummond. It is obvious to me that you love your daughter.'

'More than you or anyone will ever know. She has been my whole life. When she was ill as a child, I nursed her; when she was sad, I comforted her. In good times and bad, and there were plenty of those, we soldiered on, but this is something altogether different. Somehow I've got to get her over it. She has to put it behind her.' She had disposed of all the food and all that was left was a heap of little parcels. The cake still sat under its cardboard cover. She took it out and put it in a cake tin. 'It'll keep for Christmas. Oh, the flowers! I forgot them.' She dashed into the front room and came back with the lilies and the posy of carnations. The latter had wilted badly and she put them in the bin under the sink. The lilies she dismantled and put into a vase of water. 'I'll put them in the shed for now and take them to Tom's grave tomorrow. Laura was going to do that anyway.'

Steve sat sipping his tea while Anne bustled outside with the flowers and the cardboard cake, half of him wishing he could go and leave this unhappy house behind him, half of him wanting to see Laura again and do what he could to comfort her. But why would she take comfort from him? As far as she was concerned he was simply Bob's friend, who was to have been his best man. He ought to go. But he had not yet been given the names of the people to take the food to, and so he sat and waited for Mrs Drummond to come back.

It was growing dusk and she carefully pulled the curtain over the door after shutting it, then lifted the wooden frame on which she had tacked blackout curtaining, intending to fasten it on the window with the butterfly nuts that had been screwed into the frame. He took it from her and did the job for her. She switched on the light. 'Are you hungry, Flight Lieutenant? I've kept some of the ham. I could make you a sandwich.'

'No, thank you. I really should be on my way.'

'Oh, the names and addresses.' She went to the dresser drawer and pulled out a notepad. 'Some sent presents too. Laura's already written a list of those. She was going to write and thank them personally when she came back from her honeymoon. You could take some of them back with the food. I'll sort the rest out later.'

'Don't you think Laura would want to do that herself? When she's feeling better, I mean.'

'No, best done now.' She was busy writing as she spoke. When she finished, she ripped off the page and handed it to him, together with Laura's list. Then she went into the front room and came back with an armful of gifts. 'The names are on the cards. I'd better find you a couple of carrier bags.'

It all felt wrong. Mrs Drummond was taking everything out of Laura's hands in a misguided effort to save her daughter pain, trying to put the clock back to a time before Bob had come on the scene, trying to wipe him from her daughter's memory. Steve wanted to weep himself for the grieving bride. And for Bob.

His task was complicated because at every house he visited he was bombarded with questions. What had happened? How was Laura taking it? Could they do anything to help? And no, they did not want their gifts returned; they had been given. One day Laura might be able to make use of them. It meant he was obliged to return to the house.

It was not surprising that he could see no chink of light; the blackout was complete. If Mrs Drummond had followed her daughter to bed he would have to bring the parcels back another day or leave them on the back step. He was trying to calculate when he could expect to be off base next when the door opened. The figure before him was too tall to be Mrs Drummond.

'Bob?'

He stepped forward. 'It's me, Steve. I had to come back—'

'Oh.' Laura put her fist up to her mouth and her dressing gown fell open. 'I thought—'

'I'm sorry. I wish I could be the man you hoped for.'

'Come in.' She turned away so that he could enter the kitchen. He shut the door and pulled the curtain across. She switched on the light and stood looking at him in bewilderment. 'I was asleep and having an awful nightmare that everything was ready for the wedding and Bob had been shot down. I came down here and the house was as it always was. It could have been a dream. I almost convinced myself it was. But it wasn't, was it? It was real. You did come and tell me Bob...' She choked and rallied. 'Bob is gone.'

'Yes, I'm afraid so.'

She sank into a kitchen chair, seemingly unaware that her open dressing gown revealed the white silk underwear which had been under her wedding dress. 'How long ago?'

'Since Bob was shot down?' He looked at his watch. 'Just over twenty-four hours.'

'Is that all? I thought it was longer than that, it feels like a week.' She looked at the table. It was set with cups and saucers and cutlery for breakfast for two. Her mind, still functioning in a strange disaffected sort of way, registered the fact that it was not as it had been when she went upstairs. 'Where is everything?'

'Your mother sorted it out. She asked me to take some of the presents back, but most of the people didn't want them back, so I've still got them here.' He held up the carrier bags. 'They said you might find a use for them.'

'People are kind,' she said dully. Then she gave a cracked laugh. 'There's one that can go back because I'll never find a use for it. Come, I'll show you.' She took his hand and led him into the front room. He knew she was putting on some kind of act to deaden her pain, that inside she was falling to pieces, and he wanted desperately to put her together again. He went with her because there was nothing else he could do. Laura pointed to the monstrous glass punchbowl, surrounded by a dozen matching glasses with handles. It took up half the table. 'See. It came from Bob's sister. It's obvious she has no idea what sort of home I come from. She thinks I live in a mansion like her parents.' Her laughter was a harsh cackle.

'Laura, stop it.' Steve put the carrier bags on the table and took her hands in his.

'Stop what?'

'Stop pretending.'

'Mum is pretending, isn't she? She's pretending it never happened.

55

She's swept it all away, except that monstrosity, and gone to bed. Is that what I'm supposed to do?'

He didn't know what to say. And suddenly she crumpled. He took her into his arms and held her while she wept again. But these tears were different from her earlier hysterical sobs; these were quieter, as if she had come to accept the inevitable and was mourning what might have been. He held her for a long time, breathing in the sweet scent of her, feeling the softness of her hair under his chin, the dampness of her tears falling on his hand. At that moment he was a comfort, someone big and warm and blessedly silent. Oh, yes, he was silent. There was nothing he could say. But he would hold her as long as she wanted him to, even if he stood there all night.

Her tears slowed to an occasional sob and then stopped. She stood back. 'I've made a mess of your uniform.'

'It doesn't matter. Do you feel better now?'

'Better?' She gave him a twisted smile. 'Do you mean have I stopped crying?'

'I can see you have.'

'I'm not being fair, am I? Bob was your friend and no one has given a thought about you. We've leant on you and sent you on errands and never said how sorry we are that you have lost your friend.'

'It doesn't matter. I understand.'

'Oh, Steve, what are we going to do without him?' It was a wail and he was afraid she was going to start crying again, but she made a visible effort not to.

He took a deep breath to steady himself. 'We'll do what countless others have done through the ages, what so many are doing now and many more will do as this war goes on: we'll gird our loins and carry on.'

'Yes.'

She was calmer now and though he didn't want to leave her, he felt he must. If he stayed with her, sharing her grief, he would end up in tears himself, and what a fool that would make him look. He managed a smile and put his hand under her chin to lift it. 'I'll have to go. Duty calls.'

'Yes. Thank you for everything. You will keep in touch, won't you?'

'Yes, if you want me to.'

'Of course I do. You are my link with Bob.'

He found his cap in the kitchen and let himself out of the back door.

The Rawtons arranged Bob's funeral. If they had not put a notice in the personal column of *The Times*, Laura would not have known when it was. After an eulogy of praise for a loving son and brother who had lost his life in the service of his country, the time and place of the funeral was given. 'Family and close friends only,' it said.

'They might just as well have said straight out, "Laura Drummond, keep away,"' Laura said dully when she read it. 'It's what they mean.' She had written them a letter of condolence, told them how she felt for them in her own grief, and had received a printed acknowledgement, such as everyone else had received; there had been no personal message. It had hurt her, knowing they thought her of so little consequence in their son's life that they could dismiss her like that. A wicked little thought entered her head, that perhaps they were glad he had died rather than marry her. It was banished in a trice as not worthy of her.

'So, are you going?' After another night in the shelter, Laura and Anne were sitting over a breakfast of cornflakes and toast, spread very thinly with butter. 'Scrape it on and scrape it off again,' Anne would say, laughing, though she was not laughing now.

Laura had not cried again, not publicly, and she appeared to be mastering her grief, but there were hours when she simply stared into space, her mind spinning with memories of Bob: jokes they had shared, plans they had made, plans which could never come to fruition. And sometimes when something happened – a Hurricane flying across the sky, trailing vapour, or a piece of news on the wireless – she would think that Bob might have been there; or if someone told her an amusing tale, she would smile and think, 'I must remember to tell Bob.' Then it would come to her, as if for the first time, that she could not tell Bob; he was not there to tell. He was gone. For ever. The only thing that kept her going was the child growing inside her, a child who would be part of Bob, his legacy to her. 'Of course I'm going. He was to be my husband. If fate hadn't been so cruel we would have been married and I would be his next of kin.'

Knowing how toffee-nosed the Rawtons were, she would not let her mother go with her. There were a great many mourners, taken to the church in a fleet of limousines. Some wore black, but many were in one kind of uniform or another, high-ranking most of them, with black armbands. Laura, carrying a single deep red rose, slipped into the back of the church after they had all gone in. While they sang hymns, read passages from the Bible and told everyone what a brave and patriotic man Bob was, she sat with head bowed and relived every moment of the time she had spent with him. She heard his infectious laugh; listened to his tales of life in the air force, the silly games the young men played when they were off duty; heard him tell her how much he loved her, how he looked forward to making her his wife; how they would have a handful of children, all as beautiful as she was. It was an indulgence she did not allow herself at home. Her mother always knew when she was brooding and would do everything in her power to snap her out of it. But she did not want to be snapped out of it; she wanted to remember, she wanted to remember the pleasure of knowing him, of loving him and being loved by him, not have it taken from her.

She recited his last letter in her head, every word indelibly printed on her brain. 'My dearest, dear, my love, my wife. If Steve has given you this letter, then you will know I am gone from you, gone with your name on my lips, but please, my darling, do not grieve for long. I will always be with you in spirit and you must move on. Be happy for my sake, but do not forget me altogether. We crammed so much happiness into a short time and I am grateful for that, for the joy you brought me, for your courage in taking me on. Go on being brave. And laugh. I loved you in all your moods, but especially when you laughed. Goodbye and until we meet again, God keep you safe. Your devoted husband.' He had not expected tragedy to strike before they were married and had not foreseen the letter being delivered to her on their wedding day. On the other hand he had always said she was already his wife and perhaps that was what he meant. And here she sat, listening to his funeral oration, shut out and grieving alone.

But she would not be alone; Bob would live on in their child. And soon she would have to tell her mother she was pregnant. But not yet, not until she was absolutely sure. She smiled a little quirkily when she thought of how Lady Rawton might react to the news. If she told her, which she might not.

The service ended and she stayed in her place until everyone had followed the flower-laden coffin to the churchyard for the interment, then she walked out into the sunshine and stood a little way off. Lady Rawton was hanging on to the arm of her husband, her face heavily veiled. On either side of them, family members gathered.

'You should be there with them.'

She turned to find Steve beside her. A slight breeze was ruffling his fair hair. His face looked grey with fatigue, his blue eyes dark-rimmed. His left leg was in plaster and he was supported on crutches. 'What happened to you?'

'Bad landing,' he said laconically. 'Broken leg.' He didn't tell her that it had been hit by an enemy fighter and had limped home on one engine. It didn't do to remind her that he had been luckier than Bob.

'Oh, you poor thing. You look done in.'

'Hardly surprising. We get very little respite.'

'Squadron leader now, I see.'

'Yes.' His promotion had come as a direct result of Bob's death, but he did not tell her that either.

The parson was intoning, 'Ashes to ashes, dust to dust,' and Lady Rawton had stooped to pick up a handful of soil and scatter it on the coffin. 'Go on,' Steve urged her. 'Go and say your goodbye.'

She walked forward slowly. The congregation were beginning to turn away, all except Sir Peter and Lady Rawton. They looked up as Laura approached, but did not speak. Laura dropped the rose onto the head of the coffin and stood a moment, her lips framing the words, 'Goodbye, my love.' And then she turned and stumbled back into Steve's arms.

Chapter Two

STEVE COULD NOT fly with his leg in plaster, so he was given a temporary desk job: working out rosters, lecturing on aircraft recognition, chasing up spare parts for the maintenance crews, filling in forms. It was frustrating when he would much rather have been in the air. He was glad when, three weeks later, he was given leave and told by the MO to see his own doctor and come back when the plaster was off and he was ready to fly again. Hobbling on crutches, he hitched into London with one of the others also going on leave who had a car and had wangled some petrol for it. He was dropped off at Liverpool Street and managed to scramble onto a train, which he left at Attlesham and from there took a taxi the four miles to Beckbridge.

His mother was at the kitchen table filling some flasks with tea and putting them in a canvas bag when he arrived. She turned with a cry of joy and ran to embrace him, then stopped when she saw the crutches. 'What happened to you?'

She was thinner than he remembered and had had her fair hair cut short and permanently waved. It had a few strands of grey in it, he noticed, and there were fine lines about her eyes which were new. 'I made a bad landing,' he said, propping the crutches against the table to hug her. There was no sense in adding to her worries by telling her he'd crash-landed because his kite was full of holes.

'I was just going to take this down to the top field,' she said, indicating the bag. 'I won't be long, then we can have a long talk.'

'I'll come too.' He picked up his crutches and followed her.

The village seemed as tranquil as ever, hardly touched by the war. Steve leant over the field gate to watch the haymaking. His father was driving the tractor, a new Fordson Steve hadn't seen before. Two land girls in brown dungarees and hair in headscarves, helped by Josh and hindered by a couple of evacuees, were busy raking it. The boys, Lenny and Donny Carter, were flinging the cut grass all over the place, smothering themselves. To them it was something new to play with, a fine joke. Boy, the family collie, circled them, trying vainly to round them up.

'It's good to see them laughing,' his mother said.

'The girls or the boys?'

'All of them, but the twins especially. You should have seen them when they first arrived. They were filthy and Lenny had wet himself and tears had made streaks in the dirt all down his face. No one wanted them and I couldn't just leave them, could I?'

'Leave them where?'

'In the school assembly hall. We'd taken them there from Attlesham Station; fifty altogether, boys and girls, all wearing luggage labels like a lot of parcels. Everybody who'd agreed to take a child came to pick the ones they liked the look of. It seemed a very unfair way to me, but you couldn't make someone take a child they didn't fancy, so all the pretty girls went first and then the more angelic looking boys. They were all marched away by their new foster mothers and Lenny and Donny were left in the middle of the hall with two pitiful bundles of clothes and their gas masks. The elbows were out of their jackets and their socks were down round their ankles. Lenny's were wet. He's the softer one of the two.'

'I don't know how you tell one from the other.'

'Lenny's hair is a little darker and he has a mole on the side of his neck. Donny is very proud of the fact that he's ten minutes older; he thinks that gives him the right to boss his brother about.'

'What about their parents?'

'Father's in the Navy, mother works in a factory somewhere in London. She came down once – last November, it was. I couldn't take to her. She seemed very off-hand, didn't seem to have much time for them. I wanted to yell at her to give them a cuddle, that's all they wanted, but all she could manage was a peck on the cheek, as if she was afraid of smudging her lipstick. I thought she'd stay the whole day and I'd cooked a roast – we'd killed a pig the week before – but she said she had to get back. The boys had been so looking forward to her visit and had planned to show her round the village, and they had drawn some pictures for her of cows and pigs and chickens in the farmyard. They'd never seen anything like them before. As far as they were concerned milk comes in bottles and you buy eggs and bacon in the corner shop. They were full of all the new things they'd seen and done, but she didn't seem interested. Two hours she was here, just two hours; came on one train and went back on the next. Poor little devils, I could have cried for them. I think they hoped she would take them back with her, a lot of the evacuees went back when there was no bombing. She's never been since.'

'They seem happy enough now,' Steve said, looking across at them.

They were rolling in the cut grass, which was too much for Josh. 'Dozy buggers!' he yelled, waving his rake at them. 'Git yew outa it, 'fore I tek this here to yar breeks. How's a body to wuk when it all git mussed up agin?'

The boys sat up and looked at each other, not understanding the broad Norfolk dialect of the old man; to their ears, he could have been talking a foreign language. 'Boys, come here,' Katherine called to them.

They obeyed, arms outstretched, making aeroplanes of themselves, imitating engine noises. Josh shrugged his shoulders and resumed raking the cut grass.

'Come and say how do you do to my son,' Kathy said. 'Squadron Leader Steven Wainright.'

'A pilot?' Donny asked, looking up into Steve's face and noting the smile of amusement and the clear blue eyes.

'Yes,' Steve said.

'You got a Spitfire?' This from Lenny.

'No, it's a Hurricane.'

'Ain't as good as Spitfires.'

Steve smiled. 'They both have their good points. The Hurricane is the stronger of the two, or I wouldn't be here now.'

'You got shot down?' Donny squinted up at him, his admiration growing.

'No, I made a bad landing,' he said, repeating the tale he had told his mother.

'Have you shot an enemy plane down?'

'I might have had a hand in downing one or two, and they're aeroplanes not planes.'

'Our dad's in the Navy.'

'Good for him.' He paused. 'What have you been doing today?'

'Mooching.'

'No school?'

'We went to school this morning. It's only a titchy little school and we have to share it with the Beckbridge kids. They went this ar'ernoon. Next week it's the other way about and we go ar'ernoons.'

He smiled. 'When I went there, I had to go mornings *and* afternoons.'

'With Miss Elmfield?'

Steve smiled, remembering the stern disciplinarian that was the village headmistress. 'Yes. Does she teach you?'

'Nah, we've got our own teacher, Miss Gosling. She's nice, she takes us big ones. The little ones go in with Miss Wainright's lot. Next year we're going to sit the scholarship, but we don't reckon we'll get it. Ma says it's a waste of time; kids like us don't go to grammar school.'

'You do if you're clever enough.'

'Which reminds me,' Kathy said. 'Have you done your homework?'

'Can't do it,' Donny said.

'Would you like me to help you?' Steve asked.

They looked at him quizzically, unsure whether he was bluffing. 'You mean it?'

'Yes, come on, let's go and get it over with. When I was a boy, I always did the things I didn't like doing first, then they weren't hanging over me when I wanted to play.' He began hopping back to the farmhouse on his crutches, a boy on each side of him and Boy hard on his heels. Kathy followed, smiling.

Wounded or not, it was good to have Steve home. She hadn't wanted him to join up but he had been mad on flying ever since he was a nipper and there was no holding him back. She worried about him, worried all the time. Whenever the BBC newsreader said, 'Two of our aircraft did not return', or 'Six enemy aircraft were destroyed for the loss of one of ours', her heart went into a spin. If she was in the middle of a meal, her appetite disappeared and she pushed her plate away, unable to continue eating. If she was sitting by the fireside knitting, she dropped her needles and imagined the horror. If she was ironing a shirt, she was in danger of scorching it until William spoke to her in his normal voice or one of the twins demanded her attention. She would come back to earth and get on with whatever she was supposed to be doing, but until Steve telephoned and she heard his voice, she was on tenterhooks. She supposed it was like that for every mother. How glad she was that William would not be called up. To have both son and husband in the firing line would fray her nerves to pieces.

As soon as they reached the house, the twins fetched their homework books and a maths textbook and settled at the dining table with Steve between them. They had had to number the pages of the exercise books as soon as they received them, so there was no tearing out the middle pages to use for drawing or making paper aeroplanes. And they had to cover them in brown paper or wallpaper and write their names on the outside. Exercise books were scarce and not to be treated roughly. Miss Elmfield had even dug out the old slates the children had used donkey's years before and brought them into use again to save paper. Kathy, smiling indulgently at their bent heads, went into the kitchen to prepare the evening meal.

Living as they did on a farm, food was not a severe problem.

Sugar, butter, cheese and tea were rationed, as were bacon and ham, but farmers were allowed to kill their own pigs under strict regulations. They had milk from their own cows and made their own butter, though again the regulations meant there was not an unlimited supply; the Ministry of Agriculture and Fisheries saw to that. Things like oranges, lemons, bananas and tinned fruit had disappeared altogether, but they had plenty of home-grown vegetables and fruit in season. She was lucky, Kathy thought; people who lived in towns were not nearly so well off. When the twins' mother had come on that short visit, she had offered her a bag of vegetables, but the woman had turned it down. 'Wouldn't know what to do with them, duck,' she had said.

This statement was borne out by the twins, who had obviously not been familiar with fresh vegetables and had demanded fish and chips and cake. Katherine, to mitigate their homesickness, had obliged them by queuing up for an hour and a half for two pieces of cod and producing fish and chips, only to be told, 'They're not like the ones we get from the fish shop at 'ome.' They'd enjoyed it in spite of that, but there was a limit to the number of times you could obtain fish and, besides, William said they must learn to eat what everyone else had. 'Everyone else' being William; their daughter Jennifer, who taught the infants at the village school; her elderly mother, who lived with them; the land girls, Meg Saunderson and Daphne Halligan; and now Steve. Josh lived with his wife in a tied cottage at the end of the lane that led down to the farm, and he was often given a dish of something to take home with him. She was glad that when William inherited the farm and its huge kitchen, he had also inherited the large pots and pans to go with it. She set to with a will, happy to have all her family round her.

'I suppose it's too much to expect that you're home for good,' William asked Steve over the meal, which was taken round the kitchen table. The schoolbooks still littered the table in the dining room. 'I could do with some help around the place.'

'Hey,' Daphne said. 'That's what we're here for.' She was in her early twenties, dark-haired and brown-eyed, and had been totally ignorant of country ways when she first arrived. Having been born and brought up in a London suburb, the milk she drank, like that of the twins, had always come in bottles. Her mother had persuaded her that working on the land was the least dangerous job of those she was offered and so she had opted to be a land girl and wear their far-from-glamorous uniform. She was a willing worker and was prepared to try anything, even the milking, though the cows had frightened her at first.

'I know that,' William said. 'And a fine job you're doing, but it's not like having a young man working alongside you.'

Meg laughed. She was blonde and vivacious, the daughter of wealthy parents. She had chosen the Land Army instead of one of the other services because she was mad on horses and thought work on the land might afford her a chance to ride. It hadn't turned out that way. Bridge Farm had been mechanised and the only horse in the stables was an ancient carthorse. 'We look more like boys than girls these days,' she said. 'I never thought I'd end up wearing breeches and thick socks.'

'I expect you look very glamorous when you dress up to go out,' Steve said.

'Thank you, kind sir,' she said. 'I could prove it to you, if you care to take me to the local hop on Saturday.'

Steve laughed. 'You'd know all about it if I trod on your toe, this plaster weighs a ton.'

'Oh, I forgot. Sorry.'

'Nothing to be sorry for.'

He looked up as his sister breezed into the room carrying a pile of exercise books. She was eighteen months younger than he was but, in his eyes, cleverer. She was also very pretty with fair hair rolled up over a thin scarf, and clear blue eyes, which lit up at the sight of him.

'Steve! You're home.' Jenny dumped the books on the dresser and ran to put her arms about his neck from behind and kiss his cheek.

'I'm so pleased to see you. When we heard you'd been wounded, we were on tenterhooks until we heard you were OK. What happened?' She left him to take her place at the table and her mother fetched her dinner from the oven of the kitchen range, where it was being kept warm.

He repeated the tale of the bad landing. 'What about you, what have you been up to?'

'The usual. Trying to instil a little learning into reluctant children when they would rather be out playing. And coping with shortages. Look what we've had to do.' She leant across and picked up one of the exercise books, which had been neatly cut in half. 'Not enough to go round. We've even had to saw pencils in half.'

'One of the twins told me you were teaching some of the evacuees.'

'So I am. It must have been a shambles getting all those children out of London. We didn't get the school we were expecting and the ones that came lost half an infant class and their teacher, who were carried on to somewhere else, but we're managing.' She laughed suddenly. 'You'd never believe we all speak the same language. It took ages for everyone to begin understanding each other.'

'But you enjoy it?'

'Yes. It's rewarding to see the children's faces light up when they suddenly see what you've been driving at.'

'Is that all? No boyfriends?'

Jenny laughed. 'No time. What about you?'

'No time. Besides, it wouldn't be fair on any woman to tie her down when you never know what's round the corner. Look what happened to Laura...' He had told them in his letters about being best man for Bob, and how he had been shot down on the eve of the wedding. Since he had left Laura after Bob's funeral, they had been keeping up a correspondence of sorts, though her letters revealed little of what was happening to her, what she was thinking or how she felt, and his were constricted by censorship. He'd go and see her on his next leave when he wasn't hampered by the plaster and the need for crutches; he had promised Bob he would. He often wondered if Bob had had a premonition of disaster.

'Poor thing. How is she coping, do you know?'

'We write now and again. She doesn't say much, but something like that must take a bit of getting over. I can't forget it myself.'

'Do you think there'll be an invasion?' His mother asked, changing the subject abruptly.

'Not if I can help it. Hitler won't come if he can't beat us in the air.'

The Luftwaffe had been hitting shipping in the Channel, Dover and the Kentish coast had been bombed continuously until it became known as Hellfire Corner and now they had turned their attention to airfields. The general consensus was that Hitler had to destroy the RAF before he could invade and so night after night waves of bombers came over and made huge craters in the runways, demolished buildings and any aircraft on the ground that had not managed to scramble into the air, killing and injuring ground staff as well as fliers.

People nearby stood with their heads tilted upwards, hands shading their eyes, and watched the aircraft twisting and turning, firing at each other until one or the other was hit. They saw them spiralling towards the ground in flames. Some of the pilots bailed out and landed in trees or back gardens, or in the middle of fields where farm labourers worked. British pilots were cheered and carried shoulder-high to the nearest house to be bombarded with tea and cake, or taken to the pub where they were plied with beer while they waited for transport to fetch them back to their station. Enemy fliers were surrounded by belligerent workers, wielding whatever weapons came to hand, more often than not pitchforks, with which they threatened the men until the local bobby or a member of the Local Defence Volunteers came and took charge of them. Every night, news broadcasts told of enemy aircraft brought down and allied losses, though the more astute suspected the figures were doctored.

'He's having a good crack at it,' his grandmother put in. Alice

Cosworth was an older version of Katherine. Although her hair was pure white and there were more than a few wrinkles around her mouth and eyes, she was very regal and upright and nothing much escaped her. She remembered the time before the last war, the one fought, so they said, to end all wars. And what had happened? Another, even more bloody, and one where civilians were suffering more than servicemen. She was glad she was no longer young.

'That's defeatism, Gran,' Steve said.

'I'm only stating a fact.'

'Then here's another,' Kathy said, getting up and gathering together the used plates. 'It's time the twins were in bed.'

'But it's still light,' Donny grumbled.

'Draw the blackout curtains. You'll never know the difference. Now, clear up the schoolbooks and off you go.'

It was a signal for everyone to disperse. Katherine and Alice set about the washing-up, the twins went reluctantly to bed, the land girls went to their quarters above the stable block, which had been refurbished into a snug little flat, and Jenny offered to drive Steve to the village pub for a drink. William had a small petrol allowance that just about kept the family Ford on the road.

'Mum looks tired,' he said, as they drove.

'She is. We all are. And you are not immune. You are beginning to look old before your time. Is it very bad?'

'Can be. We try not to think about it. The job's got to be done.'

'How long are you going to be home?'

'Until this plaster comes off. I've been told to go to the local hospital to have it taken off, and then I've got to do a bit of exercise to get the leg muscles working again.'

'And all the time you're here, you will be itching to get back, won't you?'

'Yes, but don't tell Mum that, will you?'

'I won't. You've changed, but then it's hardly surprising. We are none of us the same as we were.'

'Oh, I don't know. Underneath we're the same. I'm the same

Steve you quarrelled with as a child—'

'The same one who rescued me from the river, covered in weed; the one who punched his best mate because he said something about me he didn't like.'

'A typical brother,' he said laconically. 'And many's the time you've saved me from a beating.'

'Dad never beat you. They were all empty threats.'

'Childhood,' he said. 'All gone, but at least we had one. What sort of memories do you think those twins will have?'

'Happy ones, I hope. Mum's done her best for them. They cried every night when they first came. Donny pretended it was only Lenny, but I know he did too. They said they didn't like the noises.'

'It's the middle of the country, what noises?'

She laughed. 'I think what they really meant was the lack of noise, or noises they could not identify: the occasional owl and a dog barking, which they insisted was a wolf; Dad going round checking the animals last thing at night and clattering about in the yard; cows lowing, pigs snorting; things you and I would never notice. But they're miles better now, even manage to get up to mischief.'

She drew up at the door of The Jolly Brewers, one of two pubs in the small village of Beckbridge. There was also a butcher, a blacksmith, a cobbler and a post office and general store, which sold everything from food to candles and accumulators for those who had a wireless but no electricity. You could buy a kettle, a length of rope, wooden pegs, blue bags for the weekly wash, soap, sweets, newspapers and comics, and, if you were registered there, sugar and cheese and other rationed foods.

Inside the pub several customers were nursing a single glass of beer and trying to make it last. It wasn't just the shortages; most of them had never had much money and an evening at the pub was for social contact, for grumbling and a game of darts, not serious drinking. Steve was greeted with cries of recognition and a grilling about what he had been up to and if he thought the RAF could outwit the Luftwaffe, to which he replied with a definite yes.

'Spot of leave, Steve?' Ian Moreton asked when he hobbled to the bar to buy their drinks. 'Or are you home for good?'

The man was in his mid-forties, with thin pale hair, a thin body, thin compressed lips and thin hands, but with the thinness came wiriness. He wasn't particularly muscular, but he was strong and he could run fast enough when there was a bobby on his heels. He lived on what he was pleased to call a smallholding, which was in fact a very small cottage in a couple of acres, half of which was an orchard and the other half used to keep chickens and a couple of pigs. It had never provided enough of a living for him and his family of wife, son and daughter, so he supplemented his income with casual labour and trading anything he thought might have a saleable value. The idea of taking regular employment was anathema to him. The war, the shortages and the blackout provided him with endless possibilities.

'No, going back as soon as I'm passed fit.'

'More fool you.'

'Then perhaps it is just as well there are a few fools about or you might be sharing your bar stool with a Jerry.'

'That's right, you tell him,' Joe Easter said. Joe had been landlord ever since Steve could remember, long before he had been old enough to come inside and buy a drink. 'I'm sick of him leaning on my bar putting everyone off their beer with his long face.'

'I can't help having a long face.'

'True enough.' Steve winked at the publican, as Jenny picked up the glasses of beer for him and carried them to a table.

Ian, who had been hanging around waiting for it to get dark, went round to the back of the pub and picked up a kitbag. Kitbags were innocuous enough, except when they clinked, and this one clinked very loudly. He held it close to his chest and set off down the road. He daren't take it home. Joyce had nearly brained him the last time. 'You'll hev the police on us,' she said, guessing he had purloined the stuff from the airfield where he had a job helping to maintain the runway. 'Get rid of it.'

'That's just what I mean to do, but I've gotta put it somewhere 'til I find a buyer. You'd think old Joe Easter would be glad of a few extra bottles to put on his shelves, wouldn't you.'

'He's got more sense. Askin' for trouble, that'd be. You're not hiding it here.'

'No one's looking for it.'

'How do you know?'

''Cos the crate got broke and there was glass everywhere and it was written off.' He grinned suddenly. 'I took some empty bottles from the back of The Jolly Brewers and broke them in the crate. After I'd taken out the whole bottles, o' course.'

'You daft lump, Air Ministry stuff is marked. The bottles i'n't the same as the ones in the pub.'

'They got better things to do than sift through a heap of broken glass looking for marks. Besides, there's tons of stuff goes missing—'

'Yes, and if you bring any of it back here, I'll throw it out and you alonga it.'

She had sounded as though she meant it, so ever since then he had found other places to hide the stuff: barns, sheds, even a haystack. It was never hidden for long; there were always willing customers who didn't ask too many questions about where it came from. It wasn't only drink, 'either; there was jam and syrup and chocolate bars, all stuff that was either rationed or becoming scarce.

He hurried up the road and turned down the lane that led to Beckbridge Hall. The gates of the Hall, once kept closed and only opened by the lodge-keeper to people he knew or was expecting, were gone, taken away as scrap metal for the war effort. Now the lodge was empty and the way lay open. Ian set off up the drive until the big house came into sight. Once a stately home giving work to half the village, it was now badly neglected and occupied only by Lady Helen Barstairs and her elderly butler and his wife. It was in darkness, not a glimmer of light showing, which was as it should be. The blackout was his ally.

He left the drive and struck off across the park, though you could hardly call it a park now there were no animals to graze in it and no one to cut the grass, which was almost knee high. He had once been employed on the estate and knew exactly where he was going. In the middle, hidden by trees, there was a small lake with an island and a boathouse. It was not the boathouse that interested him because that would be too damp, but a summer house, which stood on slightly higher ground and looked out over the lake. Its door was padlocked, but it had rusted so badly a good wrench soon forced it open. He went inside, dumped the kitbag on the floor in the dust and took a torch from his pocket.

There was only one room, though it was a fair size. Half a dozen mildewed deckchairs were stacked against one wall. On the side opposite the door there was a long bench with a hinged seat. Ian went over and lifted the lid to reveal cricket pads, also mildewed, some stumps and bails and a couple of bats. There was also a croquet set. He hauled it all out, took the bottles from the kitbag and carefully stowed them inside with the pads, bails and stumps on top. There was no room for the bats and the croquet set, so he piled them neatly beside the deckchairs and shut the lid of the bench. A quick look round satisfied him that his hiding place was secure and he slung the kitbag over his shoulder and left, shutting the door behind him and replacing the padlock so that it did not look as though it had been disturbed. He set off home thoroughly pleased with himself. It could stay there until he sold it, and that should not take long.

Helen could not sleep. There was nothing new about this sleeplessness; it had plagued her most of her life, but since the beginning of the war it had become worse. She got up and padded across to the window where she drew back the blackout curtains and stood looking out. The familiar scene was bathed in moonlight. A tree-lined drive from the lane to the front door ended in a wide turning circle just below her window. To her right was a swathe of parkland and then a small wood. Beyond that was a lake; she could just see the glint of water between the trees. The summer house was down there too, but could not be seen from the house. It was becoming dilapidated now; she could not remember the last time it had had a lick of paint. She used to go down there a lot at one time, when the dream was still alive, the dream of being reunited with Oliver and her daughter, a dream which she thought had died a slow and painful death. But it hadn't. The past kept coming back, now more than ever…

Under the influence of the sedative, she had only a hazy memory of the journey back to Beckbridge after her confinement. Her father drove the car with her mother silently beside him, while she sobbed in the back. She imagined the woman she had seen from the window of the clinic taking her baby home and feeding her from a bottle when her own breasts were achingly heavy with milk. The clinic had given her tablets to dry it up. What had they told that woman? That she didn't want her child, that she wanted to be rid of her?

'Shut up, Helen, for goodness sake!' her father said irritably.

She was tempted to open the car door and fall out. She would undoubtedly be killed, considering the speed they were doing, and that would end her misery, end her father's embarrassment, too, but then she thought of Olivia and her determination to be reunited with her and subsided into her seat. She did not cry again, not when anyone could see or hear, at any rate.

She had no one she could talk to, no one to tell how miserable she felt, no one to commiserate with her, not even Kathy. They had once been close, told each other all their secrets, but now all her cousin could manage was a frosty 'Hallo' when they met in the village. Life went on as if she had never been away and the baby had never been born, though her father no longer invited servicemen to the house. Oliver's name was never mentioned, nor Olivia's. She asked her mother once, and once only, the name of the woman who had taken her daughter, but Mama had assured her she did not know it, that it was not the policy of the clinic to divulge such information. 'Better that way, darling,' she said. 'No good tormenting yourself over it. Think of Richard coming home. You will enjoy setting up home with him and you will have more children.'

Richard coming home worried her. Could they possibly make a life together? Would she be able to live with him in any kind of normality and keep her secret?

She didn't have to. Richard was taken prisoner in the summer of 1918, but it was not until the war was drawing to a close that she was informed of his death in captivity. She did not know how that had come about until a fellow officer who had been with him in the POW camp came to see her. Richard had spotted a column of enemy infantry on the road and dived to tree-top height to strafe it with a Lewis gun. His engine had been shot up by a German plane, his observer killed, and he had been forced to land behind the German lines. He had been wounded and taken to a dressing station and from there to a POW camp, where he died of his wounds. 'Thought you might like to know he was constantly thinking of you and talking about you,' her informant had said. 'He would not contemplate not coming home to you even when he was dying.' She was touched by that, but wickedly relieved he would never learn about Oliver or Olivia.

She pretended to put it all behind her, celebrated the Armistice with everyone else, spoke civilly to her parents, went to social occasions with them and engaged in charitable work, almost as if she were treading water, waiting for something to happen.

Three months later both her parents died in the space of a week, struck down by the influenza epidemic that was sweeping the whole of Europe, leaving Helen feeling... She did not know what she felt. Abandoned? Lonely? Left to her own devices to make what she could of a life already blighted? Freed to do what she most wanted to do? Or tied by convention, promises made under duress, the futility of it all?

The funeral was attended by Great Aunt Martha, brought down from Scotland by Cousin Cyril; countless distant relatives she hardly knew; friends of her father and mother; William and Kathy, who was hugely pregnant, making Helen feel sadder than ever; Kathy's parents;

villagers; the local doctor and the family lawyer. They stood around the double grave in driving rain turning to sleet while the parson murmured the words of the interment, then returned to the house to be plied with sherry, tea and food, and talk over the lives of the two who had died. 'Together in life, together in death,' someone said. 'Better that way. They were so devoted.'

None of the mourners asked how she would manage without them, how she would cope with this great mausoleum of a house with its depleted number of servants and the need for repairs becoming urgent. She supposed they assumed she would marry again. Great Aunt Martha even said it aloud. 'You shouldn't have any trouble finding yourself another husband, Helen,' she said. 'You can't manage this great house all on your own. There would be no need to say anything about you know what.' The last sentence was said in a whisper.

Marriage was the last thing on her mind. Her baby daughter filled it to the exclusion of all else. Olivia would be a year old in two weeks' time, a year lost to motherhood, never to be recovered, a year in which she had missed her first smile, her first baby tooth, her efforts to sit up and crawl, perhaps hauling herself to her feet. She might even have been trying to say her first word. Would it be 'Mama'? She ached for her, ached even more than she had for Oliver, though she still dreamt that he would turn up one day and claim her, and together they would find their daughter and bring her home to be a proper family. It was a dream that slowly faded as month followed month and the surviving servicemen came back and dispersed to their homes. She had no idea whether he was alive or dead, but if he were alive he had made no attempt to contact her.

But now her parents were gone, was she any longer bound by that promise not to try and find her daughter? She gave no thought to how that was to be achieved, nor the legal consequences or the effect her sudden arrival would have on the adoptive parents, nor, for that matter, what her friends and relations in Beckbridge would make of it. Olivia was hers and no one had the right to take her child from her.

After a week spent with the family lawyer sorting out her father's affairs – there was no new Earl of Hardingham, the title had died out with her father – and discussing her inheritance, which was barely enough to keep the house going, she was on her way to London.

Her first stop was the St Mary and Martha Clinic, but they would tell her nothing. 'That information is entirely confidential,' she was told by a haughty matron who refused to let her see the doctor himself. 'You undertook never to enquire into what had happened to the infant; that promise is binding. In any case, I am not sure we even keep records of that nature.'

She tried examining the register of births in every parish in the area close to the clinic. Her father would not have registered the baby under her own name and so she tried the name she had been given in the clinic. Mrs Jones! There were several of those, but none with a child called Olivia and none on the right date. She returned home to Beckbridge weary and frustrated, wondering if she was on a hiding to nothing. But the search was becoming something of an obsession and a few days later she was back in London, widening her enquiries to neighbouring parishes. When that failed to produce results she simply looked for girl babies born on the right date. She found a few but when she investigated further, none proved to be the right one.

She spent weeks going back and forth, and after each trip she made her way home, tired and miserable, made worse when she learnt from the local newspaper that Kathy had had her baby. 'To William and Katherine Wainright, a girl, Jennifer Alice, sister to Steven, seven and a half pounds. Mother and baby are both well.'

Reluctant to give up her search, she advertised in the personal columns of the newspapers, wrote to the governors of the clinic, decrying their methods and demanding answers, but received no replies. It was then she decided she had better sort out her mother's clothes and personal belongings, something she had been putting off doing and then wondered why she had not thought of it before. Among her mother's letters she found the account from the clinic for arranging the baby's adoption. The amount made her eyes goggle and simply proved how desperately anxious her parents had been to rid themselves of the shame she had brought upon them. But more than that, there was an accompanying letter from the doctor who ran the clinic.

'I can assure you, my lady, that your concern that the infant should never be in a position to be seen and identified by anyone in your circle of family and friends has been fully taken account of. The home she is going to is in Stepney in the East End of London. The family are poor, but we have been assured that she will not be ill-treated. I have taken the liberty of asking Mrs Bates, the midwife who attended the birth, to keep an eye on her and report to me if she has any reason to suspect the child is not well cared for. She knows the family. That being so, I consider I have done as much as could reasonably be expected and therefore submit the enclosed account as agreed. Yours faithfully...'

Why had her mother kept it? Why had it been addressed to Mama and not her father, who was the one who had dealt with the clinic? Had she thought that one day she might show it to her? Poor Mama, she would never have dared do it, but she had left it for her to find. Helen lost no time in following it up.

Locating Mrs Bates was not difficult. Any mother of child-bearing age in Stepney could have told her where the midwife lived. It was one of a terrace, tall and narrow, only one degree above the dockland slums a few streets away. Mrs Bates came to the door in answer to her knock. Helen recognised her immediately as the woman who had taken her baby out of her arms and carried her away. 'Mrs Bates, do you remember me?'

'No, should I?'

Helen smiled. 'Perhaps not. You were more interested in the lower half of me and it was eighteen months ago.' She paused while the woman puzzled over her identity. 'I'm...' She stopped. 'No, you would not have been told my real name. Never mind. I need some information. May I come in?'

She was admitted into the sitting room and invited to be seated. 'What information do you want?'

'I am trying to trace a child born at the St Mary and Martha Clinic on the fifth of March, 1918. You were there at the time. In fact you helped to deliver her.'

'How do you know this?'

'I was there, breaking my heart at having her taken from me. We had a real fight and she was forcibly removed from my arms and handed to you. Look at me. Do you remember me now?'

Recognition dawned. 'Yes. But you undertook not to trace the infant. You signed a paper.'

'It was signed under extreme duress, as you well know.'

'I can't tell you where to find the child, even if I knew.'

'You do know. The doctor wrote a letter to my mother saying you would keep an eye on her to make sure she was well looked after.'

'And I did and she is. I can tell you no more than that.'

'I believe you can.'

'Well, I won't. What do you think it would do to the poor child and her mother if you went barging into their lives? The home is a stable one and they are a happy family. Do you want to destroy that?'

'No, of course not. I only want to see her. She is my daughter and I can never forget her or the cruel way she was taken from me.'

'You agreed to let her go.'

'I never did. I was forced and you knew it, and so did that doctor. Good heavens, I kicked up enough fuss.'

The midwife smiled. 'Yes, you did, didn't you? More than most.'

'So are you going to tell me?'

'No.'

'Then I have no choice but to go to the police and complain about the way the clinic is run and how newborn babies are bought and sold and poor pregnant girls exploited.' She stood up to go. 'Even if the police are not keen to act, I think the newspapers will be interested.'

Mrs Bates looked worried. 'It was done with the best of intentions. Mrs...the mother was desperate for a child. I had no idea that you had not agreed, not until you struggled so hard to keep her, but your parents were there and I couldn't go against them, could I? And you can't expect her to be handed back, just like that.'

Helen supposed that was just what she had hoped for, but was sensible enough to realise it would not do to admit it. 'I wouldn't ask *that, but I would like to see my child, to judge for myself that she is well cared for and if I can help at all, even secretly, that's what I want to do. Can't you understand that?'*

'Yes, I suppose so.' It was said reluctantly.

'Then tell me where I can find her.' She opened her handbag and took out a bundle of five-pound notes as she spoke and watched the woman's eyes widen.

'You promise, you promise faithfully not to upset them, to stay out of sight and never, ever attempt to take the little girl from the woman she thinks is her mother? If you don't swear it, I'll be damned if I'll tell you anything.'

'I promise.'

Money changed hands and she was given a name and address: Mrs Anne Drummond, 18 Prince Albert Street, Stepney.

When Helen made her way there after asking directions several times, it was to find a narrow street full of slum dwellings, with dirty steps and grubby curtains. There wasn't a blade of grass to be seen. She was appalled. Her baby, her beloved daughter, was living here in squalor. She stood across the street from number 18 and stared at it, willing someone to come out with a child. Perhaps it wasn't her daughter; perhaps Mrs Bates had got it wrong? As she stood there, uncertain what to do, a man in overalls came down the road and opened the door. She glimpsed a woman holding a baby, ready to welcome him home. The baby waved a chubby hand at him and he took hold of it and bent to kiss her, laughing at something his wife had said. Then the door was shut and she saw no more, would not have done anyway because her eyes were full of tears. It was only afterwards she realised the house was cleaner than its neighbours, its step was scrubbed and the net curtains were snow white. The baby had looked well fed and, she had to admit it, loved. She turned away and went home, back to her empty mansion, knowing she had achieved nothing except more heartache...

There was a man walking across the grass, from the direction of the lake and the summer house, carrying something over his shoulder.

Helen's heart began to pound. Coming on top of her foray into the past, she immediately thought of Oliver. But of course it wasn't Oliver. The man looked nothing like him. Was he an enemy spy who had landed by parachute to create mayhem? Or a fifth columnist? Could it be an English airman who'd had to bail out? But she hadn't heard an aircraft, much less the sound of gunfire. The idea of going down to challenge him she dismissed; he was too far away and she was unarmed. She could always fetch her father's shotgun, but would she have the guts to fire it if she had to? As she watched, he turned and looked up at the window and she shrank back out of sight, but not before she had recognised Ian Moreton, who had once worked for her father before being dismissed for dishonesty. What was he doing? She noticed the sack over his shoulder and smiled suddenly. He had been after rabbits or perhaps fishing; he had come from the direction of the lake. In the old days, when her father's keeper raised pheasants, he would have been prosecuted for poaching, but what did it matter? There were no pheasants now, nor trout come to that, but a rabbit in the pot would be a welcome meal for his family and she did not begrudge it. She went back to bed.

For the rest of the week Steve hobbled about the farm and listened to his father grumbling about the regulations that dropped on the mat almost daily, not to mention the inspectors who turned up now and again and tried to teach him his job, a job he had had ever since he left school at the age of thirteen, a job he had been born to. 'Dozy lot, don't hev the sense they were born with,' he said in his inherent Norfolk brogue. 'They think you ken plough up a medder and grow wheat straight off. I told them the ground were boggy, not fit for crops, and where did they think I was going to put my cattle? It was the same in the last war. Men from the Ministry telling farmers how to run their businesses, just as if they were a lot of schoolboys. I remember your grandfather sending one of 'em off with a flea in the ear.'

'Not a good idea,' Steve said. The farm had been in the family for several generations and Steve knew his father wanted him to take over one day. He supposed he would; he could think of nothing else he wanted to do. But first there was a war to win. He followed the news assiduously and knew that the airfields were being pounded and every available pilot was needed. He could not sit at home, pretending to be an invalid. There was nothing wrong with him.

The plaster was taken off at Attlesham Cottage Hospital later that week and, after a few days getting used to being without it, he returned to duty.

The airfield was in a mess. Everywhere there were craters being hastily filled in. Some buildings were severely damaged; most had their windows blown out. Where once there had been a gun emplacement was now a hole filled with metal and concrete. There was evidence of aircraft being hit on the ground, although others appeared to be in a state of readiness. 'We copped it yesterday afternoon,' the wing commander told him when he reported for duty. 'We managed to get most of the squadron off the ground before they arrived but there are four aircraft completely useless and several more needing repairs.'

'Any casualties?'

'Two ground staff killed and one pilot, caught trying to take off. Several WAAFs from the ops room were cut by flying glass.'

'Have you got a kite for me?'

'We'll find one, even if we have to take it off one of the new boys. Grab a bite to eat and get into flying kit, then go over to dispersal. They'll be glad to see you.'

Steve went to his room and sat down on his bed. Beside it was a small cupboard and next to it a wardrobe. A chair stood at the end of the bed. Everything was neat and tidy. Across the room an identical set of furniture which had once served Bob was now used by Flight Lieutenant Brand. This was far from tidy. A jacket was hung over his chair, a pair of shoes lay on the floor just as he had kicked them off. The locker was covered with knick-knacks, an empty Craven A packet, a cigarette lighter, a single cufflink. Steve smiled and opened his kitbag. Soon his things were back where they belonged and his bedside locker was sporting the photo of Laura he had purloined from Bob's kit and a snapshot of his mother and sister, posing with Boy. He changed into flying kit, pulled on his boots and made his way over to the hut close to where the aircraft were parked.

'Ah, the wanderer returns,' Brand said, waving his hand at two flying officers he had not seen before. 'Come over and be introduced.' Steve walked over to join them, trying not to limp. 'This is Flight Lieutenant Steve Wainright, chaps. He's been on holiday, but now he's back we can get on with this war.' He waved a hand at his companions. 'Steve, let me introduce Flying Officers Olliphant, known as Jumbo, and Bullimore, known as Oxo.'

'Hallo,' they said together.

The telephone shrilled suddenly. Steve went to answer it. 'Scramble,' he said.

There was a mad dash for the door and in thirty seconds the room was empty.

Steve forgot his leave, forgot his injuries, as he sprinted for the aircraft and climbed inside. Three minutes later he was airborne. He was back in the thick of it and there was nothing in his head but the need to bring down the enemy.

Chapter Three

THE HALF-HEARTED raids on London, which had been more like gnat bites than real wounds, suddenly assumed a more sinister aspect. Instead of bombs falling on London as a result of bombers being lost or damaged so they had to jettison their cargo, the Luftwaffe turned on the capital with a vengeance. In the middle of a sunlit Saturday afternoon in early September, the sirens wailed, first one and then another, area after area, and the population trooped to the shelters, grumbling about the time being wasted. Laura was on duty and set about the well-rehearsed routine of taking her patients to safety, helping those patients who could walk and others who could be taken in wheelchairs to the basement shelter. The beds of those who were bed-bound were wheeled into the corridors away from the windows. If a surgeon was in the middle of an operation there was nothing to be done but carry on. The whole process went into reverse when the all-clear sounded.

She had returned to work, knowing that if she stayed at home she would mope about and weep and it was better to be somewhere where she could do some good. Everyone was kind to her, but she could tell they were afraid to mention Bob, that they measured every word in case it might upset her. Sometimes they forgot, and she would smile at their look of embarrassment and tell them it didn't matter. Work was her panacea, but she wondered for how much longer. She had committed the worst transgression an unmarried woman could commit and there were those who would brand her a fallen woman and walk by on the other side of the street. She dreaded that, but she dreaded telling her mother even more.

Would she welcome the baby? She would not expect her to have it adopted, would she? They would have a serious falling out if she did; nothing on this earth would persuade her to part with Bob's child. It would be hard because she did not know how they would manage financially, but her mother had brought her up without a father, at least since she was ten, and she could do it too. She would work until she could no longer do so and save every penny.

She was too busy to see the aircraft, but she heard them. She could not break herself from the habit of thinking of the airfields and the fighter pilots and Bob whenever the siren sounded. But Bob was no longer there. Bob was where they could not reach him. Steve would be up, taking Bob's place, and she prayed for him, as she did all the young men in danger.

She heard the *crump, crump*, nearer than she had heard it before, and then she heard the jangle of a fire engine's bell. How close were they? She paused on the way back from escorting a patient to the basement and stepped outside. The drone of hundreds of aeroplanes, the shriek of bombs followed by the earth-shaking blast of explosions which made the ground shake and the windows rattle, the bells of fire appliances and ambulances tearing off towards the trouble, blended into a cacophony of sound. This was no gnat bite. She went to a phone box to ring home. There was no answer. Her mother ought to be in their Anderson shelter, but was more likely in the thick of it, doing what she called her 'bit' in the Women's Voluntary Service. It was just like her to put herself out to help others; she had always been like that, always thinking of those less well off, always sewing or knitting or baking cakes. She hoped fervently that Mum had not put herself in danger, for what would she do without her? How was she going to cope with her pregnancy and a baby without her support? She really must pluck up her courage and tell her. 'Oh, God, don't let me lose her too,' Laura prayed, before going back inside.

The casualties started arriving a few minutes later and for the next few hours Laura, no longer on the airmen's wards, treated broken limbs, lacerations from shattered glass, wounds to heads and eyes and stomachs, and dreadful burns. She nursed patients who had had emergency surgery, including amputations. They were not all adults, either. Seeing the poor wounded children broke her heart. She knew many must have died but she did not ask about those.

'They've gone for the docks,' one of the ambulance men told her when they brought in a man with an arm hanging by a thread of muscle and flesh. 'It's an inferno.'

The all-clear went at six o'clock, the new admissions trickled to a stop and the patients were returned to their wards. They were hardly back and tucking into their tea when the siren went again and the whole process was repeated. A new wave of enemy aircraft flew in and pounded the docks, the gasworks and the Arsenal. Laura, who should have gone off duty, worked on. There was no escape from the noise, the whine of falling bombs, the explosions, the crash of falling buildings which seemed frighteningly close. And added to the unrelenting noise was fire. Incendiaries mixed with high explosives sent flames and dense black smoke high into the sky, first in little pockets, then joining up to make a wall of fire and, though it was some distance from the hospital, Laura imagined she could feel the heat.

At five o'clock in the morning the drone of the bombers faded and the all-clear sounded. Everyone was worn out: doctors, nurses, ambulance men, police and especially firemen. Some were casualties themselves. Laura went home for a couple of hours' rest before she was due back on duty. Miraculously, the buses were running. She climbed aboard one and collapsed into a seat, so exhausted she could have slept there and then.

Anne, who had been one of the first to join the Women's Voluntary Service, had been working all night at an East End school where the homeless were brought to be given clothes, blankets and hot food. The wounded had been taken to first aid posts or the hospital, so the people she saw were uninjured in the physical sense, but they were bewildered, wandering round in a daze, their eyes gazing almost sightlessly out of faces blackened by smoke and dirt. It was from these she learnt that Stepney had been one of the areas worst hit.

Stepney, where she had lived when she was married just before the Great War. The houses, commonly called 'two-up, two-down', were crammed together, back to back, with no inside taps, let alone bathrooms. The lavatories were in the tiny backyards. There were cockroaches and mice, even rats sometimes, and the drains stank. Keeping it clean had been a nightmare, which she supposed was why so many in the neighbourhood didn't bother. But one thing the orphanage had taught her was that cleanliness was next to godliness and she had done her best to keep their house and herself neat and clean. She had been laughed at for it. 'Miss Whiter than White,' her mother-in-law called her, as much for her insistence on attending church as for her obsession with cleanliness. She had hated having to bring Laura up there, and she swore that one day they'd get out.

It had taken years of scrimping and saving, but they had achieved it in the end. Her mother-in-law, who had always lived in Stepney and said she wouldn't live anywhere else, had been left behind. Anne had been guiltily glad of that. They had not spoken to each other since the awful row they had had at Tom's funeral. But the woman was Tom's mother when all was said and done, so as soon as she came off-duty Anne went to see what she could do.

The bus was stopped short of her destination by an ARP warden and she had to walk the rest of the way. She passed houses with all their windows blown out and doors off their hinges; some had their fronts blown off, revealing their interiors like open dolls' houses. Fireplaces hung on papered walls, beds stood covered in debris, ripped curtains were snagged where there had once been windows. The air was so overlaid with smoke and brick dust it made her eyes stream and got into her lungs and made her cough. Everywhere fire appliances, some antiquated and pulled by London taxis, were directing their hoses against the flames. Whole houses were nothing but rubble. Policemen and wardens were busy everywhere, some directing those who stumbled about unable to comprehend what had happened to them, others digging in the rubble for survivors. After picking her way over broken glass and bricks and snaking hoses, she stopped by a warden. 'You can't go any further, missus. Too dangerous.'

She pointed down the street, only it didn't look like a street, more like an untidy builder's yard. 'I am looking for Mrs Drummond from number 18.'

'Relative, was she?'

'Was?'

'Yes, sorry, love. She wouldn't go to the shelter. I warned her enough times but she took no notice and she was inside when the house took a direct hit. They got her out but it was too late. She's been taken to the mortuary. Are you next of kin?'

'I'm her daughter-in-law, but she has a daughter. Maisie Youngs. Lives in Essex.'

'Perhaps you could make sure she is informed.'

'Yes.' She turned and left. The past was gone, wiped out in a single night, and now there was no one to accuse her, no one at all. Except... Anne shook the thought from her and clambered onto a bus to take her home.

Laura was making a cup of tea and a sandwich when she arrived. 'Thank goodness, I was beginning to wonder where you'd got to.'

'I've been helping out at a rest centre down the East End. There's hundreds killed and thousands homeless. It seems as though half the East End has gone.' She sighed. 'Granny Drummond with it. The warden told me she refused to go to the shelter. That's just like her, stubborn old fool, never would listen to reason.'

'Oh, Mum, I'm sorry. Is there anything we can do?'

'No. I saw Maisie as I was leaving. She said she'd see to everything.' She paused and changed the subject. 'What about you? What sort of night did you have?'

'Pretty horrible. I only got off an hour ago. I thought I'd have a couple of hours' sleep before going back.'

'You do that. I think I will too. You never know when the devils will be back. I reckon last night was only the beginning.'

During the course of the day, they learnt a little of the extent of the damage on carefully monitored BBC news bulletins, laced with encouraging homilies about not being beaten and everyone pulling together and helping those in need. Instances of bravery were cited, instances of looting glossed over. Much of the real news was passed on by word of mouth from people who arrived at the hospital and had witnessed it. Laura, back at the hospital treating casualties, pieced it together bit by bit as the day wore on. They spoke of whole streets going down like ninepins, of dead bodies and bits of bodies being thrown about like rag dolls, of people staggering about covered in brick dust and soot; of dockside warehouses containing barrels of rum, tins of paint, rubber, pepper, timber and food all going up in flames, the smell of their contents adding to the general stench. The Royal Victoria Docks and Surrey Commercial Docks were sheets of flame. The mooring ropes of barges had burnt through and sent the blazing vessels drifting down the river. They came back when the tide turned, still blazing.

Telephone lines, gas and water were cut off and the only means of communication were dispatch riders and messengers on yellow bicycles wearing tin hats and armbands. Firemen at Woolwich Arsenal were fighting flames surrounded by live ammunition and stores of nitro-glycerine. In Hackney, a brick road shelter had a direct hit. It was crowded and the blast from the explosion sucked the walls out and the concrete roof fell in and crushed the people inside.

It was all very well to say, 'London can take it' but how much could they take? It wasn't the whole of London; it was the fact that the damage was concentrated in a particularly poor area, as more than one person pointed out to her. 'And where were the bleedin' RAF?' someone asked. 'And the guns. They've left us unprotected.' Laura treated their wounds and soothed their anger until four o'clock that afternoon, when she returned home utterly exhausted.

They ate tea quietly and sat listening to ITMA on the wireless before deciding to have an early night. They weren't given the opportunity. At eight o'clock the raiders returned. Gathering up their belongings, all ready to hand, Laura and her mother trooped out to the Anderson shelter and sat, sleepless, listening to the now familiar hum of aircraft, the explosions, the crash of falling masonry. Anne picked up her knitting, but Laura sat doing nothing but rehearse in her mind how she would tell her mother she was pregnant. She had to do it soon because someone more observant than the rest might notice, or she might be ill or injured in an air raid. It would be terrible for her mother to find out from an anonymous doctor.

'Don't dwell on it, dear,' Anne said.

Laura, startled out of her reverie by the thought that her mother could read her mind, pretended to be searching in her pocket for her handkerchief. 'Dwell on what?' she asked.

'I don't know, do I? Whatever it is that's bothering you.'

She wasn't ready yet, she truly wasn't. 'Nothing's bothering me. I'm just tired.' She was a coward, a yellow-bellied coward, ready to deny her child when that child would be the most welcome, the most wonderful thing that had happened to her, except meeting its father. Bob still filled her thoughts. It was as if he were still there, somewhere up in the sky, watching over her, protecting her just as he had done in life.

'Still thinking of Bob, are you?'

'Yes, all the time. If he were alive now, he would have been so angry at all this destruction, all the people being killed and injured.' If he were alive now, she would be Mrs Rawton and everyone would be delighted that she was expecting a baby. What a difference a wedding ring would have made!

'And you would still be worrying about him. At least you've been spared that.'

'Yes, I suppose so. But I think of the others too. Steve and the rest of the squadron. I haven't heard from Steve for ages and it makes me wonder if he's still alive. If he is, he must be just about exhausted.'

'We all are.' Anne was knitting a pair of socks with oiled wool, intended for some unknown seaman, but it was horrible stuff to handle and she was glad to lay it down and give her fingers a rest. She unscrewed the cap of the Thermos. 'Can't you get a spot of leave, you look all in.'

'I can't ask for time off when there's so much to be done.' She took a huge breath before continuing. 'Anyway, I'll be getting plenty of leave soon. I'll be giving up my job.'

'Why?' Anne asked in astonishment, handing Laura a cup of tea from the Thermos. For the first few weeks of her pregnancy she hadn't been able to face tea and had gone to great lengths to keep the fact from her mother, but the nausea had passed and now she was able to drink it with pleasure. 'I thought you enjoyed your work, though goodness knows, it was never meant to be like it is.'

'It's not the job, but I can't go on. You see, I'm going to have a baby.' There! It was out. Not the way she had intended, but out. She waited because her mother was sitting staring at her in the feeble light of the oil lamp, her cup halfway to her lips, frozen in shock. 'Well, say something.'

Anne put the cup down carefully on the little table they had brought into the shelter a few days before. 'What do you expect me to say? "Well done, dear"?'

'Don't be like that, Mum. It's not the end of the world.'

'It's the end of your world,' Anne snapped. 'How could you do it?'

She couldn't help it; the words flew off her tongue. 'Don't you know?'

'Don't be coarse. I brought you up to be ladylike with a proper sense of right and wrong. A handsome man comes along and it all flies out of the window.'

'No, it didn't. I am still the same, still your daughter—'

Anne opened her mouth to say something and shut it again with a snap. She looked across the tiny space to where Laura sat watching her in the dim glow of the lamp, while all around them the bombs fell and people were dying. 'I'm disappointed in you,' she said quietly. 'I thought you knew better.'

'I loved Bob. We would have been married, if—'

'Would have been, might have been, but that's not good enough, is it? What will people say?'

'I'm not interested in what people say. I want to know what you think about having a baby in the house.'

'Here?'

'Yes, of course. What do you expect me to do, go to some back street woman for an abortion? Give it away? What sort of mother gives away her own flesh and blood? I couldn't do it. It is Bob's child, a child made in love, and it will have all the love I can give it. I knew you would be upset but I never thought for a minute you'd be so unforgiving. I loved Bob, surely you can understand that? We jumped the gun, that's all.'

'How can you be so shameless?'

'I don't feel any shame, only sadness that Bob isn't here to share my joy. Mum, please don't condemn me. You loved Dad, didn't you?'

'Yes, but we didn't—'

'You might have done if you hadn't already been married when he was called away to war.' She attempted a little joke. 'I might have arrived a little too soon.'

Anne's reaction was to burst into tears. Desperate to make amends, Laura fell on her knees beside her and took her hands. 'Mum, I didn't mean it, I know you would have been stronger than I've been, but can't you forgive me? I want this baby so very much and I can't bear to think you will not welcome it too. Babies are precious.'

Anne continued to sob. She was sobbing for herself, for what had happened in the past, for the hurt she had caused Tom, for the lies she had told and continued to tell, for broken promises, all piling up to be answered on Judgement Day. What right had she to condemn when her own soul was black with guilt?

'Mum?' Laura was becoming seriously concerned. She had never expected it to be as bad as this.

Anne sniffed and attempted a smile. 'It's all right, love, I've had my say. And I do understand. But it won't be easy, you know. People will condemn. All those who bought you wedding presents will walk by on the other side of the road with their noses in the air.'

'I don't care, as long as you stand by me.'

'Of course I will. It's what mothers are for.'

'Thank you.' Laura reached up and kissed her mother's wet cheek. 'I'll try not to be a burden to you.'

'You are not a burden, you have never been a burden. You have always been *my* joy. We'll manage.' She picked up her cup of tea and pulled a face. 'Ugh, it's gone cold.'

Laura, too relieved to hide the fact, laughed. 'I could go indoors and make some more.'

'You'll do no such thing. We'll wait until the all-clear.'

They settled down to sleep, but as far as Anne was concerned, sleep was impossible, not only because deckchairs do not make comfortable beds but because Laura's revelation had shocked her, sent her hurtling back into the past, reminding her of her own spartan upbringing and inability to conceive a child of her own. More and more she found herself dwelling on it and tonight, with the uneven drone of bombers, the *ack-ack* of guns, the crashing of walls and windows and the clatter of debris on the outside of their shelter, she found herself going over it again, as if that would change one iota of it.

Tom's answer to her letter telling him she was pregnant was to tell her to give up her job and take care of herself and their precious child. Because it was wartime and women were needed when once they would have stayed at home and kept house, she had learnt to drive an ambulance. It was not something people of her class would normally do, but war had a way of turning everything topsy-turvy. She would meet the troop ships and transport the wounded to hospital. It was a job she enjoyed and made her feel as though she was doing her bit and bringing her husband safely home again. It also meant she could save a little money towards their dream home. But she realised cranking the starting handle of an ambulance and humping injured soldiers about was not a good idea for a pregnant woman, so she stopped working and instead made baby clothes, bought a second-hand cot and pram and watched the bump in her abdomen grow, waiting for her baby to start kicking. But it never did.

She was scrubbing her front step one day when she felt a sudden spasm of pain, like a very bad period pain. She got to her feet, picked up her bucket and went back indoors, leaving the step half done. A few minutes later another pain gripped her and then she felt a wetness between her legs. She could not believe she was losing her longed-for child and for a moment could not make up her mind what to do. She would not go to her mother-in-law for help but trudged down to the midwife's house, hoping against hope Mrs Bates would be able to stem the flow and save her pregnancy. She couldn't; the baby was lost on the midwife's spare bed. It was, so the widowed Mrs Bates told her, a girl. She lay there and sobbed and sobbed.

'Give over, dear,' Mrs Bates said, when it seemed she would never stop. 'Cryin' like that won't alter anything.'

She tried hard to pull herself together. 'Will I be able to have more babies?' she asked, mopping her eyes and blowing her nose.

'Can't say. Ask your doctor. If you can't, you can always adopt. There's poor motherless babes crying out to be given good homes…'

She knew that. When she was a little girl she would have given anything to have had parents and an ordinary home. Oh, how she had envied those who had! She would have been overjoyed if someone had taken her in and adopted her. She dried her tears, accepted the rags Mrs Bates gave her to sop up the blood and left in a state so numb she could not remember how she got home. The nightmare was made worse the next day when the doctor told her she would never have children. She didn't want to accept it, wouldn't accept it; it was a mistake. The next time she saw her mother-in-law she told her everything was going on normally. And that was when the deception began.

She carried on pretending, bulking herself out with more and more padding as the weeks progressed, shutting her eyes to the fact that at the end of the waiting, there would be no baby. It was crazy, mad, wicked.

One day she met Mrs Bates in the street. The midwife stopped and looked her up and down. 'Mrs Drummond, just what do you think you're playing at?'

Anne stared blankly at her; it was the first time she had been challenged and had almost come to believe there really was a child growing inside her. 'I don't know what you mean.'

'Yes, you do. Come home with me and tell me all about it.' She relieved Anne of her shopping basket and took her arm. Anne went with her like an automaton. Once in Mrs Bates's kitchen, she was pushed into a chair and given a cup of hot strong tea. 'Now then, out with it. I know you lost your baby and you can't have got that big with another one so soon. Besides, your 'usband's in France, ain't 'e?'

Anne suddenly deflated like a pricked balloon. The tears flowed and she could not hold the cup, which rattled in its saucer. Mrs Bates took it from her. 'Pretending, are you?'

Anne nodded dumbly.

'It's not uncommon, but usually the truth comes to light before this. You look ready to drop it.'

Anne smiled weakly. 'Everyone tells me it must be a big baby.'

'Remind me. When was it supposed to be due?'

'The middle of March.'

'That's less than a month away.'

'I know.'

'What were you thinking of doing, dumping the padding and saying it was stillborn?'

'I wasn't thinking at all.'

'Well, think now. You can't go on like this, can you?'

'No.' It was said with infinite weariness.

'I can get you a baby, a real live baby.'

'Adopt one, you mean? Tom won't have that. He's said so enough times.'

'He's away, isn't he?'

'Yes.'

'Then don't tell him.'

'I can't deceive him like that. And wouldn't he know?'

'Not necessarily, men can be incredibly stupid, you know.'

'But I'd have to sign papers and things like that, wouldn't I?'

'No. I know a doctor who runs a clinic for unmarried mothers and he arranges private adoptions. It's not strictly legal, you understand, but it goes on and he does it for the sake of the babies. They have loving parents and a good home instead of being sent to an orphanage.'

Mrs Bates knew nothing of Anne's life before she arrived in Stepney, but mention of an orphanage was the deciding factor. She agreed to go with Mrs Bates to the clinic and talk to the doctor.

'I have a young mother-to-be in here who is due to give birth at roughly the same time as yours,' he told her. 'She comes from an upper-class family who are anxious to keep the birth a secret. If you wish, we can arrange for you to have the child.'

'Oh, yes please.' Anne did not ask what it would cost; she didn't care. She went home and waited and when Mrs Bates came to tell her the mother was in labour, she booked into the clinic. It cost her every penny of the money she had been carefully saving to leave Prince Albert Lane for a new home, but once the decision had been taken, she could not, would not, back out. Two days later, a baby was put into her arms by Mrs Bates. 'She's all yours. She hasn't even been registered, so you can do it.'

Anne looked down at the tiny infant, less than a day old, and wondered how any mother could bear to part with something so wondrous. She had a quiff of dark hair, huge violet eyes and a rosebud mouth. Her tiny fingers gripped Anne's thumb with surprising strength. She was dressed in the most beautiful white cotton nightgown, hand embroidered with white daisies and drawn threadwork, and wrapped in a knitted shawl of the finest wool. It was more than Anne could afford to buy; the child's real mother was obviously not short of a shilling or two. That was just like the upper classes; they took their pleasures where

97

they found them and when the consequences became inconvenient, they disposed of them like unwanted puppies. She could almost hate the mother for her callousness, but for the fact she had given her this priceless gift. She would love this child, take care of her through thick and thin, and when Tom came home... She did not want to think of what she would say to him. She walked out of the hospital in a dream. The child was hers. She had seen nothing of the unknown mother, would not even think of her.

It was just as well her mother-in-law did not expect to visit her in hospital; she could not afford to stay there, so she went to Mrs Bates's for a couple of days. The midwife taught her how to mix up the powdered milk to give the baby a feed and bring up the wind afterwards, how to change her nappy and bathe and dress her. Every little task was a joyous revelation. Then she took her daughter home, a proud mother.

Mrs Drummond and Tom's sister, Maisie, came round the next day to view the new arrival. The expensive clothes and the shawl had been packed away and she was dressed in the little garments Anne had prepared for her: a cotton nightgown, a knitted matinée jacket and bootees. 'I can't see anything of Tom in her,' her mother-in-law said, peering into the pram, which Anne had wheeled through the house to the kitchen, not having a back entrance. 'She's got dark hair. You're both fair.'

Anne was prepared for that. 'Maybe she takes after someone on my side of the family.'

'Maybe. We'll never know, will we?'

Anne ignored the jibe.

'What are you going to call her?' Maisie asked. She had recently married a tailor's shop assistant and lived a few streets away. She was also hugely pregnant.

'Laura.'

'Laura! What a high falutin' name. Did Tom help you choose it?'

'Yes.' How could she tell him of her deception? How could she disappoint him? He would be furiously angry. He might even want to give Laura back.

Anne registered Laura as her own, and almost managed to deceive herself that she was. When Tom came back from the war, he was disabled by mustard gas and his sight was badly affected. He was also impotent, so she did not have to tell him she could not have another baby. Laura would be their only child.

She was healthy, in spite of Mrs Drummond's dire warnings that she would be a weakling on account of being bottle-fed. She grew quickly and by the time she was toddling about it became evident she would be taller than either of her parents. Tom laughed at his mother when she said Laura was none of their breed and there must have been a mix-up at the hospital. 'That's the trouble with having babes in 'ospital,' she said. 'You never know what you're going to be saddled with.'

'Do you think I don't know my own child?' Anne demanded, swallowing down the guilt. 'Fine mother I'd be.'

The all-clear brought her out of her reverie. Laura sat opposite her, reading, knowing nothing of what had been going on in her head. They picked up their belongings and returned thankfully to the house. It was three in the morning.

The raids were repeated every evening for fifty-seven consecutive nights until both Laura and Anne were almost asleep on their feet. They went to work numbed by what was happening around them, wondering each night as they made their way to the shelter if it would be their last. They installed a couple of camp beds, which left a tiny gangway between them, but at least they could lie down and try to sleep. They rose each morning bleary-eyed and went about their allotted tasks like automatons, wondering how much longer it would go on. But Laura had the consolation of knowing that she had no secrets from her mother. They would get through it somehow and Bob's child would be born and grow up loved and happy. She prayed for it every night, she thanked God every morning when they emerged unscathed.

Steve's eyes were so gritty with tiredness he could not stop blinking. The fact they had clear warning that the bombers were on their way did little to help. The squadron got off the ground, but it was almost impossible to see the enemy. Occasionally, more by good luck than anything else, they encountered an enemy aircraft and there was a dogfight which resulted in bringing one down. One out of hundreds! He felt angrily helpless. Occasionally the searchlights picked up a Dornier or a Heinkel, but it usually escaped by flying higher out of range of the lights. Night after night was the same; he wouldn't have noticed his twenty-third birthday come and go if he hadn't had cards from home.

He worried about those on the ground, worried that he could not do anything to help them. He worried about Laura. He had seen nothing of her since Bob's funeral. Bob had asked him to look out for her, but not even Bob could have foreseen the unremitting ferocity of the Luftwaffe's attack. When the bombers left, the squadron just had time to land and refuel before they came back again. He was becoming very concerned for the health and safety of his men and by the end of October, he knew they were all at the end of their tether.

The raids on London dwindled only because the Luftwaffe turned their attention to other industrial centres and ports, which were being heavily bombed, but it was enough for Steve to be given a week's leave. It was never more welcome. He decided to go and see Laura on the way.

Crossing the city was an eye-opener. He had seen the bombers coming in, of course, and looked down on the conflagration from above, but what he saw on the ground shocked him. There were great gaps where houses had once stood. Inside walls had become outside walls, propped up by baulks of timber when the house next door was demolished. Many of the basements of these had been filled with water ready for firemen to use. Roads were roped off because there was the danger of falling masonry, or because there was an unexploded bomb which hadn't yet been dealt with.

The extraordinary thing was that people were going about their business, walking, or taking a bus or tube, notwithstanding that the Underground stations were being used as shelters and were crammed with sleeping bodies every night. He didn't know what sanitary arrangements had been made, but the stench, even during the day after they'd all gone home, was pretty bad. Delivery vans, coal lorries, taxis and buses were working; newspaper sellers stood on corners, their four-page newspapers being eagerly snapped up. Shops had had their fronts blown out and although some had been forced to close, others were open with chalked notices on the boards that had taken the place of windows, saying 'Business as usual', which was ironic, considering they had little on their shelves.

He went to the hospital first, where he was told Laura was not on duty, so he took the tube to Burnt Oak and hurried on foot to Axholme Avenue, wondering what he would find when he got there. The house, he was thankful to see, had not been bombed. She answered the door to his knock, wearing slacks and a loose shirt. Her hair was combed back into a ribbon, which would have been severe if several shorter ends had not escaped and curled about her head. She looked tired, her eyes dark-rimmed. 'Steve! What a surprise. Come in.'

He stepped inside and took off his cap. 'I was on my way home on leave and thought I'd pop in and see how you were.'

'We're fine. Tired of spending our nights in the shelter, but otherwise OK. Would you like a cup of tea?'

'Yes please, if you can spare it.'

'Oh, I think we can manage that.' She smiled and some of the tiredness vanished from her eyes, leaving her looking more like the Laura he remembered, the one in the photograph he had on his locker. 'It's a poor do if we can't find a cuppa for one of our brave fliers.' She led the way into the kitchen as she spoke.

'I don't know so much about the brave bit. It seems to me it's the civilians that are bravest in this war.'

'We haven't got much choice, have we?' She filled a kettle, put it on the gas and turned to put cups and saucers and a milk jug on the table. 'Sit down, Steve, and tell me what you've been up to.'

'Nothing to tell. We take off, we buzz about the sky trying to shoot down the enemy, then we land, eat and sleep when we can, and then fly again. I feel so helpless not being able to prevent what's happening to London. How do you put up with it?'

'Because we have to.'

'I suppose so. But haven't you got relatives or somewhere you could go to in the country?'

'No, none at all.' She was tempted to tell him she was pregnant, that before long she would have to give up work altogether, but she decided against it. Although she was not exactly ashamed of her condition, she didn't want to shout it from the rooftops. 'This is my home, Steve. I've lived here since I was eight years old. I don't see why Adolf Hitler should drive me out. Besides, Mum won't go and I'm certainly not leaving her here alone.'

'Is Mrs Drummond still working for the WVS?'

'Yes, she's been given a paid post, which means even more work, but I think she enjoys it, though she comes home very tired. I wish I could do more to help her, but she never complains.'

He smiled. 'Mothers are like that.'

'Yes.' She poured the tea and handed him a cup. 'I know your father is a farmer, but what about the rest of the family: mother, brothers, sisters?'

'My mother is a bit like yours, I think, never so happy as when she's helping other people. She's looking after a couple of evacuees from the East End who are a bit of a handful. I have a sister, Jenny, who's a schoolteacher, but no brother. I suppose Bob was as near to a brother as anyone.' He stopped suddenly. 'Oh, I'm sorry.'

'What for? Please don't feel you can't mention his name to me. I like to talk about him, but there's no one…' She stopped before adding. 'Mum doesn't find it easy. I expect you miss him.'

He was reminded of Mrs Drummond's reaction to Bob's death and the swift way she disposed of the evidence of the wedding breakfast. 'Yes, every day. He was always so cool in a crisis, so good at getting the best out of everyone.' He turned and got to his feet as the back door opened and Mrs Drummond came in.

'Flight Lieutenant, it's good to see you safe and sound.'

'Mum, he's not a flight lieutenant now, he's a squadron leader.'

'It doesn't matter,' he said. 'How are you, Mrs Drummond?'

'Oh, we're all right, aren't we, Laura? Tired, but in one piece.'

She looked more than tired, she looked ill. Her complexion, which he remembered as rosy, was pasty, and her well-rounded figure was thinner. The contrast between mother and daughter was marked. Anne seemed to have shrunk, while her daughter, always much the taller of the two, was expanding. 'I'm glad. But it must be pretty bad, what with the air raids and everything.'

'Can't do much about those, can we? Do sit down again. I see Laura has given you a cup of tea.'

'Yes, thank you.'

'Can we offer you something to eat? A sandwich, perhaps?'

'No, thank you, Mrs Drummond. I've got a spot of leave and only popped in on my way through London to see how you were. I believe there's a train from Liverpool Street in an hour.'

'Then you won't want to miss it. But thank you for coming.'

'My pleasure.' He picked up his cap and bag. Laura went with him to the front door.

'Look after yourself,' she said, softly.

'And you.' He bent to put a butterfly kiss on her cheek and, before she could express either surprise or outrage, he turned and strode off down the street. He did not look back so he did not know how long she stayed at the door before retreating inside.

It had been a strange, very unsatisfactory visit in many ways. Laura had been polite, even welcoming, but there had been no warmth there. *What did I expect?* he chided himself as he made for the Underground; did he think she would fall into his arms as she had done at Bob's funeral? She had only been taking comfort from him then, comfort he had been glad to give and would again if she

103

ever asked it of him. He was glad he was going home to all things familiar; to his parents and sister, the village and the farm. He'd help with the ploughing if that had not already been done, milk the cows and trudge over the countryside with Boy at his heels, and sleep and sleep, which should make him feel better.

The twins had disappeared again. Kathy, almost ready to dish up the evening meal, sighed. They had been going off a lot lately. It was disappointment, she supposed. They had had a few postcards from their father, and that cheered them up a bit, but it was their mother they really wanted to hear from; only their mother could say when they could go home again. All but a handful of their classmates had gone back and that included their teacher, so the twins had been integrated into the village classes, which added to their feeling of abandonment. They had looked for a letter every day from the beginning of the summer holidays, expecting to hear that she was coming, but day after day there was nothing. Kathy had begun to wonder if the woman had been bombed out or even killed when, in the first week of September, two days before the boys were due to go back to school, a letter arrived. Overjoyed, they rushed upstairs to read it in the privacy of their room. When Kathy asked them later if their mother was well, Donny told her tersely that she was but she couldn't come. 'She's goin' to try and come down for Christmas,' he added.

'She's busy,' Lenny added.

It had been the beginning of their naughtiness. After settling down so well, they had become irritable and uncooperative, refusing to lift a finger to help either in the house or on the farm, and Lenny started wetting the bed again. Kathy didn't know what to do. How could she scold them when their tantrums were due to their unhappiness? But she couldn't let them run wild. They had missed school several times and would not tell her where they'd been. Supposing they decided to run away, really run away, not spend a few hours hiding themselves somewhere, how would she know until they had been gone for hours and hours and the trail had gone cold? Supposing they tried to go home to Stepney; the air raids were as bad there as anywhere. If she had their mother in front of her now, she would cheerfully shake her until her teeth rattled.

Jenny came in the back door, left her shoes in the scullery and padded into the kitchen in her socks, pulling off her headscarf. 'It's raining cats and dogs.'

'Oh dear, and the boys are out. I wonder where they've got to?'

'No telling with them.'

'I'm worried about them. I don't want Mrs Woodrow on my tail for neglecting them.' Mrs Woodrow was the welfare officer for the evacuees in Beckbridge and she occasionally paid visits to make sure the children were being properly looked after and were behaving themselves. 'I couldn't live with myself if they were taken away and sent to one of those hostels for problem children that no one wants.'

'Shall I go out and look for them? I can go on my bike.'

'OK, tell them it's nearly suppertime.'

'Donny, let's go 'ome. Me feet are wet.' They were walking down the lane that ran alongside the big house. It was full of muddy puddles into which Donny, in Wellington boots, jumped now and again, spattering his brother, who was wearing plimsolls because he had a blister on his heel and they were the most comfortable footwear he had. The hedges, bare of leaves, dripped moisture into the ditches, now full to overflowing. The country had not been too bad in the summer, when the sun shone and the air was warm and they could go exploring and find things to do, but now it was wet and grey and miserable and matched their mood exactly.

'It ain't home. I hate it.'

'Ma said it was 'ome for us now. She said there weren't no winders in our house and no gas and she had to stay at 'ome while the builders were in.'

'I know what she said.'

'Let's go then. I'm all wet.'

'No. I want to think.'

'You can think in our bedroom.'

'No, I can't. Aunty Kathy always wants to know what we're doing and calling us down to do our 'omework or 'ave our dinner. I need peace and quiet to think.'

'What about?'

'We can't go 'ome 'cos we ain't got money for the fare, so we've got to think of a way of gettin' Mum down 'ere. Then we'll make 'er take us home.'

'She said she might come for Christmas.'

'She said she'd come in the 'olidays an' all, but she never did.'

'She couldn't 'elp not 'avin' any winders or gas.'

'No, I know.' Donny sounded sceptical.

'Me feet are wet and I'm cold.'

'Good.' Donny jumped in another puddle and water cascaded over his twin. 'If you're ill, Aunty Kathy will send for Mum. It might even turn to pneumonia and then she'd 'ave to stay 'til you was well again.' He stopped suddenly. 'I got an idea. Come on.' He turned in the gates of the big house and struck off across the park towards the lake, followed by a reluctant Lenny. They had ventured in the grounds several times in the past, on one occasion, in the summer, going as far as the lake. It was fringed with reeds and had big yellow water lilies in the middle and ducks swimming on it. There was a kind of shed there with a boat in it and a landing stage, but it was all very rickety.

Donny stood at the edge of the lake surveying the water. Rain was ruffling the surface and now it looked cold and uninviting. 'If you was to slip in I could go in and save you. If we was both at death's door, Mum'd blame Aunty Kathy and she'd fetch us 'ome.'

'No, Donny, we'll be drownded.' He was on the verge of tears, but he manfully held them back, knowing they made his brother cross. 'Le's go 'ome.'

Donny, who didn't really fancy jumping in the water, which looked decidedly uninviting, turned away. They were passing the summer house when Donny stopped and pointed. 'Look at that. Someone's bin 'ere. The grass is all flattened.'

'So what?'

'It could be a spy. There's lots of spies about, they come down by parachute and they have wirelesses and signal to the bombers where to drop their bombs.'

'How d'you know?'

'Everyone knows. Le's go and investigate.'

'I want to go 'ome.'

'So do I. If we catch a spy, then they'll be so pleased with us, they'll send for us to go to Buckingham Palace to get a medal from the King, and then Mum will be proud of us and let us go 'ome.' He didn't wait for Lenny but ran to the door. 'Someone's broke the padlock.' He took it off and opened the door. 'There's footsteps all over the place.' He went inside, followed more slowly by his brother. There were indeed footprints in the dust of the floor. There were deckchairs stacked against a wall and some cricket pads. 'There's gotta be a wireless somewhere.' He began poking about behind the deckchairs and looking up into the rafters. A bat flew out, making Lenny scream. 'Oh, shut up, Lenny, it's only a bat. You remember Aunty Daphne showed us one in the barn the other day. They're only mice that c'n fly.'

'Le's go,' Lenny said. 'Supposin' someone comes.'

'In a minute. Crikey!' He had discovered the bench seat was hinged and had lifted the lid. 'Jus' look at this!'

Lenny crept forward and peered over his brother's shoulder. What he saw made his eyes open wide in surprise. There were bars of chocolate, bottles of whisky, tins of peaches, golden syrup, lipsticks and bottles of scent. '*California Poppy*, Mum's favourite,' he said in wonderment. 'How did it get there?'

'I don' know, do I?' He had found a flat packet which he was undoing. A pair of silk stockings tumbled to the floor. He picked them up and tried to stuff them back, but they wouldn't go, not like they'd been before.

'Do spies have things like that?'

'They might, if they wanted to bribe someone for information.'

'What information?'

'Anything they wanted to know.'

'I don' believe that. I reckon it's loot. Someone's nicked it and 'id it. Shut the lid, Donny, and come away. If someone comes—'

'It won't 'alf make a good present for Mum, don't you think?' Donny persisted 'Scent and stockings. She'd be ever so pleased. She'd come to see us then, wouldn't she?' Donny did not wait for his brother's agreement but put two bottles, one *California Poppy* and the other *Evening in Paris*, into a pocket of his raincoat.

'We can't take them, it's stealing. If we're catched, Aunty Kathy will beat us.'

'Don't be daft, she don' believe in hitting kids, she said so.'

'She might if she was angry enough. That's what Mum always used ter say: if we didn't make her angry, she wouldn't 'ave ter 'it us.'

'Tha's different, mums can do what they like. Aunty Kathy's not our mum, not even a relation. We don' 'ave ter say 'ow we got them. We can pretend we saved our pocket money and bought 'em.' He picked up two lipsticks, one ruby red, and one natural pink, and the already opened packet of stockings and stuffed those in Lenny's pockets. Then he took a bar of Cadbury's milk chocolate and shut down the lid.

'We'll get caught and go to prison,' Lenny said, following his twin outside and watching as he replaced the padlock.

'Who's goin' to tell on us? You think a Jerry spy is goin' to go to the coppers and report it? Or a thief. "Please, sir, me loot's bin took." Use yer loaf.' He unwrapped the chocolate and broke off two squares, one of which he handed to Lenny. Then he carefully re-wrapped the rest and put it into his other pocket. 'We wanted something to make Ma come and this is it. Now, le's get goin'. But act natural. We don' want Aunty Kathy gettin' suspicious.'

Helen, walking home after a visit to the village shop, encountered the two ragamuffins as they ran down her drive. One was wearing Wellington boots and the other plimsolls but apart from that they were as alike as two peas in a pod. They were wet and filthy, their faces and hands black with what looked like coal dust. Their knees were grazed and their socks were wrinkled round their ankles. Seeing her they scuttled to a stop.

'What are you doing here?' she asked them.

'Just lookin',' Donny mumbled.

'Explorin',' Lenny added.

'Are you twins?'

'Yep. I'm Donny and this 'ere's Lenny. We've been evacuated.'

'From London?'

'Yeah. Stepney.'

Stepney. She had never lived there, but she had spent hours and hours tramping its streets looking for a lost daughter and had come to know it well.

'Who are you staying with?'

'Aunty Kathy. Mr and Mrs Wainright. Bridge Farm. Do you know them?'

'Oh yes, I know them. Run along now and say hallo to Mrs Wainright from me.'

She watched them go and then, instead of continuing up the drive to the house, she turned across the grass and went to the summer house. The boys had been coming from that direction and she wondered what they had been up to.

The grass around it was trampled and the padlock broken; she must remember to have it replaced. She went inside and sat down. Inside, apart from footprints in the dust of the floor, no doubt caused by the two evacuees, everything was as it should be, just as it had been all those years ago when she and Oliver would fly into each other's arms and make love, unheedful of the consequences. Why hadn't he come back?

Sitting in the dilapidated summer house with its flaking

paintwork, its murky windows and mouse-nibbled cushions, she wondered what had happened to him. Had he survived the war? Had he gone home to Canada? Had he married? Did he ever think of her? She had schooled herself not to think of him, but how was that possible when every day, through news of the war and worry about their daughter, the past was brought home to her, as if sleeping ghosts had been reawakened by the new conflict? It was as if one were merging into the other regardless of the twenty-odd years that had passed between them. And still the pain was there and, for some reason, it was especially bad now.

Whenever she could, Helen travelled up to London and made her way to the park, knowing that the woman habitually took Olivia there to run about and play. She would follow them, just to see the child and watch her sturdy toddler's legs running after a ball or perhaps a sparrow that had come for crumbs. She was beautiful, dark-haired, rosy-cheeked, and obviously loved. Her dress, though poor, was clean. Helen's heart had been twisted with pain to think of someone from those terrible slums bringing up her child when she could give her so much more: a room of her own, more than one if you included the nursery and schoolroom; toys; beautiful clothes; shoes, lots of shoes, not the thin-soled ones she had seen her wearing; and good schooling when the time came. But the toddler's obvious contentment was the twisting of the knife in a wound that would never heal.

One day she was careless and the woman turned round and confronted her, demanding to know why she was following her.

'I was admiring the little girl. She is so pretty.'

'God, you're perverted. I've a good mind to call the police.'

'Please don't do that. I mean no harm, I promise you.'

'Why pick on my child?' She waved her arm to encompass other children playing in the park. 'There are dozens to choose from.'

'She is my daughter.'

'Rubbish. Where did you get that idea?'

'Oh, but she is. My flesh and blood. She was born in St Mary and

Martha Clinic on March the fifth, 1918, and handed over to you by an unscrupulous doctor and his assistants.'

The woman was obviously flustered, but was not going to give in without a fight. 'No. Laura is mine, mine and Tom's. I have her birth certificate to prove it.'

So that was why her search of the records for Olivia had been so fruitless! The child had been registered as Laura Drummond. 'Then you falsified it. That is surely a crime.' She did not know why she was being so belligerent, except that seeing the child run to the other woman with a buttercup she had picked and calling her 'Mummy' was breaking her heart.

'Who's going to prove that? Not you. You gave her away. You didn't want her.'

'That's not true. I did want her. If you only knew—'

'I don't want to know. If you do not go away and leave us alone, I'll call a bobby.'

'Do that, if you like. You are the one who has broken the law, Mrs Drummond, not me. And I could go to the newspapers.'

'You wouldn't.' The woman had gone very pale. 'If you love her, as you say you do, you would never subject her to that.'

Unfortunately that was true. As a blackmailer, she was a complete failure. 'No, I don't think I would. But let me tell you what happened—'

'I don't want to hear it.'

'Why not? Are you afraid you might start feeling sorry for me?'

'No.' Helen, watching her draw Laura onto her lap and cuddle her, wished she could wrest the child away from her, but knew it would be an act of stupidity. 'Did you mean it when you said you did not want to give her away?'

'Yes.' She began slowly, but little by little the story came out, all of it; she held nothing back and ended with her last sight of her daughter being carried away. Anne listened, grudgingly, it was true, but in the end she admitted Helen had been hard done by, though in no way relinquishing her right to Laura. In her place Helen wouldn't have done either. 'You can't have her back. She is happy with me and Tom, it would break her heart to be separated from us. Surely you can see that?'

'Yes, but I want to keep in touch, to know that she is well and happy, and if there is ever anything I can do to help, I want you to tell me. I am not without means.'

There was no immediate answer and Helen watched the expressions flitting across the woman's face: sympathy, doubt, fear, mostly fear. At last she said, 'I will let you know from time to time how Laura is getting on, if you promise never to contact me again, never try and see her or speak to her. Ever.'

How could she make such a promise? But what else could she do? Her child's happiness was more important than her feelings. 'Very well. I will stay away, so long as you promise to tell Laura the truth when she is old enough to understand. Will you do that?'

'I don't know. You are asking a lot.'

'You are asking a lot of me. And surely she deserves to know the truth. There may come a time when she may need me.'

'I doubt it.'

'All the same, will you give me your word?' She dug in her handbag and brought out her card with her name and address embossed on it, and a snapshot of herself, taken in front of the summer house, and offered them to her. 'Show her these, tell her I loved her.'

'All right. You keep your promise and I'll keep mine.'

It was all she could do. With a last anguished look at her child, she returned home to the problems of day-to-day living, things like disappearing servants, how to keep the house going on the money she had inherited, and fielding questions from Great Aunt Martha as to why she had not found a nice young man to marry. She shut up half the house and managed with Mr and Mrs Ward as butler and cook/housekeeper and a daily woman to do the rough cleaning and laundry. It was as if her life were on hold.

The chill in the rain-laden air brought her back to the present and she stirred her cramped limbs and returned to the house. Here she was rattling round in a huge mansion, apparently safe and sound, when Anne and Laura were in the thick of it in Stepney. The thought that her daughter might be hurt, even killed in an air raid and she not know a thing about it, made her quake with fear. If she had not made that promise to Anne, she could have invited her and Laura to stay with her. Surely that would be better than living in air raid shelters? Was she justified in breaking her word on those grounds? Had Anne kept hers? Had she told Laura the truth? The thought that her daughter might have been told and did not want to know her hurt. It hurt badly.

Chapter Four

'STEVE!' JENNY, ENCASED in a yellow oilskin cape with a hood, had been all round the village searching everywhere she thought the twins might be and, drawing a blank, had decided to cycle to Attlesham Station in case the boys had decided to try and board a train. Halfway there she had seen the tall, uniformed figure of her brother striding towards her. 'Does Mum know you're coming?'

'No, I thought I'd surprise her. Anyway, I couldn't be sure I'd get away. Where are you off to?'

'I'm looking for the twins. They've gone off again and Mum is worried. You didn't see them skulking about on your way, did you?'

'No. Do they often run away?'

'Not run away exactly, but they do go missing for hours at a time.'

'Nothing new in that. I used to do it myself when I was their age. I always came home when I was hungry.'

'Yes, they are probably at home now.' She turned the bicycle round and he put his bag on the carrier and took it from her to wheel it to towards home. 'Couldn't you get a taxi from the station?'

'Not a one to be had, so I decided to walk. How is everyone?'

'Same as usual. Josh still grumbles, Meg and Daphne still laugh at him, Dad still fills in endless forms and Mum is mum to everyone.'

'But the boys are a handful?'

'Yes. Their dratted mother hasn't been to see them and all they've had is one measly letter saying she might come at Christmas.

You should have seen their faces. Poor little devils, they had been counting on her coming for the summer holidays, especially after all their pals went back to London and they were left behind.'

'Perhaps it's just as well they were. I had to cross London to catch my connection. It's a mess.'

'How long have you got?'

'Seven days.'

'Then you'll be here for Saturday's dance. Daphne and Meg are going. I can guarantee you won't be without partners.'

'Thanks, Sis. Speaking of the twins, look over there.'

She looked up and saw the two bedraggled boys apparently coming out of the gates of the Hall. They had their hands in their pockets. 'Donny, Lenny, where have you been?' she called out. 'I've been looking everywhere for you.'

'We went for a walk,' Donny said, falling in beside her.

'I've got wet feet,' Lenny informed them.

'I'm not surprised,' Steve said. 'It's too wet for plimsolls. Why didn't you wear your wellies like your brother?'

''Cos I've got a blister on me 'eel.'

'Then going for a walk was hardly a sensible thing to do, was it?'

'Nothing else to do.'

'Where did you go?'

Lenny opened his mouth and was silenced by a look from Donny, which was not lost on Steven. He was not so old he couldn't remember the things he used to get up to as a child and he guessed they had been doing something they knew they shouldn't. 'Let me guess. You've been exploring the grounds of the Hall and found the boathouse.'

Lenny gasped and Donny managed a grin, though he could feel the loot in his pocket weighing it down. 'Yes, but we didn't take the boat out, honest.'

'I'm glad you didn't. I'd be surprised if it's watertight. But you know you aren't supposed to go in there. It's private property.'

'We weren't doin' no 'arm. An' the lady didn't mind.'

'You mean Lady Barstairs?'

'Dunno her name. She said to say hallo to Aunty Kathy.'

'Then I expect it was. Run along now and get out of those wet clothes before you catch your death of cold.'

'Can you die from a cold?' Lenny asked.

'I shouldn't think so.'

'Oh.' He paused. 'But you can get ill though?'

'Oh yes. Headache, stuffed up nose, aches and pains, but you needn't worry, Aunty Kathy will cure you.'

'Can we take the bike?' Donny asked. 'We'd get 'ome quicker on that.'

Steve removed his bag and the boys got on the cycle, Donny on the pedals and Lenny on the saddle. They wobbled off down the lane. Steve laughed. 'They'll probably end up in a heap on the road.'

'No, they've become quite adept. They seem more cheerful than they have been, which is strange considering how wet and bedraggled they are. I'd guess they've been up to something.'

That was a view shared by Kathy when she scolded them for disappearing without saying where they were going and getting soaked into the bargain. Donny had slipped out of his boots as soon as he entered the house, but Lenny had to sit on the scullery floor to undo his plimsolls.

'Take your coat off first,' she said. 'Then go upstairs and change. Put your pyjamas on. You can have your tea in your dressing gowns.' Dressing gowns were garments they had never had before coming to Beckbridge, but Kathy had gone to the WVS clothing exchange and found a couple, together with some other items of clothing they needed. Steve came in the door at that point so she did not immediately notice that, instead of hanging their raincoats on the rail in the lobby, they ran upstairs with them on. 'Steve! Oh, how lovely to see you.' Eyes alight, she ran and embraced him. 'Why didn't you say you were coming? We could have met you at the station.'

He kissed her cheek. 'I didn't know which train I'd be on and, anyway, I enjoyed the walk.'

'In the rain? You are as wet as the twins. Go up to your room and change. I'll do a few more vegetables and make the meat go round. More gravy and dumplings should do it. Oh, it's so good to have you home safe and sound. Jenny, be a dear and go and tell Dad and the girls Steve's home and we'll be eating in half an hour.' She bustled about peeling potatoes, shredding cabbage and laying an extra place at the table, humming happily to herself, while upstairs the twins emptied their pockets and hid the contents on the top of the wardrobe.

'Now what?' Lenny asked.

'Get into jim-jams and go down for supper.'

The taxi Helen took from Liverpool Street Station stopped at the end of Prince Albert Lane. 'Can't go any further, missus,' the cabbie told her. She got out, paid him and set off up the street. Except there was nothing left of it. A few walls still stood, carefully roped off, and the craters where some houses had been were half filled with dirty water. The street itself had been swept clean and a coal cart, pulled by a horse, trundled along it. At the far end, one house, with its windows boarded up and its sidewall propped up by large timbers, had a notice pinned to its door. 'Still living here.' She knocked and waited.

A voice from inside called. 'This door don' open. Come round the back.'

She stepped gingerly round the foundations of what had been the house next door and was met by an elderly woman with two small children clinging to her skirts; her grandchildren, Helen surmised, and wondered where the mother was. Killed or at work? All were ill-clad. 'I'm looking for Mrs Drummond and her daughter, Laura,' she said.

'Don't know nuffin' about anyone called Laura; her daughter's name is Maisie, but Mrs Drummond copped it when her 'ouse 'ad a direct 'it.'

Helen felt herself begin to tremble. Surely, surely not? She would have known, somewhere inside her a voice would have told her that all she lived for had been brought to a sudden and bloody end. 'I'm sure she was called Laura. Mrs Drummond would be about my age, not very tall, fair hair, a little plump.'

The woman eyed Helen up and down, taking in her fur coat and stylish hat, and the look was one of curiosity. 'Oh, then yer must mean the other Mrs Drummond. Tom's wife. They moved away, years ago.' She stopped to think. 'The little girl had just started school, as I recall.'

Helen's had heart plummeted into her boots. 'Do you know where they went?'

'No. Maisie might know where to find 'er.'

'Where does she live?'

'Dunno. Not round 'ere. Moved up in the world, she 'as, married to a tailor.' She laughed. 'Making uniforms for the troops fit to bust, 'e is, so she told me when she came up to arrange the funeral. The war ain't bin bad for everyone.'

'Do you know her surname?'

'Not that I c'n recall. Sorry I can't 'elp yer.'

'Thank you anyway.' She pressed some coins into her hand. 'For the children.'

The woman accepted them and ushered the children back into the house and Helen trudged back down the street, ready to howl. She was very, very angry. And it hurt to think she had scrupulously kept her word and been rewarded with betrayal.

There were no taxis to be had and she caught a bus back to the station. She found a seat in a crowded carriage and sat down to endure the return journey. She was not aware of the slowness of the train, the frequent stops, the growing dusk and the feeble yellow light in the carriage. Her head was spinning. Why had Anne never told her of their change of address? Had she gone up in the world or down? Was she in want? Did she need help? To find out, she had to find her again, but the memory of the weeks and weeks of searching before – the letters, the questions, the disappointments when a promising lead came to nothing, the bribery and bullying tactics and the sheer expense of it – daunted her. Could she find her again? Did she have the stamina to do it? But if she did nothing, her daughter would be lost to her for ever.

'Are you all right?' The woman who was sitting opposite her leant forward and touched her hand.

Startled out of her reverie, she blinked to clear her vision and realised silent tears were running down her cheeks unchecked. She smiled wanly. 'Yes, thank you. I'm afraid I've had bad news. The war, you know—'

'I'm sorry. It's the same all over. If I had Hitler here, I'd strangle him with my bare hands. All this suffering, lives gone, houses demolished… There, there, dear, don't cry, I'm sure you don't want to hear me rabbiting on.' But she did rabbit on, which, in some measure, saved Helen from brooding. She left the train at Ely and boarded another for Attlesham. It was gone midnight when she arrived, but the stationmaster called up a taxi for her and twenty minutes later she was home. It had been a long, long day and nothing achieved. Perhaps she was not meant to achieve anything.

The twins, who were too healthy and well-fed to catch cold, waited until after Steve had returned from leave the following Sunday to pay a return visit to the summer house. It looked exactly as they had left it but they approached cautiously, Lenny dragging reluctantly behind his brother. It was all very well for Donny to say they could get some more things but they still had to hide them. He was terrified of being caught. Aunty Kathy would tell Mum, and Mum, instead of coming down to give them a hug and a kiss and take them home, would give them a belting. Beltings hurt. Donny didn't agree; he said Mum would be so pleased she wouldn't care where the stuff came from, and maybe he was right. In any case, he wouldn't have dreamt of letting Donny go alone; where his twin went, he went.

With a quick look round him, Donny took off the padlock and opened the door. 'It's OK,' he said, walking straight over to the locker. Lenny followed. The door banged behind them, making them jump out of their skins. They whipped round to find Ian Moreton grinning at them.

'Well, well, the little magpies. I thought it might be you.' He had been mystified to find some of his hoard missing. It was annoying because the summer house had been a particularly good hideout, sheltered from the elements, cool and dry and, as long as he kept an eye out for Lady Helen, he could come and go undetected, taking out what was needed for customers and putting in any new stuff he had acquired. Puzzled and angry, he had been about to bundle all that was left into his bag and take it somewhere else but changed his mind. If the thieves were clever enough not to take the lot, it meant they intended to return and all he had to do was keep his eyes peeled.

The boys stared at him in consternation. 'Narth'n to say for yarselves?' he asked.

'We weren't doin' no 'arm,' Donny said. 'Jus' lookin' round.'

'Lookin' round and helping yarselves, eh?'

'Helping ourselves?' Donny queried, trying to brazen it out.

'To suff'n that don't belong to you.' He was speaking quite reasonably, but they both recognised the underlying threat.

'We thought it belonged to a spy, Mr Moreton,' Lenny put in. 'We was going to catch 'im and turn 'im in.'

Ian laughed. 'Spy, eh? Well, I'll tell you this fer narth'n, that stuff don' belong to no spy. It's mine.'

'Why you 'idin' it 'ere?' Donny's cheek worried Lenny, but he admired his brother for his courage. 'I reckon you don' want people to know about it.'

'Have you told anyone?'

'Wouldn't do that, Mr Moreton. It'd all be took away if we did.'

'Ah, I see, you don't want to kill the goose that lays the golden egg.'

'Don' know what you mean.'

'Never mind. How good are you at keepin' secrets?'

'Very good, Mr Moreton.'

'You swear it. You swear you'll never tell a soul what's in this 'ere summer house.'

'It depends.' Donny was pushing his luck and it made Lenny gasp with fear. Mr Moreton was not a very big man, but he had a temper, everyone in the village knew that.

Ian gave a great guffaw. 'Man after me own heart,' he said. 'I like that. Now, this is the deal. You say nothing about this to anyone, anyone at all, and I'll make sure you don't lose by it.' He opened the locker and took out a bar of chocolate. 'I know you like chocolate, you've had one already.' He put the chocolate in Donny's hand. 'Now, I'm relying on you.'

'We wanted something for our Pa. One o' them bottles of booze.'

'Cheeky bugger! If you want any more, you have to earn it.'

'We don' mind workin', do we, Lenny?' This was said eagerly. 'What you want us to do?'

'Narth'n right now. Later, perhaps. Now cut along and not a word. You'll know what to expect if you let me down.' He picked up one of the cricket bats and stroked it gently. They knew exactly what he meant and scuttled away, glad to have escaped in one piece. The sound of Mr Moreton's laughter followed them as they fled.

Steve had returned to his squadron to discover there was a new intake of pilots. 'Babes in arms' was Oxo's comment, which made Steve smile, considering the boy had only been operational himself a few months. He had survived his first few critical weeks and was now a seasoned and sensible pilot. Brand had been shot down over the Channel and Oliphant had been grounded on medical grounds and now spent his time in the ops room. There were changes in the rest of the squadron too. Pilots were shot down or transferred for one reason or another, and others arrived, young, fresh-faced and eager. Steve was beginning to feel like an old man. Patrolling the skies, peering through the darkness for the familiar formations of Heinkels and Dorniers, he knew from the information radioed to him that the raid was a heavy one.

London, after a few weeks of respite, was having another pounding.

'Skip, there they are!'

He saw them at the same time, dozens of them. Angry and frustrated he might have been but he was not reckless; his training and experience kicked into action and he went after the last one in the formation with cool precision. He had no hatred for the enemy airmen, tried not to think of them having families, just as he did. What he was after was an aeroplane, a thing made of metal and other inanimate materials. When it went down in flames, he rejoiced that it would never invade the skies above his homeland again, could not threaten Laura. She was constantly in his thoughts. He found himself thinking of her trim figure, her violet eyes, the sheen of her dark hair, her smile, and looked forward to seeing her again. When he had time off.

'Why don't you go into the country?' Anne asked Laura. They were sitting in the Anderson shelter, listening to the sounds of a raid, trying to ignore the thumps and whistles and crashes. They had heard it all before and though they could never be blasé about it, they had come to accept this semi-underground existence as normal. Each morning they woke and went out into the early morning dawn to find their house still intact, though they had lost a window on one occasion and the garden had been showered with shrapnel more than once. Judging by the noise, this was an especially heavy raid, which was what had prompted Anne's question.

Laura, like her mother and everyone else, was tired. Her pregnancy was obvious to everyone now but she stuck at her job, shifting uncomfortably when hours of sitting at a table sorting piles of resistors into boxes by size and colour made her back ache and her bottom numb. She had given up nursing and taken factory work as soon as she realised that long hours on her feet and lifting heavy patients was too risky for her unborn child. She needed to keep going until after Christmas at least, so she wore loose smocks over a skirt she had let out and hoped the manager would not look too hard at her and decide she was corrupting the morals of the other girls in the factory. That was a laugh. Some of them were far more immoral than she was. They talked of nothing but the pictures and the dance halls and boyfriends – where they had gone with them and what they had done; it seemed to be all they lived for. She ought not to blame them when death stalked them every night and their daytime jobs were so repetitively boring. She missed the hospital. There she felt she had some purpose in life, that she was helping people and making a difference. The work she was doing in the factory, so they were constantly told, was vital to the war effort, but it didn't feel like it; it was deadly dull. She listened to *Music While You Work* and *Forces' Favourites* relayed over loudspeakers and dreamt of the child she was expecting.

'Mum, how can I go? At the moment I've got a job of sorts and I must work as long as I can. Where would I find work in the country? Any employer would take one look at me and shake his head.'

'You'll have to give up work sooner or later.'

'I know that.' When the time came, the responsibility for their keep would devolve entirely on her mother with the help of the small savings she had managed to accumulate, and the prospect of that worried her constantly. Mum was looking tired, almost gaunt. The fat had dropped off her, so there was nothing much left of the plump, cheerful woman she had once been. She said it was the war, but Laura suspected it was more than that. She had tried several times to persuade her to see a doctor, but she had refused. 'I'm not going to the doctor just because I've lost a bit of weight. They'd laugh at me and tell me they've got more important things to do with their time. Anyway, I was always too fat.'

'I'll go if you come too,' Laura said.

'I can't leave here, it is my home, the one your dad and I worked so hard to get. It's more than bricks and mortar and a few sticks of furniture to me. It's my life.'

'Mum, you can't say it's your life, that's morbid. It could be bombed out of existence, but that doesn't mean you can't survive without it. Now, stop talking like that and tell me where you think we should go.'

'I'm going nowhere.'

'Then neither am I.'

Anne gave up for the moment, but she was worried. She worried about Laura, about the baby, about her own failing health, about what would happen if she could no longer work. Some days she had to drag herself out of bed, she felt so exhausted. And hiding the pain from Laura was becoming more difficult. Sooner or later something would have to be done to make sure Laura and her child were cared for. She thought she had shaken off the past, but she was going to have to face it again.

Laura was three years old, nearly four, when Anne found herself face to face with Helen Barstairs. She had been sitting on a park bench watching the child play when she became aware that they were being watched. The woman was tall and dark, wearing a fur coat and a felt cloche that shouted money and privilege. 'Who are you? What do you want?' she asked.

'I mean no harm. You see, I had a little girl once...'

'Oh, I'm sorry.'

And then her world fell apart when the woman said she was Laura's mother, that she had given birth to her at the St Mary and Martha clinic on the fifth of March, 1918. 'She was taken from me,' the lady said. 'Pulled out of my arms and carried away. Given to you.'

Anne desperately wanted to get rid of her, and was worried that Laura might overhear. She might not understand, but she might say something about a strange lady to her daddy. 'You didn't want her.'

'That's not true. I did want her very much. Shall I tell you about it?'

'I don't want to hear it.' She could have stood up and walked away, but something kept her glued to the seat. And the woman who was Laura's mother told her a tale of such heart-breaking misery it brought tears to her eyes. Lady Barstairs! She had known Laura's mother was well off, but that she might be titled had never entered her head. That

she had wanted to keep her child was something she had never allowed herself to dwell on. Lady Barstairs had been hard done by but that did not mean Anne would ever relinquish Laura. Never. Never. What she did was to offer her a little consolation, a promise to keep in touch if she left Laura alone. Reluctantly, Lady Barstairs agreed, but Anne did not feel safe after that.

She grew over-protective, hardly liked to let Laura out of her sight, afraid that Helen would break her promise and try to take Laura from her or come to the house when Tom was there. What would he do about it? When Laura started school, she had to leave her there, terrified someone would tell the child, 'Your mummy is not your mummy.' Though she tried to hide it, she was jumpy and irritable, and Tom soon realised there was something wrong. It came to a head one evening after Laura had gone to bed.

'What's the matter, love?' he asked, putting his arm round her and drawing her away from the sink where she was washing up. 'You've been edgy for months. Are you ill?'

'No, I'm just tired.'

'It's more than that. Come and sit down and tell me what's wrong.'

'I c-c-can't.'

'Of course you can. Come on, out with it.'

She took a deep breath. 'I've done something wicked.'

'You? Wicked?' He laughed. 'I don't believe it.'

'But it's true.'

'And you are afraid of what I will say?'

'Terribly afraid.'

He led her into the front room and sat with her on the sagging second-hand sofa, taking both her hands in his. 'Now, tell me what this wicked thing is.'

Little by little, it all came tumbling out: her dejection at losing her own baby; how she was told she couldn't have any more and couldn't accept it; about the lifeline offered by Mrs Bates and how she had meant to tell him when he came home from the war, but when it came to it, she couldn't find the courage.

He was silent for a long, long time and she wondered if he would ever speak to her again. When, at last, he did it was not to offer words of forgiveness but to ask about Laura's real mother, something she had studiously avoided mentioning. 'Who is she?'

She had planned to tell him the whole truth, but balked at the last hurdle. 'I don't know. I was told she passed away on the day Laura was born. They were going to put her into an orphanage, Tom. Even if the mother hadn't died, she had no intention of keeping her. I couldn't let her go into a home, could I? I know what that's like.'

'So why tell me now?' His voice was controlled but she could see the angry colour mounting in his face and it frightened her.

'It's been on my conscience.'

'I should just about think so. All these years! Living a lie, letting me think the child was mine. I don't know how you could do it.'

'I know I should have told you, but I wanted her so much. You should have been there when she was put into my arms. She was so tiny and helpless. I simply couldn't let her go and I'm sure you wouldn't have been able to either. I hoped you would understand.'

'Who else knows you've made a complete fool of me?'

'No one.'

'Mum said she wasn't mine, but I didn't believe her.'

'She was only guessing.'

'What else don't I know?'

'Nothing. You love Laura, don't you? You can't suddenly turn off that love because she's not your flesh and blood.'

'Ah, but is she your flesh and blood?'

'What do you mean?'

'You know what I mean. How could you pull the wool over everyone's eyes for nine months if you weren't really pregnant? People round here are not that stupid. Who was he?'

She could not believe he had asked the question, that he could even consider that she had been unfaithful and stared at him in shock. 'There's no one, there's never been anyone but you, surely you know that? I stuffed myself with padding. I was deceiving myself as well as everyone else. Try to understand. Please don't let this make any difference. Laura doesn't know, there's no need for her ever to know. Please, Tom…'

He pushed her away and stormed from the house. Wearily, she climbed the stairs and went to bed, laying awake, listening for him to return and worrying what she would do if he never did. She heard him come in at two in the morning and collapse on the sofa. She went down to find him snoring in a drunken stupor, covered him with a blanket and went back to bed. At least he had come home. He had gone to work when she came down the next morning; the blanket was neatly folded over the back of the sofa. She spent the day on tenterhooks, trying to do all the things she normally did, taking Laura to school, doing the shopping, a bit of dusting and ironing, cooking the evening meal, wondering if he would come back for it.

He came in the back door at his usual time and went through to the dining room, where Laura was laying the table for her. She hardly dare breathe, listening to what they were saying.

'Have a good day at school, love?'

'Yes. I came top in English. Miss gave me a gold star.'

'Well done, sweetheart. What else did you do?'

'Sums. I got some of them wrong. I'm supposed to do them again tonight.'

'Would you like me to help you after we've had our tea?'

'Oh, yes please.'

Anne breathed a sigh of relief. At least if he was angry it was not with Laura. She took the casserole into the dining room, trying to put on a cheerful face. They ate together as they always did, and if there was a constraint between her and Tom, Laura did not seem to notice it. The child helped her wash up and then settled down to her homework. It was so normal, Anne began to hope.

Tom never really forgave her, but in the end he told her coldly that considering she was in every other way a good wife and an exemplary mother and Laura's happiness was important to him, they would try and make a go of their marriage. But it was nothing but a pretence and *their relationship was never the same again. Soon after that they moved into the house in Burnt Oak, and two years after that Tom died from a chest infection, made worse because of the mustard gas he had inhaled.*

She had kept her secret, was still keeping it, years after Tom's death, even after her mother-in-law had confronted her at Tom's funeral, calling her a tart, saying she'd killed him with the worry of it, and she never wanted to see her or her bastard again. She had been sending Helen the occasional snapshot of Laura but she stopped sending them after that. Helen didn't know their new address and she hoped that was an end of it. But it wasn't, was it? But not yet, please God, not yet.

Ian had not been joking when he said he would put the twins to work, not because he particularly needed them, but by involving them, he could control them. He used them as messengers; a couple of evacuees wandering about the village attracted less attention than he would. 'Tell Mr Wareson I've got a few bottles of whisky in,' he would tell them. 'Catch him coming outa his house, don't speak to anyone else.' Or, 'Tell Mrs Cook, her in that big house on the Attlesham Road, I can get her two jars of jam and a tin of golden syrup. Tell her it come to four and a tanner in advance.'

All their business was done in the summer house. Here the boys received their instruction and were paid their 'wages', usually chocolate, but sometimes other things which they intended to use for Christmas presents. They had even inveigled a half bottle of whisky out of him to give to their dad. Always there was the threat of what would happen if they told anyone. 'I'll see you go to clink for thievin',' he warned them.

'You stole the stuff in the first place.' Donny was always one to push his luck, though he usually backed away when he saw Mr Moreton's face turn red.

'No, I did not. It's honest tradin', that's what it is. I don' make a song an' dance about it on account of everythin's in short supply an'

I have to choose who I let hev it.' He had reached out and grabbed the lobe of Donny's ear. 'You c'n understand that, can't you?'

'Yeah.' It was a squeal of pain as his ear was twisted.

'Then run along and do as you're bid.'

Today, they had skipped Sunday school and would have to invent something about the hymns they had sung and the lesson to tell Aunty Kathy. They had become adept at that. Donny was blasé about it, but Lenny was deeply unhappy. He hated telling lies and usually let Donny do all the talking.

'Are we going home now?' he asked, scuffling his feet in the fallen leaves which had collected at the side of the road. It was nearly dark and he hated to be out in the dark when there were no street lamps and the bare trees, moving in the wind, cast strange shadows, and owls hooted and things scuffled in the undergrowth. He knew Donny didn't like it either, though he pretended not to care.

'Might as well.'

'How many days to Christmas is it?' Christmas was large in their minds. Mum had said she would come down and perhaps, if Dad's ship came in, he would come too. When they asked Aunty Kathy if that would be all right, she had said, 'Yes, of course. They will both be welcome. We'll have a grand time, won't we?'

'One day less than it was yesterday when you asked.'

'Mum will come the day before, won't she? She won't leave it until Christmas Day. I want her here when we open our stockings.'

'How do I know? She never said which day. You saw the letter.'

'Perhaps she'll write and let us know. Or she might telephone.'

'She might.'

Kathy washed the flour off her hands and went to answer the front doorbell. Mrs Woodrow, the welfare officer for the evacuees, stood on the step and Kathy's heart sank. Had she heard about the trouble she'd been having with the twins? 'Mrs Woodrow, come in. If you've come to see the twins, I'm afraid they are at Sunday school.' Sunday school was where she had sent them, but she was not at all sure that was where they had gone. They had been more than usually secretive lately.

'Oh.' She was a very big woman, always dressed in country tweeds with her hair rolled up tightly under a man's pork pie hat. She had a booming voice, but that little word had been said unusually softly. 'Perhaps it's just as well.' She followed Kathy into the little-used drawing room, where Kathy turned to face her. 'It'll give you time to decide how you're going to tell them.'

'Tell them what? Do sit down.' Kathy waved her to an easy chair on one side of the hearth.

'I'm afraid, there's very bad news. Their mother was killed in an air raid last Sunday night. Her house received a direct hit. It was completely demolished, so I am informed, and there were no survivors.'

Kathy sank into the chair opposite her visitor. 'Oh, the poor, poor boys.'

'I'll tell them if you don't feel up to it, but it would be better coming from you.'

'What else do you know? They're bound to ask. Why has it taken a week to tell us?'

'I'm told the ARP and rescue squad had to dig in the ruins for days before they got the bodies out and then there was a question of identifying them.'

'Them?'

'Mrs Carter and a man.'

'Her husband was on leave?'

'No, I was told he's at sea. He will be notified and no doubt will get compassionate leave as soon as his ship docks. Of course, no one could say when that would be.'

'Oh, I see. I don't think I'll tell them about their mother's visitor.'

'No. Very wise.'

'They will be heartbroken. They had a letter from her a few weeks ago, saying she hoped to come for Christmas.'

'It will be a very sad Christmas for them. Let's hope Petty Officer Carter can get leave.'

'How does it affect their evacuee status? I mean, they will stay with me, won't they?'

'For the time being. We shall, of course, consult Petty Officer Carter, when he comes home.'

'I understand, but it would be a pity to uproot them when they have settled down so well.' Even as she spoke, Kathy wondered about that. She had done her very best to give them a stable and comfortable home, by all accounts more comfortable than the one they had come from, but was that enough?

'Yes, I agree, and my recommendation will be that they remain here. We have funds to tide you over until arrangements can be made about their keep.'

Kathy had not even been thinking of that. Mrs Carter was obliged to send seventeen shillings a week for their board, lodging and clothes, but she often missed. Kathy had never reported this. 'That's not important, Mrs Woodrow. What is important is their happiness, and I fear this will be a terrible blow to them. They talk about their mother constantly, more than their father.'

'He was a peacetime sailor, Mrs Wainright, and would often be away from home. They are no doubt used to not having him around.' She stood up. 'I'll be off, but if you need me, you know how to contact me.'

'Yes.' She saw the woman to the door and then turned back indoors and wandered in a daze into the kitchen. How was she going to break the news to the boys? What words should she use? Did they understand about death? At nearly eleven they surely must.

'Who was that?' William looked up from his newspaper. For once he was not busy on the farm; the threshing was done and the grain sent off to market, the straw stacks had been built and the potatoes harvested with the help of Meg and Daphne and the schoolchildren, given time out of school to do it. If you could call it help. The crop had been turned up by a digger on the tractor and the children had been stationed along the rows with baskets and paid a copper or two to pick up the potatoes and fill the baskets. All his forms had been filled in and sent off to the Ministry, and all he had to do later that afternoon was the milking. For a precious couple of hours he had done nothing but toast his toes on the fender and read the paper.

'Mrs Woodrow.' Kathy sat down heavily at the table. 'The twins' mother has been killed in an air raid.'

The paper dropped in his lap. 'Good God! Poor kids. And you have to tell them.'

'Yes.'

Kathy followed the boys up to their bedroom when they came home. They did that a lot lately: going straight up without even taking off their coats or coming into the kitchen. Donny was stowing something in the back of their wardrobe when she went in and scrambled out with a guilty look on his face when he saw her; she had given them a little money to buy Christmas presents for the family and she supposed that was where they were hiding them. She pretended not to notice and sat on one of the beds. 'Boys, come and sit here with me. I have something important to tell you.'

They moved over and sat one on each side of her and she put her arms about them. Donny shrugged her off, but Lenny allowed it. 'You must be very brave because the news I have is very bad.'

'Dad's boat's been torpedoed,' Donny interrupted her.

'Why, no,' she said in surprise, though on reflection she supposed that would be their conclusion. Their father was away at war and therefore the one at risk. 'I'm afraid it is your mother. Your house was bombed. I'm so dreadfully sorry, my darlings, but she died.'

She felt Lenny stiffen beside her but it was Donny that yelled out his disbelief. 'No! No! I don' believe yer. Yer makin' it up.'

'Why would I do that, Donny?'

'I dunno, do I? She's coming down for Christmas, she said so, and then she'll take us home. I hate this place! I hate you! I hate this war!' And then he burst into tears.

That set Lenny off and the pair of them sat and sobbed. She could do nothing but sit there with them, fighting back her own tears, not at the loss of Mrs Carter but in sympathy with two little boys who had so cruelly been deprived of their mother. She couldn't tell them not to cry, so she dabbed their wet faces with her handkerchief until the sobs subsided into an occasional hiccup.

'Who told you?' Donny demanded when it seemed he had no more tears to shed.

'Mrs Woodrow. You remember her? She was the one who met you at Attlesham Station when you first came and brought you to Beckbridge. She looks after all the evacuees and keeps in touch with their parents. She told me that your father would be notified and he would probably come home.'

'When?' Lenny asked, seizing at a straw.

'I don't know. It depends when his ship docks.'

Lenny sighed and sniffed. 'Mum always said that when we asked her. "When his ship comes in," she always said.' The memory was too much for him and he began to cry again.

Kathy hugged him. 'Perhaps it will come in soon.'

'I want me mum,' Lenny's voice was muffled against Kathy's bosom. 'She can't be dead.'

'I wish that were true, Lenny, I really do. But we can't wave a magic wand and make it all right again.'

'What's going to happen to us?' Donny asked. 'Will we have to go to one of those places where they put kids with no mums?'

'No, you'll stay here with me, at least until your dad comes home. You've still got him, haven't you? You're not orphans.'

'Might just as well be. He's always at sea.'

'He'll be back soon.'

'In time for Christmas?'

'I don't know. Perhaps not.' She could not let them build their hopes on that, as they had on their mother coming; it was best to be honest, even if she sounded unsympathetic.

Lenny was no longer sobbing, but silent tears still coursed down his face and dripped off his chin. Donny had stopped crying altogether and was looking mulish. 'Do you want to come down for your tea?' she asked.

'No,' Donny snapped. 'Go away. Leave us alone.'

Silently she stood up and watched them for a minute, before going downstairs. Meg and Daphne had come in and were laying the kitchen table.

'How did they take it?' William asked.

'I'm not sure they've taken it in yet.'

The sound of banging and crashing and yells came to them from the direction of the boys' bedroom, which was directly above the kitchen. Kathy looked up at the ceiling. 'What on earth are they up to? They sound as if they're wrecking the place.'

'I'll go,' Daphne said, and disappeared in the direction of the stairs.

She opened the bedroom door to a scene of devastation. The covers had been stripped from the bed, the stuffing pulled out of the pillows and feathers were flying everywhere; the curtains hung in ribbons. The wardrobe door stood open and the little stash of Christmas presents, not only those intended for their mother and father, but for everyone else in the house, had been pulled out and systematically destroyed. There were streaks of lipstick on the mirrors and paintwork, a jar of jam had been flung at the wall and broken against it. The room was filled with the scent of lily of the valley and raspberries. Daphne stood and stared.

Donny, seeing her, stopped with his arm raised to throw a half bottle of whisky at the window. She ran forward and grabbed it from him. 'Donny, stop it, stop it at once. It won't help.' She looked round for Lenny and found him cowering in a corner, his knees up to his chest and his head in his arms. She didn't know which to go to first.

'It ain't fair!' Donny shouted. 'It ain't fair. Ma said if we was good, she'd come for Christmas.'

'It's not her fault she can't.'

'No, it's ours.' This was a mumble from Lenny.

Daphne went and knelt beside him. 'How can it be yours, sweetheart?'

'We wasn't good.'

'Oh, Lenny, of course you were.' She folded him into her arms and rocked him. 'It was no one's fault. If you want to blame anyone, blame Hitler and the Germans, they started this war.'

He sobbed against her jumper and in a little while Donny crouched down beside them and pushed his way up into her arms as well and the three of them cried together.

At last they became quiet and Daphne eased herself away from them. 'Just look at this mess, boys. Are you going to help me clear it up?'

They nodded.

She went down and fetched a brush and dustpan and some warm soapy water in a bucket and set about picking up the feathers and broken glass, scraping the jam off the wallpaper and washing the mirror. The boys half-heartedly set about remaking their beds, though they weren't sure what to do about the ruined pillows. Kathy came up while they were doing it. She was shocked by the mess, even more by the things the boys had used for missiles. Where had they come from? They could not possibly have afforded to buy them. Surely they hadn't taken to stealing? Half of her wanted to give them a good scolding and demand to know, the other half wanted to cry out in pity. She found new pillows and put them on the bed without a word.

'Sorry, Aunty Kathy,' Donny mumbled.

Kathy picked a feather out of his hair. 'I'll forgive you, this time. Do you want some tea?'

'No. I'm going to bed.'

'What about you, Lenny?'

'I'm going to bed too.'

She and Daphne helped them into their pyjamas, which at any other time they would never have allowed, tucked them in and returned downstairs, taking all that was left of the loot with them.

'They'll wake up in the morning, hoping it was a bad dream,' Daphne said as they returned to the kitchen, 'Poor mites. And just before Christmas, too. They had been so looking forward to it. And what about all that stuff? Lipstick and jars of jam, and whisky, for goodness sake. How did they come by it? Surely they didn't steal it? Was that why Lenny said they hadn't been good?'

'I don't know. We can't ask them, can we? Not now.' The laddered stockings had given Kathy an idea where the stuff might have come from and something had to be done about it, but she wouldn't say anything to the boys until she had spoken to Joyce Moreton. Joyce had worked at the local post office and general store since the postman had joined up the previous year. She sorted and delivered the mail on a bicycle and afterwards served in the shop. She must have been privy to a lot of other people's personal business, but she was never heard to speak of it. She was as universally liked as her dissolute husband was disliked.

The shop was busy. Kathy had to wait several minutes until there was a lull between customers and Mrs Galloway, the sub-postmistress, had gone out to the back room to make a pot of tea before she could get Joyce to herself. And now she wasn't quite sure how to begin. She picked up a tin of peas and put it down again. What did she want tinned vegetables for when they grew all they needed?

'Is anything the matter, Mrs Wainright?'

'I don't know. I want to ask your advice.' She dug in her shopping bag and produced a lipstick. 'Do you recognise this?'

Joyce picked it up and examined it. 'Not one we sell.'

'I was afraid of that. There was more, all sorts of things: jam, chocolate, whisky, scent, silk stockings – though they were already laddered.'

'Oh, I think I see what you're driving at.' Ian had come home the previous week with a whole bag full of silk stockings which he swore he'd bought cheap off a market trader. 'You can have a pair if you like. Here, take two pairs.' He had thrust a couple of envelopes into her hands. Both pairs had been laddered and she suspected every other pair was too, and that inclined her to believe he hadn't nicked them. He hadn't shown her anything else, though. 'Where did you find them?'

'In the twins' room.'

Joyce was shocked. 'How did they get there? Have you tackled them about it?'

'No, they've just learnt their mother's been killed in an air raid and they're both very upset. I couldn't, could I?'

'No, of course you couldn't.' She'd give that no-good husband of hers what for when she saw him, selling dodgy stuff to children. 'Will you leave it with me?'

'Yes and thank you.' Kathy gladly handed over the bottle of whisky and the stockings. Joyce put them with the lipstick in her own handbag, just as Mrs Galloway came back into the shop. Kathy asked for a tin of condensed milk, which was still free of rationing but was in short supply and reserved for 'registered customers only', a phrase everyone heard more and more as the war progressed. 'I'm going to make the boys some fudge', she said to explain why someone who had a herd of cows should be buying milk in tins.

When Ian went home that night, Joyce was at the range, prodding at some boiling potatoes with a fork. Ken was sprawled on a grey horsehair sofa studying a book on aircraft recognition. He did not look up as his father came in. He hated him. Now he was as tall as his father, the beatings had stopped and been replaced by taunting jibes. If he wasn't goading him about his reading matter, it was over his lack of girlfriends – as if he would bring a girl back to this dump! He couldn't wait to get away and join up. He had asked Steve Wainright about joining the RAF, but Steve had advised him to wait until he was called up. It was all very well for Steve; he didn't have to live in this place with a pig of a man who didn't know the meaning of words like honesty or decency. One day the old man would over-reach himself and they'd all be free of him.

Stella was standing at the mirror over the mantel brushing her hair. She had a round, rosy face and pale hair, which she supposed was better than the ginger of her mother and brothers, but she wished it was dark and wavy like Vivien Leigh's. She did not turn round but her brushing slowed as she watched in the mirror, waiting for the explosion and hoping Ma would get the better of Pa this time. She'd like to see him get his comeuppance. He'd stopped her going to Attlesham Grammar School when she won a scholarship, telling her she was getting too big for her boots and the village school had been good enough for him and it was good enough for her. She had turned fourteen in the summer and left school for a job at a butcher's in Attlesham, where she doled out the meat ration and kept hard-to-come-by unrationed sausages and offal under the counter for favoured customers. If only she was a bit older, she could leave home. As soon as the opportunity arose, she would.

'What's this?' Ian asked, pointing at the little heap on the table which should have been laid ready for his tea. Instead, the brown chenille cloth sported, not a plate of meat and two veg, but a lipstick, a bottle of whisky and an opened envelope from which the pale silk of a stocking protruded. Had the old witch found them in her summer house and brought them to Joyce?

'You tell me.' She waved the fork at him and a lump of hot potato landed on the back of his hand. He lifted the hand and everyone in the room waited, expecting it to land on Joyce's face, but he simply put it to his mouth and sucked the potato off.

'Me? They hin't got anythin' to do with me.' He laughed. 'What would I want things like that for? Tek me for a pansy boy, do you?'

'Nothing so refined. I know you for a wide boy, on the mek at the expense of everyone else and tradin' with innocent children. Teachin' them your wicked ways is the last straw. Do your dirty deals if you must, but not with my friends or my friends' families. If I hear you have, I'll be down that police station quicker than you can say Jack Robinson.'

Stella put down her brush and crept quietly from the room. Ken looked up from his book, ready to defend his mother, but to his surprise, his parents simply glared at each other in hostility. He wanted to say, 'Go on, Ma, don't back down, you've got him on the back foot,' but he said nothing. Time for that when it became necessary to divert his father's wrath.

'Keep yar hair on,' Ian mocked. '*If* I had anything to deal with, which I i'n't sayin' I hev, I wouldn't deal with yar friends. Askin' for trouble, that'd be. They can't bear to see a man doing well for hisself.'

Joyce turned back to the fire to hide the laugh that almost escaped her lips. She didn't suppose for a minute she had achieved anything, except to let him know she was on to him, but whether she would really turn him in, she didn't know. They'd been married nineteen years and she had stuck with him. It was a kind of habit, and she wouldn't do anything to jeopardise her home, such as it was, because of her children. A wayward husband was better than no husband at all, or so her mother told her. But then, her mother liked the little treats Ian took her now and again.

Chapter Five

CHRISTMAS 1940 WAS a miserable time; there didn't seem to be any good news anywhere. The whole of Europe, including the Channel Islands, had been overrun and U-boats were sinking allied shipping at an alarming rate. Great Britain was isolated and there were many miserable pessimists who said she was lost, especially as the United States refused to become involved. Everyone had to tighten their belts as rationing bit deeper and shortages of those things that were not rationed meant that unscrupulous men like Ian Moreton could fleece the public. Prices went sky high and to add insult to injury income tax had gone up to seven and sixpence in the pound. Rural Norfolk was saved most of the bombing, but it wouldn't be long before more new airfields were ready and then it would be a target just like London and the cities.

Kathy, who had cooked a large cockerel she had been fattening up for the purpose, tried to make it as festive as she could with holly and mistletoe and paper chains, which she had hoped to persuade the boys to make, but they had been so listless she had ended up making them herself. Meg and Daphne had been given leave to go home for Christmas, Petty Officer Carter had not arrived and neither had Steve. She was glad when the holiday was over.

'Drat that siren,' Anne said, as the wailing penetrated the blacked-out windows. She was just going to dish up the evening meal: a couple of sausages she had begged off the butcher, some mashed potatoes and cabbage. They had had a tiny, scrawny chicken for Christmas dinner, which, try as she might, she had not been able to make last more than two days. Getting the sausages had been a bonus for when the chicken ran out. Not that she cared for herself; she never felt very hungry nowadays, but Laura needed her food if she was to have a healthy baby. 'You'd think they'd give it a miss over Christmas, wouldn't you?'

'They did.'

'What, for two days? No doubt Jerry was enjoying himself with plenty to eat and drink and decided to take a holiday.'

'Well, the holiday is over. I wonder if 1941 will be any better than 1940.'

'I don't know. I sometimes wonder if anything will ever be the same again.'

'I don't think it will. But we've survived and we'll go on surviving.'

'God willing,' Anne said fervently.

They sat down to eat but had hardly put a fork to their mouths when they heard the uneven drone of enemy aircraft. The sound went on and on, and then there was a tremendous crash, not far away, and all the doors and windows rattled. 'God! That was a near one,' Anne said. It was followed by several more in quick succession. 'We'd better get out of here.' She stood up and grabbed the bag containing a Thermos, two mugs, some milk and sugar, a packet of sandwiches and her little case which was always kept ready, then she put out the light and opened the back door. The sky was full of aeroplanes and criss-crossed with searchlights. Over the rooftops they could see smoke which was more orange than grey. The raid was nearer than it had ever been before. And bigger. They had never seen so many aircraft at once; the sky was black with them. They could hear the clang of a fire engine's bell, as more fires sprang up. And in the light of these, the bombers could easily see where to drop their high explosives.

'Come on,' Laura said, pulling on her mother's arm. 'Let's get into the shelter.'

They dashed across the few yards of garden to the Anderson

shelter, ducked inside, just as a dreadful screaming whistle assailed their ears. It was enough to frighten the hardiest. They stood, waiting for the explosion, but nothing happened. 'It didn't go off,' Anne whispered. 'I wonder where it is.'

'I'm not going out there to find out. Shut the door and draw the curtain across. I'll light the lamp.' She looked round puzzled when her mother burst out laughing. 'What's funny?'

'You, worrying about showing a light when the whole city is lit up like day.'

The laughing set Anne coughing and she couldn't get her breath. Laura sat her down and poured her a drink of tea from the flask. 'Sit still and drink this, and then you're going to tell me what's wrong.'

'Nothing.'

'Mum, I'm a nurse, I know when someone is ill. Now tell me.'

'I don't know. I'm tired.'

'It's more than that. Are you in pain?'

'Now and again.'

'Where?'

'In here.' She put her hand to her left breast. 'It's not all that bad.'

'Rot. I've seen you wincing and trying to hide it. Now there's to be no more arguments. When we get out of here, you're going straight to see the doctor. I'll come with you, if you like.'

'No, I'll go after you've gone to work.' She didn't want Laura with her. If there was something seriously wrong, she wanted to tell her in her own time and in her own words.

They emerged the next morning to a devastated city. A pall of smoke, brightened now and again by a tongue of flame, hung in the air like thick fog; smuts tumbled down like black snow. The warden came to warn them not to go down to the end of the street where a bomb disposal squad were defusing an unexploded bomb. They would be well advised to stay indoors with the doors and windows shut, just in case it went off.

'That's a laugh,' Anne said. 'We've lost most of our windows at the front.'

'You're not the only ones. I'll send the men down to you but you might have to wait a bit. Half the city's been flattened. Can you nail some boards up for the time being?'

They did the best they could, which meant the front sitting room and Anne's bedroom were in permanent darkness. Laura insisted on going to work and trekked down to the opposite end of the road and took a detour to reach the factory. The fire service and the Civil Defence worked among the ruins, hoses were still being played on fires, the police were directing the traffic, refusing drivers access to streets where there were unexploded bombs or unsafe buildings. Even so, people were going about their business, picking their way over broken glass, brick rubble and firemen's hoses to get to their work, going into shops which more often than not had their windows boarded up, pushing prams, riding bicycles, stopping now and again to tell each other what they knew.

Anne swept up the glass and when the warden came along, telling everyone the bomb had been made safe, she set off for the doctor's surgery, knowing she couldn't duck out of it. Laura would insist on knowing the verdict.

The talk in the waiting room centred on the raid. Incendiaries, high explosives and parachute mines had destroyed a large part of the old city and a large area surrounding it had sustained damage. It was the old buildings that fared the worst; the new ones, the ugly blocks of steel and concrete, could withstand a certain amount of fire, but several churches and the Guildhall had gone up in smoke and fire burnt all round St Paul's Cathedral, which had somehow managed to survive. 'Talk about the Great Fire of London,' someone commented. 'The whole city's gone up in flames. My Rodney's in the AFS and he said the hoses ran dry on account of the river being so low.'

Back at home, musing on what the doctor had told her, which was no more than she expected, Anne tried to make herself a cup of tea but found there was no water and no gas. It was all part of her punishment. She went out again, made her way to church and knelt there in the cold, to pray, to ask what to do, to beg forgiveness. But she knew what she had to do even before she got there.

Helen put down her knitting and went into the hall to answer the telephone. 'Helen Barstairs speaking.'

'Helen. It's Anne Drummond.'

'Anne Drummond?' It was a second before the name registered, and then her heart started to beat frantically. 'Is anything wrong? Laura—'

'Laura's fine. But I need to see you. There's something I want to tell you. Can we meet?'

Helen sat down heavily on the chair beside the telephone table and forced herself to sound calm though questions tumbled over themselves in her head. 'Of course. Where and when?'

'Can you come up to London?'

'Yes.'

'Lyons' Corner House. Tomorrow at eleven?'

'Yes, I can manage that. Can't you tell me what it's all about?'

'I'd rather not over the phone. Don't worry, it's not the end of the world.'

Helen put the receiver down and wandered into the drawing room, picking up ornaments and putting them down again. She fetched a photograph album from a drawer and sat on a sofa to look at them: pictures of Laura as a toddler; her first day at school, proud in her new uniform; getting a school prize; another with her adoptive father – sent, Helen suspected, to prove to her she had a daddy who loved her, which is something Helen could never give her. Nothing after she was seven or eight, which she supposed was when they had moved house. She had assumed that was when Anne had told Laura the truth and she didn't want to know her. It hurt, hurt terribly, and it was a long time before she could even begin to accept it. But had she been wrong? Did Laura want to see her after all? She could not settle to anything, didn't want to talk to anyone. She put the album away and went to the cloakroom, threw an old black cape over her shoulders, took a key from a nail just inside the scullery door and went to the summer house.

She was so immersed in Anne's call that she did not see that the knee-deep grass had been trampled round the door of the building. She did not even notice that the new padlock had been forced and she did not need the key. She sat down in the corner, but this time there were no ghosts, no visits into the past; for the first time she felt brave enough to look into the future. Her head was filled with questions. When had Anne told Laura about her birth? Could it have been recent? Did it mean she could at last see her daughter? Her daughter, her precious daughter! Oh, the joy of that!

Suddenly realising how cold she was, she stood up to stamp her feet and bang her arms against her sides to restore the circulation. It was then she noticed the footprints and the cricket bats and the croquet hoops, which were normally kept in the bench. She bent to lift its lid and stared in disbelief at what she saw. The whole space was packed with tins, jars and packets. Kneeling on the dusty floor, she took them out one by one. Every item was something in short supply, things most women would give their eye-teeth for. There was drink and chocolate, stockings, make-up and perfume. Someone had stashed it all there, but who? A black marketeer, someone who knew the summer house was there, someone who felt able to come and go as he pleased. Ian Moreton! He had been creeping about at night and she thought he was after rabbits!

Now what should she do? Confront the man? Inform the police? Tell his wife? Supposing she was wrong and it wasn't Ian at all but a gang of crooks? She put it all back and put the lid down, then left, carefully hanging the broken padlock back as she had found it. Then she went back and rang Constable Harris. He was out, his wife said, but she would tell him to come up to the Hall the minute he returned. He hadn't arrived by the time she went to bed and the next morning she forgot all about him in her eagerness to catch her train.

When she arrived at the café and saw Anne sitting alone she

felt disappointed, even though she had said nothing about Laura accompanying her. Helen did not recognise her at first, expecting the young dumpy woman she had been eighteen years before, forgetting to take account of the intervening years. This woman had wispy grey hair and was as thin as a rake. And her face was devoid of colour. Helen was shocked.

As soon as Helen joined her, Anne beckoned the waitress and ordered tea and scones. 'How are you?'

'I'm fine but, forgive me, you don't look at all well.'

'I've got breast cancer.' She spoke quietly, but there was no tremor in her voice, no sign that the diagnosis had hit her like a ton of bricks. She might just as easily have been saying she had a cold.

'Cancer? Are you sure?'

'Yes. I've known something was wrong for some time. I noticed a lump, you see, but I didn't do anything about it until it became painful. I have to go into hospital for a mastectomy.'

The waitress brought the tea tray and they waited while she set everything out on the table. Helen reached across to put milk in the cups and pour the tea. 'Oh, Anne, I am so sorry. Does Laura know?'

'Yes, I told her yesterday, just before I rang you. I don't think she can quite take it in. To be honest, neither can I.'

'What can I do to help?'

'If anything happens to me, look after Laura, please. She'll have no one else. I have no family and there's only Tom's sister and I don't expect her to be sympathetic.'

Helen felt desperately sorry for the woman and yet, deep inside, there was a spark of joy, a tiny hope that flickered and was instantly extinguished. It was wicked to feel pleasure at such a time. How could she wish for someone to die, especially someone who had brought up her daughter with such loving care. 'You know I will. Does that mean you've told Laura about me?'

'No. I keep trying, but then I can't seem to get the words out. It's been so long.'

'You want me to tell her?'

'No, it's something I have to do.'

'Let me pay for the operation.'

'I couldn't let you do that.'

'Why not?'

'Why should you? I imagine you would be dancing on my grave. I took your child—'

'You took a child, the fact that she was mine has nothing to do with that.'

'That's not what you said the last time we met. Threatened me with the police, as I recall.'

'Let's say I've mellowed.'

'You kept your promise.'

'Yes. To be honest, it was less painful that way. And I did have the pictures you sent. I wept when they came, but in a way they have been a comfort to me. But why did you stop sending them? And why didn't you tell me you'd moved house?'

'How did you know I had?'

'I was worried about the bombing. I went to your old address but it wasn't there any more. I spoke to a neighbour. She said you'd moved, but she couldn't tell me where.'

Anne sighed. 'I was afraid you would tell Tom—'

'You mean he didn't know?' She was astounded.

'Not at the beginning. He didn't want to adopt, you see, so I pretended Laura was mine. Then when you turned up out of the blue I had to tell him. It was awful. You have no idea how bad. He asked a lot about you. I told him you had died giving Laura birth and they were going to put her in an orphanage. I'm not a very good liar, Helen, and it was easier to forget you existed. In the end, because we both loved Laura, we stayed together. Moving house was supposed to be a new beginning for us. Unfortunately, he only lived two years after that and I was left to bring her up on my own.'

'Why didn't you tell me? I could have helped, would have been glad to do it.'

Anne smiled, though the sparkle had gone from her eyes. She

looked gaunt and worried. 'We managed.'

'And you still didn't tell her?'

'No, I was afraid she would want to meet you and you had so much more to offer—'

'That's silly. You gave her a stable family life and a loving father. I could not give her that. It was the only reason I kept my promise.'

'Now it's time to keep mine.'

'Just like that!'

'No, I'll have to work up to it. I've been thinking about it and the first thing is for me to be suddenly reunited with a close friend I knew during the last war. You could visit us. It would give you and Laura a chance to get to know each other—'

'You sound as if you don't expect to get over this. You mustn't think like that. You must fight it.'

'Oh, I shall fight every inch of the way, and I shall probably survive the mastectomy, but I think it will only be a reprieve. Just long enough for me to put my affairs in order and for you to become part of our lives.'

'Oh, Anne!' Tears she hadn't shed for years toppled over Helen's lashes and ran down her cheeks. She fumbled for a handkerchief to wipe them away. 'It's so dreadfully sad that what I want most in the world has to be paid for at such a terrible price. But are you sure?'

'I'm sure. I'm going home now. Laura will be wondering where I've got to. I shall be full of the extraordinary way in which I bumped into an old friend I haven't seen in donkey's years and how we have vowed not to lose touch again. I'll say I've invited you to come and have a meal with us. You'll do that, won't you? Will Tuesday lunch suit? We'll take it from there. Do you agree?'

'Yes, but please let me pay for the operation. The sooner it's done, the better. You can tell Laura you've got an insurance policy to cover it.'

'Thank you.' She fished into her handbag and withdrew a piece of paper. 'That's the address.'

She paused, watching Helen put it in her own bag. 'There's something else you should know.'

'Oh?'

'Laura's pregnant. It's due in March.'

Helen, who had half risen, sank back into her seat, knowing there was more to come.

'She was a nursing sister at the Middlesex, a good one, too. She got engaged to a pilot. He was shot down on the day they were going to be married. Unfortunately they had anticipated the wedding.'

Helen's mind flew back to Oliver. How easy it had been to fall in love, to let her emotions get the better of her good sense. She smiled. 'I cannot condemn her for that, can I?'

'No. I didn't think you would. Others do. It's one reason why it's important that she has someone to turn to.'

'You can rely on me.'

'Even if she is awkward about it?'

'Even then.'

The two women rose. Anne turned and walked away, her head hunched into bowed shoulders. Helen, watching her go, was struck by how slowly she moved, like someone defeated, and all the bitterness she had been harbouring over the years melted away. She should be grateful. She *was* grateful. Grateful enough to spend some of her dwindling resources making sure Anne ended her days in comfort. It was little enough to pay for getting her daughter back. She would not think of the mountains they would have to climb, the obstacles they would have to overcome, before that happened.

'Steve! Fancy seeing you. Come in.'

He stepped inside and removed his cap. 'I nearly didn't knock when I saw the boards.'

'They haven't got round to putting in new windows yet. Apparently glass is scarce.' Laura laughed suddenly. 'If you don't count the broken stuff you have to walk on in the streets; there's plenty of that. Come through to the kitchen. We've got windows there. I was just making a cup of tea.'

He followed her through to the room at the back, where she filled the kettle and put it on the gas stove. 'I went to the hospital first in case you were on duty. They told me you had left.'

'Yes.' The gas lit, she turned towards him and he saw her properly for the first time. He did not know why he was so shocked, so dismayed, but he was. She must have seen his reaction in his face because she gave a little laugh. 'You can see why.'

He gulped. 'Yes.'

'You're disgusted.'

'It's not for me to judge.'

'No, it isn't.' She turned from him to warm the pot and put a couple of spoonfuls of tea in it. 'But I've decided I'm not going to hide my head in shame, nor the bit of me most people will notice.' She turned back to him. 'I loved Bob with all my heart and if we had been married, no one would have said a word. They might have thought we were foolish to bring children into this crazy world, but they would not have condemned me. To me, there is no difference.'

'Oh.' He sat down heavily at the kitchen table, wishing he had not come. 'What does your mother say about it?'

'Nothing. What did you think she said? "Go from this house and never darken its doors again"?'

'It would be a cruel mother who did that. But, forgive me, how will you manage?'

'Oh, we're managing. I've got a part-time job in a local factory, sorting resistors; all sizes, all the colours of the rainbow. It's boring as hell, but I can do it sitting down and they need workers so they'll keep me on until I'm too big to waddle about. I'm not exactly the most popular girl on the shop floor, but I can live with that. I've got to.'

'You are very brave.'

'Or brazen.' She put a cup of tea in front of him, poured herself a cup and sat down opposite him. 'I'm getting used to being cold-shouldered. People I've known nearly all my life walk by on the other side of the street, and if I stand in a queue in a shop, I'm given a wide berth. But I don't care. My baby is everything to me. It is all

I have left of Bob. You can understand that, can't you?'

'Yes, of course.' He supposed he did. She wanted her child so badly, she was prepared to take a boring, repetitive job and endure the silence of her workmates and the disapproval of her friends. But the birth of a baby would not be the end of it, only the beginning. She still had to bring it up, feed and clothe it and shield it from the infamy of bastardy. She was far from stupid, so she must know that. 'Is there anything I can do to help?'

'No, thanks all the same. Tell me about yourself. What have you been up to?'

'The usual. I've asked to be transferred to bombers. I'm fed up with being on the defensive. I want to hit back.'

'Someone's got to defend us.'

'Yes, but there are new pilots becoming operational all the time now and they all seem to want to fly Spitfires. I've been doing it too long. One of these days my luck will run out.'

'Don't say that,' she said softly. 'I wouldn't want to lose you too.'

He was considerably heartened by that, though his answer did not betray it. 'Nice of you to say so.'

'Mum will be in soon, will you wait and see her?'

'I'm afraid not; I've got to get back on duty.' He drained his cup and stood up. 'It was only a flying visit.'

She saw him to the door. 'Thanks for coming.'

Steve left, wondering why he felt so let down. He had no claim on her, no right to judge her. But he knew, in his heart, he *had* judged her. She had proved herself less than perfect and that was why he felt so disappointed. You build someone up in your head to be a superior being, put them on a pedestal, and then blame them when they prove to be human after all. He didn't like himself for his reaction, but he couldn't help it. Worse, he had let her see it.

Anne came into the house with a cheerful smile. She had been wearing that smile for days now, ever since she had told Laura about the operation, pretending it was nothing to worry about. It didn't

151

deceive either of them. 'You've had a visitor?' she said, noticing the two cups.

'Yes, Steve came. He was only here a few minutes. I'm afraid he was dreadfully shocked, though he did his best to hide it.'

'Funny, I wouldn't have expected that.'

'Nor me. I don't know why, but I felt hurt. Silly, wasn't it?'

'Yes. Is there any tea left in the pot?'

'It's gone cold. I'll make some more, shall I?'

'No, put some more boiling water on the leaves.'

'Where've you been? Standing in queues again?'

'No. I went to buy myself a new nightdress for when I go into hospital and then I bumped into an old friend I haven't seen for years and forgot all about shopping. We had tea at Lyons' and talked and talked.'

'Do I know her?'

'You met her once when you were a toddler, but I don't expect you remember her. We met during the last war, got to know each other well, but then we lost touch.'

'That's not like you.'

'No, but we were poles apart in every way. She came from a wealthy background; her father was a lord or something and she lived in the country, and what with looking after you and your dad, I never did take up her invitation to visit her. To tell the truth, I would have felt uncomfortable—'

'Why should you? You're as good as she is any day.'

'Oh, she isn't a snob, Laura. Far from it. You'll like her, I'm sure.'

'I'll like her?'

'I've asked her to come for a meal.'

'Mum, are you well enough? You should be resting, not entertaining.'

'I'd like you to meet her.'

'Why particularly?'

This was the tricky bit. Anne sipped her tea while she formed the words. 'She is a friend, one to whom I owe a lot; she helped me when your dad was away in the last war. Besides, she has a huge house in the country and if we are ever bombed out of here, it will be somewhere for us to go.'

Laura laughed. 'Oh, Mum, you are as transparent as glass. You want me to evacuate myself into the country. I wouldn't go before and I certainly won't go now when you have to go into hospital. What sort of daughter would that make me?'

'I don't mean now, I was thinking about after the operation. We could both go. I could convalesce there.'

Laura remained unconvinced. She had no idea what her mother was up to, but she was up to something. For someone who had steadfastly refused to budge, she had suddenly developed a yen to live in the country with an old friend, one of the upper classes, whom she purported to despise, someone she had never mentioned before. It took a lot of swallowing. 'When is she coming?'

'Next Tuesday, for lunch, then she can catch a train back home before the sirens go.'

'Then I'll have to think about what we are going to give her to eat. If she's posh—'

'She won't want anything special. I told you, she's not a snob, she'll take us as she finds us.'

That was bravado on Anne's part; she was worried to death and the nearer the time came, the more agitated she became. Laura noted it and wondered…

Helen took a taxi from Liverpool Street to Axholme Avenue. It was a suburban street of semi-detached houses, all much the same, all with small front gardens and bay windows, except that many of the windows had lost their glass and were nailed up with plywood. Some had lost tiles from the roof and one a chimney. But they were infinitely superior to those hovels in Prince Albert Lane.

'Here you are, missus,' the taxi driver said, stopping outside one, boarded up like the others. She paid him and, taking a deep breath, made her way up the path. This was it. This was the moment she had been waiting for and suddenly she was afraid. She stood a moment to gather herself before lifting her hand to the knocker.

'Helen, you came.' Anne stood there looking tiny and anxious.

'Did you think I wouldn't?'

'No. Come on in. Let me take your coat. We'll go through to the dining room. We've still got windows in there and a good fire. You must be perished.'

'No, it was quite warm on the train.' She had deliberately not worn her fur coat, which would have kept her warm; it didn't seem appropriate somehow. She handed over the blue herringbone tweed she had had for years, aware that someone had come out of a room at the far end of the hall. Heart thumping, she turned to face her.

Here was a young Helen Barstairs, heavily pregnant and defiant. Here was the same dark hair – though she noticed a slight sheen of auburn which was so like Oliver's – the same widow's peak and amber eyes. It was so startling, she almost gasped, but managed to turn it into a smile.

Anne looked from one to the other and suddenly wondered if she was doing the right thing. But it was done now. 'Laura, this is Lady Helen Barstairs.'

Helen moved forward and offered her hand. 'How do you do,' she said. 'Your mother has told me so much about you.' She was amazed how normal she sounded.

'Nothing bad, I hope.' Laura's hand was warm and firm.

'No, all good, I assure you.'

'Go through to the dining room. Lunch is nearly ready.'

Laura went back to the kitchen, leaving Helen to precede Anne into a small room in which a coal fire burnt. The table was laid with a white cloth and sparkling cutlery and glasses. Besides four dining chairs, there was a sideboard and a drinks cabinet. Helen moved over to stand looking out of the window at the back garden, somewhat lifeless in the middle of winter. There was an Anderson shelter halfway down it.

Anne came to stand beside her. 'We spend most of our nights in there.'

'It must be frightening.'

'You get used to it. You get used to anything in time. What do you think of her?' The last was said in an undertone.

'What do you expect me to think? She is my flesh and blood and I'd love her whatever she looked like or whatever she did. She reminds me of me when I was expecting her. What have you told her?'

'Only that we were friends in the last war and lost touch. I didn't say how we came to be friends, you'll have to think of something.'

'Driving ambulances?'

'Good idea.'

'What are you two whispering about?' Laura came into the room behind them bearing two tureens.

'We weren't whispering, we were reminiscing about our time driving ambulances,' Anne answered.

'Is that how you met?'

'Yes,' they said together.

'Come and sit down to eat and tell me all about it.'

Helen could not remember afterwards what they ate, or even if she ate at all; she joined in the fiction of the ambulances, letting Anne do the talking since she knew what she was talking about. When she was asked about herself, she spoke of Beckbridge Hall and her life in the village, of her parents and Richard, but it was a kind of waking dream. She felt that if she pinched herself she would wake up in her own bed.

'You never had children, then?' Laura asked.

Helen was startled. It was a question for which she was not prepared. She glanced across at Anne who was looking troubled, no doubt expecting her to blurt out the truth. 'I had a daughter,' she said slowly. 'But I lost her in infancy.'

'Oh, I am sorry. It must be terrible to lose a child.'

'Yes, it is.'

'Have some more vegetables, Helen,' Anne put in suddenly.

Helen declined politely and turned back to Laura. 'When is your baby due?'

155

'Towards the end of March. And before you ask, I'm not married and never have been.'

'Laura!' Anne protested.

'I wasn't going to ask,' Helen said. 'It's your business.'

'I think she should get out of London to have it,' Anne said, moving to safer ground. 'What with the air raids and everything—'

'Mum, you know we are making no decision about that until you've had your operation.'

'You are both welcome to come and stay with me,' Helen said.

Laura laughed. 'Has Mum put you up to that?'

'Not at all. I have a big house and no one to share it with. In fact, I have been thinking of offering it as a nursing home for recuperating servicemen. I believe you are a nurse. You could help me set it up – after the baby is born, of course. In fact, your being there would help me. The WVS have been asking me about taking in a bombed-out family. I would be able to say I'm making private arrangements to utilise the house.' She was making it up as she went along but she noticed the look of gratitude Anne gave her.

'That's very kind of you,' Anne said. 'We'll think about it, won't we, Laura?'

Laura felt she was being driven into a corner, but the proposition made sense. And it would be lovely to be nursing again, something she had not thought would be possible with a child to look after. 'Yes, we'll think about it, but let's get Mum's operation over with first. Has she told you about that?'

'Yes. If I can do anything—'

'Thank you,' Anne said. 'I've been advised to find a hospital away from London. Many of the London ones have been badly damaged and, in any case, they've got their hands full looking after casualties. Trouble is, I'm not sure where.'

'What about Addenbrooke's in Cambridge?' Helen suggested. 'That's considered a safe area and it's easily reached from London. I have connections there. I could make enquiries and let you know.'

'Would you? That would be very kind.'

Laura looked from one to the other. She could not help feeling that this was all a put-up job, that the words were carefully rehearsed. It was all to do with getting her out of London, she was sure of it. She also knew that her mother was seriously ill and the operation might not be the end of it. She guessed her mother knew that too, though she pretended otherwise; they both did. And why did Lady Barstairs look so familiar? Mum had said she had met her when she was a toddler; did that mean the memory had stayed in her subconscious over the intervening years and that was why she felt she ought to recognise her?

The meeting had been a strain on all of them and Helen, seeing how tired Anne was becoming, did not stay long after the offer had been made. She ought not to have felt disappointed. After all, she could hardly have expected Laura to fall on her neck. She had been polite, friendly, hospitable, and that was all she could expect. Laura was no longer a child, she was a grown woman, soon to be a mother herself; the baby Helen had called Olivia was lost for good and the years could not be grabbed back.

The man standing on the doorstep with his kitbag at his feet was in the uniform of a petty officer. 'Dad!' Donny yelled. 'Lenny, Dad's here.'

Kathy came to the door when she heard Donny's shout and smiled at the man who had lifted Donny off his feet and was whirling him round. Lenny flew past her and flung himself at his father, who was almost toppled over by the onslaught. He hugged them both and then turned to Kathy. 'Mrs Wainright?'

'Yes, you must be Petty Officer Carter.'

Kathy shook his hand and invited him into the kitchen, where William was just taking off his boots and Alice was stirring the gravy on the top of the stove. Kathy introduced them and invited Alec to eat with them, since she was about to dish up Sunday lunch. He had a week's leave, he told them, and he wanted to spend it with the boys. 'Do you think they'll let them off school under the circumstances?'

'I'm sure they will. You can ask my daughter when she comes in. She's one of their teachers. Have you got anywhere to stay?'

'No, I was hoping you might recommend somewhere, the local pub perhaps.'

'You are welcome to stay here. You can have Steve's room. He's away in the RAF.'

'Thank you. If it's not too much trouble. I've got my ration book.'

'Donny, go and tell Meg and Daphne I'm dishing up,' Kathy told him, as Jenny came in.

Introductions were made all round and it was a happy party that sat down to eat roast pork and apple sauce and a mountain of home-cooked vegetables. The boys talked nineteen to the dozen; Kathy hadn't seen them so animated since they learnt of their mother's death.

Afterwards, they took their father on a tour of the village and showed him the church, the school, the shops and the common. 'Anyone can go on it, but it's not a park, 'cos the grass ain't cut and there are cows and horses on it,' Donny told him. 'Lenny was afraid of the cows to start with—'

'So were you.'

'No, I weren't!'

Alec laughed. 'I take it you've got used to them now.'

'Yes. Uncle William's got a lot. He milks them twice a day. He gets gallons and gallons of milk from them. And it goes off in big churns to the dairy.'

'He's got pigs, too,' Lenny put in. 'And he grows things. We helped lift the spuds and got paid for it.'

'That's good. So, you are happy here?'

'It's all right,' Donny admitted. 'Not like home though.'

'Home is gone, lads. Flattened.' He had gone there first after his ship docked. It hadn't been much of a house; two up and two down with a privy in the back yard. In the early years of his marriage, he had been ambitious, wanting to better himself and improve the lives of his family. 'We'll save to find somewhere better,' he had told

Doreen. 'I can't spend much at sea, and I'm not a drinker, so I'll send you all the money I can spare and you can put it into savings. We'll build up a nice little nest egg for when I leave the service.' It hadn't worked like that. She hadn't saved a penny and complained he never sent enough, that the boys grew out of their clothes faster than she could replace them. He might have accepted that if she had made an effort, but the boys were poorly clad in someone else's cast-offs and she had a wardrobe full of clothes for herself. Well-meaning neighbours had told him she was out every night, leaving the boys on their own, and though she said she was with girl friends, she had been seen more than once with a man. When he taxed her with it, it had caused a row and she accused him of believing gossips before her. If it had not been for the twins he would not have come home at all. Now she was gone, he really could not be sorry, except, of course, she was the boys' mother.

'So Mum really is dead?' Lenny queried.

'Yes. I'm sorry, boys.'

'What's going to happen to us, Dad? We won't have to go into one o' them orphanages, will we?'

'No, of course not. Has Mrs Wainright said you will?'

'No, she said we could stay with her, but I don't think she meant for ever.'

'I expect she meant until the war ended and I came home for good.'

'But you're in the Navy.'

'I'll have to come out of it, won't I? We'll find another house. Don't worry.'

'Mrs Wainright's nice,' Lenny said. 'She don't ever beat us. She gets cross sometimes, though.'

He smiled. 'I expect you deserve it.'

'Yes, I 'spec' so.' This was said with a huge sigh. Donny gave him a nudge with his elbow and he fell silent.

Alec noted it but did not comment. 'What about the others?'

'They're all right,' Donny conceded.

'I like Aunty Daphne the best,' Lenny said. 'She don' grumble at us and she 'elped us clear up our bedroom when—'

'Shut up, Lenny,' Donny said. 'Dad don' want to know about that.'

'Ah, but supposing I do?'

'It weren't nuffin. We made it untidy, tha's all. And there's Miss Wainright.' Donny attempted to change the subject. 'She teaches the infants. Sometimes she 'elps us wiv our 'omework, 'cos we're going to sit the scholarship. If we pass we'll go to the grammar school in Attlesham next September.'

'Then you must work hard and pass it. A grammar school education will make all the difference when you grow up.'

They walked on. 'Tha's where Lady Barstairs lives,' Lenny said, pointing to the drive of the Hall. 'Miss Wainright said she's Aunty Kathy's cousin. It's enormous, as big as a palace, but there ain't no princesses there. She's got a big garden too, big as a park, with a lake an' a summer house an' all.' Another dig in the ribs from his brother and he stopped.

'We collected pans and things for a Spitfire,' Donny said. 'They said whoever collected the most would get to name it. We was goin' to call it "Doreen", but we didn't win.'

'Never mind. I'm sure Mummy would have appreciated the effort.'

'Do you think she c'n see us?' Lenny asked, with a worried frown. 'Can she look down and see what we're doin'?'

'I don't know. Do you think she can?'

''Course she can't,' Donny said dismissively. 'Tha's poppycock.'

They turned in at the farm gate just as Daphne was coming across the yard, rolling a churn of milk towards the gate. Alec hurried to help her with it, then they all trooped in for tea.

That evening, after the boys had gone to bed, Daphne and Alec strolled down to the pub. They sat in the bar chatting, mostly about the boys. 'I'm so glad you came and you're going to stay a little while,' she said. 'They've been so homesick.'

'What's this about the big house? Lenny wanted to talk about it, but Donny stopped him. And they said something about making their room a mess and you helping to clear it up.'

Daphne told him about their reaction on being told of their mother's death without mentioning the small hoard of booty they had stored in their wardrobe. 'Don't tell the boys I told you,' she ended.

'Poor little devils. It isn't as if their home life was anything to shout about. I hate to say it, but Doreen wasn't the best mother in the world.'

'I'm sorry.'

'Tell me about yourself? How did you come to be a land girl?'

They moved on to easier subjects and on the way home she told him about the dance in Attlesham that Saturday. Alec said he'd like to take her, and Daphne said yes.

They went out walking with the boys several times in the week that followed and when the time came for him to go back to his ship he asked her to write to him. 'You could give me all the news and tell me what the boys are up to,' he said. 'I'll try to write to them more often. I feel guilty that I haven't done so before but I thought their mother was writing and visiting, and when you're at sea—'

'Of course I will,' she said. She liked Alec Carter and she really wouldn't mind if what looked liked the beginning of a friendship developed into something more.

Helen heard the drone of an aeroplane just as dawn was breaking. Everyone in Beckbridge heard it. It was flying low, circling round and round. She wondered if it was in trouble and peered out of her bedroom curtains to look. It seemed right overhead. She could see the cross on its fuselage. There had been no alert, so this one must be lost. She wished it would go away. And then she saw the bomb, saw it as clear as day, and it seemed to be coming straight for her, screeching like a banshee. She flung herself under the bed as the explosion rocked the house to its solid foundations. The noise was followed by the sound of breaking glass and debris falling to earth. Something big landed on the roof; she heard it sliding down and then crashing to the ground. And then there was an eerie silence. She waited. Nothing. She waited a little longer, hardly daring to breathe.

'My lady, are you all right?' It was Mrs Ward outside her bedroom.

Feeling foolish, she scrambled out of her hiding place and went to open the door. Mrs Ward was standing in a dressing gown, her long grey hair hanging down in plaits. She was carrying a candle in a metal candlestick and her face, in its glow, was as white as the winceyette nightdress she wore. 'Yes, I'm fine Mrs Ward. What about you and Mr Ward?'

'We're right as rain but the electricity's gone off. I'm going to stir up the embers and put the kettle on the range. Shall I bring you a cup of tea?'

'No, I'll come down and have it in the kitchen. Then I'll have to inspect the damage.'

'I think it's mostly broken windows and tiles off the roof. John's gone out to look.'

'I'll be down in a minute.'

The housekeeper went downstairs, the guttering candle casting her shadow on the wall as she went. Helen went to the window. There was no glass in it and the frame was twisted. She dare not touch it. Over two hundred years the house had stood, defying wind and weather and the ravages of man, but now it, too, was a casualty of war. The aeroplane had gone. She could see where the bomb had dropped because there was a gap in the trees that ringed the park and there was the flicker of flames, like a large bonfire. She dressed in trousers and jumper and went downstairs.

Mrs Ward was sitting at the kitchen table drinking tea. She poured one for Helen and offered her the biscuit barrel. 'Oh, I'm sorry, my lady, I should ha' put them on a plate. I wasn't thinking.'

Helen smiled. 'As if that mattered at a time like this.' She dipped her hand in, brought out a digestive and bit into it.

Mr Ward came in the back door dressed in trousers and dressing gown. 'There's hardly a complete window in the front of the house and a lot of tiles off the roof, and a chimney's come down. If I could get my hands on that there Hitler, I'd string him up myself.'

Helen smiled suddenly, thinking of her father. He would have been angry, not afraid, and she was angry too, railing against the injustice. How could she ask Anne and Laura to come and live in a place with no windows and half the roof open to the sky? Anne had had her operation three weeks before and appeared to be getting over it, though she was still in hospital. Cambridge was no more than forty miles away and Helen had been to visit her and had seen Laura several times. Laura was always friendly but there was a wariness about her, as if she could not quite believe the story her mother had told her. On the other hand, she had never hinted that she did not. Anne might say she wasn't a very good liar, so perhaps she had not quite explained away the sudden affluence to Laura's satisfaction. Helen wondered if Anne was simply sticking her head in the sand. And, strangely, Helen herself was beginning to wonder how badly she wanted Laura to know the truth. All the years of wishing and longing and feeling angry had suddenly dissipated. Wouldn't it be better simply to be a friend of the family, someone who could be relied on to help when help was needed, perhaps a confidante? Wouldn't that be easier than all the upset telling the truth would surely bring about?

'I'm just going to see what's happened,' she said, pulling on Wellington boots and tucking her trousers into them.

She knew where to go, the gap in the trees had told her plainly enough. Walking across the damp grass, she was reminded of the last time she had been there. It was when she had discovered that hoard of contraband. She had been so full of her meeting with Anne she had forgotten all about ringing Constable Harris, and he had not come to see her, so she supposed Mrs Harris had forgotten to pass on her message. It had gone clear out of her head since then, which wasn't surprising considering she had been occupied with arranging

Anne's operation and going to visit her, musing on her relationship with Laura and wondering if it would be in order to remember her birthday.

The explosion, which had uprooted a tree and set fire to its dry branches, had burnt itself out. The charred remains of the summer house were hanging over the edge of a huge hole. The cricket bats and croquet hoops were broken and scattered. Broken glass crunched beneath her boots. The bench had been wrenched apart and the contents had tumbled out into the bottom of the hole. She peered into it. In among the earth and rubble were broken boxes of chocolate, dented tins, smashed bottles. The smell of whisky and cheap perfume wafted up to her. She sank onto the ground and laughed aloud. It was so bizarre.

'It fell in the grounds of the Hall,' Joyce said, bringing the mail up to the farm and the local gossip with it. William and the boys were still sitting over their breakfast, talking about the explosion; Kathy was standing at the table, teapot in hand. She had heard Joyce's bicycle bell and was already pouring a cup of tea for her. 'There's hardly a winder left and half the roof's gone.'

'What about Lady Helen?' William asked. 'And the Wards?'

'I just saw Charlie Harris on his way up there to find out. I reckon they'll be shaken up even if they're not injured.'

'Did it land on the house itself?'

'Dunno, don't think so. I saw a bit of a fire in the grounds, down towards the lake. Can't think what there is down there that would burn.'

Everyone was too busy listening to her to notice Lenny's gasp of shock and Donny's vicious kicking of his shins.

'The summer house and an old boathouse,' Kathy said, remembering. They had had fun there when they were young, playing croquet and cricket and swimming in the lake. They'd take the boat out and tip each other overboard and laugh a lot, she and Helen and the young men they entertained, all properly chaperoned, of course. Another age, another lifetime ago. Another war, too. That had changed everything. Her cousin Brandon had been killed and Uncle Henry seemed to want to fill the void with other young men. Richard among them. He had come to the Hall and spent a whole leave there. Uncle Henry had given him the freedom of the stables and, as riding was one of Kathy's favourite pastimes, they frequently found themselves riding together. He was so handsome, so gentlemanly; she had fallen hopelessly in love with him. She was devastated when Helen said she was going to marry him. She wouldn't have minded, she told herself, if Helen had been truly in love with him, but Helen had seemed very cool about it. And, of course, she had to endure being a bridesmaid. She had cried buckets of tears that night.

'Get yourself another young man,' her mother had advised her, having little sympathy. She didn't want another young man, not then, although there were several about. William, for a start. She had known him since childhood; his family had been regular churchgoers, part of her father's congregation, and she had gone out with him several times. She had turned to him in her unhappiness and they had been married towards the end of 1916. But Helen marrying Richard was not the cause of the rift with her, not altogether; it was the discovery of her cousin's perfidy. Helen was married to a man fighting for King and country and yet she met Oliver secretly in the summer house. Kathy had seen them there and what they had been doing was unspeakable. She had taxed Helen with betraying Richard, called her a common tart and other dreadful names which couldn't be unsaid. Accusations of spying were hurled in retaliation.

'I'd better go up there and see if there is anything I can do to help,' William said, after Joyce had gone. 'If the place is badly damaged, I'll ask her to come and stay, shall I?' He paused, noticing Kathy's hesitation. 'Whatever happened between you and Helen was a long time ago and it's not like you to bear a grudge.'

'Go on,' her mother put in. 'She is your cousin after all. She can have my room. I can manage in one of the attic rooms.'

Alice had always deplored the estrangement of the two families who had once been so close. Her sister, Louise, had married the Earl of Hardingham and gone to live at Beckbridge Hall, which elevated her above the normal run of the villagers, while Alice herself had married Daniel Broomfield, a curate at a parish on the other side of Attlesham, until he took over from the retiring vicar at St Andrew's in Beckbridge, bringing her back to her roots. She and Louise had remained close and their daughters had grown up together, until their lives were ripped apart by the Great War. She didn't entirely blame Helen for what happened, though Kathy had. Poor Kathy! It was just as well she hadn't married Richard, considering he hadn't survived. She was better off with William. Salt of the earth was William, even if he was a bit of a plodder.

Unable to explain how she felt, Kathy gave in, telling herself, as she had done hundreds of times before, that if Richard had been serious about her, he would not have married someone else and she had entirely misread the signs. She could not blame Helen for that, even if she did deplore her relationship with Oliver. It was water under the bridge now. 'You'll do no such thing,' she told her mother. 'If she wants to come, she can have Steve's room, at least while he's away.'

She watched William put on his boots and reach for his cap; sturdy, dependable William, the best of husbands. She turned and sent the twins off to school.

Helen was walking back across the grass when William approached her. 'Seems you've had a bad to-do,' he said. 'Are you all right?'

'Yes, I'm fine. I'm glad it didn't land on the house, though there's no end of windows broken and a chimney pot came down and brought a lot of tiles with it. There's no electricity either.' She nodded over her shoulder. 'The summer house has gone, there's nothing there but a heap of wood and a huge hole. And something else. Come and see.'

He followed her, wondering how she could be so cheerful. 'Look down there.' She pointed down into the hole.

'Good Lord! What is it?'

'I think it's black market stuff. It was hidden in the summer house.'

He scrambled down and picked some of it up. Very little of it was usable. 'Someone is going to be a touch mad when he sees what's happened to his precious hoard.'

'Yes.' She held out her hand to haul him out again. 'I hope no one thinks I knew anything about it.'

He laughed. 'I shouldn't think so for a minute.'

'I was on my way to find a phone to report it to Constable Harris. Our line is down.'

'I'll do it, if you like.'

'Thank you.'

He walked beside her to the Hall and stood outside peering up at the roof. 'We'd better get some tarpaulin over that before it rains. I'll ring the builders for you, shall I?' She followed as he walked all round the house, counting windows. 'Sixty-five,' he said. 'I never knew you had so many.'

She laughed. 'I never counted them before.'

'Well, it's clear you'll have to move out until the house is made habitable.'

'It is habitable, certainly no worse than the houses some poor Londoners are living in.'

'They have no choice. You have. Come and stay with us.'

'Oh, I don't think so, thanks all the same. Kathy—'

'It was Kathy's idea.'

She didn't believe him but pretended she did. 'That was kind of her, but it isn't necessary.'

'At least come down and have lunch with us while I sort out the builders for you.'

It was time to bury the hatchet, time to be friends again. Since finding Laura again, she had come to appreciate the importance of friendship, of not dwelling on the past. She had been living in the past too long. She smiled and accepted the invitation.

The bomb that fell on Beckbridge Hall was a nine-day wonder in the village. Everyone said they were thankful it had not landed in the village itself and the destruction of a wooden summer house was nothing, compared to houses and people's lives. Of course, they felt sorry for Lady Helen losing her windows but no one had been hurt. Mr and Mrs Ward were so terrified they had gone to live with their daughter and refused to come back. 'She'll get a taste of work now,' Ian Moreton told Joyce. 'Never done a hand's turn and now she'll have to look after herself. I'm blowed if I know why she wants to rattle round in that great place all on her own. Time they pulled it down, instead of mending it. There's others more needy who could do with a bit of building work done.'

Thanks to Donny's timely warning, he had rushed up to the summer house and cleared up every vestige of evidence, so that when Constable Harris arrived to take charge of the black market goods, there was none to be seen. Ian had laughed himself into tears over that. But he quickly sobered when he counted up the amount of money he had tied up in the stuff and none of it usable, except the tins and booze he had hidden under a tarpaulin in the boathouse. He thought it expedient to remove those, but was left with the problem of getting rid of the useless stuff and finding a new hiding place for what was left because he dare not take it home. He had put everything in a sack, buried the rubbish on the common, and taken everything else to a disused shepherd's hut on the far side of the common, helped by Donny. It was not as secure as the summer house, but it would have to do.

He'd offered the boy a tin of golden syrup for his pains, but that had been rejected. 'Got no one to give it to now,' he'd said. 'I'd rather have half a crown.' He'd had to pay the little bugger to keep his mouth shut and scared the daylights out of him to make sure he wasn't tempted to blurt out the truth.

'It's going to be turned into a convalescent home,' Joyce said, bringing him back to the subject of the Hall and its lonely occupant. 'Lady Helen told Kathy.' She didn't, for a minute, think he'd given up his lucrative sideline, though where he hid the stuff and what he did with the money she had no idea; she certainly saw none of it. Kathy had told her about the stuff her ladyship found which had suddenly disappeared again, making Charlie Harris scratch his head. They both thought the twins might know but Kathy refused to badger them about it; they'd been very quiet since their mother died and she didn't want them upset.

'I thought they weren't on speaking terms.'

'They're talking now. Funny how a bomb and a bit of danger make folks see things different.'

'What was it all about anyway? Their fallin' out, I mean.'

'I dunno, do I?'

'I reckon it was suff'n to do with men,' a voice piped up from the chimney corner.

They both turned towards Joyce's mother. Lily Wilson was sitting with her feet on the fender and her skirt pulled up above her knees to reveal voluminous pink bloomers.

'What men?'

'Oh, Richard and William and others I could name.' She tapped the side of her nose.

'What others?' Ian asked.

'Oh, those soldiers what went up to the Hall in the last war. Fine goings-on, there was.'

'How d'you know that?'

'I worked up there, didn' I? So did Valerie.'

'She married one of them,' he said. He'd always thought the wedding a rush job, held in a registry office and not the church, though not being married to Joyce at the time, he hadn't been one of the guests. The newly-weds had left for Canada soon afterwards and they hadn't seen them since, though Lily was always talking about going out there to visit them. Not that she ever would, considering she hadn't got a penny-piece to her name except her pension.

'Looks like 'istory is about to repeat itself,' he said, suddenly aware of the opportunities for trade that recuperating wounded soldiers might present. He smiled a little to himself.

Chapter Six

LAURA HAD GIVEN up work and taken lodgings in Cambridge to be near her mother. Anne had wanted to postpone the operation until after the baby was born, but the surgeon had advised against delay. The operation, so Laura had been told by the surgeon who had performed it, had gone smoothly and he thought they had removed all the tumour, but it was difficult to be sure. Laura, because she was a nurse and having her there relieved the other staff, was allowed to spend hours at her bedside. She changed her dressing, helped her to eat and drink, and talked cheerfully the whole time.

It was difficult because she was getting very near her time and she worried about what would happen if Anne took a turn for the worse while she was in labour and *hors de combat* herself. Her mother muttered a lot about Tom and Helen. Laura couldn't understand why both names should be uttered almost in the same breath, but she clearly had something on her mind. 'Mum, it doesn't matter,' she said. 'Whatever it is, it isn't important. You must get better.' The thought of losing her mother was almost too much to bear and she railed against the injustice of it. Mum had never done a bad deed in all her life. She had gone without herself to give Laura everything she needed – school uniforms, books, tennis rackets, dancing lessons – and she had done it cheerfully, without a word of complaint. She went to church regularly, helped to clean it and arrange the flowers, and whenever a neighbour needed a helping hand she had been there to offer it. She had been one of the first to join the WVS when it was formed. The prospect of going back to Axholme Avenue without her was terrifying.

Today, for the first time, Anne seemed a little better. At least, she was fully conscious and smiling. 'Still here?' she murmured.

'Where else would I be?'

'How are you?'

'As big as a London bus, but how do you feel?'

'Drowsy. Has Helen been in?'

'Not today. She was here two days ago. Her house has been bombed, she told me. Funny, isn't it? We're supposed to be going there for you to convalesce and she's lost her windows. She told me it was a stray bomber who had lost his way and decided to jettison his cargo.'

'Oh dear. Was there much damage?'

'No, only windows and a few tiles. The bomb landed in the grounds.'

'Did she say anything about us going?'

'Yes. She said the repairs are being done. She got the builders to come quickly because she told them the place was going to become a hospital for wounded servicemen. I hadn't realised she'd gone ahead with that plan.'

'Why not? No doubt the house would be requisitioned if she didn't do something.'

'Does that mean we're committed?'

'Don't you want to go?'

'I don't know. We don't know her very well do we?'

'I know her very well indeed. I hoped you'd like her.'

'I do. She's a nice person. Better than the Rawtons by a long chalk.' She had written to Bob's parents, feeling they had a right to know that they would shortly become grandparents. She had done it more for her baby's sake than her own, but the only reply she had had was a typed one from Sir Edward's secretary telling her they did not wish to communicate with her and if she persisted in harassing them, they would take legal action. They probably thought she was after money.

'Of course she is. And, Laura, I'm not going to be much help to you with the baby, am I? It is for the best.'

'I suppose so. Let's get you well first.'

'When is she coming again?'

'She didn't say.'

'I want to talk to her. It's important.'

Laura sighed. 'All right, I'll telephone her, but you've got to rest now. All this talking has worn you out.'

Laura made sure she was comfortable and left her to trudge through heavy snow to her digs in Tennis Court Road, chosen because it was near the hospital. Her mother's lack of progress worried her, as did her obsession with Lady Barstairs. Laura had never heard of the woman until a few weeks ago and yet she and Mum were supposed to be close friends. What was even more puzzling was the fact that they were a million miles apart in every way. Her ladyship had obviously been brought up in the lap of luxury while her mother was living in an orphanage and enduring the privations of life as a skivvy, which was no more than slavery. She had only recently been told about that. Mum had never talked much about her early life, but on this occasion she had wanted to chat, and Laura had listened to tales of the orphanage, where there was nothing you could call your own, and the cruelty of Mrs Colkirk. No wonder Mum hated the so-called upper classes. So why this dependence on Lady Barstairs? Was there something else her mother wasn't telling her? There must be because she had also suddenly produced an insurance policy she said she had been paying a few coppers into for years. Her mother was not a liar, so she must accept it as true, but it must have been done very secretively. Perhaps she had taken it out in order to have something to leave in her will, but if that was so Laura was glad she had decided to use it for the operation.

The chimney was rebuilt, the tiles were replaced and the windows re-glazed. There had been some compensation from the war damage people, but it hadn't covered the special bricks to match the existing ones, nor all the windows, and Helen had paid the extra in order to have the house ready for Anne and Laura. She had made enquiries about making it into a convalescent home and discovered the Air Ministry were looking for beds for airmen who had been shot down and needed long-term treatment for burns. They were doing wonderful things with a procedure called plastic surgery, where they took skin from other parts of the men's bodies and grafted them onto their burnt faces and hands. It meant a series of operations and the patients had to have somewhere to recover from one before they went on to the next. Beckbridge Hall, being in a relatively safe area of the country, would be ideal, they told her. She had told them Laura had some experience nursing burns cases and she would talk to her about it, but not now. Better to concentrate on Anne, who wanted to see her.

'She's bothered about something,' Laura had said the day before when she rang just after the telephone had been reconnected. 'Would you come?'

And so here she was, once more sitting in a train, taking her from Attlesham to Cambridge and wondering what the future had in store. Judging by Laura's matter-of-fact tone, Anne had not yet told her the truth, but did the summons mean that she intended to? Did she want Helen to witness it? Suddenly she was not sure that she wanted it told. It would cause untold heartache to everyone concerned.

Laura met her as she entered the ward. The baby she carried was only three weeks from being born and it made her walk awkwardly. She looked drawn, older than her years, and her eyes were dull. 'Thank you for coming,' she said. 'She keeps falling in and out of consciousness and I don't know if she will know you are here.'

She led the way back to the curtained-off area at the far end of the ward and allowed Helen to precede her to the side of the bed. Anne, always small, looked like a doll: a white-faced, pink-eyed doll. Her hands were above the covers and every now and again they twitched as if to grab something unseen. Helen sat in the chair by the bed. 'Anne,' she murmured.

The grey-haired head thrashed from side to side. 'Tom, Laura, I'm sorry...' It was a mumble, hardly coherent.

'I don't know what she has to be sorry for,' Laura whispered. 'But it's evidently worrying her.'

'Helen, forgive me.' That was clearer, as if she knew Helen was there.

'What's to forgive?' Laura asked.

Helen didn't answer but leant forward and took one of Anne's hands. 'I'm here, Anne, and it doesn't matter any more. It's over and done with. Please don't agitate yourself.'

Anne opened her eyes suddenly. 'Helen, you came.'

'Of course I came.'

'Where's Laura?'

'I'm here, Mum.'

'Go and fetch us a cup of tea, love, I want to have a private word with Helen.' It was said quite clearly.

Laura was about to protest, but Helen's little nod sent her off in search of tea.

'Has she gone?'

'Yes.'

'I haven't told her, Helen. I couldn't.'

'Doesn't matter. I don't want you to. It won't change anything and it will make her very unhappy.'

'I've written her a letter to read after...after, you know...' She paused. 'Cowardly of me, I know, but I couldn't bear to see her face when I told her. Will you give it to her?'

'Perhaps. Perhaps I won't. We'll see.'

'It's in my locker.'

Helen opened the locker and found an envelope with Laura's name on it. 'This?'

'Yes. I wrote it when I knew I might not survive the op...'

Helen put it in her handbag. 'But you have survived and now you must concentrate on getting better. The house is all ready for you.'

'Good.' She knew she was not going to Beckbridge, was not even going back to Burnt Oak; she wasn't going anywhere except in a wooden box. She suspected Helen knew it too. 'Look after her, won't you? She won't find it easy.'

'Of course.'

'She's yours now.' She looked past Helen to where Laura approached with a tray of tea things. But suddenly she was too tired to drink, too tired to do anything. She smiled and allowed her eyelids to close.

'Mum?' Laura dumped the tray down and ran round to the other side of the bed, where she dropped to her knees and took her mother's other hand.

Anne's eyelids flickered open. 'It's your birthday tomorrow, love.'

Laura smiled. 'So it is. I'd forgotten.'

'I hadn't. How could I? There's a little present for you in my locker.'

'Oh, Mum. The only present I want is for you to get better.'

'I am going to be better quite soon.' She smiled again and lifted both her hands, one clasping Helen's and one clasping Laura's, and joined them together. 'Be good to each other…'

'Oh, Mum.' Laura swallowed hard, trying not to break down.

They stayed like that a long time, one on each side of the bed, hands joined, while the fluttering breath rose and fell gently until it became almost imperceptible. There was a last huge sigh and Anne's heart stopped. It was a moment or so before her watchers realised that she hadn't taken another breath; that she never would.

Helen withdrew her hand carefully and sat white-faced and silent, while Laura flung herself forward and wept on her mother's breast.

A nurse glided silently to the bedside, felt for Anne's pulse and quietly withdrew. Helen waited, wondering what she could do, knowing there was nothing she could do to mitigate the loss of a beloved mother. And she was glad that Anne had not told Laura the truth.

♣

Laura went back to Axholme Avenue. There was, she had told Helen, things she must do. She had to arrange the funeral; Mum would want to be buried with Dad and there were friends and neighbours to invite, people who had known Anne ever since they moved to Burnt Oak, her friends at the church and in the WVS, Aunt Maisie, whom she had not seen in years. Apart from her father's sister and her children, she didn't have a relative in the world. Mum had known that and so she had looked up an old friend, an old friend who seemed ready and willing to do what she could to help. She ought to be grateful. She *was* grateful, but it didn't stop her wondering why.

'Let me help you,' Lady Helen had said. 'You shouldn't be doing all that in your condition.'

'No, thank you all the same. This is something I must do myself. I'm perfectly well and the baby is not due for another three weeks.' She gulped, determined to be practical, but the thought that Mum would never see her grandchild, never watch its first steps, hear its first words, watch it grow, had her in floods of tears again. And when, gently coaxed by Helen, she opened her birthday present, she was reduced to incoherence. It was a silver christening cup, which was really a present for her baby, but her mother could not have chosen anything better. 'Oh, Mum, what will I do without you?' she said at last, and Helen found herself turning away to hide her own tears. It was a question she longed to answer, but couldn't.

'You will come to the funeral?' Laura asked her when she had recovered her composure.

'Of course. You'll come to Beckbridge afterwards?'

'Thank you, but I'll have to sort Mum's things out and clear the house, and it doesn't seem right to do that before the funeral. I'll come when it's done.'

'Promise?'

'Yes, I promised Mum I would.'

The funeral was over, Helen had come and gone by train and Laura, dry-eyed and weary, with her unborn child growing heavier and heavier, was trying to go through her mother's things without bursting into tears, and wondering about the future. She hated the idea of giving up her home but the alternative was to shut the house up and leave everything inside to the mercy of the German bombers and the looters, who were everywhere. In any case, paying rent for an unoccupied house was a luxury she could not afford. Lady Barstairs had told her to send the furniture to Beckbridge Hall, that she had acres of room and it would be nice for her to have some of it around her. She was a very understanding person and Laura was grateful, but she could not get over her wariness. It was not distrust exactly, but a feeling that there was something she did not know, something she ought to know.

Perhaps the answer was in that little case her mother had carted everywhere with her, even to the hospital. Until now she had been reluctant to open it because it felt like prying, but it had to be done. She sat down at the kitchen table and opened it with a key she had found in her mother's handbag. It contained, as she expected, her personal treasures: her marriage certificate, her own and Laura's birth certificate: Laura Anne Drummond, born March the fifth, 1918, father Thomas Drummond, soldier; mother, Anne Drummond, née Smith. Her mother's birth certificate was a revelation. 'Father unknown,' it said. Poor Mum, no wonder she had flown off the handle when she was told her unmarried daughter was pregnant. There was a well-thumbed letter from her mother to her father and his reply, written somewhere in France, which showed how much she had been welcomed and had her in tears again. There were also snapshots taken with her father's box camera; mostly by her mother of her and her dad, but there were proper photographs of her receiving her school certificate from the headmistress of her grammar school and of the ceremony on the day she qualified as a nurse. And there was one of Lady Barstairs. She was wearing a shapeless dress with a lace collar and cuffs and a cloche hat. Behind her was a small building that looked a bit like a cricket pavilion. She turned it over. Written on the back was: Lady Helen Barstairs, Beckbridge Hall, 1921. It confirmed her mother's statement that she had known Lady Barstairs a long time and only now did Laura admit that she had not believed it.

There were other things in the case; a white crocheted shawl, so fine and soft, it made her sigh and hold it to her cheek. It smelt faintly of mothballs. Had her mother made it? In one corner, embroidered white on white, were the initials HB. Not AD or LD, but HB. It must have been a gift from Lady Barstairs, but why put her own initials on it? And then she remembered her saying she had lost a baby, so she must have handed the shawl on to Mum. Perhaps she could not bear to keep anything that reminded her of her loss. There was also a nightdress intricately smocked, knitted bootees, a matinée jacket and a little bonnet, all beautifully made, all wrapped carefully in tissue. Mum had been busy making clothes for Laura's baby and she had said nothing of having these things tucked away. She wrapped them all up again while the tears streamed down her cheeks.

If there was a reluctance to take that final step, it faded when the bombers returned. Buckingham Palace was bombed, as was St Bart's hospital and a cinema in Leicester Square. The Café de Paris, advertised as the safest restaurant in town because it was in a basement twenty feet below ground, was crowded with elegant women in evening dress and officers in uniform when it was hit by two bombs, one of which exploded in front of the band. The second, though it failed to explode, crashed through the entire building onto the crowded dance floor. The scene was one of devastation, according to the papers, who were making the most of the story, with officers carrying out their dead and injured girlfriends and ladies tearing up their expensive frocks for bandages. That same week another dance hall in the East End was hit, with far more casualties, but the frocks were not expensive and the uniforms not officers' and so it merited only a passing mention.

Her mother would have had something sharp to say about that…

Thinking about her mother set Laura crying again. She had shed gallons of tears in the last few weeks, but now it was time to stiffen her spine and get on with her life, for the baby's sake if not her own. She finished sorting her mother's clothes, most of which she gave to the WVS to help families who had been bombed out, arranged for a dealer to take the furniture and household equipment she did not want and for a van to transport the rest to Beckbridge: a three-piece suite in moquette, a set of bedroom furniture, a display cabinet and a bookcase, whose books went too, packed in boxes. There was the cot she had bought for the baby and the second-hand pram, and all the little clothes her mother had so painstakingly made, wrapped in tissue and packed, along with her own clothes, in two large suitcases. When the van had gone, all she had left to do was to take the keys to the landlord and catch a train. But the Luftwaffe had other ideas.

The siren went about teatime, just as she was leaving. She hesitated and then decided to go to the shelter and wait for the all-clear. Picking up her handbag, gas mask and the little attaché case, she went down the garden just as the drone of bombers began. She sat down, while the noisy raid went on all round her, remembering all the other nights she and her mother had spent there, buoying each other up, drinking tea from a Thermos, eating sandwiches. Mum had never shown she was afraid, but she must have been. It was here she had confessed about the baby and it was on a particularly bad night she had learnt about her mother's childhood and her first years at work before she met Dad. And the last war, which had taken his health. Poor Mum, what a hard life she'd had.

Her musing stopped abruptly when she felt a sudden contraction. It was only the beginning, but she knew without a shadow of doubt that it was the start of her labour. Her little one was not going to wait until they arrived in Beckbridge. Should she risk going out to find help, or sit it out for a while in the hope the all-clear would go? The ambulances and the hospitals would all be busy with bomb casualties. She felt desperately lonely. It was all very well to tell Lady

Barstairs she would be all right, all very well to pretend not to mind when neighbours cut her, all very well to be independent, but just at that moment she would have given anything for a friend. She longed for Bob, for the comfort of his arms, to share this time with him, to rejoice at the birth of a child with him – but Bob was gone. Mum was gone too. Outside the din was magnified as it reverberated on the metal of the shelter and shock waves from the explosions, one after another, shook the ground. Whatever was happening outside, it was worse than anything that had gone before. She was gripped by another contraction. Was she to have her baby here, all alone? Would either survive? She lay down on the camp bed and decided it didn't matter. If she died she would be with those she loved. But what if the baby was born strong and healthy and she let herself die…?

She got up, gathered up her things and went out. Searchlights swept the sky, ack-ack guns blazed though she didn't think they had hit any of the swarms of bombers that filled the night sky. There were fires everywhere and through the smoke and haze she could see parachute mines drifting down. They were silent until they hit the ground, but other bombs had a banshee scream as they hurtled downwards. They had been told the Germans put fins on them to make as much noise as possible and terrify those on the receiving end. As if they were not terrified enough! Her contractions were coming more frequently now. Clutching her handbag and her mother's case, she walked down the road, intending to go to the Edgware General Hospital, which was the nearest.

'Laura?'

The sound of her name startled her. She looked up to see a figure in a squadron leader's uniform coming towards her. Bob. 'Oh, Bob.' She stumbled forward into his arms.

Steve held her a minute, until she realised her mistake. She looked up and smiled weakly. 'Silly me. It was the uniform, I suppose. What are you doing here?'

'Going home for a couple of days. Thought I'd see how you were.'

'Having a baby.'

'I know that.'

'No, I mean now. Right now.'

'Good God!'

'Steve, walk with me to the hospital, will you?'

'Shouldn't you get a taxi or something?'

She managed a laugh. 'Can you see one?'

He looked about him. 'No, but—'

'Then let's walk. It will help a bit.'

He was confused and afraid. He knew nothing about having babies. Was she likely to have it there, in the street? Taking her case from her, he took her arm to help her along. 'Where's your mother? Surely she—'

'Mum is dead, Steve.'

'Oh God, I'm sorry. Was it a bomb?'

'No, she died of cancer.'

'Oh, you poor dear. I'm sorry. Does that mean you're all alone?'

'Yes.' She stopped and clutched his arm and hung there for a moment before carrying on. 'It's all right,' she reassured him. 'There's plenty of time.'

'What about relatives? Surely there's someone.'

'A friend. She doesn't live in London. I was going to stay with her for the confinement but the baby has other ideas.'

'What about Bob's parents?'

'They don't want to know.'

'I'm sorry.'

'Not your fault.'

'Maybe not, but Bob asked me to look after you. I haven't made a very good job of it, have I?'

'Oh, I don't know. You turned up just now, right on time. Bob sent you.'

'I suppose so.' He grimaced in the lurid light of dozens of fires. He had been going home on a forty-eight hour pass and that meant crossing London. He hadn't bargained for the air raid. He couldn't get anywhere near the station and it was then he had decided to take the Underground to Burnt Oak.

She had to stop again and he stood waiting until she was ready to go on. 'Shall I carry you?'

She laughed. 'Don't be silly. I must weigh a ton. Besides, we're nearly there.' They emerged from Bacon Lane onto the Broadway. There were fire engines and ambulances racing by, bells clanging, intent on reaching the scene of a large fire. They waited until it was safe to cross and made their way into the hospital.

'I'm in labour,' she told the receptionist. 'Can you help?'

'Are you sure?'

'I'm a nurse. And yes, I'm sure.'

She was whisked away in a wheelchair and Steve was left standing, wondering what to do.

'Are you the father?' a nurse asked him.

'No, just a friend.'

'We'll look after her now. You can call tomorrow and see how she is, if you like. I should get going if I were you. Find a shelter.' She turned away and hurried up the corridor after her patient.

Steve left and found a taxi to take him to Liverpool Street Station, only to find the last train had gone. He went down into the Underground, where thousands of people had bedded down for the night. Now that lavatories and washing facilities had been installed for them, the air was marginally sweeter. He made his way to the surface the next morning to discover more devastation and wondered how much longer the people of the beleaguered city could endure it. He tried telephoning the hospital but he couldn't get through, so he took a taxi there.

'She's not here,' he was told. 'They took her by ambulance to another hospital, away from the danger zone.'

'Where?'

'If you are not a relative and not the father, I can't tell you.'

He regretted denying he was the child's father. 'Is she all right? Has she had the baby?'

'She hadn't when she left here.' The receptionist was obviously not going to tell him anything. It made him angry, but being angry only made her dig in her toes. 'Look, Squadron Leader, if I were you, I'd go back to where you came from and no doubt she will contact you if she wants to. If not...' She shrugged.

Defeated, he turned on his heel, went back to Liverpool Street and caught a train for Attlesham.

It was good to be home and he just had time to unwind, have a good dinner, catch up on the local news, take the girls to the pub and have a good night's sleep before he had to leave again. His transfer to bombers had come through and he was reporting to a new posting at Scampton in Lincolnshire.

Robert Thomas Rawton Drummond was born in the early hours of the morning of Sunday, 16th of March in a hospital near Epping. The journey out of London had been a nightmare and would not ordinarily have been attempted, but they needed all the London beds they had for casualties. As soon as they arrived Laura was rushed to the delivery room and it was not until some time later – after her baby had been put into her arms and she spent some time examining his fingers and toes, admiring his blue eyes and quiff of dark hair and given him his first feed – that she thought about Steve.

'The air force officer who brought me,' she asked the ward sister. 'What happened to him?'

'I don't know anything about an air force officer. Is he the baby's father?'

'No, just a friend. He helped me to the hospital. There was a heavy raid on.'

'Then I expect he went to a shelter, or back to his base or something.' The words were spoken curtly and she supposed they had noticed the lack of a wedding ring. 'You can always write to him.'

She supposed she could, except the only address she had was the one Bob had given her. Steve might not be based there now; people moved about a lot in wartime. She had no idea of his home address. She decided to write anyway; the letter might be forwarded. 'May

I make a telephone call. I was supposed to be going to stay with a friend for the confinement. I must let her know where I am.'

'I'll do it if you give me her number.'

Laura provided it and she went off down the ward, starched and upright. A few minutes later she came back, in a much more benign mood. 'Lady Barstairs said to tell you congratulations and you are to go to her as soon as you are fit to travel. She says she'll fetch you by car.' She smiled suddenly. 'I am assured that everything is in hand for you to be looked after, so if you feel up to it, you can go the day after tomorrow. We could use your bed…'

She was a grandmother! Helen put the phone down and found she was grinning with relief and happiness. She had a grandson! And he was coming here with his mother. She longed to shout it from the rooftops, to tell everyone, 'I'm a granny!' But there was no one she could tell. She did what she used to do when she was young and wanted a little secret time to herself; she made her way to the summer house. Only it wasn't there any more. The builders had broken it up, dropped it in the bottom of the crater and filled the whole thing with earth. She went and sat on the tree stump facing the water. The wind was keen but she was well wrapped up. She wished she could tell Oliver he was a grandfather. He didn't know he had a daughter, much less a grandson. But he might have others. He might have a wife and several children, even grandchildren. It probably wouldn't mean half as much to him as it did to her. *If* he was still alive. She had no way of knowing. 'Oh, Oliver,' she whispered. 'Did you mean to desert me like that?'

She had been so alone all those years, wanting something she could not have, only half alive, existing from day to day, living in the past, and only a tiny bit of the past at that. No wonder people thought she was a bit strange. But now Laura was coming with the baby, and she would enjoy her company, get to know her. And she'd have the summer house rebuilt, just to prove there were no ghosts there now.

She went back to the house and made her way round to the stables, which had once been home to several horses. Her father and mother both hunted and she liked to ride sometimes, galloping over the park and onto the common with Kathy. In the old coach house next to the stables stood the old Humber. Mr Ward had kept it clean and made sure it remained in working order, but there was so little petrol to be had, she hadn't driven it for ages. She turned and went to see Kathy, who was much more friendly nowadays, as if the bomb had destroyed the rancour along with the summer house.

'I need to use the car,' she told her, after they had exchanged greetings. 'I think it's serviceable but I wondered if William would be kind enough to check it over for me and put a little petrol in it. I've got some coupons.'

'I should think so. He'll be in soon; you can ask him yourself. When do you want it?'

'The day after tomorrow. I'm going to have a friend to live with me. She's just had a baby and I have to fetch them from a hospital in Epping.' She paused, noting Kathy's look of surprise and realised she ought to explain. 'She's the daughter of an old friend who died of cancer a couple of weeks ago, and she has no other family. The girl's husband was in the RAF; he was shot down in the sea and his body was never recovered, so what with one thing and another, she's had a pretty awful time. I shall enjoy having her to stay and helping her get over it all.'

'Oh, the poor thing. What's her name?'

'Laura Drummond.'

'Should I know her?'

'No, I don't think so. I met her mother in London soon after Mama died and we kept in touch off and on. Then I met her again recently and one thing led to another. Laura is a nurse and when I told her about the Hall becoming a hospital and the need for someone to run it, it seemed the ideal solution for both of us.' She realised she was gabbling, wanting to clarify her story in her own mind as well as Kathy's, but now she stopped suddenly. Without even discussing it with Laura she had given her a husband. Perhaps she shouldn't have done that. On the other hand, it would have been unkind to have blurted out that her new lodger was unmarried. Laura had told her a little of the unkindness of neighbours and so-called friends and she wanted her to start again in Beckbridge with a clean slate.

'You don't mind me saying that?' she asked Laura as they left Epping behind them. She drove carefully because although the snowploughs had cleared the road, there was still snow lying on the verges. 'Beckbridge is a close-knit community where everyone knows everyone else's business. It's not prying, at least most of the time it's not, they are simply being friendly, but I didn't want you to start off at a disadvantage.'

'No, I don't mind. I always think of Bob as my husband. He always said I was his wife. I would have been married, legally and all that, if it hadn't been for the Luftwaffe.' She looked down at the sleeping Robby and smiled. Wrapped warmly in a shawl, he was fast asleep in her lap. 'I'll wear my mother's wedding ring. She would have liked that.'

Helen had been shaken to the core to see the baby swathed in the shawl Laura had been wrapped in when she had been wrenched from her arms. It was like being jolted back into the past and reliving that awful time. She had felt an irresistible urge to scream and scream and wrestle the child from his mother. Her consternation must have shown because Laura had begun apologising. 'I'm sorry. I shouldn't have put him in these clothes, but I didn't have any others with me. I sent all my baby things on ahead with the van.' And then she had gone on to explain how she had found them and assumed she had given them to her mother.

'Yes, I did,' Helen admitted, surprised that Anne had kept them, unused, but she might not have wanted to let family and friends see them and ask questions. By all accounts Stepney was as full of busybodies as any other community. 'It was a bit of a shock seeing the shawl again, but don't worry about it. I am happy for you to use them. Do you call him Robert or Bob?'

'Bob was his father's name, so I thought Robby.'

'Then Robby, he is.'

'Tell me about Beckbridge,' Laura said now.

'It is only a small village, so everyone knows everyone.' She laughed suddenly. 'But living in what they like to call the "big house", I've never really socialised with them. It was not my choice but the way things were in the old days; the village was the village, the big house was the big house, and they don't seem able to break out of the habit. There is my cousin, Kathy, who lives just down the road. She's married to a farmer. I'll take you to meet her when you're ready.' She stopped speaking to overtake a military convoy and Laura bent her head to kiss Robby's cheek. Her breasts were feeling heavy and she would need to feed him as soon as they arrived.

'Your furniture arrived safely,' Helen went on, as they passed the leading vehicle. 'I've had it put in the east wing. I thought you might like a little self-contained apartment, so when the builders were doing the repairs, I had them install a kitchenette and bathroom for you. But that doesn't mean you have to stay there. You are free to go anywhere you like in the house; it is your home, yours and Robby's. Any time you feel like company, I'm always somewhere about and you'll soon make friends with the people in the village. But if you want privacy, you can just shut yourself away.'

'That's very kind of you, Lady Barstairs.'

'Not at all. You are doing me a favour. A big one. But please don't call me Lady Barstairs, it sounds so stiff.'

'What shall I call you then?'

Helen longed to say 'Mother, of course,' but that was not an option, not now, perhaps not ever. 'Please call me Helen,' she said.

'I gather you have already been in touch with someone about using the house as a hospital?'

'Yes, they've inspected everywhere and they think it will be ideal. It has to be equipped, of course, and there might need to be a few partitions, more electrics and plumbing and things like that, so when you feel up to it, you can liaise with the medical people.'

'I'm raring to go. I hated giving up nursing but if I can get back to it and help our injured airmen into the bargain, it will feel as though I am doing something to help the war effort.'

'You have to get over the birth first.'

'That won't take long.'

'I wondered if you might like a little help with the baby. I thought perhaps a girl from the village, just to mind him when we are both busy.'

'Yes, it would help, but I'm not sure I can afford it.'

'I think we can manage that. We'll talk about it later when you've rested and fed the baby and settled him.' They were driving down a gentle hill towards a village. Like everywhere else they had passed, it was devoid of a signpost. 'This is Beckbridge.'

Laura looked about her as they drove down the main street. There didn't seem to be much of it: a church, a school, a couple of pubs, a butcher, a blacksmith, a cobbler and a post office cum general store. There were a few cottages and one or two more substantial houses and little else.

'We go into Attlesham for anything the village can't provide,' Helen said as they left it behind. 'It's a typical market town, but it does have a cinema and a railway station. Oh, and a petrol station, when they have any petrol, that is. Do you drive?'

'No.' She didn't add that they could never have afforded a car, so what was the point?

'Might be a good idea to learn. You could use the car then, so long as we can get a petrol allowance. Might be able to swing that, if we are doing essential war work. That's the lane to Bridge Farm on the right.'

Five minutes later she was turning left into the drive of the Hall. Laura leant forward to catch her first glimpse of her new home. She had known it was large because her mother had told her so, and Helen's nonchalant reference to the east wing seemed to confirm it, but she was unprepared for the sight that greeted her at the end of the half-mile drive. It was massive. And old. Its red brick walls were covered in creeper; its rows of sash windows gleamed in the sunlight, making her think what a headache organising the blackout must have been. The huge oak door was in the centre of the front elevation under a columned portico and was reached by a wide sweeping carriage drive.

'Beckbridge Hall has always been handed down from father to son ever since the Restoration, when it was given to my ancestor by Charles II as a reward for his loyalty to his father – the one the Roundheads beheaded, you know,' Helen said. 'It was only a small house then, stone-built, solid as a castle. It looked a bit like a castle, too, with crenellated walls and a tower or two, and a baronial hall, but over the generations, more has been added until it has become a conglomerate of several styles, but I think it is still a beautiful building. My Regency forebears refurbished it, lined some of its walls with panelling, plastered and painted others, enlarged the windows, which had been kept small until then, and added carpets and curtains, chandeliers and fine furniture. They made the cold castle into a comfortable home. My home, Laura. And now yours.'

She stopped the car at the front door and Laura, carrying Robby, was ushered inside. She found herself in a huge entrance hall; the house in Axholme Avenue would have comfortably fitted inside it. Immediately opposite her was a staircase with an ornate iron balustrade. To her right and left were doors.

'I'll show you round after you've settled Robby,' Helen said, leading the way down a corridor to the left of the staircase and through a door at the end, which gave onto a long gallery going to the left and right. It was lined with antique chairs, wall tables and niches containing statues and seemed to stretch forever. 'The house is built on four sides of a square,' Helen explained, turning left. 'The front elevation has the hall in its centre. What was the baronial hall and other smaller rooms are on one side, and a large reception room, the main dining room and the domestic offices are on the other. This gallery runs behind those and joins the two wings. On the opposite side of the square is a row of rooms which form offices and workrooms for the domestic and outside staff. It has an archway through to the yard, stables and kitchen garden. It was a very inconvenient arrangement to have the dining room and parlours so far from the kitchens and so over the years it has been changed about and now I live on one side only. That's why it will make such a good hospital; it will be easy to divide it off from our living quarters.' She made her way up another set of stairs and along a corridor. 'Here's your apartment.' She flung open one door to reveal Laura's sitting room furniture. 'This was once a bedroom but I thought you might like it as a sitting room. It has a nice view over the park. Next door is another bedroom with an adjoining dressing room, which I thought might make a nursery. On the other side of the corridor is a small kitchen and bathroom. Of course, if you want to change anything, feel free to do so.'

'Oh, no, it's wonderful.'

'You'll find your cases in the bedroom. Is there anything else you need?'

'No, thank you. I'm overwhelmed by your kindness. It's like a dream.' Impulsively, she leant forward and kissed Helen's cheek.

Helen rubbed the spot thoughtfully. Her daughter had kissed her! Oh, she never thought it would ever happen. She blinked back tears. 'Oh, please don't keep thanking me. I shall love having you here and I'm sure we'll make the hospital a great success.' She had to continue the charade that it was the hospital that mattered. 'I'll leave you to sort yourself out and look after that young man. When you're ready, come back downstairs and at the bottom turn right. You'll find me in the kitchen.'

Laura found her cases, took out a clean nappy and some gentle skin cream and went into the bathroom to change Robby. The bathroom was big, obviously converted from another bedroom. The bath stood to one side of the window under which was a central heating radiator which was hot to the touch, making her wonder how much it cost to heat the whole place. There was a large cupboard from floor to ceiling, a WC and a washbasin. Against one wall was a table, which was just the right height for changing nappies. Laura set about making Robby feel and smell fresher, then lodging him on her shoulder and supporting his head, she went to explore the kitchenette. Helen had equipped that too. Its window overlooked the courtyard. There was a disused fountain in the middle and a small triangular flowerbed in each corner. There were rose bushes in need of pruning in the centre of each and they were surrounded by daffodils. The cheerful yellow blooms poking out of what was left of the snow seemed to tell her that life was most definitely worth living. It was down to Mum, of course, who had looked after her through life and continued to do so even as she lay dying. Dear Mum. The best of mothers.

Robby's grizzle, reminding her he was hungry, saved her from shedding more tears. She went back to the bedroom and sat on the bed to feed him and, when he was replete and winded, she put him on the middle of the double bed while she made up his cot, which Helen had put together for her. Or perhaps she had instructed servants to do it. A place like this would need servants. Lots of them. He was asleep almost as soon as she had tucked him in, and she crept away in search of her hostess.

She found her in the kitchen cooking. 'Sit down,' she said, indicating a place at the big table. 'I rarely use the dining room nowadays. It's only mince. I thought I'd make a shepherd's pie.'

Laura sat down and wondered again about staff. 'That's lovely. I'll give you my ration book later. And rent.'

'The ration book I'll take, the rent, no.'

'But I can't stay here for nothing. It's not fair on you.'

'You won't be staying here for nothing. You will be paid a salary by the Air Ministry, and that includes board and lodging. They will pay me, so there's no need for you to.' She brought the dish to the table and spooned some of it onto two plates.

'We shall need staff.'

'Yes. We used to have dozens in the old days but they drifted away one by one until there was only Mr and Mrs Ward. Then when the bomb dropped, they took fright and left too.'

'You mean you are managing this great place all alone?'

'That's just it, I'm not managing. I've shut up all but a few rooms. The poor house has a neglected air, but I hope that will change when we get it up and running. It's going to be quite a challenge.'

'Yes, but I think it will do me good.'

'Would you like some more to eat?'

'No, thank you, that was delicious.'

'I used to like to help our cook when I was a child. My mother didn't approve and we had to keep it a secret from my father, who considered it degrading, but I'm certainly not sorry. The ability to produce a meal has stood me in good stead since this war started. I've got an apple crumble and I begged some cream from William. He's my cousin's husband. Would you like some?'

'Please.'

They moved on to talk about the war in general and life in the village until the washing-up had been done, then Laura said she would like to have a little rest and went up to her room. Robby was still sleeping. With a bit of luck he'd be a good baby, but Helen was right, they would need some help with him when the Ministry people came and laid out their plans for the hospital. She took off her dress and crept under the eiderdown, but her head was buzzing too much to allow her to sleep. After an hour or so, she got up and decided to explore the house.

There were three storeys and dozens and dozens of rooms, some small, some vast with ornate ceilings and huge gilt-framed pictures. Helen found her in what must have been the baronial hall, converted into a ballroom with plasterwork and chandeliers and cherubs painted on the ceiling. 'They will give our brave airmen something to think about as they lie on their backs staring at the ceiling,' she said.

'Yes.' Laura laughed suddenly. 'I remember one of my patients regaining consciousness and saying he had gone to heaven and I was an angel—'

'Was he your…Robby's father?'

'No. Bob was never a patient.'

'I'm sorry, perhaps I should not have mentioned him.'

'I don't mind talking about him. At first it was difficult, but now I can look back on the happy times and thank God I had that little time with him and that he left me a precious keepsake. Robby is all the world to me.'

'I am sure he is.'

They were silent for a time, each thinking their own thoughts. Laura realised that what she had said was true; she *could* look back and be thankful, even smile a little at the jokes she and Bob had shared. Helen, too, was glad, as she realised that she was no longer dwelling on the past, but looking forward to the future. She had spent years and years of her life in idle longing, wishing and dreaming of being reunited with her daughter, of hearing her call her 'Mother'. Twenty-three years gone in a flash, gone while she vegetated. Was that indolence or a perverted sense of justice – that she had no right to happiness because she had betrayed her husband? They were wasted years. It did not seem to matter any more whether Laura called her 'Mother' or not. She was here, and they had established a relationship which promised to be close, and that was enough. She had been telling herself that ever since Anne died, but now she realised it was true.

'Kathy, I've brought Laura to meet you.'

Kathy looked from Helen to the young woman who stood beside her and was taken aback because she was so like a young Helen it was uncanny. She was smiling and holding out her hand. Kathy recovered quickly and shook the hand. 'Do come in. I'll put the kettle on.'

Laura picked Robby out of his pram and the two women followed Kathy into the sitting room, where she invited them to sit down, then she left them to go and make tea. Laura wandered to the window to look out on a substantial garden, alive with daffodils. 'Kathy's like you,' she said. 'Not quite so tall and a little plumper.'

'Our mothers were sisters. Mine was the elder.' She smiled suddenly. 'They said she had made the best marriage when she married an earl and moved to Beckbridge Hall, but Uncle Daniel was a parson and a good man and Kathy had a happy childhood.'

Laura turned from the window and wandered round the room with Robby in her arms, looking at the photographs that stood on the mantelshelf. 'Steve!' She picked one up, as Kathy returned carrying a tea tray. 'This is Steve, isn't it? Steve Wainright.'

'Yes, he's my son,' Kathy answered, setting the tray down on the table. 'Do you know him?'

'Yes, he was a friend of...' There was a slight pause, which only Helen understood. Laura covered it by returning the picture to its place on the mantel. '...my husband.'

'Was it Steven who helped you when Robby was born?' Helen asked.

'Yes. He was on his way to see me when he found me struggling to get to the hospital. He saw me safely there and went away before I could thank him properly.'

'What a small world it is, after all,' Helen said, though she, like Laura, was wondering about the implications of claiming Laura was married, when Steve knew perfectly well she was not.

'He didn't say a word to us,' Kathy said, pouring tea. 'He said he'd been delayed on the way home by an air raid.'

'That was certainly true.' Laura laughed. 'It was a particularly bad one. They shipped me out to Epping to get away from it. I wrote to Steve to thank him, but I wasn't sure he was at the same base.'

'He's just been moved. He decided to transfer to bombers, though I don't suppose they are any less likely to be shot down than fighters. I worry about him all the time.'

'I'm sure you do. When you write to him, will you tell him you've met me and how grateful I am?'

The door opened and William came in. He was wearing green corduroy trousers and a jumper and thick socks, having left his boots on the kitchen doorstep. He was introduced and shook hands with Laura. He was followed a few minutes later by Kathy's mother, who stared long and hard at Laura. 'Did you say Laura was the daughter of a friend?' she demanded of Helen after the introductions had been made.

'Yes, I knew her years ago.'

'Not a relation?'

Her aunt's bluntness took Helen by surprise but she answered quickly enough. 'No, why do you ask?'

'She is uncannily like you. She has that little widow's peak in her hair, hadn't you noticed? I've got one, so has Kathy.'

Helen had been so happy to have Laura with her, she hadn't thought of anyone noticing a family likeness. If too many people commented on it, she might be forced into telling Laura the truth. At one time it was what she wanted more than anything but now she was afraid. Her relationship with Laura was still too new and untried for upsets. She looked apprehensively at Laura, but the young woman didn't seem unduly perturbed. 'Lots of people have those.'

'I suppose so.' But Alice didn't sound convinced.

They heard voices in the kitchen. 'That'll be Meg and Daphne,' Kathy said. She went and called them to be introduced. They stopped long enough to say hallo and admire Robby before going back to work.

After that the twins arrived, but they soon disappeared again, passing Jenny on the way. She did not immediately notice they had visitors, being more concerned with detaining the boys. They were about to sit the scholarship exams and she had been coaching them. They were bright kids and ought to pass but she wondered what they would do if one passed and the other did not. They were not so bound together as they had been and were developing separately, but going to different schools, one academic where the leaving age was sixteen and the other a secondary school where pupils left to find jobs at fourteen, might not go down too well. Would the one who passed expect to have to forgo his place at grammar school? If it happened, it was likely to be Donny who was successful; he was altogether more self-assured. For that reason she had been concentrating a little more on Lenny's weaknesses. 'Where are you two off to?'

'Out,' they said in unison.

'What about your revision? The exam is only a couple of days away.'

'What they don't know now, they'll never know,' Alice put in. 'You can't cram any more into them.'

'Tha's right,' Donny said. 'I'm stuffed up to here.' He indicated his throat.

Jenny smiled and let them go. It was then she noticed the visitors. 'Jenny, this is Laura,' Kathy said. 'And this is baby Robby. Isn't he a poppet? And so good, we haven't had a peep out of him.'

'Hallo, Laura,' Jenny said, bending over to admire the baby contentedly asleep in his mother's arms. 'He's gorgeous. How old is he?'

'Three weeks tomorrow.'

'And isn't it a strange coincidence, Laura knows Steven,' her mother put in.

'Really?' Jenny went to sit at the table to drink the tea her mother had poured for her. Laura was the name of his friend's bride, the one he was going to be best man for. She was tempted to say something but decided it would be tactless.

'Laura has come to live with Aunt Helen,' Kathy explained. 'The Hall is being made into an Air Ministry hospital and Laura is going to be in charge.'

'That will keep you very busy,' Jenny said, addressing Laura.

'Yes, but I shall enjoy the challenge.'

'Does Steve know you are here?'

'No. I had no idea he lived in Beckbridge, nor that he is related to Helen. Perhaps I shall see him when he comes home on leave.'

'Whenever that might be,' Kathy said. 'You can never tell these days. The news is terrible, isn't it? What with the Blitz and our boys being shot down and U-boats sinking our ships. The twins' father is on a destroyer and I worry about him as well as Steven. They have already lost their mother as a result of the bombing.'

'Poor boys,' Laura said. 'I know what that's like. My grandmother was killed by a direct hit.'

'And there's the rationing,' Alice piped up as the others murmured condolences. 'Jam and syrup and coal now on top of everything else, and the meat ration down again. One and ten pence-worth a week, I ask you! It's hardly enough for one meal let alone for a week, and I'm fed up with rabbit.'

'Sitting here chatting won't buy the baby a new bonnet,' William said, getting up and putting his cup and saucer on the tray. 'I must get back to work. Nice to have met you, Mrs Drummond.'

'Oh, Laura, please. I expect we'll meet again.'

William left and it was a sign for Laura and Helen to depart. As they were going to the door, Helen turned back. 'Kathy, do you know anyone in the village who might give Laura a hand with the baby? If she's busy with the hospital, she'll need someone reliable.'

'Not offhand. You could ask Joyce Moreton. She's bound to know.'

'Good idea. We were going to do a bit of shopping and register Laura's ration book.'

On the way to the shop, with Helen pushing the pram, she explained to Laura who Joyce was and all about Ian Moreton and his hidden stash of black market goods. 'He's as slippery as an eel,' she said. 'How he managed to get rid of the evidence so quickly is a mystery.'

Laura smiled; they had spivs like that in every community. 'Fancy Steve coming from this village,' she said. 'We talked about his home and his family but he never said where it was. And I didn't mention your name either when he helped me to the hospital. Do you think he'll let the cat out of the bag about my not being married? I wish now we hadn't started that fiction.'

'I'm sure he won't. He's a nice lad. He was always friendly to me, not one to bear grudges.'

'Grudges?'

'Yes. Kathy and I fell out, years ago it was, but it's all right now. The war sometimes brings people together as well as throwing them apart.'

Laura wondered what the two women had fallen out over, but didn't like to ask. 'Like you and Mum.'

'Yes, and you and Steven.'

'There was never anything between me and Steve. He was Bob's friend. Mine, too. He always seemed to arrive when I needed someone.'

Helen smiled but said nothing.

Chapter Seven

STEVE, TAKING A break from training on the Lancaster he was going to fly, was reading his mail in a corner of the mess and as he read his eyes opened wide and his heart began to beat faster. Laura was in Beckbridge living with Cousin Helen and they were going to run a hospital for injured airmen. It was unbelievable! And she had a son called Robby, who was a little peach. She asked to be remembered to him and said how grateful she was for his help. 'She says she hopes to see you when you are next on leave,' his mother had written. Next on leave. He wanted to dash off home straight away to see for himself that it really was Laura, but he had only just come back and it would be ages before he got more time off. He read on. 'She is uncannily like Helen, had you noticed? Granny saw it at once and said so aloud, but Helen says there's no relationship. I can't think there is either, because I'm sure I know everyone in the family.' He stopped reading to consider the question and decided any resemblance was superficial. What was more important was how he felt about Laura.

Over the months since Bob's funeral, when he had held her in his arms to comfort her, his feelings for her had grown, become more than mere friendship. He supposed that was why he had been so shocked by her pregnancy, but the night he had helped her to the hospital he had realised nothing could change the way he felt for her. But he could not tell her so, not yet.

He put the letter in his breast pocket and strolled outside. A new intake of airmen had just arrived and were tumbling out of the back of a truck, laughing and talking. They were young, fresh-faced and eager. One, with a shock of red hair and a sergeant's stripes on his arm, looked familiar. Steven waited to be seen and recognised.

Ken Moreton, grabbing his kit from the back of the truck, turned and saw him. 'Steve Wainright! Would you believe?'

Steve smiled. 'So you made it into the RAF then?'

'Yes, but not a fighter squadron. What are you doing here? I thought you were flying fighters.'

'I transferred. Thought I'd like a crack at giving Jerry a bit of his own medicine.'

'How are you finding it? The change, I mean?'

'It's a bit like going from driving a racing car to a London bus, but I haven't been passed for ops yet. We've yet to assemble our crews. I imagine that's what you lot are.'

'Yes. I'd be honoured if you'd have me as navigator.'

'Let's have a run together and see how we get on.'

'Thanks.'

'Been home lately?'

'Just got back. Nothing much has changed, except the Air Ministry bods and builders are swarming all over the Hall. It's being made into a convalescent hospital. Stella was full of it. She's got a job up there looking after Mrs Drummond's baby. I reckon she only went so that she could flirt with the patients, but there aren't any there yet. She loves the baby though, says he's no trouble and Mrs Drummond is nice to her. Her husband was in the RAF and got shot down, so Ma told me. She said you knew her.'

So Laura was pretending she'd been married. He could not blame her for that, considering how narrow-minded people could be, how narrow-minded *he* had been. 'Her husband was my squadron leader.'

'Small world, eh?'

'Very.' Steve was thinking about Laura and was barely listening.

'Who'd have thought we'd end up on the same station? In the same aircraft perhaps. I think I'll like flying with you, being as you're an old hand and know the ropes.'

Steve smiled. Sometimes being an old hand had its disadvantages;

you knew the pitfalls, when perhaps it might be better to be ignorant. Fearfulness brought its own risks. 'Perhaps, but when we're on the base, it's "Skip" not Steve. Remember that, will you?'

'Yes, sir!' Ken sprang to attention and saluted, making Steve laugh. The young man was exuberant, cheerful and incredibly young. Steve wondered if he'd still be like that after a few weeks on ops. It made him feel old himself and he had to remind himself that he was only twenty-three. He prayed he would see his twenty-fourth birthday and a lot more after that. There was so much he wanted to do, so much to see, so much to think about. Laura, for one.

He excused himself and returned to his room, where he re-read his mother's letter and then sat gazing at the photograph of Laura, which stood on his locker where he could see it every morning when he woke. Was it fate that had sent her to Beckbridge? It meant he was almost sure to see her the next time he went on leave and he could take it from there. It would be some time before that could happen, so he contented himself with writing to her and getting on with the job in hand.

He assembled his crew and they became a well-knit team and flew on several operations over Germany. It was no less hazardous than flying fighters; what with flak and the fighters sent up to intercept, he felt a bit like a sitting duck. But Ken was a good navigator and they both took a savage joy in finding their target and returning some of the terror that had been inflicted – and was still being inflicted – on London and elsewhere.

In May the Blitz reached a new peak and on one bitterly cold night it seemed the whole of London was in flames. Returning safely from a mission, he could see a pall of black smoke and the lurid glow of flames over the city from many miles away and wondered if anything could possibly be left standing. The following day, the newspapers made much of the fact that St Paul's still survived among the ruins, though Westminster Hall, the Houses of Parliament, the British Museum and every main-line station had been hit. No figures were published, but it didn't take a genius to realise there must have been appalling casualties. Steve was glad Laura was safe in Beckbridge.

It was the beginning of August before he could get home again and by then the Luftwaffe's attention had been directed elsewhere and everyone breathed again. His father was glad to see him, not only to know that he was safe but because he was about to start harvesting the wheat and an extra pair of hands would be useful.

'William,' Kathy protested. 'How can you put the boy to work the minute he comes home? He looks exhausted.'

'I'll be all right after a good night's sleep, Mum, and a little healthy work out of doors might be just what the doctor ordered.'

'How much longer is it going to go on?' Kathy asked, as she set about preparing the evening meal. 'There doesn't seem to be any end in sight. Germans in Yugoslavia and Crete and Russia. Churchill was right, it's nothing but blood, sweat and tears and no good news anywhere. And when I see some of those poor boys they've got up at the Hall, it makes my blood curdle.'

'You've seen them?'

'They go down to the village sometimes. I don't know how Laura can stand it day after day, but according to Helen she's marvellous with the poor fellows and they're all falling head over heels in love with her.'

'That's par for the course,' he said noncommittally.

'She's a nice girl. Where Helen found her, I've no idea. They are so alike in looks and yet nothing alike in their ways. Helen is still the lady of the manor even if it is now a hospital, while Laura is down to earth, but gentle with it.'

'And the baby?'

'He's good as gold, which is something to be thankful for, considering how young Stella is. The arrangement seems to work, though. Will you go up and see them?'

'Yes, I expect so.'

He strolled up to the Hall the next day and was struck by the change in the place. The carriage drive had been weeded, the lawns cut and the borders were alive with lupins, delphiniums, stocks and lilies. Two or three men in hospital blue were on their knees weeding. He stopped to chat, noting with a kind of revulsion he did his best to hide how disfigured they were, some more than others. And yet they seemed cheerful. He left them and went on to the front door, which stood wide open. He stepped inside to find the vestibule looked as it always had, with its ornate staircase and paintings on the walls, but now it had a polished, lived-in feel about it and there was a reception desk in one corner. It was unattended but there was a bell on it, which he picked up and rang. After a minute a young nurse came down the hall.

'Is Staff Nurse Drummond about?'

'Sister Drummond, you mean. I'll see if she's free. Who shall I say?'

'Tell her Steve.'

She disappeared and a few minutes later his heart gave a jump as Laura came towards him, dressed in navy blue with a wide silver buckle to her belt and a frilly white cap on her dark hair. 'Steve! How nice to see you.' She leant forward and kissed his cheek.

'I've got a spot of leave, thought I'd drop by and renew the acquaintance.'

'Of course. I should have been disappointed if you hadn't. Come through and have a cup of tea with us.' She led the way past the staircase to the east wing and into a cosy sitting room, which in the old days had been known as the morning room. If he had hoped for a quiet tête-à-tête with her, he was disappointed; Helen was sitting at a bureau intent on some paperwork. 'Helen, look who's here.'

She rose to greet him. 'Steven, it's good to see you, but you're looking tired.'

He kissed her cheek. 'Aren't we all. I've been hearing a lot about the changes to the Hall and thought I'd come to see for myself.'

She laughed. 'And here was me thinking you had come to see us.'

'That too, of course.'

'Sit down. I'll go and fetch the tea things.'

When she had gone he turned to Laura, suddenly tongue-tied, which was so unlike him he found himself blushing. 'How are you?' he asked lamely.

'I'm very well. And you?'

'Well.'

'But tired, I can see. It doesn't get any easier, does it?'

'No.' She had meant his job, but he was thinking of how to break the ice. But ice wasn't a fair word; she was smiling and friendly. 'Fancy you knowing Aunt Helen; she's really Mum's cousin but we all call her Aunt Helen. When Mum wrote and told me you were here, I could hardly believe it.'

'Nor me. I was glad because it meant I could thank you for your help the night I had Robby. I don't know what I would have done without you.'

'Think nothing of it. I wanted to find out how you got on but when I went to the hospital the next day they were decidedly unhelpful.' He had explained that in his letter to her, but now, in his awkwardness, he could find nothing else to talk about. 'I never thought I'd find you here.'

'Helen offered me a home and a job I love, and I'm grateful for that.'

'And the baby?'

'Robby? He's three months old now. I'd introduce you to him, but Stella has taken him out in his pram. By the way, Helen told everyone I was a widow. She said she wanted to save me embarrassment and stop awkward questions. Would you mind playing along with that?'

'Not at all, Mrs Drummond.' He laughed and the tension eased a little. 'Tell me about the hospital. I gather it's mainly for burns victims?'

'Yes, there's a very clever surgeon called Mr Archibald McIndoe doing pioneer work repairing scarred faces with a process called plastic surgery, and healing sick minds into the bargain. Some of the men have to have several operations, and they have to get over one before they can have the next. That's where we come in. It's a sort of home from home, where they can have constant nursing care but the freedom to come and go if they are well enough. The main reception rooms, the big hall and the rooms above have been converted into a working hospital. It's fully equipped and staffed and I've been put in charge of day-to-day nursing. The RAF has provided a resident doctor, two nursing sisters and two nurses, and Helen persuaded Mr and Mrs Ward to return, so we have a handyman, a cook and three village women who do the cleaning.'

'It must keep you very busy.'

'Yes, it does. Fortunately, I have Stella to look after Robby. She's very young and I wondered how she'd cope but she took to Robby straight away. I gather her brother is in your crew.'

'Yes, he's a good chap, we get on well.' He paused, then plunged on. 'Do you have any time off? I mean, would you come out with me while I'm home? The pictures perhaps, or a dance. You say which…'

Helen came back at that point carrying a tray and he jumped up to take it from her and put it on the table. It was in turning from her to Laura that he was struck by their likeness to each other. Gran was right; you could almost mistake them for mother and daughter. 'What do you think of our little set-up?' Helen asked him. 'Don't you think Laura's doing a grand job?'

'Oh, no doubt of it.'

'I keep telling her to ease off a bit, but she doesn't seem able to. It's as if she's being driven, though it's certainly not me who's doing the driving.'

'So can you persuade her to come out with me? I've got a week's leave.'

'I don't need persuading, Steve,' Laura put in. 'It's just Robby—'

'I'll gladly look after Robby when Stella's not here,' Helen said. 'You go, my dear, it will do you good. Take the car.'

'You know I can't drive it.'

'But Steve can. Let him teach you.'

'I'll be happy to,' he said. 'As long as I spare a bit of time to help Dad with the harvest.'

During the following week, they were together whenever Laura was free of her duties, and Steve suspected that Helen was doing more than her share to make it possible. They went to see Charlie Chaplin in *The Great Dictator* at the Attlesham Odeon, and on three afternoons he took her out to quiet country lanes and taught her to drive the Humber. 'It's not exactly the best car to learn in,' he said. 'You'd be better off in a little Ford or an Austin Seven.' But as it was the only car available and Helen had been given a petrol allowance for it, Laura set about learning to use the clutch, change gears, make hand signals and steer in a straight line.

Steve was introduced to Robby and agreed with everyone that he was a lovable little chap, but he was no nearer to Laura. She was still the same at the end of the week as she had been at the beginning; friendly but slightly distant. He knew she was still thinking of Bob. On the last evening of his leave they went to a dance, taking the Humber into Attlesham. It was the usual small-town hop but the band was reasonably good and they danced almost every number together. He even risked a little cheek-to-cheek in the last waltz and was encouraged when she did not draw away. She drove him home afterwards and stopped the car at the farm gate. He did not immediately get out and they sat for a moment in silence. He knew what he wanted to say, but could not make up his mind how to say it. 'Thank you,' he said.

She laughed. 'For driving you home without crashing the car or for not standing on your toes?'

'Everything. I've enjoyed this week.'

'So have I.'

'You will go on writing to me?'

'Of course, but don't expect long epistles. I shan't have the time.'

'I realise that, but a few lines will do, just to let me know you are thinking of me, because I shall be thinking of you.' He picked up her hand from her lap and put it to his lips. 'You know I am in love with you, don't you?'

'Are you?' she asked, guessing what was coming and shying away from it. She didn't want to get too close to anyone when the memory of Bob was still so fresh and the manner of his death so frighteningly real. At least it was a quick, clean death and not the half-life of the poor fellows she nursed.

'Oh, yes. Have been for some time, I think.'

'Steve, please don't expect me to reciprocate. I can't. I like you a lot, but that's all it is. It's less than a year since Bob died and I'm only just beginning to put my life together again. I simply will not risk it happening again. You are my friend, Steve, perhaps my best friend, let's leave it at that, shall we?'

He leant over to give her a chaste kiss on her cheek. 'Whatever you say.' He got out of the car and walked up the path to the door. The next morning he went back to Scampton.

Although he had two weekend passes in the meantime, it was Christmas before he got his next full leave. Meg was spending it at home, but Daphne, whose mother had died in a road traffic accident in the blackout the previous summer, opted to stay at Bridge Farm with the boys. The twins, having had their first term at grammar school, were disappointed their father could not get leave, but he was out in the Atlantic somewhere on convoy duty. Kathy did her best to make it a happy occasion in spite of the war and the shortages, and indeed, it did look as though things might be looking up with the entry of the USA into the conflict after the Japanese raid on Pearl Harbor. But the euphoria was short-lived. Hong Kong surrendered on Christmas Day, the Germans were at the gates of Moscow and the British fleet in the Mediterranean sustained terrible losses trying to get to the aid of beleaguered Malta. But Christmas was Christmas and Bridge Farm was a haven of gaiety, even if it was a little forced. Steve was determined to enjoy it and refused to think about bombing raids and flak and anything except that he was home and that he could see Laura.

They had been corresponding but that was hardly satisfactory. He could not tell from the written word what she was really thinking and feeling; her letters were newsy and affectionate, but as one friend to another. He lost no time in walking up to the Hall with Christmas presents. She was expecting him and was dressed in a pretty blue silk dress with a matching bolero. Aunt Helen was there too, a little greyer, a little thinner, but that wasn't the only change. She seemed to glow with something he might have called love in anyone else. The nearest he could think of was fulfilment. After years of living the life of a recluse, she was busy, and glorying in it. He kissed them both on the cheek.

'How are you?' Laura asked.

'Fighting fit. And you?'

'Ditto.'

He lifted the parcels he was carrying. 'Christmas presents.'

He watched them unwrap them. A scarf for Helen and a silver brooch in the shape of wings for Laura. For Robby he had found a teddy bear, dressed in a flying jacket and helmet. The two women thanked him and kissed him, and Laura fetched Robby to receive his. He was growing into a sturdy boy, able to crawl all over the floor and pull himself up to his feet if he had something firm to hang onto. On this occasion it was Steve's knee. This, he realised, was the test. Could he love the little lad, could he forget he was Bob's and that Laura held Bob's memory sacred? If he showed the slightest hesitation about that, Laura would know. He picked him up and sat him on his knee. Robby grinned up at him, revealing tiny white teeth.

'The men all spoil him,' Laura said. 'He doesn't care what they look like.'

It deflated him. He was one of many. Nevertheless, he asked her to go to the New Year dance with him.

Midnight struck during the last waltz. Everyone turned to everyone else. 'Happy New Year!'

Steve held her in his arms and kissed her. 'Happy New Year, love.'

'And to you.'

He drove her home in the Humber and stopped outside the coach house. 'Back to the grind tomorrow. I have to catch the six-thirty in the morning. It was a smashing evening, I really enjoyed it.'

'So did I.'

'Nothing's changed, you know, not on my side…'

Laura ignored that. 'Another year gone, who's to tell what we'll be doing this time next year. My wish is that this dreadful war will be over and there will be an end to all the carnage.'

'Amen to that,' he said, though he didn't see how it could be. She wasn't going to tell him what he most wanted to hear. He got out and opened the car door for her. They walked across the cobbles of the yard to the kitchen door. 'Goodnight, sweetheart,' he said and took her into his arms to kiss her again. She responded with more warmth than she had done before and then gently pushed him from her. 'Go on. It's getting late. You've got to get up early in the morning, and so have I.'

Reluctantly, he turned to go. Almost as an afterthought, she said, 'Steve, you always wear gloves and goggles when you're flying, don't you?'

He knew the reason she asked, but chose to answer flippantly. 'You bet I do. It's damned cold up there.'

He went home humming 'Goodnight, sweetheart' to himself.

What made Jenny decide to go into the café on that Saturday afternoon, she did not know. A jaunt into town, especially when she had the use of the car, meant she had several errands to run, not only her own, but for everyone else in the house. Her mother had asked her to try and find some shampoo since the village shop had run out of it, and to see if the twins' school trousers had arrived at the outfitters. They were continually going through the knees of their trousers and, what with clothes rationing and shortages, replacing them was causing headaches. Many boys were being kept in shorts in spite of the school rules stating they should wear long trousers, but Donny had been looking forward to going into proper grown-up trousers and her mother had given in to his vanity, and, naturally, Lenny had to be treated exactly the same. Meg had heard there were stockings in at Woolworth's, Daphne wanted a lipstick and she herself was looking for a couple of maths textbooks to supplement those she had been provided with. Having accomplished as much as she could, she had turned into the café, her coat flapping open in the first mild day of the year.

She didn't see the soldier with a captain's pips and the Canada flash on his shoulder, carrying a plate containing a sticky bun in one hand and a very full cup of coffee in the other, as he made his way from the counter to a table where he had left his haversack and cap. They collided in a bump that sent the cup flying and the coffee down the front of her skirt and blouse.

'Gee, I'm sorry.'

'My fault.' The hot liquid was seeping through to her underclothes, almost scalding her. She tried to hold the blouse away from her body until it cooled. 'I wasn't looking where I was going.'

'It's burning you.' He had reddish hair, an open sort of face, clear blue eyes and a wide mouth, which looked as though it laughed a lot. He was not laughing now as he surveyed the damage.

'It is a bit hot.'

'Here, let me help.' He put the crockery down on the nearest table and produced a big white handkerchief.

Afraid he was going to start rubbing her down she stepped back half a pace. 'It's all right. Please don't worry about it.'

He handed her the handkerchief and watched as she dabbed at the stain. 'It's not going to come out, is it?' he said.

'I'll put it in to soak when I get home. It's not the end of the world.'

'Do you live far? Let me take you. Better still, let me buy you a new outfit.'

'Nonsense, this is nothing special. I'll go home and change. Thank you for your concern.'

211

He picked up his haversack and cap and reached the door before her. 'I ruined your clothes, so come on, let me buy you a new dress.'

'Clothes are rationed.'

'So I heard, but how do you ration clothes?'

'You have so many coupons in a year and you hand them over when you pay for whatever you've bought. A dress costs eleven coupons if its made of wool, nine for cotton. A blouse is about five, a skirt a little more, depending on the amount of material in it. A coat is eighteen. And there's underwear and stockings, even handkerchiefs, they all need coupons.'

'That doubles my culpability. Let me make amends.'

'You don't need to. It was my own fault.'

'I insist. Please let me do it. I shan't sleep tonight if you don't.'

She decided it would be churlish to continue arguing. With him at her side, she crossed the road to Bonny's dress shop, where she tried to select the cheapest blouse and skirt she could find, but he gently steered her in the direction of the top end of the merchandise. 'This green skirt would suit you, and how about this blouse to go with it?' He took a cotton blouse in a swirling pattern of green, black and tan from the rail and held it against her. It was perfect, but the price appalled her.

'But I can't accept anything so expensive.'

'But the quality's good. Go on, try them on.'

While she was in the changing room, he asked the assistant to wrap her stained skirt and blouse, so that she had no choice but to hand over the coupons and put her coat on over the new clothes.

'Are you always so masterful?' she asked, as they emerged from the shop.

'Only when I have to be.' He had picked up her shopping basket and obviously had no intention of handing it over and disappearing. She could not have allowed it if he had.

'Let me buy you a coffee,' she said. 'Since I spilt the one you had.'

He laughed. 'Thanks, I'd like that. I ought to introduce myself. My name's Wayne Donovan.'

'And I'm Jenny Wainright.' Solemnly, they shook hands.

They went back into the café and sat talking over a cup of coffee, which made him grimace. 'Not what you're used to,' she said with a smile.

'Oh, it's not so bad.'

'How long have you been in England?'

'A few months. I came hoping to see some action, but up to now, nothing.'

'Perhaps you should be thankful for that. What are you doing in Attlesham, or shouldn't I ask?'

'I had a spot of leave and thought I'd look up my mom's folks. I've gotten their address and I know it's near here, but that's all. You can maybe help me. How do I get to Beckbridge?'

She laughed. 'Well, you could come with me. That's where I live.'

'Is that so?' he said in delighted surprise. 'Then maybe you know my aunt. Her name's Joyce Moreton.'

'Oh, everyone knows Joyce and Ian. I'll take you to them, if you like. I've got Dad's car.'

'Gee, that would be great.'

They finished their coffee and made their way to where she had left the Ford. A few minutes later they were cruising towards Beckbridge. 'Have you been to England before?' she asked him.

'No. Mom's always said she'd bring me to visit and show me where she was born but we never made it. She met Pop in the last war when he was stationed near here and she went back to Canada with him after he was discharged.'

'Then you've never met any of your relations?'

'No.' He laughed. 'Is there something I should know?'

'Not at all. Stalwarts of the village, they are, especially Joyce. She is the postwoman and works in the village shop.'

'So Mom told me. I believe her husband has a small farm.'

'You could say that.' Jenny could not help the smile. 'He does a bit of everything.'

'My cousin Ken, I know, is in the Royal Air Force.'

'Yes, he's in my brother's crew.'

'What are they flying?'

'Steve started out in Hurricanes, but for some reason known only to him he switched to Lancasters, and that's when he and Ken found themselves on the same station. Steve's a bit older than Ken and he's been flying since before the war, so he tries to look out for him.'

'What about you? What do you do?'

'I teach at the village school.'

'And your folks?'

'My father is a farmer, we live at Bridge Farm. It's been in the family for ages. I expect Steve will take it over one day.'

'What do you do for entertainment?'

'Go to the pictures in Attlesham, sometimes to the Saturday hop. There's not much in Beckbridge itself. Walks and whist drives at the church hall and the pub of an evening. Quiet really.' She laughed suddenly. 'We did have a bomb drop in the grounds of the big house. It demolished a summer house.'

'The big house. Is that what you call Beckbridge Hall?'

'Yes. My mother's cousin owns it. It's been in her father's family for generations. Her husband was killed in the last war and they never had any children, so she stayed living at home. It's recently been made it into an air force hospital.'

'I've heard my mom speak of it. She used to work there, it's where she met Pop.'

'Then perhaps you'd like to visit it while you're here.'

'Sure thing.'

They were driving down the hill into the village. 'This is Beckbridge.' She laughed. 'You're in it and out again before you know where you are.' She negotiated a right turn into a narrow rutted lane and drove carefully along it for a couple of hundred yards, then she stopped at a green-painted gate. 'Here you are. Beck Cottage.'

Wayne leant forward to look. He didn't know what he expected, but this place was tiny. Made of brick and flint, it had six little windows and two doors, which suggested it had once been two even smaller dwellings. His idea of a farm it certainly was not. No wonder Miss Wainright had smiled. He got out of the car, fetched his haversack from the back seat and bent to thank her. 'I'll see you around perhaps.'

'Oh, more than likely.'

While he went to the door she drove on a few yards, turned the car in a farm gate and stopped again. She saw him at the door and Joyce flinging herself into his arms, and then quietly drew away.

'Wayne, why didn't you let me know you were coming?' Joyce cried, dragging him inside. 'We could have killed the fatted calf. Or at least a pig.'

'I wasn't sure when I'd get leave. It came unexpectedly and I figured I'd surprise you.'

'You've done that all right. Here, let me look at you.' She held him at arm's length. 'Goodness, you're the spitting image of Valerie. Come in and sit down. I'll make some tea. You do like tea?'

'Sure.' He sat down and looked around him. He was in a small living room which contained a horsehair sofa, two matching armchairs, a dining table and six dining chairs. The chimney alcove on one side was filled with shelves cluttered with ornaments, vases, a letter rack stuffed with correspondence and a bowl containing wrinkled apples. On the other side was a cupboard on which stood a wireless set, powered by accumulators. The single window was tiny and the room cool and dim.

They heard the sound of someone coming into the next room, which he assumed was the kitchen. She went to the connecting door. 'Ian, look who's here. It's Valerie's boy, Wayne, come to see us.'

Ian, dressed in corduroy trousers and a collarless shirt, came into the room. Wayne stood up and shook his hand. 'Glad to meet you, sir.'

'Sir!' Joyce giggled. 'He's your Uncle Ian, for goodness sake. I'm just going to make a cuppa,' she informed her husband. 'Do you want one?'

'Won't say no.'

'Go and call Ma while I make it.' To Wayne she explained, 'She has her own place over the lane, but she spends half her time here with us.'

Ian disappeared and in no time at all, Wayne heard an excited cry and a little old lady dashed into the room and flung herself at him. He was rocked by the onslaught but held her firmly and bent to kiss her. 'You must be my gran.'

''Course I am.' She grabbed his hand and put it to her cheek. 'I never thought I'd see the day. Let me get a proper look at you.' She stood back, still holding his hand, and looked him up and down. 'He's the image of Valerie, don't you think, Joyce?'

Joyce, who had just come back into the room with a tea tray, agreed. 'Yes, I saw it straight off.' She set out cups and saucers, milk jug and sugar basin and went back into the kitchen to fetch a cake on a plate. 'How do you like your tea?' she asked Wayne.

'Not too strong,' he said. 'I can't get used to the way you English drink tea.'

'Would you rather have coffee? It's only that bottled Camp, I'm afraid.'

'No, tea is fine.' Camp coffee was the equivalent of dishwater as far as he was concerned. He went to his haversack and produced a packet of real coffee, a tin of peaches and another of corned beef. 'I thought you could use these.'

'Peaches!' Lily exclaimed. 'I hen't had any o' them since the start o' the war.'

'Ma, course, you hev,' Ian said. 'I give you a tin only a month ago.'

Joyce turned to him. 'I didn't know that.'

'No, well, what the eye don' see the heart don' grieve over.'

Joyce hurriedly changed the subject. 'How long can you stop, Wayne?'

'I've got seven days' leave. I thought I'd find a hotel or something in the village, then I could explore.'

'I'n't narth'n *to* explore,' Ian said.

'Don't be silly, man, he wants to see where his mum was brought up and married, i'n't that so, Wayne?'

'Yes, and to visit with you, of course.'

'Then you don't need a hotel, you can have our Ken's room,' Joyce said.

'I don't want to put you out.'

'You i'n't puttin' us out. We're glad to hev you. It's Sunday tomorrow, so I c'n take you around and introduce you to people.'

'I already met Miss Wainright. She gave me a lift from Attlesham.'

'Oh, what did she tell you?' Lily asked.

'Only that she's a schoolteacher and her father's a farmer and her brother and Cousin Ken are serving together.'

'That's right,' Joyce said. 'I'm glad Ken is with Steve; he'll look out for him. Couldn't bear it if he got burnt like them poor devils up at the Hall. Makes you shudder to see them.'

'Miss Wainright mentioned that it was being used as a hospital. I'd like to see it. Mom's talked so much about it.'

'Hev she so? What about your father, does he talk about it?' This from Lily.

'Not so much, but he never lived there. Mom said he went there with some pals because the old fellow, Earl somebody or other, let them have baths and gave them tea, and she was working there and that's how they met.'

'The Earl of Hardingham, that was his name,' Lily said. 'I was working there too, under cook, I was. No end of servants, they had then: kitchen maids, parlour maids, chambermaids, butler and cook, not to mention outdoor staff. Not a one left now except Mr and Mrs Ward, and they took theirselves off when the bomb dropped and had to be persuaded to go back. Lady Muck was left all alone 'til she got that Laura to live with her. Bit of a mystery, that.'

'Why?' Joyce demanded. 'What's so mysterious about having someone to run the hospital? She couldn't do it, could she? And

Laura Drummond's not the only one, there's several nurses there and a couple of doctors.'

'Laura's the only one that's the spitting image of Lady Helen.'

Wayne looked from one to the other, unable to follow the conversation, but it intrigued him. According to Miss Wainright, nothing much happened in the village, but it seemed to be a hotbed of gossip. He was looking forward to his tour of the village and more revelations. It would be something interesting to tell when he wrote home.

'You'll never guess who I picked up in town,' Jenny told her parents at dinner. 'A Canadian Captain—'

'Picked up, Jen?' her mother enquired. 'Was that wise?'

'Oh, it wasn't like that. He spilt coffee down my front and insisted on buying me a new skirt and blouse.'

'I wondered why you suddenly decided you needed a new outfit. You have to be careful with clothing coupons, you know. *And* picking up strange men.'

'He was most insistent. But you haven't heard the interesting bit. He asked me how to get to Beckbridge and it turns out his name is Wayne Donovan. He's Joyce Moreton's nephew.'

'Good God!' Alice said, which struck Jenny as a strange reaction.

'He's on leave. I took him to Beck Cottage. He says he wants to meet his folks and explore where his mum and dad met.'

'That'll put the cat among the pigeons,' Alice said.

'What do you mean, Gran?'

'Oh, nothing,' she said vaguely, looking at Kathy, who was concentrating on eating and would not meet her eye. She knew perfectly well what had happened all those years ago. She'd had the devil of a job persuading Kathy that what the eye didn't see the heart wouldn't grieve over and she certainly should *not* write to Richard on the subject of his wife and Oliver Donovan. She suspected Louise had sent Helen to Scotland to separate her from him. Poor girl! Aunt Martha had been a tyrant and lived in seclusion in a remote village in the Highlands; if it was meant to be punishment, it was certainly that. And the irony was that Richard hadn't survived. Oliver had come back at the end of the war, married Valerie and taken her to Canada. Alice doubted if Helen, living in seclusion as she did, close-watched by her parents, knew anything about that.

Meg and Daphne looked at each other and shrugged. There was an atmosphere around the table that could be cut with a knife. 'I'm going to the dance tonight,' Meg said, deliberately changing the subject. 'You coming, Daphne?'

'Might as well.'

'What about you, Jenny?'

'I ought to do some marking, but I can do it tomorrow. Dad, can we borrow the car?'

'Is there any petrol in it?' he asked mildly. 'You've already taken it to Attlesham and back today.'

'Oh, go on, Dad. You can get some more, can't you?' Although the threat of invasion had faded, the Local Defence Volunteers, now renamed the Home Guard, were still recruiting and he was involved with that, for which it was conceded he needed extra petrol. He complained about the time it took up, but it never occurred to him to try and get out of it.

'All right, go on with you. I don't want you walking home.'

When they got there, they found Stella with Wayne, who promptly joined them.

'I didn't think when I set out this morning that I'd end up with a bevy of beauties at a dance,' Wayne said, after he had been introduced to Meg and Daphne.

He had accepted his aunt's offer of accommodation because it would have been rude to refuse, but he had been taken aback by the primitive state of the place. They had no electricity and no water laid on, let alone a flushing lavatory. He found he was expected to make his way down the garden path to a little shed, which had a bucket under a wooden seat with a hole in it. He dare not conjecture how that was emptied. He had been given a kettle full of hot water to

219

take up a narrow winding stair which led directly from the sitting room to his bedroom, where he found a jug of cold water standing in a china bowl on a marble-topped table and a waste bucket underneath it. Chuckling to himself, he had set about having a wash and getting himself ready for the evening meal, which he learnt was cooked on a range, heated by coal. How his aunt managed he did not know, but she produced a feast of roast chicken and vegetables, which was followed by the tin of peaches drenched in cream. It was good and he had complimented her on it. His grandmother joined them and entertained him with stories of the village and what it was like working at the big house, some of which he had heard from his mother.

It was Stella who had suggested the dance. She was a forward little miss for her age, made up with face powder and bright red lipstick. She wore high heels and no stockings, admitting that the colour was painted on her legs and her mother had drawn the seam with an eyebrow pencil. For the dance she had put on a flowered cotton frock with a square neckline and the waist cinched in with a wide bright red belt. Jenny's outfit was more muted: she wore the skirt and blouse he had bought for her and though she used lipstick it was pink rather than red. But then she was older, and a schoolmistress at that. But she danced well.

'I didn't thank you properly for giving me that lift,' he said, as they danced a foxtrot.

'Oh, I am quite sure you did. I bet your aunt was surprised to see you.'

'She was. I met my grandmother, too. She's a character, isn't she?'

'Yes, one of our older inhabitants. What she doesn't know about Beckbridge and its people isn't worth knowing.'

'She was talking about the Hall and how she and Mom used to work there when Mom met Pop. Hinted at a mystery, something to do with the lady who owns it and the one who runs the hospital.'

'There's no mystery that I know of. Aunt Helen and Laura's mum were friends, and when her mum died, Aunt Helen asked Laura to live with her and help with the hospital, seeing as she's a nurse.'

'Aunt Joyce says she'll show me round the village tomorrow and she'll take me up to the Hall to have a look round. Do you think your relative will mind?'

'I shouldn't think so. While you're out, ask Joyce to bring you to see us. I know Mum would like to meet you. She was a bit surprised when I turned up this afternoon in this skirt and blouse.'

He smiled. 'They suit you.'

'I'm sure I did not express my gratitude sufficiently.'

'Think nothing of it. It meant I got to know you, didn't it?'

'I've no doubt you would have done anyway if you're staying in the village. It's a small place, everyone knows everyone else and most of their business too. It's hard to keep a secret in Beckbridge.' Speaking of secrets reminded her of Gran's comment, that his arrival would put the cat among the pigeons. And now he had said Lily Wilson had hinted at a mystery. It was all very intriguing.

The music ended and he returned her to their table and then danced a quickstep with Stella, did a foxtrot with Daphne and stumbled over a valeta with Meg, before returning to Jenny for a waltz. At the end of the evening they all crammed into the Ford and Jenny drove them home, singing as they went, though they were all as sober as when they started.

Small as it was, it took ages to see round the village because Joyce kept stopping to introduce Wayne to all and sundry, many of whom were on their way home from church. 'This is my Canadian nephew,' she said. 'He's spending his leave with us.' The result of that was that he was pumped about life in Canada and if he had yet seen any action, and the older inhabitants who had known his mother asked after her, all of which required answers. It was midday before she stopped at the end of the drive to the Hall.

'It used to have big iron gates,' she told him. 'But they took them away, alonga the railings round the vicarage and the school playground to make ships and aircraft. At one time there was someone living in the gatehouse who opened the gates when people came to call in their carriages.'

'Do you remember that? The carriages, I mean.'

'No, but Mum does. She'll tell you all about the grand life they used to live up there. The Earl and Countess have been dead over twenty years and there's only their daughter up there now. She's a widow from the first war and, just like everyone else, she's trying to make ends meet and cope with rationing. I'll take you to meet her.'

He followed as she set off up the drive. 'Won't she mind?'

'No, course not, not when she knows who you are. She'll mebbe remember your father. You'll have something to talk about.'

There were men in blue suits and red ties strolling or sunning themselves about the grounds. Some were in wheelchairs or on crutches, one had lost a hand, most were scarred about the face. He stopped to talk to some of them.

'Canada, eh?' one queried. 'Been here long?'

'A few months.'

'What do you reckon to old England?' asked another. 'Not beat yet, are we?'

'Not by any means.'

'He's half English,' Joyce put in. 'His mother's my sister.'

He looked up to see Stella coming towards him carrying a baby. 'You came then,' she said. 'This is Robby.'

He put his finger under the baby's hand and found it gripped firmly and an attempt made to convey it to a rosebud mouth. Stella laughed. 'Everything goes into his mouth.'

'He's a handsome little feller,' he said, repossessing his finger.

'Come and meet his mother. She's over there.' She nodded towards a woman in a navy blue uniform and a frilly cap who was bending over a patient in a wheelchair, tucking a rug about his legs.

Followed by Joyce, Stella led the way. 'Sister Drummond, this is my Canadian cousin I told you about. He's come to look round.'

Laura straightened up and held out her hand. 'How do you do, Captain.' She found herself looking into clear blue eyes which were regarding her with undisguised admiration. For a moment it unsettled her, which was surprising considering her patients often looked at her like that. It meant nothing except that she was young and female and lavishing attention on them. 'Stella tells me your parents met here at the Hall.'

'Yes, during the last war. Mom's often spoken of it and I couldn't go home without saying I'd seen the place.'

'I haven't lived here very long, Captain. The person you should speak to is Lady Helen. I think she might be in the kitchen helping Mrs Ward. Come on, I'll take you. And Stella, don't carry Robby about, he's getting too heavy. Put him in his pram and take him for a walk.'

Laura took him to the kitchen door and ushered him inside. The kitchen was vast, the ceiling so high that a clothes line strung across it was out of reach above their heads and lowered on a pulley. A huge dresser displayed crockery and a long shelf on another wall held a row of gleaming pans. There was a very upright, middle-aged woman standing at the kitchen table shredding cabbage and a woman in a white apron was basting something on a huge black cooking range.

'Helen, this is Captain...' She stopped and turned to Wayne. 'I'm sorry, Stella didn't say your name.'

'Wayne,' he said. 'Wayne Donovan.'

The cry Helen emitted was because she had cut her finger. She sat down suddenly and put it into her mouth, where she sat sucking it and looking up at him, trying to tell herself it couldn't be, it just could not be. There must be hundreds of people called Donovan and he wasn't a bit like Oliver, not with that carroty hair. He was looking a little disconcerted. 'I didn't mean to startle you, ma'am.'

She took her finger from her mouth and wrapped her handkerchief round it. 'Careless of me,' she said. 'I know that knife is sharp. How do you do.'

'This is Lady Helen Barstairs,' Laura completed the introduction. 'She has lived in this house all her life, so she can tell you anything you want to know.' And to Helen. 'Shall I find you a plaster?'

'Please, before I bleed all over the place.' She waited while Laura fetched a plaster from the first aid box in the cupboard and wrapped it round her finger. It gave her a little time to compose herself, though she was still shaking.

'There, that should do it,' Laura said. 'Shall I make the captain a cup of coffee?'

'Oh, please don't trouble,' he said. 'I only came up to say hallo.'

'Hallo,' Helen echoed. He may not look like Oliver, but he certainly sounded like him. It was the accent, she told herself, trying to still the swift beating of her heart.

'He's my nephew,' said Joyce, who had followed them into the kitchen. 'His dad married my sister, Valerie. You remember Valerie, don't you, my lady? Valerie Wilson. She used to work here in the old days alonga my mum.'

'Yes, I believe I do.' This wasn't happening, she was having a nightmare. She forced herself to speak normally. 'Wasn't she one of the chambermaids?'

'That's right. She married Oliver Donovan. He came up here during the last war when all those officers used to come for tea and sandwiches and hot baths. You remember, don't you?'

'Oh yes, I remember.' It was said with a kind of weariness. She knew it would hurt, but she had to know more. 'I believe he went to France.'

'So he did,' Wayne said. 'He was wounded towards the end of the war and came back here. That's when he and Mum decided to get married.'

So he *had* come back, but not to her. She gulped at the cup of coffee Laura had put in front of her, glad she was sitting down because her legs would not have supported her if she had been standing. As it was she had to use two hands to get the cup to her lips. 'Were they married here in Beckbridge?'

'I believe so.'

'Not exac'ly,' Joyce put in. 'It was the Registry Office in Attlesham. It was a quiet do, 'cos Oliver didn't have no relations to see him married and they decided to have a church service when they got to Canada.'

'I didn't know that,' he told her.

'What a small world, it is,' Laura said, looking from him to Helen and back again. She knew her friend well enough by now to know that something about the visit had upset her. 'Are you going to be in Beckbridge long, Captain?'

'Oh, Wayne, please.'

'He's going to stay a whole week,' Joyce said triumphantly. 'And now he's found us, I hope he'll spend all his leaves with us, then he can tell Valerie and Oliver all about us.'

Helen felt faint. How many times had she wondered if Oliver had survived? How many times had she wondered if he ever thought of her? How many hours had she spent down in the summer house holding imaginary conversations with him, talking to him about Laura, imagining his replies, always loving, telling her he had not forgotten her? But he had forgotten her. Had the affair with the chambermaid been going on before he left for France? She wanted to weep and rail at herself for believing his protestations of undying love. Great Aunt Martha had been right all along and the knowledge was as bitter as gall. And now she was paying for it all over again. Here was Laura and here was his son, half-brother and -sister. God, what was going to happen now?

'I won't keep you,' he said in the gap in the conversation, which no one seemed inclined to fill. 'It was great to have met you.'

He was going. Suddenly she wanted to detain him, to hear more. How was Oliver? What did he do for a living? Did he have other children? Did he ever mention her and if so, in what context? Did she really want to know all that? Shouldn't she hate him for marrying someone else, and one of her father's servants at that? She was so confused, she couldn't look at Wayne, lest he detect something was wrong. She found herself saying, 'Come again, Captain.' What possessed her to say that: mere politeness or some masochistic streak?

'Thank you, ma'am, I'll take you up on that.'

He shook hands with her and Laura and left with Joyce.

'Helen, you look very pale, is that cut deep?' Laura asked when they had gone.

'No. I'm not very good when I see blood, more so when it's my own. Silly, isn't it?'

'Do you want to go and lie down?'

'No.' She stood up. 'I think I'll go for a little walk. Can you manage for a few minutes, Mrs Ward?'

Mrs Ward, who had listened and absorbed every word, told her that of course she could and to run along and get some fresh air. Helen put on a jacket and slipped out of the back door before anyone could ask her where she was going. Laura guessed. She had seen Helen down by the lake beside the newly built summer house looking meditatively across the water on several occasions and concluded that the place had some significance. She would give her a few minutes alone, then go and coax her home.

'She remembers him all right.' Mrs Ward's voice broke in on her thoughts.

'Who, Mrs Ward?'

'Captain Donovan, of course.'

'Wayne?'

'No, his father. They were close at one time, though she were married and shouldn't hev bin looking at another man. Any old how, narth'n come of it. He went off to France and she went to stay with her aunt. Him and Valerie married at the end of the war.'

'Then there's no need to speak of it, is there?' Laura said.

'Weren't no secret at the time,' the cook said resentfully.

'All the same, I think we should respect Lady Helen's privacy and not resurrect whatever it was.' She spoke severely but she would have been less than human if she hadn't been curious.

Chapter Eight

'She is a stunner, isn't she?' Wayne commented.

'Who?' Joyce queried.

'Mrs Drummond. She's young to be in charge of a hospital, isn't she?'

'I suppose so, but what with the war and everything and it being an air force hospital, I suppose it's not so strange. Lady Helen no doubt pulled strings. Money still talks, you know.'

'They're mother and daughter, aren't they?'

'No, what gave you that idea?'

'They look so alike, and Sister Drummond seems to be looking out for her.'

'They're not related that I know of. Laura's mother died last year. According to Kathy, she was an old friend of Lady Helen's.'

'My mistake. Who is Kathy?'

'She's Jenny's Mum. We'll go there next. Unless you've had enough of Beckbridge and its inhabitants?'

'No, lead on. Miss Wainright is half expecting me.'

She took him round to the back door, that being the way she always went herself. Jenny dragged them both into the kitchen where Kathy was basting a small joint and Alice was laying the table for Sunday lunch. William, in his Windsor chair by the hearth, was hidden behind a copy of the *Eastern Daily Press*. The headlines told of the Luftwaffe's attack on Norwich two nights before, when the city had been bombed and machine-gunned for over an hour and a whole terrace of houses had been destroyed. Revenge attacks for the bombing of German cities, so it was said. It made him think of Steve and though he said nothing to Kathy, he prayed fervently for his safety. The fall of Singapore in February had been a national disaster, but it was especially poignant for local people because the Royal Norfolks had been out there and many of their sons and husbands had been taken prisoner. He knew some of them, had seen their families struggling to come to terms with the prospect of not seeing loved ones again for years. Shipping was still going down at an alarming rate and the siege of Stalingrad continued, but with the spring thaw, that was likely to change. Rationing was being tightened and now included coal, gas and electricity and all kinds of soap. Even those things not rationed had been put on a points system, leaving few things unrestricted, and they were in such short supply long queues formed within minutes of a shop receiving stocks: the arrival of tomatoes, onions, sausages and offal had housewives standing in line for hours.

Black marketeering was reaching epidemic proportions and to deal with it the maximum penalty had been increased to fourteen years' penal servitude. William wondered what Ian Moreton made of that. The man was so greedy he'd expect to get away with it for ever. Conscription had been extended to men up to the age of forty-five and women were being called up too. He was too old and in any case farming was a reserved occupation, but it meant more men would soon disappear and he would be left scratching his head how to get the harvest in.

'We're not stopping,' Joyce said. 'We've just been up to the Hall and thought we'd call in on the way home.

Kathy looked up from her work to greet the newcomer. 'Mum, this is Captain Wayne Donovan,' Jenny said.

'How do you do, Captain.' Kathy wiped her hands and shook hands with him. He was not like Oliver to look at, which came as a relief. His bright hair was characteristic of the Wilson side of the family.

William put the paper down and stood up to shake Wayne's hand. 'Like a beer, Captain?'

'Thanks. But I'm Wayne.'

William went to the pantry where he kept a few bottles of home-brewed beer on the cold stone floor and brought one back. 'You been here long?' he asked, pouring the amber liquid into two glasses and handing one to the visitor. Joyce, on being asked, declined.

'Came to England a few months back,' Wayne answered his question. 'This is the first chance I've had to visit Beckbridge.'

'What do you think of it?'

He took a mouthful of beer and nearly choked, it was so strong. 'It's just like Mom described it, but I wasn't prepared for how small it is, except the Hall. That's some big house.'

'Yes. Of course, it's nothing like it was.'

'It used to be grand in the old days,' Alice said. 'Henry was the Squire, the whole village belonged to him and everyone looked up to him. His wife, Louise, was my sister, you know.'

'Is that so?'

'Yes. Did you meet Helen and Laura?' Alice was determined to wrest the last ounce of information from him.

'Certainly did. I thought they were mother and daughter, but Joyce says they're not related.'

'You're not the first to make that mistake,' Alice said.

'We'd better be going,' Joyce put in. 'Don't want to keep you from your dinner. Wayne is staying the whole week, so I expect you'll be seeing him again.'

Wayne shook hands with everyone and they took their leave, leaving a strange uncomfortable silence behind them.

'Helen, it's too chilly to sit out here and lunch is ready.'

'Yes, I was just coming back.'

'Do you feel better now?'

'What do you mean?' It was asked sharply, confirming Laura's idea that there had been something wrong.

'You felt faint. The sight of blood, you said, though I was surprised at that. You've helped me with dressings more than once when we've been short-handed.'

'That wasn't my blood.'

'No. So, do you feel better?'

'Yes. I'm stupid, I know.'

'Whatever you are, you are certainly not stupid, Helen. Nor am I, so are you going to tell me what's wrong?'

'Nothing's wrong.' She stood up to prove it. 'Come on, let's go back.'

Laura walked beside her. 'He's going to come back, you know.'

'Who?'

'Captain Donovan.'

'So? I invited him to.'

'Yes, but why? You didn't need to and I could see his visit upset you.'

'Don't be silly. I never met the man before today.'

'No, but you did meet his father.'

'Yes. He was one of many who came to the house when my father was alive.'

'Would I be wrong in thinking he was special?'

Helen hesitated. 'No, you wouldn't be wrong, but it was a long time ago. Water under the bridge. I didn't know he'd survived the war, nor that he'd married the chambermaid, that's all. Let's drop the subject, shall we?'

'Sorry. I didn't mean to pry.'

Laura's hurt expression filled Helen with remorse. If only she could tell her the truth. But she could not, she was too afraid. The last year had been the happiest of her whole life and she dare not risk endangering that. 'No, I'm the one who should be sorry. You look after me so well and I do not deserve it.'

'Nonsense. It's you who has been good to me and I bless the day Mum met you again. Now cheer up and come back for lunch. Afterwards, I've got to see that Flying Officer Grant is ready for his trip to East Grinstead tomorrow.'

It was at East Grinstead where Mr McIndoe did his skin grafting operations, and the Flying Officer, who had already had operations on his eyes, was going to have work done on his nose. It should mean he'd look a little less ghoulish. His young wife, though she had been warned, had been horribly sick when she saw him just after the first operation. But mention of the young man served to make Helen pull herself together. She would show Oliver's son round the house and garden and she would chat as if his father had been no more than a passing acquaintance, and she would smile while she did it. None of it was his fault, any more than it was Laura's. 'Yes,' she said. 'Back to work.'

'I'm off to the pub,' Ian said. 'You coming, Wayne?'

'Yes, if Aunt Joyce doesn't mind?'

'No, course not.'

He fetched his cap and the two men strolled down the rutted lane and turned into the High Street. 'I've got a bit of business to transact,' Ian told him. 'So if I disappear for a while, you'll be all right on your own?'

'Yes. Is there anything I can do to help?'

Ian laughed. 'You can say I never left your side, if you're asked.'

'Might I be asked?'

'Shouldn't think so. Just in case.'

'What's it all about?'

Ian tapped the side of his nose. 'I do a bit of trading, things that are hard to come by, know what I mean?'

'Yes, I think I do. Isn't it a bit risky?'

'Not really. People i'n't about to cut off their source of supply by shopping me. War makes criminals of us all, bor.'

'I see. Where do you get your supplies?'

'Oh, here and there, mostly up at the airfield. The Yanks have taken it over and they've got plenty. Seems to me they ought to be sharing it around a bit, so I buy and sell and everyone's happy. You got anything surplus to requirements up your way?'

'Can't help you, I'm afraid.'

'Don' mek no matter. Better not involve you anyhows. Joyce'll have me guts for garters.'

They wandered into the bar to find several elderly locals who could be found there every evening, making a pint last two hours, and a group of airmen from the Hall, enjoying a drink and playing a noisy game of shove ha'penny. One of them looked up as they entered. 'Hallo again,' he said. His eyes, in a pinkly scarred face, were lashless slits and the tip of his nose was missing.

'Hallo.' Wayne recognised one of the men he had spoken to that morning. 'They've let you out, I see.'

'Shhh. I'm supposed to be resting for my trip tomorrow. Going to give me a new nose.'

'Can I buy you a beer?'

'Thanks. I'm Colin by the way. This is Charlie and this is Bertie.'

They both said hallo and he asked them what they wanted to drink and then turned to include Ian, but he had disappeared. He shrugged and joined the airmen.

'Enjoying your leave?' Charlie asked. One side of his face was a ribbed pink scar, the other showed the handsome young man he had once been. His hands were like claws, but he had somehow mastered the art of picking up a glass with both hands.

'Yes. My mom came from this village. She met my pop at Beckbridge Hall in the last war, so I wanted to look round the place.'

'It's changed a bit, though I can imagine what it was like in the old days. Lady Barstairs is a bit of an autocrat, but she's OK. What we must be doing to her lovely home must make her want to weep, but she never turns a hair.'

'And Mrs Drummond?'

'She's a marvel,' Colin said. 'If it hadn't been for her I'd have thrown in the towel long ago.'

'Nothing's too much trouble,' Charlie said. He had a pair of crutches propped against his seat. 'Another beer?' He went to pick up one of the crutches and made to stand up.

'No, please, I'll get them,' Wayne said, putting a hand on the young man's shoulder.

'Let the lazy bugger get them in,' Colin said. 'He sits around and expects everyone to wait on him.'

'That I do not. Who was it that brought your tea to you this morning?'

'And spilt most of it in the saucer.'

'Do you want another drink or not?'

'Yes, I'll have a beer.' He grinned and winked at Wayne as Charlie manoeuvred himself onto his crutches and hopped across to the bar. 'I'll go and help him bring them back, don't worry.'

'Tell us about yourself,' Charlie said, when they were all sitting with brimming glasses in front of them. 'What unit are you in? What d'you do before the war? That sort of thing.'

'I'm a motor engineer. My father owns garages and motor workshops and I worked for him until I joined the Engineers last year. I got shipped over here a few months ago. Been kicking my heels ever since.'

'Won't last,' Bertie said. 'They'll find something for you to do.'

'There were Canadians with the BEF in France,' Charlie said.

'Yes, I know. I would have come at the outbreak of war, but Mom was against it. I had to get Pop to persuade her.'

'He didn't mind you coming then?'

'He was in the last lot. Fought in France and caught a bullet in his thigh. They shipped him back to England and he recovered. It was after that he met with Mom and they got married. He's a real patriot, wouldn't surprise me if he didn't find some way of getting over here himself.'

They went on to exchange gossip and information, and because Joe Easter had only that morning taken delivery of two barrels of beer and he couldn't refuse 'those poor devils', as he described them, they went on topping up their glasses all evening. By the time Joe called 'Time, gentlemen!', Ian had not come back and they were all very merry. And that was how Laura found them.

'Shame on you, gentlemen,' she said. 'Lieutenant Grant, you've a long journey tomorrow, you were going to have an early night as I recall. And you, Captain.' She rounded on Wayne. 'You should not have encouraged them. They are supposed to be recuperating.'

'Best way to recuperate,' Charlie put in, picking up his crutches. 'Convivial company and a pint of ale.'

'You've all had more than a pint. It's a good thing I guessed where you were and brought the car.' Her words were severe but she could not conceal the fact that she was smiling. Charlie was right; it did help their recovery to be accepted and treated like normal human beings, which of course they were. 'Now get in the car, there's good chaps. You too, Captain Donovan. I'll drop you off at the end on Beck Lane.'

He was fitter and stronger than they were; the beer had had less effect and the arrival of Laura had sobered him almost completely. He followed as she shepherded them to the big car. 'I'm supposed to be out with Ian,' he said. 'He disappeared early on. Do you think I should go home without him?'

She laughed. 'That's par for the course. He'll trip over his own shoelaces one day. He can find his own way home. Come on. I want to talk to you, anyway.'

'Oh ho!' Colin said. 'Either you're for a wigging or you've struck lucky. Which is it, Sister?'

She did not answer, but indicated Wayne should get in the passenger seat beside her while the others crowded in the back; it was plenty wide enough for three and they sat with Charlie's crutches across their knees.

'I'm sorry,' Wayne said, as they set off, afraid he had blotted his copybook. She had something special about her: a way, a look, a smile; whatever it was, he wanted to probe it further. 'But they're grown men and if their supervision is so lax they can escape and spend an evening in a bar, it's not down to me, is it?'

'No, of course not. I spoke hastily. Forgive me.'

'Nothing to forgive. Was that what you wanted to talk to me about?'

'It doesn't matter. Just a silly idea I had.' She had started out with the intention of suggesting he should not return to the Hall, but how could she do that without explaining and betraying Helen's confidence, making a mountain out of a molehill?

'What idea?'

'Nothing. Forget it.'

She would not be drawn and the three in the back began singing lustily enough to drown out any attempt at normal conversation. When they arrived at the Hall she stopped outside the front door. 'Home gentlemen,' she said. 'I trust you can put yourselves to bed.'

They answered her cheekily as they tumbled out. She waited until they had disappeared inside, then drove round the sweeping circle of the drive and back out of the gates. 'I can walk from here,' Wayne said, though it was said half-heartedly. He was not anxious to leave her.

She did not take the car down Beck Lane but stopped at the top. He made no move to get out. 'Now, tell me about your silly idea,' he said.

'It was something and nothing.' She paused before continuing. 'Your sudden arrival was a bit of a surprise to everyone.'

'It was and perhaps I should have written first, but Aunt Joyce gave me a right royal welcome.' He stopped, wondering whether to mention it, but curiosity got the better of him. 'Lady Barstairs seemed – how shall I say? – taken aback, a bit shocked.'

So he had noticed it. 'I suppose seeing you reminded her of the last war, when her parents and her husband were alive. He died in France, you know. Perhaps he and your father knew each other...' She limped to a halt.

'Did she tell you that?'

'I'm only guessing.'

'What is it with everyone round here, dropping hints, tapping their noses, playing guessing games?'

'I don't know, Captain. I've only lived in the village a year and by their standards, I'm a newcomer. I believe it takes at least a generation to become one of them.'

'So, what are you asking me? That I shouldn't visit again?'

'No, of course not.' She gave a light laugh. 'It's just that I want to protect Helen from memories that are painful, but we all have those, don't we? We can't shy away from them.'

'You are very fond of her?'

'Next to my mother, my son and my...' She paused. '...my son's father, God rest him, she is the dearest person in the world to me.'

'I'm sorry about your husband,' he said, then waited. If she wanted to talk about him, he would listen, but it was up to her.

'He wasn't my husband,' she told him, surprising herself. Why confess that now when she had been accepted by everyone as a widow? It was as if she couldn't bear to have an untruth between them, as if they had always known each other and their lives were in tandem. 'He was shot down on our wedding day.'

'Gee, I'm sorry. I don't know what to say. It must have been damn awful.'

'It was. No one knows we weren't married, except Helen and Steve Wainright. He was going to be best man.'

'I shan't say a word, but I'm privileged you told me.'

'I don't know why I did.'

'Steve won't say anything?'

'No. He was Bob's best friend, and now he's mine. A rock if I need one.'

'You're not in love with him?'

'How could I be? I loved Bob.'

'Of course, but that shouldn't mean denying yourself for the rest of your life. He would not have wanted that, would he?'

'No. Perhaps in time...' She laughed lightly. 'Right now, I'm too busy keeping those airmen in order.'

'Do you have any time off?'

'I manage a few hours now and again.'

'When?'

'Are you asking me out?'

'Guess I am.'

'What did you have in mind?'

'Anything. Whatever you like.'

'Tuesday afternoon,' she said. 'We could go for a walk. There are some pretty walks hereabouts.'

'It's a date.'

He left her and wandered down the lane to Beck Cottage. Ian had not come back.

'Do you think that's wise?' Helen asked, trying to keep the panic from her voice. They were rolling bandages at a table at the end of one of the wards. One or two of the beds were empty but they would unfortunately soon be filled again. The day was warm and the windows were wide open and the soft breeze was lifting the curtains, making dancing patterns on the floor. Outside in the courtyard they could hear the muted voices of the nurses talking to those patients fit enough to be wheeled out to take the sun.

'Why not? He's at a loose end and it's my afternoon off.'

'You don't know anything about him.'

'I know enough to know he's a gentleman and a long way from home. It doesn't hurt to be friendly.' She paused. 'Unless you know something I do not.'

'You know I don't. Oh, Laura, I'm afraid for you.'

'Afraid? What of?'

'You might become too fond of him and—'

'You're afraid it's like father, like son, is that it?' Laura leant forward and touched the back of Helen's hand in reassurance. 'Don't worry, I'm not about to fall head over heels in love with him.'

'What if he falls for you?'

'Oh, Helen, I'm sure such a thing has never entered his head.' She laughed suddenly. 'You know, you are nearly as transparent as Mum was. You're afraid he'll carry me off to Canada and you'll lose me and Robby. Don't think I don't know how you dote on him. No granny could be more doting.'

'Yes, well…' Helen stopped, realising what Laura had said. *No granny could be more doting.* But she *was* his granny. Oh, how she hated keeping that secret! Did the advent of Oliver's son mean that it could no longer be kept quiet? She dreaded Laura's reaction when she found out. She could guess most of it. Disbelief at first, then denial, then anger, and the result would be alienation. She would lose her then, and Robby too, and she didn't know how she could go on living if that happened. If only there was a way of making it all right. Should she tell Wayne, warn him off, swear him to secrecy? How would he react? In the same way as Laura, she guessed. And how could she be sure he wouldn't run with the tale to Joyce, or worse, tell his parents? It felt as if she was standing beside a ticking bomb. 'I'm being silly, aren't I?' she said. 'Meeting trouble halfway.'

'Yes, I do believe you are. Cheer up, we've got work to do if I'm to get off on time. And when we come back, I'll invite him in for tea and you can show him round like you promised.'

Helen pretended to be satisfied. Trouble was coming, she could feel it in her bones and there was no need to meet it halfway, it was hurtling towards her.

The clear moonlit sky was black with aircraft whichever way you looked. Steve didn't need to be told that it was the biggest raid the air force had ever mounted. Their new boss, Air Marshall Harris, seemed to think he could bomb the enemy into submission, that they couldn't 'take it' as Londoners had done. Whether he was right or not, Steve didn't know, but his mouth had gone dry and it had been a job to stop his hands shaking as he settled himself in the cockpit. Once he'd gone through the familiar routine of taking the Lancaster into the air, he settled down to join the throng and take his aircraft and crew of seven over hundreds of miles of enemy countryside to drop his payload on Cologne. The raid was timed to take exactly ninety minutes and they had been ordered to set course for home after that time whether they had reached their objective or not. 'We don't want any stragglers left over the target when it gets light,' they had been told at the briefing.

The Lancaster had been in service since the previous September but already it was proving its worth. It was very different from flying a Hurricane or a Spitfire, being more cumbersome, especially with a full payload, but he liked flying it and he liked the comradeship, the feeling that he was not alone up there, although he was ultimately responsible for his crew and the rest of the squadron. They were good lads. He grinned a little to himself; lads! It made him feel a hundred. They were flying steadily over East Anglia and apart from keeping his distance from other aircraft, he could relax a little until they hit the Dutch coast.

Beckbridge was somewhere below him. They could not fail to hear the aircraft going over and, as it was such a cloudless night, could probably see them too. Would they guess he was up here? His mother would worry and his father would tell her not to, which was a futile thing to say because she couldn't help it. Would Laura be thinking of him or the fact that there were bound to be casualties who would need her nursing? He didn't want to think of that; better to remember his last leave, the quiet understanding they had achieved. She hadn't committed herself, but he was hopeful that the ghost of Bob might have been laid to rest. That is, if Wayne Donovan hadn't turned her head and achieved in a week what had taken him over a year of treading on eggs to bring about.

Everyone had a different view of the man. Mum had mentioned him in passing, Meg had written that he seemed a friendly chap and popular in the village, though what he made of Joyce and Ian she could not be sure. Jenny was more forthcoming. She had been to a dance with him and to the pictures, and she obviously found him fascinating. He hoped that Laura didn't think so too. It would be a tragedy for him if, having wooed her out of almost two years of mourning Bob, he was to lose her to someone else.

He could see the coastline below him and then they were over the North Sea, over a thousand aircraft, swarming like a plague of locusts. 'They say there's safety in numbers.' Ken's voice came to him over the intercom.

'Let's hope so, though we can hardly keep our arrival a secret, can we? So keep your eyes peeled everyone. We'll be dodging flak.' He pushed thoughts of home from him to concentrate on trying to avoid the anti-aircraft fire without colliding with one of the other aircraft doing the same thing.

He was not the first to arrive over Cologne, others had been there before him and he could see the fires long before he arrived over the target. It reminded him of the sight he'd had of London on that last big raid just over a year ago. The memory stiffened him against feeling sorry for those on the ground. This was payback time. He flew over the target, listening to his bomb aimer's calm voice guiding him in, and tried to ignore the gunfire coming up from the ground and the *rat-tat* as his rear gunner kept the fighters off their back.

'Bombs away.'

'Right, let's go home.'

After a minute or two, Ken's voice came over the intercom with their course and they arrived back at base in one piece, though on inspection later Steve discovered a few holes in the fuselage. Over a thousand aircraft had set off to drop nearly fifteen hundred tons of bombs; forty-one of them had not returned, two of them having collided in mid-air. The fires were still burning the next day and dense smoke prevented the reconnaissance people from taking photographs, but they became available soon afterwards and made Steve wonder if anything could have survived; the destruction seemed total. Two nights later their target was Essen and at the end of June it was the submarine base at Bremen. Each time they scraped home, he found himself wondering how much longer his luck would hold. He was never more glad of seven days' leave.

He and Ken travelled home together. 'I've heard about a new unit being formed,' he told Steve as they settled in their seats on the train for Attlesham. 'Thought I might give it a go.'

'New unit?'

'Yes. You know how difficult it is sometimes to find the target in the dark and you end up dropping your bombs just anywhere, which is a terrible waste if all they do is kill a few cows, not to mention the number of aircraft and men being put at risk for no strategic gain, so they've hit on the idea of being guided in. They are going to be called Pathfinders. They'll go in low and quick to find the target, drop flares and incendiaries to light the way for the big boys coming on behind, and then get out again pronto. I thought I might fancy that.'

'I shall miss you.'

'Don't have to. Come too. I reckon we'd stand a better chance of getting back in one piece…'

Steve didn't agree with that last statement, but he could see the sense of doing it. How many times had he cursed the fact that on a dark night it was almost impossible to pick things out on the ground and he could never be sure his bombs had been dropped in the right place. 'I'll think about it.'

Ken settled for that answer. 'What are you going to do this leave?'

'Nothing, if I can help it. Might help Dad, see Laura, go to a dance.'

'Laura? You mean the nurse up at the Hall? Your girl, is she?'

'I'd like to think so.'

'I reckon she's OK, though my gran keeps hinting at a mystery about her.'

'Why?' He remembered his own grandmother saying something of the sort.

'Dunno. Gran said Lady Helen was a recluse for years and years, never went anywhere, never had anyone to stay, drove all the village kids away from the Hall grounds. That's true because I remember her coming after me once 'cos I went for a swim in the lake—'

'No doubt she was concerned she'd be blamed if you drowned.'

'Maybe, but after years of being cantankerous, she suddenly produced an old friend no one's ever heard of who was so close to her that when she died her ladyship took the daughter and the new baby under her wing and opened up the house to a bunch of injured airmen. It's a monumental change for her, and according to Gran, very fishy.'

Steve pretended to be amused. 'So what's her theory?'

'She won't say, just taps her nose and says it'll all come out in the wash.'

'Some people like to make a mystery out of nothing. I met Laura's mother. She was a nice woman and she and Laura were as close as any mother and daughter could be. And Laura's doing a grand job at the hospital.'

'Too true. I just hope I never end up there.'

'Amen to that,' Steve said with feeling.

The train stopped at a station and he watched people getting on and off for a minute before the doors were slammed shut, the whistle blew and they were on their way again. 'Did you meet your Canadian cousin?'

'No, but he caused quite a stir, I believe. According to Mum, it was a case of "mothers, lock up your daughters".'

'Is that so?'

Ken laughed. 'Mum's biased. Gran even more so. He's probably perfectly ordinary.'

They lapsed into silence until the train drew in at Attlesham, when they collected up their kit and made their way out of the station to find a taxi. It dropped Ken off at the top of Beck Lane and continued on to Bridge Farm with Steve.

The farm was his bolt-hole, his safety net, the place to unwind and forget the sound of aircraft engines, the searchlights and flak, the noisy banter of other airmen pretending they weren't scared out of their wits, the tight feeling in his gut and the dry mouth, the sheer weight of being responsible for a squadron of men and aeroplanes. His mother could spoil him all she liked and he would wander about the village, lend a hand on the farm and see Laura. He smiled at the prospect as he made his way across the yard to the back door; she was becoming more and more important to him. And then he was in the kitchen with everyone talking at once and he knew he was home.

Ian was sitting over a breakfast of bacon and eggs when Joyce came into the kitchen at the end of her round of delivering the mail to snatch a cup of tea and a bacon sandwich before going back to the shop for the rest of her day's work. 'There's a letter for you,' she said, throwing a brown envelope down in front of him. OHMS, it had stamped on it. He knew what it was and was reluctant to open it.

'Go on, it won't bite.'

He wiped his greasy fingers on his corduroys and slit it open. A single sheet of paper fluttered out. This was it, this was his call-up. He'd been expecting it ever since men up to forty-five had been required to register. He'd asked Bill Wainright to certify that he was an agricultural labourer whose skills were needed and therefore made him exempt, but he had turned him down on the grounds he did not employ him, except on a casual basis when he was short-handed. He had even laughed and said a spell in the army might do him good. Damn the man! Sitting on his thousand-acre farm, he could afford to scoff. He didn't have to try and make a living out of half a dozen acres, nor was he expected to turn up for a medical in less than a week.

Could he find some ailment that might make him fail that? Flat feet? A persistent cough? He didn't want to fight, the whole idea was abhorrent to him, and Joyce didn't seem to care that he might be killed. Serve her right if he was. And there was a whole hoard of black market stuff buried under the trough in that old hut which he could not abandon. He'd have to get young Donny to help him dispose of it. The boy knew the ropes by now and was proving himself useful. He would wander about the village, his hands in his pockets, socks round his ankles, kicking stones with his sandals and looking for all the world as if he had nothing better to do, when all the time he was acting as look out while deals were being struck and goods delivered. The boy didn't know where the stuff came from and Ian didn't propose to tell him, but there was a certain quartermaster up at the airfield who wasn't averse to earning a bob or two.

Everyone had hoped the arrival of the Americans would mark a turning point in the war but he had seen little evidence of it. Still, he couldn't complain; their appearance had been a stroke of luck for him. They had everything, stuff people in Britain hadn't seen for years and would pay almost anything to get. Tinned fruit; oranges; stockings called nylons which didn't run into ladders as soon as you looked at them; coffee; cigarettes which tasted foul but you got used to that after a time; booze, stacks of it, and now it looked as though it was all coming to an end.

'When do you go?' Joyce's voice broke in on his reverie.

'Medical next Wednesday. After that…' He shrugged.

'Good, you'll be able to spend some time with Ken while he's here.'

'The lazy bugger is still in his bed and I've got work to do.' He stood up. 'I promised to help Wainright with his haymaking.'

He didn't go anywhere near Bridge Farm, but made his way up to Beckbridge Hall. There was a good market up there, young fellows kicking their heels, tongues hanging out for a drink, with wives and sweethearts who wouldn't say no to chocolates or perfume or stockings. That chap Grant was back and now he had a new nose, he looked almost human again. He had met him in the pub a few days before and he was looking forward to going home to his wife and little boy. He would want presents to take with him. He'd have to run the gauntlet of Lady Barstairs and the Drummond woman, but he wasn't worried about them. He'd spent a profitable hour with his mother-in-law, who had explained, amid much chuckling and innuendo, why, in her opinion, Laura Drummond looked so much like Lady Helen. Ma had a long and accurate memory when it came to dates. It was only conjecture but it made him look at the old battleaxe in a different light, almost admiration.

The airmen who were not bedridden spent much of their time lounging or walking about the grounds or being wheeled about by their comrades. The more active ones played croquet on the lawn or their own version of cricket: one batsman against the rest, which was played well away from the house. No one stopped him as he strolled up to them. Business was brisk and he soon had a handful of orders which he said he would leave in the summer house for them to pick up at their leisure. Then he went belatedly to help William with his haymaking but was told he wasn't needed because Steve had arrived.

'Mr Moreton was up here talking to the men this morning,' Laura told Helen. The two women were in the kitchen drinking coffee over the remains of their midday meal. Stella had left them to put Robby down for his afternoon nap and Mrs Ward had gone off duty for the afternoon, before coming back to prepare the evening meal. 'I can't think what he wants with them.'

'Oh, I can. He's up to his usual tricks, selling black market goods. I wonder if… No, he wouldn't be so brazen.'

'Are you going to say something to him if he comes again? After all, he's making use of us and some people might think we condone it. You know the penalty for black marketeering is fourteen years?'

'Is it?' Helen was surprised that it was so severe. 'The trouble is, if he goes to jail, Mrs Moreton will be the one to suffer. It's probably why no one has turned him in before now.'

They were interrupted by a knock on the door and a voice calling, 'Anyone at home?'

Laura jumped up and turned as Steve came into the kitchen. 'Steve! I didn't know you were home. Come in.'

'I'm already in.'

He held out his hands to her and she grasped them, holding him at arm's length. 'How are you? When did you arrive? How long have you got? You look tired.'

He laughed. 'I'm fine and if I look tired it's because I've been deprived of the sight of you. Hallo, Aunt Helen, how are you?'

'I'm fine, Steven. Tell us what you've been up to while I make a cup of tea.'

'Oh, the usual. Flying aeroplanes. Nothing out of the ordinary.'

'We won't talk about that then. We've just been discussing Ian Moreton and what to do about him, if anything.'

He didn't fancy that subject either but was too polite to say so. 'What's he been up to?'

'Selling black market goods to our airmen,' Helen said. 'I wouldn't say anything if it was away from the Hall, but he has come up here quite blatantly and you never know when the Air Ministry people might decide to come and check up on us.'

'I'll talk to Ken, see if we can come up with something.'

'Thank you.'

He turned back to Laura. 'When are you going to come out with me?'

Laura looked at Helen, who laughed and said, 'You know best when you can get off. I'll look after Robby if that's what's stopping you.' She put a cup of tea down on the table in front of Steve. 'Sit down and drink your tea. I've got work to do.' She smiled and left them.

He turned to Laura and held out his arms. She went into them as if it were the most natural thing in the world. He kissed her, tasting the tea on her mouth, smelling the faint perfume of recently shampooed hair. 'It's too long,' he said, at last.

'What's too long.'

'The time between kisses.'

She laughed. 'You didn't say how long you've got.'

'Seven days and I want to spend every minute of it with you.'

'You've got to go home to bed every so often.'

'True. Wouldn't it be grand if you could share it with me?'

'Now you're being silly.'

'Am I? Perhaps I am. So, are you free this evening?'

'Afraid not, but tomorrow's my day off.'

'A whole day. Where would you like to go?'

'You choose.'

'OK. I'll put my thinking cap on.'

She watched him pick up the cup of tea and drain it. 'I'll walk down the drive with you, then I must get back to work.'

They set off hand in hand with the sun hot on their backs, followed by the wolf whistles of some of the patients who were strolling about the garden. 'There's still no shortage of patients,' he said.

'No, more's the pity, but we're learning all the time and Mr McIndoe is a marvel.'

'Do you miss London?'

'Not now. There was a time…' She paused, leading him off the drive and across the grass towards the lake. He went without demur. 'But then there's nothing there for me now, no family, no close friends, and I've made Beckbridge my home.'

'You wouldn't consider going to Canada then?' He made himself speak lightly.

'Canada?' she queried, puzzled.

'Yes, with a certain Captain Donovan.'

'You're as bad as Helen; she said much the same thing. I only went out with the fellow once and we had an enjoyable afternoon, but that doesn't mean I'm about to throw all this up…' She waved her hand at the house and the airmen behind her. '…just because a handsome soldier asks me out.'

'Oh, so he is handsome?'

'Yes.' She laughed. 'You're jealous!'

'Too right, I am.'

'You shouldn't be.'

He wasn't sure what she meant by that, but before he could ask her, they arrived at the summer house and stood looking at it contemplatively. It had been rebuilt, slightly to one side of where the original building had been, probably because the rubble and earth that filled the crater wasn't stable enough for the foundations.

'I'm sure the place has some significance for Helen,' Laura said. 'That's why she had it rebuilt exactly as it was.' She turned to face him. 'Do you know anything about it?'

He knew she was deliberately changing the subject. 'No, but I think the older members of the village might. Does it matter?'

'Only in as much as it makes Helen unhappy, and yet it is a

sadness she seems to invite, as if she's punishing herself. Doesn't make sense, does it?'

'I suppose not.'

She went inside and lifted the lid of the bench, but it was empty. 'Thank goodness for that.'

'Why, what did you expect to find?'

'Black market stuff.'

'You mean Ian? Surely, he'd never be such a fool as to try the same trick twice.'

'Helen wondered if he might. Her civic duty has been doing battle with her reluctance to upset Joyce. She'll be glad I found nothing.'

They went outside again and stood looking at the water. Yellow flag irises bloomed among the bulrushes at the water's edge and further out a handful of mallards dipped their heads in the water, making gentle ripples. He put an arm about her and she leant her head against his shoulder 'You'd never know there was a war on, would you?'

She had hardly uttered the words when a squadron of Spitfires zoomed across the sky, shattering the peace. 'Oh, well,' she said, as they both shaded their eyes with their hands to look up at them. 'Back to the real world.' She turned and he followed her to the end of the drive, where the iron gates had once stood.

'Tomorrow,' he said, bending to kiss her lightly. 'I'll call for you at nine o'clock.'

'I'll be ready.'

He strode off and she turned back to the house.

Donny breathed a sigh of relief that he had seen them coming in time and emerged from his hiding place in the garden of the lodge. He hoisted the heavy kitbag over his shoulder and made his way across the grass to the summer house.

Steve borrowed his father's car and took Laura to Cambridge, where he hired a rowing boat. Most of them had been put up for the duration, but there were still some for hire, not taken by undergraduates because it was the long vacation, but by servicemen, mainly Americans, keen to experience all that England had to offer and that included weekends in London going to shows and touring the landmarks, visiting Stratford-upon-Avon, walking in the hills, and boating on the rivers. Cambridge was conveniently near their airfields, so it was a popular destination.

Steve took the boat down towards Ely. Laura, relaxing in the stern, was content to let him do all the work, watching his muscular body as he wielded the oars. 'You're no novice, are you?'

'I did a bit of rowing while I was here. It seems a lifetime ago now. Before the war.'

'What did you study?'

'History and English. Silly subjects for a farmer's son, I suppose, but they were the subjects I was best at in school. I had some idea I might like to teach, but then I realised what a disappointment that would be to Dad, and shelved it. Anyway, the decision was taken out of my hands by the war. Besides, Jenny is the teacher, not me. I'll take over the farm some day.'

'Will you like that?'

'Yes. There was a time when I rebelled against it – it's what most sons do at some time or other, I suppose – but now the prospect of a rural life, governed by nature and the seasons appeals no end.' He pulled into the bank under some willows, jumped out and tied the boat up. Then he held out his hand to help her out and retrieved the rug and picnic basket he had brought with him. 'We are fugitives from the war,' he said. 'We are going to sit here to eat cold chicken and drink warm wine and pretend it doesn't exist.'

They settled themselves on the rug and enjoyed their picnic. But in the back of his mind were words he wanted to say, words that had to be got off his chest. 'Going back to the subject of the rural life,' he said, twisting a stem of grass in his fingers. 'Are you really at home away from the bright lights of the city?'

'Yes. Do you find that strange?'

'No, but I wanted to be sure.' He paused and then went on. 'Laura, when I said I wished you could come to bed with me, I wasn't trying it on, you know. I was thinking of something…more permanent.'

'I know.'

'What do you say? You know I love you, so will you consider marrying me?'

'Steve, this isn't the time. We've both got work to do and until this war is over—'

'God knows when that will be and it isn't an answer to my question.'

'True.' She paused. 'Steve, you are my rock. Apart from Robby and Helen, you are the most stable thing in my life—'

'Do you mean that?'

'Of course. Whenever I've been in trouble, there you've been, supporting me: the day Bob died; again when I was feeling especially down because I had to work in that factory and everyone was shunning me; the night Robby was born. And when I arrived in Beckbridge and was beginning to wonder just what I'd let myself in for, there you were—'

'But…? There has to be a but after a statement like that.'

'Steve, I can't think about getting married now, really I can't.'

'Is there someone else?'

'You know there is not.'

'Except the ghost of Bob Rawton.'

'No, it isn't that, at least I don't think so. I'm simply saying let's wait.'

He sighed. 'You're probably right. I might get shot down and it wouldn't be fair to put you through that a second time.'

'Steve, please don't say that, please don't tempt fate.' She leant over to kiss his cheek. 'You said we were going to pretend the war doesn't exist.'

'We can't though, can we? It doesn't matter where we go or what we say, we can't hide from it. We might ban it as a subject but it won't be banned. Damn it!'

She laughed and edged herself over to him and snuggled her head into his shoulder. 'It's lovely here.'

'Yes.' He put his finger and thumb under her chin and tilted her face up to his. 'When the war ends, however long it takes, I shall bring you back here and ask you that question again.'

'You'll wait that long?' she queried.

'For ever if I have to. At least, until and unless you marry someone else.'

'There's not much fear of that.'

'Not even a handsome Canadian?'

She pummelled him in the shoulder with her fist. 'Tease!' She sat up straight and began gathering up the remnants of the picnic. 'It's time we went back.'

He sighed and helped her to her feet, realising she had not given him a direct answer – not then, nor earlier – but decided not to pursue it. He rowed them back up the river, returned the boat, picked up the car from where he had parked it, and drove her home.

'Tomorrow?' he asked, as he stopped beside the old stables.

'I'll be busy all day. There's two patients to be got ready to go to East Grinstead and one coming from there who has to be made welcome and comfortable. I'll be lucky if I have two minutes to myself. I'll have the afternoon off the day after that, but as it's Stella's afternoon off, I'll have Robby.'

'Not a problem,' he said, surprising himself. 'We'll take him with us.'

They managed, during the week, to see each other several times, though never for so long as a whole day. They took Robby, now sixteen months old, out in a pushchair and were continually being stopped by people who had come to know Laura and who wanted to admire her son. He seemed a happy lad, not given to tantrums, and Steve began to think he wouldn't mind being a father to him. If only Laura would consent to marry him. He conceded she might be right about waiting but it didn't make it any easier to bear.

If he imagined no one noticed his preoccupation with Laura,

he was wrong. Everyone watched and waited. His mother seemed concerned, Jenny amused and his father unforthcoming, unlike his grandmother who was, as usual, outspoken. 'It'll end in tears,' she said, one evening after he had come back from taking Laura to see Noël Coward in *In Which We Serve* at the Attlesham Odeon.

'Why?' he demanded.

'You don't know anything about her.'

'I know as much as I need to know, more than anyone else round here.'

'Don't you believe it, boy. You mark my words, she's not what she seems—'

'Rubbish.' He thought she had guessed that Laura had never been married, but as he had promised to respect Laura's confidence he could not tell them he didn't care a hoot about it. 'We've got no secrets from each other. If you are referring to the fact that she went out with Wayne Donovan—'

'Well, there is that,' she said. 'And that will *certainly* end in tears.'

'I wish you'd stop dropping hints and say straight out what you mean,' he said angrily.

'Not for me to say,' she said. 'Ask your mother. Or ask Helen.'

But he wouldn't do that and so he went back to Scampton unsatisfied.

Chapter Nine

IT HAD BEEN light for a long time but you would never have known it; the pall of smoke was so thick. You couldn't see the ships, though Wayne supposed they were still there. If he couldn't see them, they couldn't see where to aim their fire. Nor could the supporting aircraft do their job. He didn't know what was happening in Dieppe itself – he had heard heavy gunfire and explosions for hours, but here on the beach the tanks were bogged down. Only ten of the twenty-four tank landing craft had managed to disgorge their cargo onto the beach; the rest had been sunk even before they reached the shore. If the poor beggars in Dieppe were waiting for their help, they would wait in vain. He had his engineers do their best to get the twenty-odd tanks that had managed to land going again, but they were subjected to murderous fire and coils and coils of barbed wire. A few had managed to get off the shingle and make it into Dieppe but he had no idea what had happened to them after that.

It was only supposed to be a raid, an in-and-out operation, to test the German defences and give them a fright, but it was not the Germans who'd had the fright. He'd been terrified, and still was, as shells and bullets spattered around him. Major-General McNaughton had been campaigning for months for his Canadian troops to be given something useful to do and he had got his way. But Wayne wasn't sure that what they were doing could be classed as useful, nor sensible; he was beginning to think of it as a fiasco. They had set out full of good spirits, a force of over six thousand men: mostly Canadians, some British commandos, a few Americans and

Free French, ferried across the Channel by a fleet of ships to be put ashore on an eleven-mile front to put the wind up the Hun. They had been told at the briefing that their task was to destroy the shore batteries, a radio-location station and German Divisional HQ in Dieppe itself. Above them, to give them air cover, had been several squadrons of Spitfires. In addition, sixty fighter squadrons and seven bomber squadrons had been put on standby to support them. They had felt strong and invincible, and that was borne out by the code-name of the operation. 'Jubilee' they called it. That was a laugh!

Their troubles had started even before a man had landed. One of the Commando force had run into armed German trawlers and exchanged gunfire, which those onshore could not fail to hear, and the element of surprise had been lost. Now, here he was, kneeling on the shingle of a French beach, trying to free the track of a Churchill tank, and wishing he was anywhere but where he was, preferably in Beckbridge. If he was taken prisoner, he wouldn't see the village or Laura again for a very long time. The ships were supposed to take them off, but he couldn't even see them. He could hear them plainly enough. And the yells and groans of the men around him who were being mown down.

'Pull out. Get yourselves back to the water.' The command was passed from man to man.

'What about the tanks?'

'Leave them. Go on, now. Get back to the ships.'

Most of the tanks were already bogged down but they did their best to demobilise them and then ran, dodging bullets, back to the water's edge. There were a few boats waiting to pick them up, but not nearly enough. It put him in mind of the stories he had heard about Dunkirk. What a nightmare that must have been. 'Come on!' he urged his men. He went back and forth, urging on those who could walk, helping to carry those who could not, then stood up to his armpits in water, hauling them over the gunwales until the boats were filled to overflowing. 'We can't come back, Captain,' he was told by one of the sailors manning the one nearest to him. 'The rest of you will have to take your chances with Jerry.'

'Not on your Nelly,' he said, repeating a phrase he had heard Ian Moreton use, and pulled off his boots and struck out for the nearest ship. He hadn't gone far when he felt something sting his arm and realised he had been hit. There was a neat round hole in his jacket sleeve. He ploughed on but soon found the arm would not obey him. He rolled over on his back and kicked out with his legs. He'd get back to England if he had to swim the whole bloody way.

Swimming on his back, he was facing the shore. It was littered with burning tanks, submerged landing craft, and he dreaded to think how many bodies. The pall of smoke still hung over the town and he could see boats trying to get in close enough to take the men off; they were being subjected to murderous fire. He redoubled his efforts. August it might be, but the water was cold and his uniform was hampering him. He had to stop every now and again to tread water and rest. Then he ploughed on again. That destroyer, which had seemed so near when he set out, now looked more distant than ever. His limbs felt numb, but his brain was active, active in a useless kind of way. He was thinking of Mom and Pop, safe home in Canada, of Jenny and Laura in Beckbridge. He'd taken them both out while he'd been on leave. Jenny was tender-hearted, bright and wholesome and he liked her a lot, she brought out his protective instinct, but what he felt for Laura was different. He couldn't describe it accurately, it was a kind of chemistry, a melding of minds. She was intelligent and kind-hearted – she had to be to do the job she did – but she was perhaps a bit more worldly-wise than Jenny, which he put down to losing her man and her mother and having to deal with badly injured airmen, some of whom were mentally, as well as physically, scarred. He remembered that afternoon when they had walked for miles.

The countryside was gently undulating, there was nothing you could call a hill. Most of it was arable, divided into quite small fields, but there were meadows where cows and sheep grazed, cottages with gardens ablaze with flowers. 'We are supposed to dig up our flowerbeds and grow vegetables,' she had said. 'They call it digging for victory, but country people love their flowers and they won't be persuaded to sacrifice them all. Even at home – in London, I mean – we kept one border for blooms and dug up the lawn to grow vegetables. Puny little things they turned out to be. The soil wasn't very fertile. Anyway, most of the space was taken up with an Anderson shelter.'

She had turned off the tarmac lane onto a grassy bridleway. There was a spinney on one side and a field of growing wheat on the other. He thought of the rolling wheat fields of home and for a moment felt homesick. 'Were you bombed out?'

'No, though we lost a few windows.'

He took her hand. 'That wasn't the reason you came to Beckbridge, then?'

'No.' While they walked she had gone on to tell him more about her life before the war, about Bob and her mother, and the sudden appearance of Lady Barstairs, just when everything looked blackest. 'She has been a brick,' she had said.

'Did you know you look alike? I took you for mother and daughter.'

She had laughed. 'Someone else said that. But we're not related. I think Mum would have said if we were.'

'Did Lady Barstairs say any more about why she reacted so strangely when I first arrived?'

'No. It's her business. I haven't asked for information. If she wants to tell me, she will.'

'I wrote and told Mom and Pop I'd visited and the people I'd met, but it'll be a while before I get a letter back. Perhaps when the war's over, they'll come over themselves. I'd like them to meet with you.'

At the time he had known he would be going back to start training for this raid on Dieppe, though he hadn't known the name of their objective then. If this night had been anything to go by, the struggle was going to be long and bloody. He hoped whoever was responsible had learnt a useful lesson, or all the men who had died would have given their lives in vain. He wished he hadn't come out of the dream of a sunny Beckbridge back to the cold sea. His teeth were chattering and his arm hurt like hell. Surely he must be getting near that destroyer by now. He risked turning to look. It was a little nearer. One more effort and he might make it. The trouble was he hadn't got the strength to make it. Floating up and down on the swell, he let his mind drift.

He was a child again, racing home from school so that he could join Pop in his workshop. He liked to do that, helping him strip down an engine, or fine-tune one so that it purred like a contented cat, while Pop talked. Given a little encouragement, he always had some good stories to tell, how he could trace his family back to Irish immigrants who fled Ireland during the potato famine in the 1840s and the terrible conditions on board ship, when thousands made the same journey squashed into the holds like cattle. The O'Donovans had been agricultural labourers and, on reaching Canada, had worked for a master for a time, but land was easily acquired and with hard work and prudence they saved enough to get a place of their own and dropped the initial O, claiming it was meaningless. Pop's grandparents had worked hard to give their son a good start in life, so by the time Grandpa married and Pop came along, they were in the way of being affluent enough to put him through engineering college. The First World War had interrupted his career, but he hadn't said much about that, except that it was hell. It was Mom who had told him about their meeting in Beckbridge.

'He was so handsome,' she said. 'All the girls fell in love with him, but it was me he chose. Little me, above all those grand people he could have had.' Had she meant Helen Barstairs? Was that why Lady Barstairs had reacted so strangely when he arrived? He couldn't imagine a greater contrast between the two women. Two women, he mused. Mum and Lady Barstairs; the one outgoing, noisy, her greying hair dyed the red of her youth, the other an aristocrat, thin as a rake and stiffly formal. Chalk and cheese, as his Aunt Joyce had said about Laura Drummond and Jenny Wainright when she knew he was taking them both out. Jenny. Laura. Strange, he could hear his mother weeping and Laura calling to him. 'Rouse yourself, man! Do you want to drift right back onto that beach? Get moving and come home, why don't you?' He lifted his good arm feebly and let it drop. He wasn't cold any more, just sleepy…

Daphne was reading a letter from Alec, watched by the twins. 'What does he say?' Donny asked, eager for news. The boys were in shorts and sandals, intending to go out on the harvest field after the reaper to catch rabbits. They would be in competition with the whole village, considering rabbit stew was a welcome addition to the minuscule meat ration, but they were young and strong and determined to come home with a brace apiece.

'He's coming on leave,' she told them.

'Yippee! When?'

'At the weekend. He wants to know if that's all right, Kathy.'

'Of course it is, he doesn't have to ask.'

She went on reading. 'He's seen Wayne. He says he can't say much about it until he gets here, but Wayne's all right though he's been wounded.'

'Wounded,' Jenny echoed. 'When? How?'

'I don't know. That's all he says.'

'It'll be Dieppe,' William put in. 'That was mostly Canadians, wasn't it?' The newspapers had reported the raid but little had been published about what had happened. By all accounts it hadn't been a success and was certainly not the second front everyone had been hoping for.

'Then Alec must have been there too,' Daphne said. 'I wish I'd known.'

'Why? It wouldn't have made any difference.'

'Do you think Joyce knows anything about it?' Jenny asked, thinking of Wayne, not Alec.

'Wouldn't she have said if she did?' Kathy looked closely at her

daughter, who seemed agitated. Did that mean she and Wayne…
Oh, no, not again. Ever since the Canadian had appeared in
the village, everyone had been talking about him, saying what a
handsome fellow he was, in spite of that red hair. And so polite, he
made even the old matrons feel special when he smiled at them; and
as for the young women, they lost what little sense they had been
born with. And it looked as though her daughter was among their
number. It had been the same with his father, charming all and
sundry. What had Helen made of his son's arrival? She hadn't liked
to ask, though Joyce had volunteered the information that she had
looked quite shaken. And so she might be. Suddenly to discover she
was not the only girl the man had been having an affair with must
have made a huge dint in her pride. Kathy could almost feel sorry for
her, except at the moment all her sympathy was for Jenny and trying
to prevent her from being hurt.

'I'll call in at the post office later and ask her,' Jenny said. 'Does
Alec say where Wayne is?'

'No. It's unlikely he'd know where the casualties were being taken,
don't you think? No doubt he'll tell us all he knows when he comes.'

Jenny left the house and made her way into the village, where
she encountered Joyce cycling towards Beck Lane, her round
finished. She had not heard the news. She was not Wayne's next of
kin and would not have been officially informed, a fact Jenny had
already guessed. 'I'm sorry to hear it,' she said. 'But I don't know
what we can do about it. I know the address he gave us to write to
him, but that's a forces address. If he's wounded, he'll be in hospital
somewhere. I expect he'll be in touch as soon as he's well enough.
Right now I've got other things on my mind. Ian's been arrested.'

'Arrested? What for? Black marketeering?'

'No. It was the Redcaps who came for him. He should have
reported to barracks in Wiltshire last week and didn't.'

'Surely he knew they would come for him?'

'The daft ha'porth seemed to think if he didn't live at home, they
wouldn't be able to find him.'

'Where was he living then?'

'In Lady Barstairs' summer house.'

'He never was!' Jenny could hardly suppress a smile. 'That must have been more uncomfortable than being in the army.'

'Anyway, it didn't do him a ha'porth of good, someone let on where he was and Charlie Harris, who had been told to look out for him, told the military.'

'You can't blame Charlie. He has to do his duty.'

'I know that. But, Jenny, I'd have a word with young Donny, if I were you, before the constable comes looking for him.'

'Donny? I thought that had all been nipped in the bud.'

'Seems not.'

Jenny returned home to find Helen sitting in the kitchen drinking tea with her mother. 'Ian Moreton's been arrested by the military police,' she told them. 'Dodging his call-up.'

'I know,' her mother said. 'Helen just told me, but it isn't only that. He was using the twins again. Constable Harris says they've got to be taught a lesson and he's all for dragging them up in front of a magistrate. And Alec's coming on leave in a couple of days. What will he think of me?'

'I hope he has more sense than to blame you, Mum. Aunt Helen, how long have you known about this?'

Helen was embarrassed by the direct question. She had been condoning Moreton's occupation of her summer house for several days, ever since she had come upon him sleeping there. He'd made himself at home, too. There were cushions and blankets and a Primus stove, a mug, a plate, packets of tea and sugar and goodness knows what else. Her furious indignation and her demand that he should take himself off before she called the police had been met with laughter. 'I don't think you'll do that,' he had said, so calmly she was taken aback. 'You wouldn't want your dirty linen washed in public, would you?'

'I don't know what you're talking about, you obnoxious little man.'

'Oh, come off it. Don't tell me you haven't got a skeleton in the cupboard you wouldn't want rattled.' He paused to light a cigarette and let his words sink in.

'I can't think what you mean.'

'A sad little tale of a man and a woman, not free to love but loving too freely, if you get my meaning.' And the horrible man had tapped the side of his nose.

Added to her fury that her privacy had been invaded and the one place she held in some reverence had been violated was the dreadful knowledge that her secret was no longer safe, and it wasn't Wayne Donovan who threatened it but this worm of a man. 'You are talking rubbish,' she said.

'Am I? Call the police then.'

'I would, but it wouldn't be fair on your wife and daughter.'

'Nor on yours. Though I fancy she's already getting her pound of flesh out of you.'

She only just managed to stifle the gasp that came to her throat and hoped he would not notice she was shaking. 'What on earth are you talking about?' She didn't know why she continued to answer him when a dignified silence might have served her better, but she had to discover how much he knew.

'I am talking about the madam who's taken over the Hall. The loss of your home was a high price to pay for her silence, wasn't it?'

She had wanted to kill him, she really had, and if there had been a weapon to hand, she might have attempted it. Instead she told him in her haughtiest lady-of-the-manor voice that she would give him twenty-four hours to pack up his stuff and leave, and if he had not gone by then, she would send for the constable. That had been several days ago and she hadn't dared carry out her threat.

She became aware of the two women looking at her in some puzzlement for her answer. 'I suspected he was hiding stuff in the summer house again, but as for living there… Who would want to do that when he's got a perfectly good home?'

'Was it you who sent for Charlie Harris?' Jenny asked.

'No.' It had been Laura who had come across the man making himself at home in the summer house and had taken it upon herself to ring the constable. What Helen was not sure about was if Moreton had told Laura what he had guessed. If he had, surely she would have said something?

'But what do we do about the twins?' Kathy asked. 'I begged Charlie Harris not to do anything. After all, if Ian is safely out of the way, they won't be tempted to do anything like it again. In fact, I promised him they would not.'

'Leave it to Daphne. She seems to be able to get through to them.'

'Leave what to Daphne?' The girl herself came into the kitchen in time to hear the last remark.

'Talk to the twins,' Jenny said. 'They've got themselves in a bit of bother.'

Donny slit the back legs of the two fat buck rabbits he had killed and threaded one leg through the tendon of the other and slid them along a pole as he had seen the men do. Lenny watched him in distaste. He'd had a stout stick and had stood with everyone else in a tight circle as the reaper mowed down the last few yards of standing wheat, waiting to chase and club the animals as they ran, but he hadn't got the heart to lash out and had let one good sized rabbit escape between his legs. Josh had been furious. 'Dozy fool,' he said scornfully. 'Tha's two hot dinners yew let go. We'll niver mek a countryman out o' yew.' He held out his hand to Donny. 'Yew did well, bor. Give 'em here. I'll tek care of 'em.'

'Not on yer Nelly,' Donny said. 'I caught 'em and I'm keepin' 'em. Our dad's comin' home at the weekend and he likes rabbit pie.'

He shouldered the pole and set off for home, with Lenny in the rear. They met Daphne in the lane. 'Good show!' she said, indicating the rabbits. 'Aunty Kathy will be pleased.' She fell into step beside them. 'Or she would be pleased if she hadn't had some bad news from Constable Harris.'

'What about?' Donny felt a frisson of fear, but refused to acknowledge it.

'Mr Moreton was arrested this morning.'

'So what?'

'I think you know.'

He remained silent and Lenny looked worried. Daphne ploughed on. 'You know what he was doing was illegal, don't you?'

'Don't know what he was doing.'

'Constable Harris thinks you do. He thinks you were an accessory.'

'What's that?' Lenny asked.

'Someone who helps a criminal. He's considered nearly as bad as the criminal himself. You wouldn't like to be arrested the day before your dad came home, would you?'

'I never done anything,' Lenny protested. 'I wasn't a...whatever it was you said.'

'Of course, if you were to cooperate, tell the constable all you know, then perhaps you wouldn't have to go to prison.' She addressed Donny because even if Lenny was involved, his brother was most likely to be the real culprit.

'Prison? You're having me on.' Nevertheless, Donny looked worried.

'No, I'm not.'

'It was only stuff from the Yanks. They've got plenty and Mr Moreton said it wasn't fair when English people were going short and he was just re...redistributin' it.'

'How do you think it gets to this country?'

'They get it sent from America.'

'How?'

'I dunno. Aeroplanes, ships.'

'Yes, ships. And who has to guard those ships and risk his life so that we can have more food?'

'Dad,' Lenny said promptly.

'Yes. How would you feel if your dad was drowned guarding

the ships bringing food to England only to have someone like Mr Moreton take it and make money out of it?' The argument she was using probably wouldn't stand close examination, but she could see that Donny had become thoughtful. 'And you helped him do it.'

'Oh, Donny,' Lenny wailed. 'I said not to—'

'Shut up!' Donny was in a fix. He hadn't connected his father's job with the stuff Mr Moreton was selling but now it had been pointed out to him, he knew he had to come clean. 'What do you want me to do?'

'Come with me to see Constable Harris. Make a clean breast of it and perhaps he'll let you off. That's if you promise never to do it again.'

Donny mulled this over for several minutes. They were turning into the farm gate before he spoke. 'You sure Mr Moreton's been arrested. They won't let him go?'

'Not until the war's over. You don't need to be afraid.'

'Ain't afraid.'

She let that go. Later that afternoon she accompanied him to the policeman's house where he told the whole story of how he had got into Ian's clutches and how he had been threatened with a beating if he didn't do as he was bid. Questioned, he told the policeman where most of the stuff had been hidden. Gamely, he insisted Lenny had had nothing to do with it. Charlie, who had had no intention of arresting the boy, was satisfied and let him go with a stern warning. Later, he went and retrieved what was still hidden and took it up to the airfield, where he asked to speak to the commanding officer. He didn't know whether anything would be done about it, but as far as he was concerned, he had done his duty. It gave him a great deal of satisfaction.

Alec, as he had come to expect, was made very welcome at Bridge Farm and was told to make himself at home, which he was very glad to do. He had no real home, nor would he have until the war was over, but an idea was forming in his mind, an idea of a future that looked far rosier than any dream he had had before. If Daphne agreed, of course; some women might not be prepared to take on two growing boys, but he was hopeful that she might. The twins liked her and she seemed to have a way with them their own mother never had. As soon as he could get her alone, he'd put it to her. In the meantime, he must be polite to everyone and answer their questions, the most urgent of which, after he had assured them he was hale and hearty, was how he had come across Wayne Donovan.

'We fished him out of the water,' he said. 'He'd been swimming for hours and was miles from the coast. The lookout spotted him first, but we thought it was a body, moving up and down on the swell, but then we saw him raise an arm as if he was trying to wave to us. We lowered a boat and fetched him aboard.'

'You said in your letter he was wounded,' Jenny said.

'Yes, shot in the arm. He was very weak and cold, but we soon had him in the sick bay, wrapped up warm, and a doctor fishing the bullet out. He'll be OK.'

'Thank God for that.'

'How did you know who he was?'

'I didn't, not right off. When he came to, he told the doctor his name but that didn't mean anything to the medics. It was only when he started chatting to Eric Marsh, the sick bay attendant, about Beckbridge and how he ought to let his aunt know he was OK, that Eric remembered I'd said my boys were in Beckbridge and I'd spent my last leave here, so he came and told me. I went to see him and we had a long chat and I promised to let everyone know he was all right. I thought you'd pass the news on to Mrs Moreton.'

'Yes, we did. Why couldn't you tell us that in your letter?'

'Letters are censored and I didn't know what I'd be allowed to say.'

'Seeing as it was a fiasco,' William said. 'You are talking about Dieppe, aren't you?'

'Yes. We took the men in and got as many out as we could, but we had to leave a lot behind. Captain Donovan was lucky.'

'Do you know where he is now?' Jenny asked.

'Sorry, I don't. They took him off on a stretcher as soon as we docked, along with all the others we had on board. He wasn't that badly hurt, mostly suffering from exposure and he was on the way to getting over that when we docked, so no doubt he'll get in touch.'

With that the subject was dropped. After a meal the like of which Alec hadn't had since the outbreak of war and even before that, he took Daphne for a stroll to the pub and asked her to marry him. 'I'll leave the Navy as soon as the war is over,' he said. 'We'll set up home anywhere you like and I'll get a job onshore.'

'Are you sure that's what you want, to leave the Navy, I mean? You're not just saying it for my sake?'

'No, it's what I want. I've spent so little time with the boys, they are almost like strangers and I want to remedy that. But I also love you and want to be with you, every possible minute not every so often when I'm on shore leave. So what do you say?'

He was not demonstrative; he didn't gush, but his quiet steadfastness was enough for her. He would never let her down and she happily agreed. Until then his kisses had been friendly pecks on the cheek rather than passionate, but now, in front of a pub full of people, he grabbed her in his arms and kissed her long and hard, to the accompaniment of ribald cheers. 'Let's go and wake up the boys and tell them,' he said, grinning at their audience.

'Will they be all right about it, do you think?'

'Yes, they'll be pleased as punch.'

'How do you know?'

'I asked them.'

She laughed and allowed him to lead her by the hand back to Bridge Farm and congratulations all round.

Wayne arrived back in the village in time for the wedding at the end of September. After a spell in hospital while his arm healed and he slowly regained his strength, he was given three weeks' leave to recuperate before returning to his regiment. He couldn't get home to Canada but Beckbridge was the next best thing. He wanted to see Laura, and as soon as he had answered all his aunt's questions and been given all the news, he set off for the Hall.

The fields, which had been growing corn the last time he had been there, were stubble now and the leaves on the trees were beginning to change colour, reminding him of home, where the fall was the most wonderful time of the year. He was feeling homesick but buoyed up by the prospect of seeing Laura and telling her what was in his mind. It had been her voice calling to him when he was ready to give up, her voice which had given him the will to wake up to the cold and pain and fight for his life. If he hadn't made that last effort, he wouldn't have been seen.

Someone had tidied up the garden of the lodge, he noticed, as he turned into the drive and walked purposefully towards the house. Most of the summer flowers had finished but there were yellow and red dahlias, bronze and white chrysanthemums, mauve Michaelmas daisies and one or two pink roses still blooming. He plucked one and stuck it in his buttonhole, sniffing its perfume. He almost danced up the steps to the front door and rang the bell.

'Sister Drummond about?' he asked the young girl who answered it, but his question was answered by Laura herself, who came from one of the downstairs rooms. He stood, grinning foolishly, drinking in the sight of her. Not even her severe hairstyle and that wide starched cap could diminish her loveliness in his eyes.

'Wayne!'

'Who else?' He flung his cap on a nearby table and moved swiftly forward to take both her hands and lean forward to kiss her lips. 'Oh, how good it is to see you again.'

'And I see you have recovered. Are you on leave?'

'Yes, three whole weeks. And don't tell me you're too busy to spend some of it with me, because I won't believe you.'

'We are quiet at the moment. Three boys who've been coming backwards and forwards for over a year have finally been discharged to return to their families.'

'That must please you.'

'Oh, it does. Everyone is over the moon when we can give a man back his pride in himself and send him off happy.'

'I hope you will send me off happy,' he said quietly, then added. 'Well, not send me off, not now, but in three weeks when I have to go back.'

She laughed, pretending she didn't understand. 'I'll do my best. Now come through to the kitchen and I'll make a cup of tea, then you can tell me all about it.'

'Now, tell me everything,' she said when he was seated at the kitchen table and she was filling the kettle. 'You didn't say much in your letter apart from the fact that you had been wounded, which Stella had told me anyway. And she got it from her mother, who got it from Jenny, who learnt it from the twins' father, who wrote to Daphne.' She laughed. 'It's better than any telegraph the way news gets round this village.'

'It was Dieppe,' he said. 'And some Jerry decided to take a pot shot at me when I tried to swim out to one of our ships standing by to take us off. Got me in the arm, which at the time was the only part of me above water. Either he was a crack shot or very lucky. Or I was, whichever way you care to look at it. I left a lot of men behind and that haunts me. God knows what the powers-that-be were thinking of; it was a hare-brained scheme. They said we had learnt valuable lessons. Too true we did.'

She turned from spooning tea leaves into the pot and put a hand on his. 'Don't be bitter, Wayne.'

'No. How does it go? "Ours not to reason why, ours but to do and die"?'

The kettle whistled and she turned from him to make the tea. By the time she had poured it and put a cup in front of him, he had regained his good humour. 'So, let me have chapter and verse,' he said. 'How are you? How's little Robby and Lady Barstairs? Where is she, by the way?'

'Gone into Attlesham to do some shopping. She's fine, and so is Robby. Stella's taken him down to the village in his pushchair. I was just about to break off for lunch. Would you care to join me?'

'Thanks.'

'You heard about Alec and Daphne?' she asked, scrambling dried egg in a small saucepan with some milk and margarine.

'Yes. I'm invited to the nuptials. I'm told the wedding breakfast is to be at Bridge Farm.'

'Have you been there yet?'

'No, I'll pop in on my way back.'

'Jenny will be pleased to see you. She wanted to visit you in hospital but until you wrote no one knew where you were.'

'Laura, you don't think... She doesn't think...'

She laughed lightly. 'You spread your net pretty widely when you were last here and left a whole heap of broken hearts behind you.'

'Not yours?'

'No, not mine.'

'Because you knew I would never knowingly break your heart or because you haven't got one to break?'

'Do you think I'm heartless?' She rescued two slices of toast from under the grill.

'Not at all.'

'So?'

'You know how it is with me? How I feel about you?'

'No, how do you feel?'

He grinned at her. 'Besotted.'

'Don't worry, it will pass.'

'I don't want it to. It's a great feeling. Do you know you saved my life?'

'Goodness, how did I do that?' It was becoming increasingly difficult to maintain the light tone of the conversation in the face of his earnestness, but something – she didn't know what, a still small voice perhaps – was telling her to beware.

'When I was struggling in the sea, cold and miserable, I almost gave up. It would have been so easy to stop trying, to go to sleep and let myself slip down. Then I heard your voice, very bracing it was, telling me to pull myself together and keep going. You said, "Come home."'

'That wasn't me, that was your own inner voice, your will to survive.'

'Same thing. Anyway, here I am. Home.'

'Your home is in Canada.' She remembered Steve asking her if she would ever go to Canada and her half-hearted denial. Had he guessed this was going to happen?

'Home is where the heart is.'

'Wayne, please don't.'

'Why not? You know I love you, don't you? It's as if I've always known you were there, in the background of my life, waiting for something to throw us together. It's a pity it had to be a war.' He looked down at the scrambled egg on toast she had just put in front of him and never felt less hungry in his life.

'The war,' she said, with a hint of bitterness. 'It tears people apart as well as throwing them together, that's what Helen said, and I remember someone else saying that we might try to forget it for a few hours, but we can't. It always comes back uninvited.'

'You are changing the subject.' He reached out and grasped her hand. 'Laura, I'm asking you…'

He never did finish the sentence because Helen breezed into the room, throwing off her hat and dumping a string bag full of shopping on the table. 'I swear the queues get longer every day. Two hours for a little bit of fish. Hallo, Wayne, you're back, I see.'

He stood up and shook her hand. 'Lady Barstairs, how are you?'

'Fighting fit,' she said. 'Fighting fit.' She had arrived home several minutes before and had been on the verge of entering the kitchen when she recognised the man's voice, so exactly like Oliver's, and stayed to listen. And what she had heard filled her with dread.

Chapter Ten

THERE WAS SILENCE in the kitchen for a moment. Helen didn't know what to say to fill the void. She had managed to stop Wayne asking his question, but he was undoubtedly on leave and would find another opportunity. She couldn't keep appearing at crucial moments. And suppose he were to mention to his aunt or grandmother what he had a mind to do, they would almost certainly tell him why he could never marry Laura Drummond. After her confrontation with Ian Moreton, Helen did not doubt they knew the truth, although it didn't look as though anyone had said anything to Laura or Wayne. But if they did? Wayne might disbelieve the story, or pretend to, but the doubt would have been planted and he would be sure to ask Laura to deny it. The thought of Laura finding out that way horrified and frightened her.

'We're having scrambled eggs,' Laura told Helen, breaking the uncomfortable silence. 'Would you like some?'

'No, thank you, I had something in the British Restaurant in Attlesham. I'll have a cup of tea, if you're making one.' If she were the tactful friend she would go and leave them to their tête-à-tête, but she dare not. She watched him eating the eggs Laura had cooked for him and wanted him gone. Guiltily, she wished he had been too seriously wounded to return to Beckbridge; she wished he could be sent back to Canada. But even that would not serve, considering the Moretons seemed to know the truth. She busied herself putting away her shopping and eventually he left, saying he would call for Laura the following morning. Having seen him to the door, Laura returned to clear the table and do the washing up.

'You told me you wouldn't consider going to Canada,' Helen said, as an opening gambit.

'You were listening at the door.'

'No, I was coming in, my hand on the doorknob, and heard Captain Donovan's last remark, that's all.'

'And immediately jumped to the conclusion that I was going to rush off to Canada with him.' Laura was almost certain Helen had been listening a lot longer than that and had timed her entrance on purpose to stop Wayne finishing what he was going to say. 'Why does it matter so much to you?'

'I don't want to lose you.'

'Helen, I didn't promise to live with you for ever. Nor that I would never marry. And you have no right to ask it of me.'

'I know. I wouldn't. But not Wayne. You can't marry him.'

'Why not?' She abandoned the washing-up, dried her hands and came back to stand over Helen. 'Because you were once in love with his father and can't accept that he married someone else? That has nothing to do with Wayne, or with me.'

'It's not that at all. Oh, this is so difficult.'

'Well, there's something bothering you, so why don't you tell me what it is.' She pulled out a chair and sat opposite Helen. 'You've evidently got something against Wayne, so out with it.'

Helen sat silent and miserable, unable to frame the words. In all the years she lived alone, while Anne was keeping a tight hold on her little girl, she imagined what she would say, knowing it would be difficult, but in her imagination it always had a happy ending. Not like this. Laura was already up in arms and she hadn't said anything yet. The tears started to roll silently down her face. Laura went into the dining room and fetched a tot of brandy which she put on the table in front of her.

'Drink this, it will steady you.' She sat down again and watched as Helen took a sip and sat twirling the stem of the glass in her fingers. She had always been upright and youthful looking, with more energy than many half her age, but now she appeared old and worn, her face and eyes betraying her anxiety. 'It can't be that bad surely?'

'Oh, my dear, I don't know how, but it's got to be said. You can't marry Wayne Donovan.' She paused and took a deep breath. 'You can't marry him because…because he is your half-brother.' There she had got it out and now there was no going back.

Laura thought she must be joking and tried to laugh. 'Tommy rot! I never heard anything so bizarre.'

'It's true. Oliver Donovan is your father.'

Laura stared at her, not at all sure she had heard right, but Helen's grey face and tortured eyes told her she had. 'You're out of your mind,' she said. 'Are you seriously trying to tell me my mother had an affair with Wayne's father? Where is she supposed to have met him? Here? And what was my father doing while it was going on? Oh, but you are telling me he wasn't my father, aren't you? It's a monstrous lie and I cannot think why you should say such a thing. I thought you were Mum's friend.'

'I was. In the end. As far as I know Anne was a loving and faithful wife and she looked after you as well as any mother, but she wasn't your mother. I am.'

Laura sat and stared at her with her mouth half open, unable to speak for a full minute. 'You're mad,' she said at last.

'No, it's the truth. I didn't want to have to tell you, but now I must.'

Laura could not take it in. She didn't believe it, not for a minute. Her mother, not her mother! It was preposterous. 'I've got a birth certificate—'

'Anne registered your birth.' Helen was calm now, calmer than Laura. It was as if she had dived into the middle of a whirlpool and come up in its epicentre, where there was no disturbance.

'Of course she did, she was my mum.' Helen had taken leave of her senses. She had lost a daughter in infancy and somehow got them mixed up and was pretending… That was it. Well, she wasn't going to condone it. 'You lost your daughter,' she said. 'You told me so yourself.'

'Yes, I lost her, I didn't mean she died. She was taken from me.'

'Are you saying… No, I won't hear of it. If you imagine—'

'I'm not imagining anything. Just listen—'

'No!' Laura stood up and rushed from the room to the sanctuary of her own quarters, where she slammed the door behind her and collapsed into a chair by the hearth. She felt her world – everything she had known and loved, happy memories of her childhood which had buoyed her up since Mum died – shattering around her, and all because Helen wanted a daughter and could not accept her own had died. Did she really believe what she was saying? She could almost feel sorry for her, but not quite.

She stood up and went towards the bedroom; she'd leave, start packing now, at once. Her hand was on the doorknob when something made her turn back and begin pacing the floor, from the window to opposite wall and back again. Where could she go? And there was Robby. He loved it here, and where could she get a job where he was so well looked after? And those poor airmen she was nursing: the one who cried himself to sleep every night; the other who had bad dreams and woke up screaming; the quiet one who stoically bore everything she did to try and help him; the joker; the one who always had his crooked red nose in a book. How could she abandon them? They needed her and she needed them; at least, she needed a well-paid job.

There came unbidden into her mind a picture of a set of carefully wrapped baby clothes and a shawl with the initials HB. Helen had been taken aback when she saw Robby wearing them. Then Kathy's mother had said how alike she and Helen were, and Wayne himself had mistaken them for mother and daughter. Why hadn't she questioned all that before? She had to get to the bottom of it. Summoning every bit of self-control she could muster she went downstairs again. Helen was sitting exactly as she had left her, except she had an envelope in her hand.

'You can't prove any of this.'

While Laura had been absent Helen had been to her room and fetched Anne's letter, realising she was going to need it to convince Laura she wasn't mad. 'Read this first, then if you like, I'll tell you the whole story.'

Laura picked it up, recognised the handwriting and opened it with shaking hands. Helen was now the one to minister; she went and fetched the brandy bottle and a second glass. She poured a tot for them both. Laura took a large mouthful and began to read.

'My dearest darling Laura. You are, and always have been, the centre of my existence, my precious daughter. And yet I have wickedly kept from you a most terrible secret which I have never had the courage to confess. I did not give you birth. I adopted you when you were a day old and pretended you were mine. You see, I could not have a child of my own and I longed for one, a baby to hold in my arms and call my own. The midwife told me of a place where mothers had babies they didn't want which were put up for adoption. I thought I was giving a home to a baby girl no one wanted. It wasn't true, as I found out when you were about three and I met Helen. Until this year when I became ill, I kept her at arm's length and made her promise not to try and contact you, and I would tell you the truth when you were old enough to understand. I didn't keep that promise, my darling, because I was afraid of what you would say. I cannot go to my Maker with this on my conscience, neither can I bring myself to confess it to you. I know you will be angry. And so, here it is in black and white. Helen will tell you the details. Listen to her and try to understand, and please try to forgive me. You have given me so much happiness, I could not have wished for a better daughter.' It was blotched with tears and signed. *'Your ever loving Mum.'*

It was too much to take in, but the question uppermost in her mind, after she had finished weeping, was why, considering Mum had been dead over eighteen months, Helen had not given it to her before. She looked up at Helen and wished she could hate her. She *wanted* to hate her. It was all her fault. And round and round in her head went the refrain: *Why? Why? Why?* She read the letter again, while the clock ticked the afternoon away. Nurse Symonds put her head round the door, looking for Laura to help change dressings. Helen looked up and put her finger to her lips. 'Make sure we are not disturbed for a little while, will you, Nurse?' The nurse went away again; it was doubtful if Laura even knew she had been.

'Have you read this?' Laura asked at last.

'No, but I know what's in it.'

'Why have you kept it so long?'

'I hoped never to have to give it to you. You loved Anne and I did not want to destroy that.'

'If that was the case, why did you make Mum promise to tell me when I was old enough to understand?'

'I always wanted you to know that I was your mother, that I loved you and hadn't willingly given you up. But I changed my mind when Anne became ill. It didn't seem to matter any more. It was more important to make a home for you and Robby. She wanted that, you know.'

'I know, but I didn't know why. You and she seemed to have so little in common.'

Helen smiled. 'Except you.'

'And my father is Oliver Donovan?'

'Yes.'

'I am the product of some sordid little extra-marital affair which had to be hushed up. It makes me feel sick.'

'It wasn't like that at all.'

'Oh, how else would you describe it? You have made a bastard of me.'

'Oh, Laura, don't say that. If I could have kept that secret for ever I would have done. If Oliver's son had not come to Beckbridge... I didn't know he'd married Valerie Wilson. But today... I knew it would all come out because you had to be stopped from marrying Wayne.'

'Oh, I can quite see that,' she said bitterly. 'And now everyone is going to know it, they will all be talking about us. Thank you for that!'

'Laura, don't be bitter. I love you, always have, and I love little Robby. I loved your father too, a little too much, as much as you loved Bob.'

God, Helen was saying Robby was her grandchild! 'There's no comparison. I wasn't married to someone else.'

'No, I know that. But you do understand what it is like to love and be loved to the exclusion of all else. You may think of me as an embittered middle-aged widow, but I was once young and I fell in love, not wisely as it turned out. But it needn't make any difference to us. We can still keep the secret; no one will say anything to your face.'

'Brazen it out, you mean, like you've been doing ever since you brought me to Beckbridge.'

'Yes.'

'I can't. I'm not like that. And in any case, I'll have to tell Wayne.'

'That's up to you. But if you don't, I am afraid his grandmother will.' She paused. 'I would like to explain, tell you how it happened. It wasn't sordid, I promise you—'

'I don't want to know.'

'Very well. I won't press you.'

'I'd like to leave here, go away and hide myself, forget you ever said anything, forget I'd ever met you, forget I'd ever met Wayne Donovan.' She gave a cracked laugh. 'By the way, I never intended to marry him. He's a nice man but I was never in danger of falling in love with him.'

'Oh, Laura, don't leave, please. You are needed here, not just by me—'

'I know that and for that reason I'm going nowhere, not right now anyhow. I have a job to do and until it's done, or someone comes to take my place, I'm staying, but it doesn't mean I have to like it. Now, if you will excuse me, I'll be getting back to work.' She got up and left Helen sitting staring into the distance. The secret was out and she wished with all her heart it had not been necessary to reveal it. The happy little world she had created in the last eighteen months had collapsed around her, and not for the first time she wondered why Oliver had come back to Beckbridge all those years ago – not only come back, but had not seen fit to call at the Hall and tell her he was marrying the chambermaid. What she remembered of her, she was common and had a raucous laugh. Mama had had to remonstrate with her more than once over it. Had Oliver made her laugh? Had they laughed at her? Even so long afterwards, she burnt with humiliation.

The arrival of Stella with Robby brought her out of her reverie. She kissed him and asked him if he had had a nice walk and found him one of Mrs Ward's homemade biscuits. Life had to go on.

'You'll have to talk to him sooner or later.' Helen had come into the sitting room to find Laura staring out of the window and had come up behind her to see what she was looking at. The window gave a view of the front lawn and drive before it disappeared round the bend towards the lane into the village. On the left was the front lawn, where the patients sometimes walked and amused themselves with croquet, though there was no one there now with autumn approaching and a cool wind blowing. On the right was an avenue of trees bordering the drive, beyond which was the park. Wayne was leaning with his back against one of the trees, one foot on the trunk behind him, smoking a cigarette.

Laura turned towards her. Nowadays they hardly spoke except when necessary to do their work or maintain a semblance of normality in front of Robby and the staff. She knew it was her fault, that if she could only unbend a little Helen would be glad to talk to her, to recapture the pleasant familiarity they had enjoyed before the bombshell. She had been forced to come to terms with the fact that Helen really was her mother, but that didn't mean she had to like it. She had been cruelly deceived, not only by Helen but by her mum. She could never think of her as anything else but Mum, whatever the genetics of the relationship. If it had been explained to her while she was growing up that she had been adopted, she would have been able to accept it. She might even have had a lively curiosity about the woman who had given her birth, but that's all it would have been. Mum would still have been Mum. There were so many questions unanswered, how she came to be registered as the daughter of Anne and Tom Drummond for one, and how, if her mother wasn't pregnant, she had been able to pass the baby off as her own, but she couldn't bring herself to ask Helen; it would be tantamount to acceptance, to condoning what had been done, and she wasn't ready for that. She hadn't talked to Wayne either, making excuses not to see him; she was too busy, or there was an emergency on the ward. He had taken to hovering in the grounds. 'I know.'

'Why not do it now?'

'It's easy for you to say. You've done your bit, shattering my happiness, now you want me to pass it on. It's like a contagion, spreading and spreading, until we're all miserable.'

'Laura, that's not fair.' Helen, who in any case never raised her voice, spoke so softly her words were hardly audible.

'I don't feel like being fair. No one's been fair to me.'

'I tried.' She paused. 'Talking of being fair, what about that young man? Is it fair to keep him hanging about like that? He hasn't done anything wrong.'

'No, you're right.' She turned away and left the room.

Helen continued to watch until she saw Laura pushing Robby in his chair down the drive towards Wayne, then she turned away and went to the kitchen to make afternoon tea for the patients.

'Laura, at last.' He threw his cigarette stub down and pushed himself away from the tree. 'What's happened? Why have you been avoiding me? What have I done to offend you? You knew I didn't intend anything improper, didn't you? It wasn't a dirty weekend I was proposing.'

'I know.'

He fell into step beside her as she went on down the drive at a rattling pace. 'Then what?'

She had almost reached the lane. To proceed would mean running the risk of meeting someone she knew. All the villagers were used to seeing her and Robby about the place and always stopped for a chat. She'd never get it off her chest if they were interrupted. She turned suddenly and made off across the grass towards the lake. He followed.

She stopped and faced the pushchair towards the water, where Robby could watch the ducks and be seen from inside the summer house, put on the handbrake and went into the building. 'Sit down,' she said, pointing at the bench with its new cushions. 'It's a long story and not particularly edifying.'

He did as he was told. She sat down beside him, leaving a good yard between them. He attempted to lighten the atmosphere with a smile but was met with a blank look and an emptiness in her eyes which alarmed him. 'It can't be that bad.'

'It is. You remember you once thought Helen and I were mother and daughter?'

'Yes. What about it?'

'Well, we are.'

This didn't register with him as earth-shattering. 'Have you only just found out?'

'Yes.'

'I can see that it might be a shock to you if you didn't know about it, but how does that justify hiding yourself away and refusing to see me?'

'You don't understand. It was Helen telling me who my father was.' She gulped air. 'His name, so Helen tells me, was Oliver Donovan.'

He stared. 'Pop?'

'Yes.'

'I don't believe it.'

'Neither did I, but she assures me it's true. She was afraid we –

you and I – were getting too close and had to stop it. According to her we are half-brother and -sister.'

'Can she prove it?' He was no more ready to believe it than she had been.

'I don't know. Why would she lie?'

'Well, I want more than her word for it. It doesn't have to be my father. She could have been with anyone.'

'I'm sure she was never like that. I believe she was genuinely in love with him, but whether he was in love with her is a different matter. But she was married and so, I suppose, it was doomed from the start.'

'Did she tell you that?'

'No, I guessed from things she's said.'

'Not good enough.' He paused. 'When's your birthday, the date you were born?'

'The fifth of March, 1918, at least that's what's on my birth certificate. I can't even be sure that's true.'

'Does it say who your parents were?'

'Tom and Anne Drummond.'

'There you are then. The whole thing is a fabrication from beginning to end. The old dear's nuts.'

'No, she isn't. She gave me a letter my mother had written a few days before she died and that confirmed everything.'

'What? About my father?'

'No, not that. About Helen being my mother. It was Helen who told me about your father.'

'Do you think she could have been crossed in love, a teensy bit jealous of my mom? Mom and Pop have always been devoted to each other and if he chose Mom over her, she wouldn't be pleased to think you and I were making a go of it, would she?'

'It could be the other way about. Your father was rejected by Helen because she was married and turned to your mother for consolation. Tell me, when were you born?'

'September 1918, after Pop was invalided out and returned to

Canada with Mom. I thought I'd told you that already.'

'You probably have, but it didn't register. You are six months younger than me, so it looks as though he was two-timing the both of them.'

'He wouldn't, he's not a bit like that. He's honest and God-fearing—'

'You don't want to believe it.'

'Too true I don't. Do you?'

'I don't want to, but I think I must.'

'Well, I'm not giving in that easily. I'm going to get to the bottom of it.'

'How?'

'Ask my father. Write to him.'

'But supposing your mother knows nothing about it, won't it hurt her rather badly?'

'Then I'll wait until this bloody war is over and I can go home and ask him face to face.'

'I don't envy you that task.' She got up to go to Robby, who was beginning to fidget. He followed her.

'Is that all you can say?'

'Isn't it enough?'

'What about us? You know how I feel about you. I thought you—'

'No, Wayne, it was never like that.' She picked up the teddy bear Robby had thrown on the ground and gave it back to him. 'I don't mind having you for a brother, though. In fact, I think I might like it. What I don't like is all the secrecy.'

'What are you going to do? Shout it from the rooftops?'

'Certainly not. The fewer people who know about it the better. I've got a job to do in this war and so have you, so we'd better get on with it.' She let the brake off the pushchair and set off back to the Hall.

They parted company when they reached the drive and she took Robby back for his tea, leaving Wayne to kick his heels in frustration. He felt as though someone had punched him in the gut, had taken the wind out of him, and he needed to think. Instead of going back into the village, he walked for hours, finding his way along little-used lanes, climbing stiles, crossing meadows, dawdling through a wood where the newly fallen leaves formed a soft carpet for his feet. He flung himself under a beech tree and lay back looking up through its branches to a sky riven with clouds. The summer was at an end and at home in Canada his mom and pop would be going about their usual tasks: reading the news, commenting on the fact that the leaves on the trees were beginning to turn colour and wondering how soon it would be before he came home. Oh, how he longed for home!

His immediate reaction to Laura's news had been disbelief. He still didn't believe it. It wasn't that he didn't believe Laura was Helen's daughter; he had always suspected something of the sort, what he couldn't swallow was that his own father was involved. What he wanted to know was why Lady Barstairs had told Laura he was. Was she a jealous old hag, fantasising about his father and ending up believing it herself? He toyed with the idea of taxing her with lying but decided against it. He got up and returned to Beck Cottage, but Joyce was at work and the house was empty. He went across the road to see his grandmother.

Built of brick and flint, her cottage was the end one of a terrace of four, intended for farm labourers. If his aunt's cottage was small, this was miniscule. Two tiny rooms downstairs and a lean-to scullery at the back, two bedrooms upstairs. There were no services laid on and the cooking was done on a kitchen range and a Primus stove. 'You are just in time to draw some water for me,' was her greeting, as she picked up a galvanised bucket and handed it to him. 'Make sure you close the lid of the well properly, don't want anyone falling in.' The well served all four cottages.

He filled the bucket and took it back to her. She ladled water into a kettle and put it on the Primus. 'There's no one at home across the way,' he said, watching her fetch a tea pot and caddy from a cupboard in the corner.

'Well, there wouldn't be. Joyce don' leave off 'til six.' The kettle whistled and she made the tea, then fetched two cups and saucers and a jug of milk. 'Now, let's sit down and have a cuppa and you can tell me what's buggin' you. Suff'n is, I know. Yew've bin like a bear with a sore head for days. Fallen out with Laura, hev yew?'

'Yes and no.' He sat at the table opposite her. It was spread with a stained check oilcloth.

'Go on.'

'She wouldn't see me and when I did at last get to talk to her she told me such a tale, I don't know what to believe.'

'She's Lady Helen's daughter.'

'You knew!'

'Don' tek a genius to work it out. Her ladyship disappeared for months and it must ha' bin about the time Laura were born. Her ma said she had gone to live near where her husband were stationed, but I know for a fact he were in France.' She poured two cups of tea while she talked and handed one to him. 'Taken prisoner, he were. Stands to reason it had to be hushed up. Didn't know she'd kept in touch with the girl though. She shouldn't hev brought 'er back here.'

'Why not?'

'Bound to put the cat among the pigeons.'

'Laura's only just found out herself. She's very upset about it.'

'Well, she would be, wouldn't she? But I don't see why you should get y'self in a tizzy over it.'

'There's more.'

'Oh.' It was said guardedly.

'Yes. Lady Barstairs told Laura that Pop was her father. Why would she do that, d'you suppose? Could it be true?'

She shrugged. 'How should I know? Oliver was often up at the Hall, but then so were a lot of others. The Earl kept open house for serving officers. Could ha' bin anyone.'

'Laura believes it, that's the trouble. She says we're half-brother and -sister. Do you think we are?'

'Dunno, do I?'

'Who does know?'

'Your pa might. There ag'in, he might not. He'd married your ma and gone back to Canada time her ladyship come back from wherever it was she went.'

'It's the devil of a mess.'

She reached out a gnarled hand and put it over his. 'Forget it, son. Put it behind you. There's others girls, just as pretty, and they don' hev someone else's nipper hangin' onto their skirts. It i'n't worth all the grief.'

It was hard advice to take but he had to accept it. He knew it was no good hanging about the village. He couldn't put on the cheerful face and broad grin everyone was used to seeing, and he might as well take himself off back to his unit. At least there no one knew what he was going through, but he'd go to the wedding, if only to prove to himself that he was in control and his grandmother was right.

He didn't see Laura again until they were filing into church. The twins, dressed in long trousers, school blazers and pristine white shirts, were full of self-importance as they acted as ushers and directed everyone to their pews. He saw her sitting on the other side of the aisle between Helen and Kathy with Robby on her lap and gave her a half smile as he took his seat between Joyce and Stella.

Alec had asked a few friends who, like him, were on shore leave while their ship was repaired after a run-in with a U-boat, and Daphne had invited one or two London friends. The rest of the church was filled with villagers, all of whom had made an effort to dress for the occasion. Laura hadn't seen so many colourful dresses or fancy hats since before the war. Ian, now a private soldier in training somewhere in the north of England, was missing, as were Ken and Steve, who couldn't get leave. They were training for some new job but were expecting to be posted to an operational unit at any time.

The bridegroom looked smart and handsome in his uniform, with his best man beside him, also in uniform, and the bride looked radiant as she came down the aisle on William's arm, dressed in pale blue satin with a saucy little pill box hat to match, with Jenny and Meg as bridesmaids. The congregation rose to their feet and the service began. It was a poignant moment for Laura because she found herself remembering her own wedding day, a day without a wedding. That was the worst day of her life, as bad as learning she was not her mother's child, even worse than the day Dad had died because he had been very ill and in constant pain and she could not selfishly wish to prolong that.

She took part in the service, threw confetti at the happy couple afterwards and went to Bridge Farm for the reception. There was plenty of food; living on a farm did have its compensations. She ate ham sandwiches, scotch eggs and sausage rolls and drank home-made elderberry wine, which was very good, talked and laughed, teased the twins, and all the while in the back of her mind was the question, how much did everyone know? Were they staring at her, talking behind her back?

She looked round the throng. Alec and Daphne, obviously happy, were circulating, accepting everyone's good wishes; Helen was helping Kathy take round plates of food; Wayne was standing between Meg and Jenny, entertaining them with some story about his arrival in England and not looking at her; Joyce was laughing at something Constable Harris was telling her and Stella was openly flirting with Alec's best man. Lenny, she supposed it was Lenny because he was the quiet one, had taken charge of Robby and they were sitting under the table playing with a toy farmyard she guessed had once been Steve's. These people had become her friends, they had taken her to their hearts in a way no one in crowded London had ever done. If they knew the truth about her, they were not showing it; she was drawn into their conversation as if she were one of them.

William called for silence and proposed a toast to the bride and groom, and the groom replied, amid much laughter. The health of the bridesmaids was drunk and then William added another toast. 'We must not forget those who cannot be with us today,' he said.

'So let us drink to absent friends.' They echoed his words and sipped their wine, each thinking of someone they knew who could not be with them, either because they had lost their lives, were missing or taken prisoner or, like Steve and Ken, on duty. Laura, raising her glass, caught Helen's eye and found herself the recipient of a tentative smile. If she were going to stay in the village, even for a short time, she was going to have to get along with her. It was the first time she had admitted to herself that she didn't want to leave, but it made her want to know the details of what she had so furiously refused to entertain before. She needed to understand, to know about her father, the father who had given her life, not the one who had loved and nurtured her in childhood. Then she would make up her mind whether to go or stay.

That evening, when she and Helen were sitting together in strained silence in the sitting room, the wedding over and the newly married couple gone off on a few days' honeymoon, the chores for the day finished and Robby tucked safely in bed, she ventured to say, 'Helen, you said you'd explain.'

'Yes, when you are ready.'

'I'm ready now. My head is full of questions, mostly about Mum and Dad, I mean Tom, of course. Did he know the truth? How did Mum manage to convince everyone I belonged to her? If you loved me, how could you bear to give me up? If someone had tried to take Robby from me, I would have fought tooth and nail to keep him.'

Helen managed a smile at this catalogue, but it showed Laura was coming round and it gave her hope. 'I'll tell you the whole story as it happened and that will probably answer most of your questions. If you want to ask more when I've finished, then I'll do my best to answer them.'

'OK.'

There was a whole minute of silence and Laura began to wonder if Helen would ever start. She got up and drained the last of the brandy into two glasses and wondered incongruously when they would be able to get any more. Then she put a glass in Helen's hands and sat down opposite her. 'I'm listening.'

Helen had been wondering where to begin. Where was the beginning? Meeting Oliver? Marrying Richard? Anne's miscarriage? Or was Laura's need to know centred only on how she came to be given to Anne and how her two mothers had met and connived to keep her in ignorance? She could baldly state the facts, but that would not give Laura a true understanding of a heartbreaking situation. She smiled suddenly. 'I feel I ought to begin, once upon a time there was a beautiful princess—'

'Dad used to start his stories like that when I was a little girl. I loved him. He'll always be my dad, whatever you say, and Mum will always be my mum.'

'Of course. But this is not a fairy story; there is no happy ending. I thought there was when you and Robby came to live with me and we got on so well together, but it was a fool's paradise. I think I need to explain the kind of life I lived as a child and as a young girl growing up. It couldn't have been more different from Anne's. We were at opposite ends of the social scale, but the harsh discipline Anne endured in the charity home and when she went out to work was matched by my father's autocratic ruling of everyone, including my mother and brother and me; both lives were loveless until your mother met Tom and I met Oliver. My father's word was law and it never occurred to us that he was ever in the wrong. I was expected to follow a strict social code and when he said Richard would make me a suitable husband, I believed him. I was only eighteen...' Now she had started, her mind went back to the time and she found herself reliving it. She forgot her audience and spoke as if thinking aloud. 'I was so ignorant of life, ignorant of everything. Until I met Oliver, I had no idea what love was. I suppose you could say I didn't know any more afterwards either...'

Laura listened without interrupting. She was reluctant to agree that Helen's life had been so strict or that Lady Hardingham had been so afraid of her husband that she could connive in the physical wrenching apart of mother and baby, but she could not doubt it had happened. And it was hard to take in the fact that Mum had deceived everyone in the way she had, pretending to be pregnant, but it was typical of Dad to forgive her and to love the daughter who had been thrust upon him. He came out of the story the best of all. Helen's description of her search for her daughter after her parents died and her confrontation with Anne was heart-rending because she could identify with both sides. 'You were a happy child, anyone could see that,' Helen said. 'It would have been cruel to try and take you from your home, even though I believed I had the legal right to claim you back because it wasn't a proper adoption. I made a promise to Anne and I kept it, not willingly, I may add, but for your sake. Anne repaid me by sending for me when she was ill and bringing us together. Only you can judge whether she was right to do so.'

'I don't want to judge anyone. I only want to understand.'

'And do you?'

'I think so. Did you ever see Oliver Donovan again?'

'No. I wrote to him as soon as I knew I was pregnant, quite expecting him to acknowledge his child, even if he could not come back immediately, but I had no reply. I didn't even know he had survived the war until his son arrived in Beckbridge. I don't even know if he knows about you. What did Wayne say when you told him?'

'He refused to believe it and talked of confronting his father for confirmation. I advised against it on the grounds it would upset his mother. There's enough people being made miserable over this without adding more.'

'Do we have to be miserable? Everyone acted for the best. No one's to blame.'

'I feel, oh, I don't know, hard done by.'

'Should you?' Helen looked searchingly at her, hoping for reconciliation, but realising perhaps it was a little too soon, but at least they were talking again and that was a step in the right direction. 'Just think what could have happened if you had been handed over to someone who didn't care, someone who, having got you, decided they could not love you. Your life might have been very different.'

'I know. I've been telling myself that over and over, that I ought to think myself lucky having two loving mothers. I suppose I will come to appreciate that in the end, but at the moment all I can think of is that I am a bastard, that my birth certificate is a forgery, and if I were ever to fall in love and want to marry, I would have too much explaining to do. And there's Robby. What will he think when he grows up?'

'Why should he think anything, except that you are his mum and you love him. And there is a much better term than bastard for both of you, and that is "love child". It is a pity they don't put that on birth certificates. And if the man you love is half decent, he won't care two hoots what happened in the past.'

'It's a good thing it's not Wayne.' Laura smiled suddenly, thinking of Steve. He knew she had never been married. Perhaps he also knew about her and Helen, or about Helen and Oliver; everyone else in the village seemed to. Poor Steve, she shouldn't have been so offhand with him. If he were to walk through the door this very minute, she would throw herself into his arms. He had always turned up when she needed him, so where was her rock now?

The year and the war ground on relentlessly – Stalingrad, Moscow, North Africa, Malta, U-boats attacking Atlantic convoys; air raids. The BBC and the papers told the population all they were allowed to. Every morning the newsreaders reported more raids on enemy targets, of damage done and how many allied aircraft had not returned. These included American Flying Fortresses and Liberators, which set off from their bases in East Anglia to pound enemy targets in daylight. The people of Beckbridge looked up as they passed over and wished them a safe return. At the end of October, General Montgomery's forces inflicted a heavy defeat on Rommel at El Alamein. It was the first good news for a very long time and everyone was suddenly more cheerful. The Government allowed the church bells to be rung on the following Sunday in celebration, though Churchill warned them it was not the end, nor even the beginning of the end, but it was perhaps the end of the beginning.

Could she say the same about her own life? Laura wondered. Helen's explanation had forced her to come to terms with the truth, and for everyone's sake she was doing her best to behave just as she always had. It was easy when she was at work; she could put her problems behind her and concentrate on helping her patients. But when she was off duty, when, at the end of a long day, she was able to relax and turn her mind to other things, it all came back to her, heaped itself in her brain and buzzed round and round like a relentless bee, until she didn't know what to think, what to feel.

The beginning was gone – Mum, Dad, Bob, Wayne and probably Steve too. Only now did she admit to herself that Steve had been more than just her rock. She had come to love him, to look forward to his letters, to seeing him on his infrequent leaves, seeing the grin spreading across his face and into his eyes, hearing his soft, warm voice, feeling his kisses, making her feel wanted and special. She was sorry she had been so off-putting when he asked her to marry him, but then again she was not. She would hate to have him change his mind about her, hate it even more if he felt duty-bound to marry her because he had asked and couldn't go back on his word. Better this way. The end of the beginning. What lay ahead she could not even guess.

It was called 'oboe', a navigational device that used radio pulses transmitted from two stations in England to the aircraft in the air. By measuring the time they took to reach the plane and return, its position could be calculated and a signal sent to tell the bomber exactly when it was over its target. Steve wasn't sure about that, but post-raid reconnaissance seemed to confirm that the bombing was becoming more accurate.

Having done their Pathfinder training, Steve and Ken had been posted to Marham and been allocated a Mosquito, which, according to Ken, looked like a pregnant duck because of its swollen belly intended to take a 4,000 lb bomb. They carried no weapons themselves and were expected to rely on speed to get them out of trouble and the fact that the Mosquito could climb higher than enemy fighters.

Tonight, the Pathfinders had gone in to mark the target with coloured target indicators just as the main force arrived over it. 'Good timing,' Steve had commented, praising his navigator, as he turned for the home run. By then the flak formed an almost continuous wall of fire and it was hell trying to get through it. They flew low, trying to keep under the guns' trajectory. Once over the North Sea, they would make height.

'Skip, I don't want to worry you,' Ken said laconically. 'But I reckon we're taking half a German forest home with us, do you think you can make a little height?'

Steve smiled to himself as he obediently lifted the nose a fraction and they left Germany behind and flew on over the Dutch countryside. This was their last op before some much longed-for leave; he would be at home for Christmas. His mother was as excited as a child. It showed itself in the enthusiasm in her letters, the plans she was making. She spoke of stirring the pudding and everyone making a wish, of finding the ingredients for making a cake, of fattening a goose and killing a pig. It was beginning to affect him. Home for Christmas, how great that sounded when said aloud. Ken, poring over his charts behind him, heard him and smiled. 'Belgian coast coming up and a lot more flak,' he reported.

Steve was relieved when they left the land behind and the sea appeared below them, glinting like pewter in the moonlight. Now he could make some height. He hardly had time to do so before they were spotted by a lone enemy fighter which dived into the attack. Steve took evasive action, but the Mosquito pitched suddenly, leaving him struggling with the controls.

'The bastard's hit us,' Ken said, as the starboard engine died and a flicker of flame appeared on the wing.

They had been flying low, too low to bail out safely. He had to climb. He could fly on one engine, but if the fire spread and they lost the wing, they would be in real trouble. 'Don't know if we can get her home,' he said. 'If I can get her up, you can bail out.'

'What do you mean "you"? What are you going to do?'

'Stay with her. I'm going to try and make it to the English coast before bailing out. If I can't, I'll ditch her in the sea as near as I can and hope Air Sea Rescue find me.' It was said breathlessly in spurts because he was busy trying to keep the aircraft on an even keel.

'And you expect me to throw myself out and leave you to it? Not on your Nelly. I'm staying with you.'

'Then plot a course to the nearest bit of England. If I can only get this crate up, I can weave about a bit and try to put that damned fire out.'

If he could stay in the air another half hour or so, they might just make land. Neither man had much to say; Steve was too busy trying to fly the stricken aircraft and Ken was wondering if he had been wise to say he would stay; the chances of them making it home were very slim. If the fire spread to the fuselage, they were done for. 'We've done it,' he said, jubilantly. 'Essex marshes below us.'

'And not a moment too soon. Get out now. I'll radio our position and follow you.'

He watched Ken tumble out and his canopy open, then radioed base with their position and began to look for a suitable field to land in. He couldn't just bale out and leave the aircraft to crash into houses or a school or something like that. Besides, he was losing height rapidly and was too low for his parachute to open properly. He steeled himself for the impact.

Ken landed awkwardly, but thanked the Lord he was in one piece, then turned to see where Steve was and realised he had not left the aircraft. Surely the silly bugger was not trying to land it? The plane was engulfed in flames. He watched it miss a church steeple by a hair's breadth and disappear behind a group of trees. It seemed a lifetime before he heard the explosion and saw a sheet of flame shoot skywards. He felt sick. He struggled out of his harness and limped across the field to meet the three men who were running towards him. He was home and safe, but Steve? He stumbled into the arms of the first man. 'My pilot,' he muttered. 'Find my pilot.'

Joyce, always the bringer of news, took the yellow envelope to the farm. 'It's not always bad news,' she said diffidently to Kathy, who held it in nerveless fingers, unable to bring herself to open it. They were, as usual, in the kitchen. The breakfast table was still littered with the used plates and dishes. Half a loaf and a scattering of breadcrumbs lay on the breadboard. A pot of homemade marmalade had a teaspoon sticking up in it. The dog snoozed under the table, waiting for his master to rise and begin his day's work. Jenny was cramming a pile of exercise books into her case. The boys were gathering up satchels and football boots ready for school. Meg and Josh were rattling around in the yard. It was a day like any other.

William reached up and took the envelope from her, slit it open and began to read. 'He's not dead,' he said, letting his breath out in a long sigh of relief. 'Wounded in action.'

'Thank God for that small mercy,' Kathy breathed, sinking into a chair. 'Does it say what his injuries are or where he is?'

'No.' He looked at Joyce. 'Was he flying with Ken?'

'Yes. Ken telephoned me at the post office. That's how I knew the news wasn't bad, at least, not as bad as it could have been. They were hit by a German fighter, but Steve insisted on trying to fly home. He got them as far as Essex, when Ken baled out. Steve was going to follow but Ken never saw him leave the aircraft. He crash landed it.' She paused. 'I don't know how badly he's injured. Ken said he'd been taken to a hospital in Hammersmith.'

'Isn't that where Laura used to work?' Kathy asked William.

'I believe so.'

'Ring them up, find out what's happened.'

He disappeared into the hall, where the telephone stood on a table, while everyone waited silently.

He came back five minutes later. 'They were a bit cagey. He has a broken arm and burns to his face and hands. But he's not in immediate danger.'

'Burns. Oh no,' Kathy said. 'William, we must go to him. They'll let us see him, won't they?'

'So they said. We'll go tomorrow.'

'The Hall,' Kathy said suddenly. 'We'll get him moved to the Hall. Laura will look after him and we can see him every day until he's well again.'

She had perked up with this and he didn't like to tell her he didn't think they would be able to dictate where their son was treated.

Steve surfaced from a drug-induced sleep only to wish he hadn't. He'd been having a lovely dream. It was high summer and he was in the air, but the aircraft he was in made no noise; it flew silently, swooping about the sky like a bird. Below him was his father's farm and in the yard stood his parents and sister and old Josh and Laura. Laura was in her nurse's uniform. They were looking up at him and waving, and he could hear them calling to him. Now all he could feel was a pain so agonising he couldn't stop himself whimpering like a child.

'Steve, can you hear me?'

That was Mum. He tried to open his eyes, but they were so filled with mucous he couldn't see properly. Instead he tried to lift his hand. That didn't work either. He groaned and mumbled, 'Mum, what are you doing here?'

'I can't understand him,' Kathy said to William. Tears were rolling silently down her face. Her son, her lovely boy was unrecognisable. His face was covered with a dressing with only a tiny hole for his mouth and slits for his eyes; his hands were enclosed in huge mittens. There was a drip attached to one arm and the other was in plaster as far as the wrist. 'Did you hear what he said?'

'No, couldn't make it out.'

'I wish I could see him properly and touch him. Do you think he knows we are here?' she asked the nurse who had shown them to Steve's bed.

'You can touch his legs. I'm sure he knows it's you. He's had quite a lot of morphine so he isn't making much sense at the moment.'

They stood and looked down at him. Kathy put a hand on his knee. 'Can you wiggle your toes, sweetheart?'

He mumbled again, but his toes did a little dance. 'Oh, he can hear us. Steve, you are not to worry. You are going to be all right. I'm going to see if we can get you to Beckbridge Hall…'

This piece of information brought on a great agitation and more mumbling. He didn't want to go to Beckbridge. He knew he must look grotesque and everyone would turn away from him in disgust. He wished he knew how badly he was burnt, but he had been refused a mirror. He had seen his hands when they dressed them. One arm was in plaster but the other was covered in weeping boils and both hands, from wrists to fingertips, were black as an undertaker's hat. 'It's only tannic acid,' he had been told. 'It acts as a coagulant and forms a kind of temporary skin while your real skin heals.' Was his face like that too? He shouldn't have been so stubborn about not bailing out. He might have escaped this agony if he had; he might have been picked up by a Dutch trawler and smuggled home. Instead, not only had he put his own and Ken's life at risk, he had hazarded the lives of a vicar and one of his parishioners who had been in the churchyard and had run to drag him out of the plane before the whole thing exploded. He had been out for the count most of the time, which was a good thing because when he came to he was in an ambulance careering at break-neck speed to the nearest hospital, and every bump in the road sent red-hot needles of pain shooting up his arms before he passed out again. At the hospital they had given him morphine, cleaned him up with saline solution to get the little bits of clothing out of his wounds, dressed them with gauze netting impregnated with paraffin and halibut liver oil, and sent him on to the Royal Masonic. Since then he had been in and out of consciousness, and he much preferred the comatose state; being awake was hell.

'He's very tired,' the nurse said to his parents. 'Perhaps you could come back another time.'

'Can we see the doctor in charge?' William asked.

The nurse took them away and then the ward sister came to change his dressings. He had to bite his tongue to stop himself yelling and, what was worse, swearing abominably. He tried to control himself by thinking of Laura. He mustn't shout. Mum and Dad were only just down the corridor and he didn't want them to hear him.

Kathy and William were shown into an office where they were joined by a middle-aged doctor. 'Mr and Mrs Wainright?' He shook hands with them both. 'I'm Dr Gibbs.'

'Please, tell us what's going to happen to our son,' Kathy said. 'How bad is he? He will be all right, won't he?'

'Eventually.' How many times had he had to say that to anxious relatives? A lot depended on what you meant by 'all right'. 'You may not believe it, but it could have been worse—'

'He could have died.'

'There is that, but I meant his injuries. He was wearing his helmet, though not his face mask, so it was his eyes, nose and cheeks that got the worst of it. His hands are badly burnt even though he was wearing gloves.' He didn't tell them they had had a devil of a job picking bits of burnt leather out of the blistered skin. 'Fortunately, a great deal has been learnt about treating burns since this war started and Mr McIndoe is working wonders—'

'Mr McIndoe?' Kathy said. 'I heard Laura mention him. He comes down to Beckbridge Hall quite frequently. It's been made into a hospital for burns casualties. Laura Drummond is the nursing sister in charge.'

'Sister Drummond. Why, I knew her. I wondered what happened

297

to her after…' He stopped, not knowing how much they knew about Laura's past.

'We were hoping he could be transferred to Beckbridge Hall. Would that be possible?'

'It isn't up to me, Mrs Wainright; Mr McIndoe will decide when the squadron leader has been to see him at East Grinstead. He will be able to tell you more, but I would be failing in my duty if I did not tell you that he is in for a long and painful journey.'

'Will he be badly scarred?'

'I'm afraid he will, but some of it can be dealt with by skin grafts and the rest will fade in time, but the important thing to remember is that he is still your son, still the man he always was. He will probably tell you differently; he will have some very black days and you will need all the patience you can muster. But he will recover and you must keep that thought constantly in front of you.'

'When is he going to be moved?'

'When he is well enough to withstand the journey. I will let you know if you leave your telephone number.'

They thanked him and wandered out of the hospital in a daze. 'As soon as we get back, I'm going to see Laura,' Kathy said, as William took her arm and guided her along the street towards the Underground station. They were so immersed in their troubles they hardly noticed that London itself was badly scarred; the spaces between some buildings were water-filled pits and many had their windows boarded up. 'She will tell us what's going to happen and whether she can get him to the Hall.'

Imagining that everyone in the village knew the truth, Laura couldn't bring herself to meet any of them and it was easy to stay in the hospital grounds and pretend she didn't have time for anything but work. Consequently she had not seen Joyce; what Wayne had told his aunt, she did not know, did not want to know. It was enough that she had to come to terms with having a new mother, one who was alive and well, without having to cope with a moody half-brother. She was unprepared for the news that Kathy brought. It was enough to drive her own problems from her head in order to concentrate on Steve's. Poor, poor man.

'Can he come here?' Kathy asked at the end of a tale that was difficult to follow, though the gist of it was plain enough. 'You'd nurse him, wouldn't you?'

'Of course I would, but it would be up to his doctors what his treatment should be.'

'Laura, I've got to do something. It was terrible seeing him like that. I'm sure he'll do better near home. I could come and see him and… Oh, Laura, I don't know which way to turn. My boy, my lovely boy is…' The tears rained down her cheeks and she fumbled in her pocket for a handkerchief.

'He is still your lovely boy, Kathy. You must always remember that. What did they tell you about his injuries?' She was trying desperately to be calm and practical but she felt a bit like Kathy did, distraught that someone she loved so dearly could be hurt and in pain. And she knew only too well what burns victims had to go through.

'Nothing much. He has to go to East Grinstead when he's well enough to travel.'

'He will be in very good hands there.'

'Will you go and see him?'

'Of course I will.' Wild horses wouldn't keep her away.

Chapter Eleven

Walking down the long ward towards Steve's bed, Laura was transported back in time. She was once again the young nursing sister, dressed in a sparkling white apron and cap so stiffly starched she crackled as she walked. It was a time when the full horror of the war and its casualties had not yet flooded the hospitals, when she could laugh and tease the patients. It was a time when she had been in love for the first time; when Bob hovered about the hospital when he was not on standby, waiting for her to come off duty; when she had a mother who loved her and whom she loved. Was that only two years ago? It seemed like an age, so much had happened – not only to her but to everyone around her. She pulled herself together as she approached Steve's bed. It was no good dwelling on it; she couldn't change one iota of it.

A nurse was helping Steve to drink through a straw placed gently between scorched lips. His face was swollen to twice its normal size and though she could not see much of it under the dressing, experience told her what it would be like. His eyes, slits in his bandaged face, were almost closed, as if he did not want to look out on a world he could no longer relate to. Silently, she took the glass from the nurse and sat on the edge of the bed to help him herself. He felt the movement of the bed, opened his eyes and spat out the straw. 'Laura, what are you doing here?'

'Come to see you, of course.'

'Mum sent you.'

'I did not need to be sent, Steve. Did you think I wouldn't want to come? You know me better than that, surely?'

'Better if you hadn't. I'm a ghoul.'

'Rubbish! You are Steve Wainright, my rock.'

He attempted a laugh and winced when it hurt. 'Fine rock I am. Couldn't lift a finger to help you.' He raised the plastered arm and let it drop again.

'Oh yes you could and I'm counting on it. In the meantime, I'll be your rock. Do you understand me?'

'Why do I have a feeling I'm being lectured?'

'Not lectured, Steve, gently chided, but if you let me down it *will* be a lecture.'

'It won't work.'

'What won't?'

'I'm not coming to Beckbridge to be viewed by all and sundry like some specimen in a glass case. "Poor Steve! He'll never be the same again. Keep the children away from him in case he gives them nightmares."'

'Now I *am* cross with you. For a start, you won't be coming to Beckbridge until you've been to East Grinstead, and only then if Mr McIndoe sends you. And secondly, do you think I would allow you to be viewed by all and sundry, as you put it. I suppose you mean your parents and sister and all the people in the village who love you.' He did not answer and she put the straw back into his mouth. 'Now drink.'

He sucked dutifully but she saw him wince; it was probably time for his next shot of morphine, without which the agony would be unbearable. She could see Dr Gibbs coming down the ward towards them. 'Here's the doctor. I'll have to go, but I'll be back.'

'Don't let Mum come again, will you? I can't bear the look on her face.' He could hardly get the words out, the pain was so awful.

'She was shocked, that's all. It would be cruel to stop her coming if she wants to, but I'll suggest waiting until after you've seen Mr

McIndoe and things have quietened down a bit.' She meant the rawness of his features and his own inner struggle to come to terms with what had happened.

'Sister Drummond, by all that's wonderful.' Dr Gibbs was looking thinner than when she had last seen him and his face was drawn, but he smiled broadly when he saw her. 'How are you? What have you been doing with yourself?'

'I'm well and busy.' She went on to tell him what she was doing. 'Squadron Leader Wainright is an old friend.'

'Yes. He's in a bit of a mess, but we'll soon have him sorted.' It was said cheerfully and made Steve grunt in annoyance. Sorted indeed! How could he be sorted when his whole world was falling apart? Laura was used to seeing badly burnt faces, but that didn't mean she wanted to marry one. He wouldn't want it either, knowing it was pity that kept her by him and not love, not the kind of love he craved. And there was Wayne Donovan, still handsome, still visiting the village... He felt the needle go in and knew that he would get a little blessed relief, not only from the pain but also from his embittered thoughts.

'How was he?' Kathy demanded. Laura had gone to the farm immediately on her return as she had promised to do.

'As well as can be expected considering his injuries. It's early days yet and he's still not able to take it in. It will take time to adjust.'

'Dr Gibbs warned us about that. Said he'd have black days.'

'It's hardly to be wondered at, is it? A young handsome man suddenly finds he's lost his looks and to him it feels like losing his identity. He doesn't feel the same about himself any more and he imagines other people don't feel the same about him either. He thinks he's repellent and that makes him resentful. He will often reject help when it's offered—'

'But you wouldn't be put off by that, would you?'

Laura looked searchingly at her, wondering if there was more to the question than appeared on the surface. 'No, of course not. Neither would you, would you?'

'No. But I was hoping if he could come to Beckbridge, we could all help him. Dr Gibbs said it was up to Mr McIndoe, so perhaps you could speak to him…'

'I'll do what I can, Kathy, because I'd like him here too, but I'll wait until he goes to East Grinstead. I know you are anxious about him, but try to stay calm. At the moment he has to come to terms with what's happened and that's a struggle he has to fight alone.'

'Are you saying I shouldn't go and see him?'

'Wait until he's seen Mr McIndoe. He has a wonderful way of being positive, bucking his patients up, explaining everything to them so they begin to realise it isn't the end of the world. It's easier for him to be objective than for relatives who are too closely involved.'

'What about you? Can you be objective?'

'I'll try.'

'You won't give up on him, will you?'

'No, Kathy, I will not give up on him.' She knew, even as she made the promise, that leaving Beckbridge was out of the question.

The boys had been anticipating Christmas for weeks, talking about it, letting everyone know that just because they were too old to believe in Father Christmas, didn't mean they didn't like having their stockings filled. Kathy, who had been looking forward to having Steve at home, suddenly felt deflated, as if none of it mattered any more. How could they celebrate, eat and drink and play games, when her beloved son lay in a hospital bed fighting for his life? And he didn't want to see her. It was her own fault for letting him see how dismayed she had been by his poor dear face. It was the shock, that was all; she would be in better control next time. She wrote to him every day but her letters had to be read to him because he couldn't pick them up and couldn't see properly, and that put some constraint on what she said. Nor could he reply, except by dictating to one of the nurses or ward orderlies. It was most unsatisfactory. How could she think about Christmas?

'I know Uncle Steve is ill,' Donny told her. 'But he wouldn't want us to be miserable, would he?'

She pulled herself together. 'No, of course he wouldn't.'

Mr Archibald McIndoe was a New Zealander in his late thirties. He wore horn-trimmed spectacles through which he seemed to view the world with a cheerful optimism that was catching. 'First things first,' he said, after examining Steve's injuries the day after he arrived at the Queen Victoria Hospital in East Grinstead. 'Eyelids first. Then you'll be able to blink properly and look out on the world again.'

He didn't know that he wanted to; his sight was a watery blur but at least he couldn't see the monstrosity that was Steve Wainright. It was a month since his crash, a month of torment interspersed with hazy drug-induced sleep, a month in which he had ridden a roller coaster of emotions: glad to be alive, wishing he were dead, relieved his mother had not come again, resentful that she didn't care enough to come and see him, wanting to hide away from everyone, wanting to go home. And there was the constant pain. But he could not help responding to the surgeon's grin, though smiling was itself difficult. 'And what will I see?'

'Well, there are some pretty nurses here and it isn't a bad place. Later we'll do something about your hands. One step at a time, eh?'

'How many steps?'

'Quite a few.'

The surgeon was not exaggerating. The heat from the fire, so he was told, had made the skin round his eyes contract so that his top and bottom lids did not meet properly. Mr McIndoe proposed to give him new eyelids using skin from beneath his arm. This he did a week later. After the dressings were removed, Steve found he could, with a little effort which became easier as the days went by, open and shut his eyes properly, could shut out what he didn't want to see. At least his face was back to its proper size and though the skin on his nose and cheeks was still pink and scarred, it was healing.

His hands were another matter. He had already suffered the

torture of having the tannic acid coating on his hands removed by soaking them in a bath of saline solution. As soon as the air had touched the exposed flesh it set his nerves jangling unbearably; even a curtain flapping created enough draught to be agonising. He had gained some relief when his hands were placed in special envelopes. Gradually, so gradually he thought the time would never come, they had healed and he no longer had to suffer the dressings. The trouble now was that the skin became hard as buffalo hide and as it contracted it drew the fingers in so that they were almost touching his palms and he could not extend them. It meant more operations but in the meantime he was able to wander about the beautifully maintained grounds of the hospital, even go out for a trip to the local pub, but that was a disaster. He could feel everyone's repugnance, especially when he tried to pick up his glass between his mangled fists and dropped it. They assured him it didn't matter, but he'd had enough and fled.

There was nothing much for him to do but submit to whatever the hospital did to him, read the newspapers and listen to the wireless, frustrated that the war was going on without him. The bombing campaign was gaining momentum; the struggle in North Africa was slowly turning the Allies' way with victory at El Alamein, and the Germans had been forced to give up the siege of Stalingrad. Its indomitable inhabitants had won that particular battle.

His parents came to see him and assured him he was looking tons better, which he supposed was true, but they carefully avoided talking about his injuries, chatting instead about what was happening in Beckbridge: the spring sowing of cereal crops; they had half a dozen new lambs, one of which Gran was hand-rearing; Ian Moreton had been home on leave and seemed a much improved character. Stella had had to register for war work and had chosen to go to a factory in Northampton making barrage balloons and was no longer at the Hall; Helen was looking after Robby almost full time now and loved it. The Yanks were everywhere and the girls had all gone to a dance at the American base to celebrate the New Year. The twins were full of mischief as usual, but doing very well at grammar school. And everyone was looking forward to having him home.

Home! He felt ambivalent about that, nervous about how people would react, hating the idea of being pitied, hating even more the thought of people avoiding looking him straight in the face. And yet he didn't want them to. He had seen himself in a mirror and knew he looked repulsive. 'Don't think it'll be just yet,' he said, lifting his distorted hands. 'Have to have something done about these.'

His mother accepted his half truth and kissed him goodbye, making him feel a heel. But he couldn't face his relatives and friends: Jenny, Meg and Daphne; the Moretons; Joe at the pub; Aunt Helen, though she must be used to burnt airmen by now; definitely not Wayne Donovan, who was, according to everyone, handsome and charming. Was Laura still in touch with him? She never mentioned him and he'd be blowed if he'd bring up the subject himself. She came as often as her duties would allow, but travel was not easy and her visits were usually made when a patient had to be brought for an operation or taken to Beckbridge for recuperation and she could ride in the ambulance. She spent a long time quizzing him about how he felt. He didn't know how he felt. He was angry and frustrated that he was such a mess and he was missing his squadron. And he would not hear of going to Beckbridge Hall.

'Why not?' she demanded. They were sitting in Mr McIndoe's office, which he had told Laura they could use. 'I'll be able to look after you until you come back to have your hands grafted.'

'I don't want you to look after me.'

'Thank you very much. I won't bother then.' She stood up and left him.

He called after her, but she gave no indication that she had heard him, and it was only when he reflected that she might not come again that he realised how much he looked forward to her visits and how, even in his blackest moods, she managed to lift his spirits. He went back to the ward, where he persuaded Johnny to go to the pub with him. Johnny looked even worse than Steve, but he was always laughing and joking. How much of it was an act, Steve could never be sure. The two of them got very drunk and rolled noisily back to the hospital after everyone else had gone to bed. The night sister pushed them into a side ward to sober up. The next morning, Mr McIndoe sent for Steve and hauled him over the coals, not for getting drunk, but for disturbing everyone late at night. 'You need a change of scene,' he finished. 'How about going to Beckbridge Hall until I'm ready to start on your hands? You could enjoy some time with your family and friends.'

'I've blotted my copybook there as well. Can't you get on with my hands straight away? Then I could get back to my job.'

'You think I'm patching you up just to have all my good work undone?'

'What else am I good for?'

'A lot, but I haven't got time to list them. You'll have to work it out for yourself.'

Steve went back to the ward and kicked the bed leg, which did nothing for his mood and only hurt his toe. 'Had a wigging?' Johnny asked.

'Yes. Being sent to Beckbridge.'

'That's not a wigging, that's a reward.'

Steve managed a laugh.

He returned to Beckbridge on Good Friday, the 23rd of April. Whoever it was that decided such things, gave him a railway warrant and left him to make his own way by train. It was the first time he had been out on his own since being shot down and it was a nerve-racking experience. He imagined everyone was looking at him, repelled by his ugly face. He was glad that the weather was cool enough for him to wear an overcoat and cap as well as woollen mittens; he couldn't get his fingers into gloves. The mittens covered his claw-like hands but they made it even more difficult to pick things up. When people saw him struggling they rushed to help, which didn't make him feel any better. He thanked them and tried to smile but smiling did not improve his looks, a fact he knew from practising before the mirror.

He had written Laura an abject apology and included a postal order for her to buy something for Robby's second birthday, and received a reply thanking him and saying he was forgiven, but she had also added he ought not to reject help freely given and though she understood his frustration perhaps others might not. She said she hoped he would reconsider coming to Beckbridge Hall; it was his mother's dearest wish, 'and I need my rock,' she had added, which made him wonder why. Was she finding the work of looking after people like him too demanding? Was it Wayne Donovan? Did she want advice about him? He had never met the man and already he disliked him. Or was it simply to get him to behave himself, trying to make him feel needed? They were questions that had plagued him ever since she had come to see him in Hammersmith and told him she needed him.

The train from Liverpool Street to Attlesham was a slow one. Not only did it stop at every station, it was more than once shunted into a siding to allow a long freight train of tarpaulin-covered wagons to pass through. Military freight, he realised; guns, bits of aeroplanes, army vehicles. The war was being waged without him. He arrived at last to find Laura waiting on the platform for him. She looked so bright and fresh in her uniform, her waist – smaller than ever, he could swear – cinched in by the wide navy belt with its silver buckle. Her red-lined navy cloak was thrown carelessly over her shoulders.

Afraid she would be repelled, he didn't know whether to kiss her or not, but she solved the problem by reaching up and kissing his scarred cheek before linking her arm in his. 'I've got the car,' she said, leading him out to where the Humber was parked. 'I managed to persuade the villagers against the welcoming committee, the flags and the brass band.'

'Good God! They never wanted to do that, did they?'

'It was mooted.'

'By whom?'

'The twins and Joyce for a start. Joyce reckons you saved Ken's life.'

'I never did. In fact, I nearly forfeited it. But thanks for stepping in.' He didn't need to ask how they had found out he was on his way home; his mother would never have been able to keep quiet about it.

Laura opened the passenger door for him, made sure he was settled before shutting it and going round to the driver's side. 'That's not to say you are going to be able to avoid seeing them altogether.'

'No, I know. But not today. I'm devilish tired.'

'I thought you might be, so I've prescribed twenty-four hours' rest. After that, limited visitors for short periods. You can cope with that, can't you?' She started the car and edged out of the car park.

'You're an angel.'

'I wish you wouldn't say that. I'm far from angelic. In fact, I've been giving everyone hell just lately.'

'You're tired too.'

'Yes, it's a national disease.'

'There's something else?'

'It can wait. My main task at the moment is to get you ready mentally and physically for your next op.'

'I'm ready now and I'll listen whenever you feel like talking, though I'd be a bit of a failure if you wanted me to punch someone on the nose.'

'Oh, I don't know,' she said laughing. 'I reckon those fists of yours are like iron.'

He smiled. She really was good at making him feel normal, even when referring to his disabilities. 'Do you really want me to tackle someone?'

'No, of course not.'

'I thought it might be Wayne Donovan.'

She kept her eyes fixed on the road ahead. It was growing dusk and the covered headlights only illuminated a few yards of the road. 'What on earth gave you that idea?'

'I dunno. I suppose it's because I'd enjoy doing it.'

'Well, you can't. He's gone back to his unit.'

'Is he coming back?'

'I've no idea.'

Steve leant forward as they passed the end of the farm drive, but there was no one about. He sat back again, half relieved, half disappointed. He was a mass of conflicting emotions. Bridge Farm was home, how could he not want to go there? His mother would be OK because she had seen him in hospital and knew what to expect, but Jenny and Meg, and Daphne, who was still working on the farm even though she was married to Alec, would have no idea how ugly he was. And there were the twins and old Josh and his wife. He couldn't bear it. And yet he longed for the warmth of the old kitchen, the quiet peace of his own room, surrounded by cricket bats, tennis rackets, golf clubs, battered train sets, model aeroplanes and books on flying. Some of his mother's cooking wouldn't go amiss either.

'I've told your mum and dad to bring Jenny to see you tomorrow afternoon,' Laura said, reading his thoughts. 'The rest can wait.'

'Must I?'

'Yes, you must.' She swung the car into the drive and up to the front door. 'Here we are.'

She ushered him inside and up the stairs to a single room. 'Get into bed,' she said, as a porter brought his bag and put it on a table at the foot of the bed. 'I'll have your supper brought up to you…'

He reached out and felt for her hand. 'Laura, thank you.'

'Only for tonight, mind,' she said, choosing to misunderstand him. 'Tomorrow you come down and have your meals in the dining room with everyone else.'

He dropped her hand and she turned away. She had made up her mind to be professional, to help him when it was necessary but not mollycoddle him. It was difficult because she felt such enormous sympathy and wanted more than anything to help him undress, tuck him in and feed him with a spoon because he found it so difficult to wield a knife and fork. But she must not do that. He had to be made to help himself, to regain his independence and self-esteem, and every task accomplished took him one step further along the road to recovery. She knew perfectly well that after the operations on his hands he would be almost back to square one, in agony again and unable to do a thing for himself. She knew exactly what the operation entailed, and it was not going to be easy. They would do the right hand first, and only after he had recovered from that would they tackle the left, but she hoped that by then Steve would be mentally stronger and his recovery all the quicker for it. Some of that would be up to her. And his family.

He did not think he would, but he slept until noon the next day and woke to find a porter bringing hot water for him to wash. The man disappeared and he was left to get on with it. He washed and dressed painfully slowly and, once presentable, made his way downstairs to the dining room, which was set out with tables for four. Laura was wandering between them having a word or two with every man. She beckoned him to one of the tables and introduced him to Flying Officer Ben Savage and Sergeant Wilcox, who had never been up in an aeroplane in his life, he informed Steve cheerfully; he was ground crew and had got his injuries during an air raid when he had tried to taxi a burning Spitfire out of harm's way. Among others whose injuries were as bad, if not worse, than his, Steve felt better, and in no time they were exchanging notes and making jokes about their treatment. It put him in a better frame of mind to meet his parents and Jenny that afternoon.

Laura found a quiet room for them and left them alone. He stood awkwardly when they entered, not knowing quite what to say, but his mother had no such qualms. 'Oh, you are up and dressed,' she said, darting forward to kiss his cheek. 'You look so much better, doesn't he, William?' If she felt any repugnance she hid it well.

So did Jenny, who kissed him on each cheek and took hold of his hands. 'Oh, your poor hands.'

'Not to worry. They're going to do something about them. I'll be as good as new.'

'You'll come home for Sunday lunch, won't you?' Kathy added, seating herself on a sofa and pulling him down beside her while William and Jenny found seats. 'Laura says it will be all right. I'd have you all the time but she says it's not a good idea at the moment.'

'I'm not fit to be seen.'

'Of course you are. Who cares about a few scars? They're not nearly as bad as you imagine, you know. Hardly noticeable. Say you'll come.'

'I hope you haven't invited the whole village.'

'No, of course I haven't. I want you all to myself. There'll be Gran, of course, and the twins, and Meg and Daphne. Couldn't send them away, could I?' She paused when she saw the consternation in his eyes. 'I will, if you insist—'

He pulled himself together. 'No, of course not. It's their home. Besides, I'd like Laura and Aunt Helen to come with me.'

She looked startled, wondering if he thought he needed to surround himself with allies, people who would protect him from his own family. Laura would be welcome, was always welcome after what she had done to help. But Helen? She couldn't leave her out, could she? 'Of course. Robby too.'

Laura arrived pushing a tea trolley. 'Thought you might appreciate a cuppa,' she said. 'Then I'm afraid Steve will have to rest. He might look strong and healthy, especially in that uniform, but it's all a con.'

'We were discussing Sunday lunch,' Kathy said.

Laura, dispensing tea, looked swiftly at Steve, hoping he had not refused to go. He was smiling. It was a strange lop-sided smile but she recognised it for what it was: a rueful admission that he was being good. 'I am sure Steve is looking forward to it,' she said.

'We want you and Helen to come too,' Steve put in.

'I'll be on duty.'

'Not all day, surely? Can't you come for tea? Bring Robby.' He laughed. 'You could make sure I was behaving myself and get me back to bed in reasonable time.'

He was covering himself, Kathy realised, a little resentfully. She wanted to nurture him, to do everything for him, feed him up, make a fuss of him. Laura had warned her against it, but surely a little spoiling would do him no harm?

Robby, used to seeing disfigured airmen, didn't think there was anything at all strange about the new arrival, except that he had a feeling he knew him. And he wandered about the part of the house where the other men did not venture, like today when he came into the sitting room Mummy and Auntie Helen used when they had time to sit down. The newcomer called Auntie Helen 'Auntie' too, so he must, the young mind decided, be family. And being family, demands could be made. He tugged on his hand and offered him a wooden brick. Steve tried to take it and promptly dropped it. 'Bu'er finners,' the little one said, picking it up and offering it again.

Steve laughed and this time he did manage to grasp it. 'What do you want me to do with it?'

Robby went on his knees below the table and brought out a truck loaded with bricks. Steve squatted down and added the brick to the pile and then Robby turned the whole thing up and spilt them all out and began building a tower. Steve watched until Robby gave him another brick. Steve's clumsiness in adding it to the tower made him knock the whole lot over. He couldn't even play with a child without upsetting everything. But Robby was giggling. He built a new pile and deliberately knocked it over. It seemed to be what the game was all about: building towers and knocking them down again. Steve joined in and they were noisily engrossed when Laura came in. They didn't notice her at first and she stood watching them, a smile playing about her lips. Perhaps a child could achieve what adults could not.

Steve saw her and scrambled to his feet. 'He's talking now,' he said.

'Yes. His favourite words are "no", "play" and "I want". He says "Mummy" and "Auntie". We shall have to teach him to say "Steve".' She picked him up and held him though he squirmed to be put down again. 'Do you know who this is?' she asked him, pointing at Steve.

'Daddy.'

'Good God!' Steve said. 'Why did he say that?'

'He's never said it before,' Laura said, almost as shocked as he was. 'I suppose it's the uniform. I show him his father's picture sometimes and tell him it's his daddy.'

'Why pick on me? There are dozens of men in uniform here.'

'I don't know. I suppose he realises you are special.'

'Am I?'

'You know very well you are. I'm going to take him for a walk. Are you coming?'

'Where to?' It was said guardedly.

'Over the common, through the woods and back home.'

He thought it was safe to say yes. They were unlikely to meet anyone and any time alone with Laura was precious.

He'd forgotten the schools had broken up for the Easter holiday, until they were crossing the common and Boy raced up to him, barking an excited greeting. He bent and hugged the dog, who licked his face. 'Where have you sprung from?' he demanded.

His answer came in the shape of the twins racing to join them. 'Uncle Steve!'

He stood up to face them and waited for the expression of horror to appear, but nothing happened. Lenny looked at him, his head on one side. 'Aunty Kathy said you'd bin shot down.'

'Yes, but it's nothing to boast about.'

'It is so!' Donny said. 'Are they going to give you a medal?'

He smiled. 'I shouldn't think so.'

'Well, I think they should. Did you come to meet us? Are you coming home with us now?'

'No, I have to stay at the Hall, but I'm coming home for the day tomorrow.'

'Good. Is Mrs Drummond going to make you better, like she does the others?'

He smiled at Laura. 'I hope so.'

He was woken the next morning by the sound of church bells and for a moment he thought he was back in his own bed. His mother would come in a minute and tell him if he didn't get a move on he would be late for church. He would get up grumbling, foregoing his breakfast in order to go with the family to church. Gran's husband had been a parson and they never missed morning service. He was sitting up with his legs over the side of the bed before he realised where he was. It brought a wry smile to his lips. He looked up as the door opened and Laura put her head round it.

'Did the bells wake you?'

'I suppose they must have. What's it in aid of, another victory?'

'The ban has been lifted for Sundays and special occasions. It must mean things are looking up, don't you think? Perhaps the war will soon be over.'

'Do you really think so?'

'Who can tell? We can only hope.'

Steve walked to Bridge Farm and arrived just as the family were returning from church. They all hugged him and he was ushered into the familiar kitchen. It was filled with the smell of roasting chicken. He sat down at the table and watched as his mother took off her hat and coat and then sat opposite him, reaching out to take his hands and looking closely into his face. 'All right, son?'

'Yes. Don't fuss.'

'I'm not.' She withdrew her hands, looking hurt, making him feel a heel. 'It was only a simple question, but perhaps a silly one. Of course you're all right, or you soon will be. Shall you sit in the other room with the others while I finish getting lunch?'

'No, I'll stay here and talk to you. You can tell me all the news.'

'Not much to tell. We muddle along. What about you? Laura has been a brick, don't you think?'

'Yes, she has.' He knew she was probing. 'What else is new?'

'Let me see. Josh says it's about time he retired. We never thought he would! He's ninety-three, you know, and as cantankerous as ever.'

'He'll have a pension?'

'Yes, a small one, and Dad says he can stay in the cottage as long as he likes.'

'He'll be up here working, retired or not,' Steve said, glad of the change of subject. 'He won't be able to keep away.'

'No, I don't suppose he will. Have you heard that, when the war is over, no one will have to work into old age just to make ends meet? There's going to be two pounds a week retirement pension, unemployment benefit, family allowances and a national health service for when you're ill.'

'It'll have to be paid for.'

'Weekly contributions out of wages, so we're told.'

'I'll believe it when I see it.' His father had come into the kitchen from outside and sat down in his Windsor chair to take off his boots. 'After the last lot we were promised a land fit for heroes and what did we get? Depression and unemployment, farms going downhill, land going to waste. Places like Beckbridge Hall being auctioned off to pay taxes. I'm surprised Helen hung on to it.'

'Steve doesn't want to know about that,' his mother put in. 'Let's be more cheerful. Pour everyone a glass of wine while I dish up.'

The wine was good and the lunch that followed excellent. Steve had trouble with his knife and fork and Kathy simply could not bear to see him struggling. She took his cutlery to cut up his food for him. 'I've got to learn to manage, Mum,' he said.

'I know you have, but not today. Today I want to spoil you.'

Laura, Helen and Robby arrived in the middle of the afternoon and stayed for a tea such as no one had seen since the beginning of the war. There was ham and salad, scotch eggs, cold pork and chicken, homemade bread – not that grey-looking National Loaf – as well as three different cakes oozing cream. How his mother did it, Steve did not know, but she must have scoured the shops for the ingredients.

The conversation was kept light and uncontroversial; he felt they were all treading on eggs, trying not to upset him. He was relieved when Laura adopted her nurse-in-charge role and said he had had enough excitement for one day and she proposed taking him back to the Hall and his bed.

'There, that wasn't so bad, was it?' she asked him, as they sat enjoying a cup of cocoa, one on each side of the table in the sitting room. Helen had taken Robby, protesting loudly, off to his bed.

'No, I suppose not, but no one was acting naturally, were they?'

'Were you?'

'How could I?'

'I remember a Steve with a sense of humour, who told jokes and laughed, a Steve who was interested in other people's problems.'

'You mean yours?'

'No, I do not. I meant your parents, who are struggling on the farm, and Daphne, whose got a husband on the North Atlantic convoys. And Joyce worrying about Ken—'

'You're a terrible nag, you know that, don't you?'

'I don't mean to be. I just want the old Steve back.'

'How? I'll never be the old Steve. Just look at me. No, on second thoughts, don't look at me.'

'Why not?' She looked into his face; there was no revulsion there, nor yet pity, that he could see. 'It's not nearly as bad as you imagine it to be, you know, and you are still Steve Wainright, still my rock…' She stopped suddenly.

'You said you needed your rock. What for?'

'Nothing specific.'

'You're a poor liar. I know there's something on your mind. If it's wondering how to tell me you don't want to marry me, forget it. I withdraw the proposal.'

'Thank you very much,' she said tartly. 'You certainly know how to make a girl feel wanted.'

'Oh, Christ, I didn't mean it like that!' He reached out to take her hand, but it wasn't easy and he ended up putting his hand over hers and imprisoning it on the table. 'I'm not myself and that proves it. You're better off without me.'

'I'll be the judge of that.'

'So?'

'So, marriage is the last thing on my mind.'

'Not to anyone? Not even the handsome Canadian?'

'No one. Least of all him.'

His heart lifted and then fell again like a stone. What did it matter? He couldn't marry her. 'Are you going to tell me why?'

'I've got too much to do to think of getting married, I told you that before.'

'So you did. But we weren't talking about Wayne Donovan when you said it.'

'Same thing applies.'

'Are you going round and round Will's mother's all night or are you going to come to the point?'

'Do you really want to hear it?'

'Laura Drummond, you are the most exasperating woman I have ever come across. You just said I ought to think about other people's problems and when I ask you to tell me yours, you clam up. Is it something to do with me? With my injuries? If you want to keep me at arm's length, that's fine by me.'

'No, of course I don't. Don't be so touchy.' She stood up and collected their empty mugs, defeat in every line of her body. He had enough on his plate without hearing her problems and, besides, he had withdrawn his offer of marriage, so it didn't matter any more. 'I think I'll have an early night. Get yourself off to bed. If you need any help, ask one of the nurses.'

He watched her leave the room, aching to comfort her, but afraid of his own emotions, afraid to let go because if he did, he would howl like a baby.

She just managed to reach the sanctuary of her room before she gave way to tears. She flung herself face down on her bed and wept: for herself; for Steve, who was busy trying to deny his feelings; for her own love which had to be denied, not because of his injuries, which meant nothing to her, but because of her past; for misunderstandings and untruths. She cried for Kathy and Helen, and little Robby, even for Wayne, who had been just as hurt as she was, though for different reasons. She wept for the mother she had known and loved and for the dad who was not her dad. In the end she didn't know why she was crying; it was like a dam bursting and she didn't know how to stop the flood.

Steve went back to East Grinstead in May on the day after the great dams of Möhne and Eder were breached and millions of gallons of water flooded the German countryside, wrecking roads and railways, bridges and homes in its path. He read about it in a newspaper he purchased from the bookstall on Attlesham Station. The Lancasters had set off from his old station at Scampton and the raid was made at extremely low level using a newly developed bomb which bounced on water. It made him wish he was back in harness, doing his bit. He would get back, he decided; he'd put up with whatever the medics did to him and he would go back.

What the medics proposed to do sounded like torture. The day after he arrived, Mr McIndoe explained what would happen, not hiding the fact that it was going to be painful. The thick leather-like scar tissue would be stripped off the back of his hand and replaced with a thin layer of skin taken from his thigh. Dozens of stitches would hold the graft in place but that would not be enough to make it 'take'. A dry sponge would be cut to shape and laid over the graft and some of the long ends of the stitches brought over it and tied. Then the sponge would be wetted and it would swell up, pressing down onto the graft helping it to weld. The whole thing would then be bandaged into place. The pressure, Steve was told, would be uncomfortable until the time came to release it and take out the stitches. Only then would they know if the operation had been a success.

Uncomfortable was not the word Steve would have used for the excruciating agony he suffered in the days after the operation. He was back where he started, needing copious doses of morphine to dull the pain and not being able to use that hand at all. He lost all track of time as he lay in his bed with his hand resting on a special pillow, which felt more like an anvil than a pillow, while an invisible blacksmith hammered his tortured flesh into it. After what seemed an eternity but could only have been a few days, the bandage covering it was removed and the stitches cut to release the pressure. He looked at his hand, expecting he knew not what, but unprepared for the gory mess he saw lying on the pillow. It made him feel sick.

'Good,' Mr McIndoe said. 'It's taken well.'

Steve had to believe him, but he was back to the torture of daily dressings. The following week, Laura, fetching another patient for Beckbridge Hall, came to see him. She was cheerful and optimistic and brought news of the village, but she was somehow detached, a professional nurse speaking to a patient. There was no kind of intimacy, no sharing of personal thoughts, no sign that she needed her rock, or indeed had ever needed him. For the first time ever, her visit did not cheer him up.

A week later, he left his bed and wandered about the hospital, talking to other patients, joining in teasing the staff except when they came to do his dressing, when his language would have done justice to a navvy. He was offered the chance of going to Beckbridge to recover before they tackled the left hand, but turned it down. The sooner it was done, the sooner he could get back to the business of winning the war.

Sicily, small though it was, was a mountainous country, but on the lower slopes vines and tomato plants grew in neat rows. There were also orange and lemon trees and from almost every vantage point Mount Etna could be seen, smoking gently on the skyline. Wayne was sitting beside his driver on the road to Andrano, munching on a handful of grapes. The campaign had been nothing like that ill-fated raid on Dieppe; the invasion of Sicily had been well-planned, well-resourced, part of the overall strategy to force Italy out of the war. He supposed the Germans had all along intended to evacuate the island but they were making it as difficult as possible for the invaders, who had to fight almost literally from one craggy outcrop to the next.

After kicking their heels in the UK with nothing much to do, the Canadian First Infantry Division and the First Armoured Brigade had been sent to Scotland for assault training, not knowing where they would be going but eager to get on with the war. No one was more glad than Wayne to be doing something positive at last. It might stop him dwelling on the bombshell Laura had dropped the last time he had been in Beckbridge. Ever since then he had been searching his childhood memory for something, anything, that could tell him whether it was the truth or not. He didn't want to believe it, wouldn't believe it. His first reaction had been to write to his father and demand that he deny it, but he knew his parents shared their letters and if Pop tried to keep one from Mom, she would want to know why. He could not risk it and would have to wait until they came face to face, and by that time it would be too late; Laura would almost certainly have found someone else. And, after all, it might be true. Strange things happened in wartime, the last conflict had been no different to this.

It wasn't that he cared a fig about his father having an affair; it was the thought of Laura being his half-sister. Surely he would not feel like he did about her if it were true; some instinct, something in the way they related to each other would have told him that it was wrong. He still thought so. And yet Laura seemed to have accepted the situation. He tried to imagine Helen Barstairs as a young woman, ready and willing for an extra-marital affair, but he just couldn't see it. He supposed she must have looked like Laura did now, and that was beautiful, but were they alike in other ways? Lady Barstairs had always struck him as cool and dignified, quietly spoken and conscious of her position as lady of the manor, while Laura was warm and loving, someone who could fly off the handle when occasion demanded. He had wanted to speak to her at the wedding reception, but never got the chance. She was chatting and laughing with everyone, just as if nothing had happened, and then left early saying she had to put Robby to bed. He hadn't seen her again.

He had returned to his unit, gone to Scotland and then embarked for active service, joining a huge flotilla of ships making for Sicily. The sea off the island had been rough and many of the men had been sick, and it hadn't helped when they scrambled down into the landing craft, which were being tossed about like corks. They were all glad when, apart from a few pot shots, they met little opposition on landing and had soon established a bridgehead from where they had set off inland, prompting his company sergeant to ask, 'D'you reckon we'll march across the whole island without a battle, sir?'

He had hardly uttered the words when the road in front of them erupted in rubble and dust. Wayne had scrambled from his truck and joined the men as they threw themselves into a wayside ditch. 'Seems you've got your answer, Sergeant.'

From then on, they had to fight every inch of the way over heavily mined mountain roads while the Germans fought delaying actions from every hillside village. Grammichele, Piazza Arerina, and Valguarnera had fallen one by one, leaving them facing the steep slopes in front of Assoro. He was reminded of General Wolfe's army scaling the cliffs of Quebec when the generals decided the only way to take the town was to climb the mountain. By the light of a fitful moon, carrying nothing but their rifles and Bren guns, they had clambered in single file along barely discernible goat tracks to reach the top. Resisting determined counter-attacks they had taken the town. Next came Leonforte and Agira, which was only overcome when reinforcements arrived after five days of fighting. With the British on the left and the Americans on the right, they had pushed on to contain the Germans into a small area around Mount Etna, where two more small places with long names fell to Canadian troops. At Agira they had suffered their heaviest losses before the town fell. Andrano was next on the list but by then Mussolini had been deposed and the Italians were welcoming the invaders with open arms, and he received the news that his troops were being withdrawn to rest.

Only then did Wayne sit down to write to his parents, telling them simply that he had been in a few skirmishes but had come through unscathed and was sitting on a beach sunbathing. He asked them how the business was doing and if the harvest was a good one. He spoke of friends he had left behind, and others he had made since crossing the Atlantic. He told them about Ian and Joyce, about Daphne and Alec. He did not mention Laura at all, which they might think strange, considering his last letter had been full of her, but whenever his pen hovered over the page, he could find nothing to say which would not reveal the tumult he felt; better to say nothing at all.

Writing to Laura was more difficult and after several attempts at trying to tell her how he felt, he gave up. With a bit of luck, they'd be sent back to the UK on leave and he could see her.

Laura sat beside Steve's bed at East Grinstead. She had promised Kathy she wouldn't give up on him, and nor would she, but he was trying her patience. Oh, she knew he was in pain, but he had been given something for it and there was no need to be so bad-tempered. Everyone was doing their best for him; his operations had so far been successful; his eyelids looked almost normal; his face, though still a bit pink and shiny, was not repulsive; he could flex the fingers of his right hand and in time he would be able to use it perfectly well. And in a few days they would know whether the operation on his left hand had been equally successful.

'You'll be coming back to Beckbridge Hall in a week to two,' she said. 'The rest is up to you.'

'I'm going back to my squadron. There's a war on, you know.'

'Yes, I do know.' If that was the only one way he could face the future, then she would not deter him, but she was afraid for her rock. She loved him and needed him, but he had gone cold on her. Had someone told him she was really Helen's daughter? It made him some sort of relation, second cousin once removed or something like that. Did he also know that her father was Oliver Donovan? If he did, he hadn't said anything, but the knowledge would be enough to drive a wedge between them. She remembered how shocked he had been on seeing she was pregnant. He seemed to have got over that, accepted what had happened and really taken to Robby. But supposing he hadn't, supposing he was so stiff with prejudice he could not accept any of it? It wasn't as if she was the only one; according to the news, illegitimate births had shot up since the beginning of the war, and who could blame couples for snatching at a little happiness when they could? Not for a minute did she regret having Robby, no matter how many people condemned her. 'Let's see how you get on, shall we?'

He couldn't explain that it wasn't the pain that was bugging him, he could endure that. He had been pleased as punch when he discovered he could use the fingers of his right hand, and with physiotherapy his dexterity was improving day by day. It meant he was not quite so helpless, and if the left hand turned out to be as good as the right, he would be back with his squadron in no time. Or so he told everyone. Inside, he was more than a little nervous, not of flying again, but of being shot at, of being confined in a burning aircraft. But he couldn't face the alternative: going home to Laura, the healer, the cool professional, whose smile had become a little forced; his mother fussing round him; other people, like Daphne, Meg and Jenny, leading their busy lives, trying to pretend he was normal, while he sat on the sidelines, smiling his gruesome smile and wishing…wishing…

He returned to Beckbridge Hall on the day the Allies invaded the toe of Italy. He was convalescing impatiently when the Italians surrendered, leaving the Germans to fight on alone. At the end of October, he returned to East Grinstead for what were called 'tidying up' operations, and then it was back to Beckbridge Hall for recuperation. He was free to do anything he liked within reason and would wander about the grounds and the village, sometimes with other airmen, sometimes alone. Sometimes on his ramblings, he met the twins.

They had become sturdy young lads, but the differences between them were more marked now; each had his own characteristics and most people who knew them could tell them apart. Donny still tried to dominate his brother, but Lenny was more independent than he used to be. Steve found them good company; they were not forever asking him how he felt. He didn't know how he felt and he wished people would not keep asking him. Not that Laura did. She was the complete professional and would treat him exactly as she did the others in her care. He didn't blame her; he had been a complete cad. He had tried apologising, but all she said was, 'Don't think about it. I don't.'

So to the boys he turned, answering their good-natured grilling of what it was like to fly aeroplanes and drop bombs and be shot at. 'How many enemy planes have you brought down?' Lenny asked him one day. It was the first Saturday in November and they were walking across the common with Boy at their heels. The object of the exercise was to gather wood for a Guy Fawkes bonfire. Donny was dragging a huge dead branch and Lenny had a wheelbarrow loaded with small pieces of wood and bark.

'I told you before,' Steve said, helping to steady the wheelbarrow with a gloved hand. 'They are aeroplanes. Planes are tools you use in woodwork.'

'Aeroplanes then. How many?'

'I don't know. Unless you actually see one go down, you can't always be sure you were the one to bring it down, and if there are several of you after one, it's impossible to say who was really responsible, so you share the honours. And since I've been in bombers, I don't think we've downed a single one.'

'You going back to it?' This from Donny.

'I expect so.'

'You don't have to, do you? I mean you've done your bit, that's what Aunt Kathy says.'

He smiled, imagining his mother saying it. 'I've got unfinished business.'

'You want to get your own back on Jerry.'

'Something like that.'

'Are you all better now?' Lenny asked.

'Do I look all better?'

'You look all right to me.'

He laughed. 'Thank you for those kind words, Lenny, but I'm not exactly Clark Gable, am I?'

'You never were,' Donny put in with blunt honesty. 'But why d'you want to be like him? I like you as you are. At least everyone can see you've done your bit. Not like Mr Moreton.'

'You're not still bothered by him, are you?'

'No, 'course not. He came home on a leave but I kept outa his way. He knows I shopped 'im.'

'You did what was right, Donny. Anyway, no one would let him hurt you. You've got Aunt Kathy and Uncle William and Daphne to look out for you.'

'And Dad,' Lenny said. 'He said he might get leave for Christmas.'

'I hope he does,' Steve said.

'He always stays in your room when he comes. Aunt Kathy said you might need it.'

He laughed. 'Is that why you've been grilling me about whether I'm going back?'

'No, it isn't. Honest, it isn't.'

'Well, you needn't worry. If I'm still around, I'll probably be at the Hall.'

They made their way to the corner of the common nearest the road, where others had gathered to build the bonfire. It was going to be enormous, Steve noted, as the twins' contribution was added to the pile. It reminded him of the bonfires and fireworks on Guy Fawkes nights before the war. The only fireworks he had seen since then had been from an aeroplane over Germany and occupied Europe, fires on the ground, flares and flak all round him. And he was fool enough to want to go back to it! The bonfire complete and the inevitable effigy of Hitler put on top, he accompanied the twins home to have lunch at the farm.

After the meal had been washed up, they all donned warm sweaters and Wellington boots and trooped onto the common to watch the bonfire, which was well alight when they arrived. The twins had brought potatoes and pushed them in at the bottom with sticks. Steve saw how close they were to the flames, which lit up their faces in an orange glow, saw the sparks flying as the green wood spat them out, saw them land on the boys' caps and shoulders, and was once again in the cockpit engulfed in fire. He dashed forward and pulled them both away. 'You silly young fools,' he shouted. 'D'you want to end up looking like me?'

They looked at him as if he had gone mad. Everyone turned to stare at him. He let the boys go. His mother moved forward but he brushed her off and walked away, passing Helen and Laura as he went, not even seeing them. They were standing on the fringe of the circle and Laura had Robby sitting on her shoulders, his plump arms round her neck. She went forward and spoke quietly to Kathy, who was all for setting off after him. 'Let him go, Kathy. He feels foolish and is best left to get over it. It's understandable, you know, being afraid of fire.'

'Do you think I don't know that? I shouldn't have encouraged him to come.'

'Yes, you should. He has to learn to get along with everyone. You can't protect him all the time. He's tougher than you think.'

'How do you know how tough he is? You didn't watch him growing up, you didn't put ointment on his scratches, you didn't comfort him when his first dog died, you didn't sit by his bed when he had the measles—'

'Not when he was growing up, I agree I didn't, but he is an adult now and I've spent hours by his bedside, more than with any other patient. I've seen the torment he has had to endure over those operations and the courage he has shown. I've seen his eyes when he's looked in the mirror and hated what he saw. I've endured his tantrums as well as his good moments. I think I know him very well indeed.' It was spoken quietly, so that no one else heard.

'Is that all he is to you, another patient?'

'You know it isn't.'

'Then what's happened to you both? I thought… Oh, I don't know what I thought. Have you quarrelled?'

'Not exactly.'

'What sort of an answer is that?'

'Ask Steve. He might tell you, and if he does, perhaps you'll tell me. Now, I think I'd better go after him. Kathy, don't worry, it'll all come out in the wash.'

A silly phrase, she told herself, as she handed Robby over to Helen and set off after Steve. She caught up with him in the lane leading to the Hall and fell into step beside him. Neither spoke. The last of the leaves had fallen from the trees and heaped themselves up beside the road in drifts. Mist-laden cobwebs decorated the dead cow parsley; rosehips grew fat and orange – the children would be out gathering those soon. A horse chestnut tree had shed its fruit and the nuts lay rich and shining among the fallen leaves.

'There's a sweet chestnut tree in the park,' she said. 'Do you like roast chestnuts?'

'Yes, we always used to roast some on the fire at Christmas.'

'And will again. Why don't we go and pick some of them up?'

'What, now?'

'Why not?'

She took his hand and led him past the gatehouse towards the lake and the summer house. The tree was a large one and had somehow survived the bomb that had ruined the summer house, but they didn't immediately begin picking up the glossy nuts which lay scattered on the ground, some still in their green casing. Instead, they went into the restored building and sat on the bench, looking through the open door at the lake. 'It's beautiful here,' she said. 'I can't blame Helen for wanting the place rebuilt. Do you remember it from when you were a child?'

'No, not really. We knew it was here, of course, but Aunt Helen lived the life of a recluse and she always shooed us off if we ventured into the grounds. Some of the village children were convinced she was a witch. She used to dress in a black cape, you see, and an old felt hat. They were terrified of her.'

'But you knew her better than that, didn't you? After all, she is your mother's cousin.'

'I saw very little of her. She and Mum didn't get on.'

'Do you know why?'

'No idea. Mum never talked about it. It's taken a war to make them speak to each other again. Of course, Gran knows, but she won't tell.'

'Was it something Helen did that upset your mother?'

'I've no idea. Mum doesn't bear grudges, never has, so I don't think it was that.'

'Aren't you curious?'

'Not particularly. Why do you ask?'

'No reason. I just wondered if it had anything to do with Oliver Donovan.'

'Who's Oliver Donovan?'

She was tempted to say, 'my father' but instead she made herself laugh. 'Wayne's father.'

'Oh. Whatever gave you that idea? Is that what Aunt Helen said?'

'No, like your mother she never speaks of it.'

He had to ask, since she had brought the man's name up. 'Where is Wayne now?'

'Goodness, do we ever know where anyone is these days? Fighting the war somewhere, I expect.'

'Have you heard from him?'

'Not recently but that's not so strange, is it?'

'I suppose not. Are you going to marry him?'

'Is that any business of yours, since you withdrew your proposal?'

'No. I apologise. I only want you to be happy.'

'I shall be happy when I see you back to your old self and content with life.'

'Then you'll have a long wait. I shan't be content until this bloody war is over and the sooner McIndoe passes me fit, I intend to do my best to bring that about. I'm not going to sit on my backside and let others, like Wayne Donovan, do my work for me.'

'You're spoiling for a fight.'

'You could say that.'

'Then save it for Jerry and not your family and me.' She stood up and went outside, and began bending down to pick up chestnuts. He followed. 'Laura, I'm sorry.'

'It's all right. You don't need to apologise to me. Here put these in your pocket.'

He took the chestnuts from her, put them in his pocket and then clasped her hands in both his own. 'You said once, nearly a year ago now, that you needed your rock. Do you still need him?'

'As much as ever.'

'For anything specific?'

'No, nothing specific. Shall we go back to the bonfire?'

He gave up and together they went back to the crowd round the fire. 'I made a fool of myself, didn't I?' he murmured, watching the twins and their friends fishing baked potatoes out of the embers. 'Pulling the twins away like I did.'

'They were being foolhardy, taking risks. You saw the danger.'

'How can I go back to flying if I'm that terrified?'

'Everyone is afraid. But, Steve, you didn't run away, you stepped forward to save them. Remember that.'

He laughed suddenly. 'Now who's the rock!'

Chapter Twelve

A YEAR TO the day since he had been shot down, Steve returned to East Grinstead, not for an operation but to be declared fit enough to be discharged. 'I'll recommend you be invalided out,' the great man said, having reassured himself that there was nothing more he could do for his patient. Steve could use his hands and hardly noticed the scars on them; the terrible pain was a distant memory, but not so distant he could forget it completely. He would never be the handsome man he once was, but the work Mr McIndoe had done on his eyes and nose had been nothing short of miraculous. He didn't like the reflection he saw in the mirror each morning but he had become sort of used to it, and he supposed his nearest and dearest had too. He often thought of what Donny had said: 'At least everyone can see you've done your bit.' He'd try very hard to wear his face with pride.

'I want to go back to flying. I've got unfinished business to attend to.'

McIndoe sighed heavily; he had heard it all before. 'If you must, you must, but it's not me you have to convince, it's the bods at Central Medical.'

'OK, when?'

'Enjoy your Christmas first. Go home on leave and I'll notify them. They'll send you an appointment.'

He really couldn't expect anything more and rose to go, holding out his hand. 'Thank you, sir. Thank you for working miracles. I know I haven't been the easiest of patients.'

McIndoe took the outstretched hand and grasped it firmly. There was a time when such a gesture would have had Steve screaming in agony; now the pressure was reassuring. 'You're not the worst by a long way and I could not have done anything without your cooperation and the help of the whole team, and that includes Sister Drummond and the staff at Beckbridge.'

'I know.'

Steve picked up his cap, set it at a jaunty angle and went out to the taxi he had ordered to take him to the station.

Joyce looked up as the door of Beck Cottage opened and a woman breezed in for all the world as if she owned the place, and stood looking round her. She was plump and wearing a thick tweed coat and a fox fur. Her hair, bright as a carrot, was arranged in neat waves under a beige felt hat with a long green feather. Joyce, rolling out pastry to make mince pies, stared at the apparition for several seconds and then yelled. 'Val! It can't be.'

'Then I'd sure like to know who it could be.' The accent was a mixture of Canadian and Norfolk.

Joyce collapsed into a chair and stared at her sister, unable to believe what she saw. 'How'd you get here?'

Valerie came further into the room and kissed her sister's cheek, wafting expensive perfume as she did so. 'If you make us a cuppa, I'll tell you. Oliver's just paying off the cab.'

'Oliver's here too?'

'Yup.' She took off her coat and hung it over the back of a chair, revealing a peach-coloured light wool dress such as would make any clothes-starved Englishwoman green with envy. Her heavy make-up covered any lines she might have had but did nothing to disguise her many chins. They seemed to be emphasised by an ostentatious diamond necklace and matching earrings. She sat down at the kitchen table as the door opened again and Oliver Donovan stood on the threshold. He was in the uniform of an army major, a little older, a little more portly, but still handsome, still easily recognisable.

'Come in, Ollie and shut the door,' Val said. 'You're letting the cold in. We've given my sister a bit of a shock.'

'You can say that again.' Joyce got up and took the kettle to the scullery to fill it from a pail of water brought in from the well down the garden. Returning, she lifted the cover off the range and set the kettle to boil. 'Now tell me how you managed to get here. And what's Oliver doing in uniform?' She opened the door of the stove and rattled a poker through the bars to stir the fire into life.

'We came over on a converted liner.' Valerie giggled, reminding Joyce of what she was like as a youngster, full of life, always laughing. 'It was full of men, there was only a handful of us women. We had a whale of a time.'

'Why?' She looked from one to the other.

'I wanted to do something for the war,' Oliver said. 'I'm not too old to be useful, so I worried the powers-that-be until they gave me a uniform and a job. It's hush hush at the moment.'

'The second front at last?'

He tapped the side of his nose, but didn't answer. She turned as the kettle whistled and set about making a pot of tea. 'What about you, Val? You haven't been given a job, have you?'

'No, not me. But I wanted to come and Ollie wangled me a berth, so here I am, for the duration. Ollie's got a few days before he has to report. We'll stay at The Jolly Brewers.'

'You can stay here. There's no one here but me, though I was hoping Ken would be home for Christmas. Ian's been sent abroad, don't know where, of course...' She poured milk and tea into the cups and put them on the side of the table away from where she was working.

'Where's Stella?'

'She's working in a factory in Northampton and lives in digs. She might get back for Christmas.'

'Aren't you lonely?'

'No time to be lonely. I've got my job at the post office and that keeps me busy.' She went back to her pastry board. 'I'd better get these mince pies done, though I was wondering why I was bothering if there was only me and Ma to eat them. Still, now you're here... Will you stay for Christmas?'

'Yes, if you'll have us.'

'Have you! I'm thrilled to bits.'

'How's Ma?'

'Same as ever. She misses Stella and Ken but she copes very well. I'll go and fetch her over when I get these in the oven.' She was busy cutting out rounds as she spoke and putting them in a bun tin.

'I'll fetch her,' Oliver said.

'Have you seen anything of Wayne lately?' Valerie asked, when the door had closed on him.

'Not since the early summer. Why?'

'I'm worried about him. He was wounded and I think he must ha' returned to duty too soon. His last letter was kinda strange.'

'What do you mean, strange?'

'Don't know exactly; it just didn't sound like him. It was all stiff, as if he had something on his mind and couldn't say what it was.'

'Well, his letters are censored, aren't they?'

'Yes, but he usually manages a bit of a joke or a tale about some of his men, and he's always written about Beckbridge and what's happening here. Not a word about that. And not a word about Laura either. He'd always said a lot about her. D'you think they had a row?'

'Don't know. No doubt you'll meet her. Perhaps she'll tell you.'

'Is she still working up at the Hall?'

'Yes. It's nuff'n like it were in the old days. There's only Mr and Mrs Ward to staff it now, except service people, o' course. No doubt Wayne told you it's a hospital for burnt airmen. Lady Helen helps to run it. Steve Wainright was a patient there. He's in the RAF, or he was 'til he was shot down. Terrible burns, he had. Hard to look him in the face at the beginning, but he don' look so bad now. I expect you'll meet him and Jenny and Kathy too.'

The back door was opened and Oliver ushered Lily into the room.

She dashed across the room and flung herself at Valerie. 'Why didn't you let us know you were coming? I was never so shocked in all my life when Oliver walked into my kitchen.' She stepped back from Valerie's embrace to peer at her. 'You haven't changed much. A bit fatter, but then you haven't had rationing like we have. And no grey hairs, but that's due to the bottle, i'n't it?'

'Oh, Ma, you do know how to make a girl feel good.'

'I speak my mind. Now, Oliver, he don't look a day older than when I last saw him, 'cept he looks more distinguished. Grey sideburns suit him.'

'Thank you, Ma,' he said.

'We'll have to celebrate. Let's all go down to the pub for a meal and a knees-up tonight. Joe will rustle something up for us seein's it's a special occasion.'

They agreed it would be a good idea, and when they had finished their tea and sampled the freshly cooked mince pies, Oliver and Valerie unpacked in Joyce's bedroom and Joyce moved her things into Ken's room. Then they set off for The Jolly Brewers. Joyce and Valerie had hardly drawn breath since they had been reunited, and by the time they reached the pub Valerie was *au fait* with everything that had happened in Beckbridge in the last twenty-five years. It had all been told in letters, but that wasn't the same as talking about it, mulling it over, offering opinions. Joyce heard all about life in Canada, which filled her with envy.

'Everyone said it wouldn't work,' Valerie told her. 'Marrying a Canadian, I mean. Ma and Pa said I was going off into the unknown and if it didn't work out I'd be all alone in a strange country, and, even if we did stay together, I'd be treated worse than a skivvy. To hear them talk you'd ha' thought I was going to marry a savage and live in the wilderness.' She laughed suddenly, a noisy genial sound. 'It was nothing like that, not for me, and I knew Oliver wouldn't let me down. We had to work like blacks to build the business, but we made it together. I'n't that right, Ollie?' Her husband nodded and she went on. 'We've got six garages now, selling cars and doing

335

maintenance. They've all got good managers, so Ollie don't really need to go to work at all. It's why he was so keen to come over. And when he told me he was definitely coming, I sure wasn't going to be left behind.'

'Weren't you afraid of being torpedoed?'

'It crossed my mind, but what the hell, you can only die once. Besides, the U-boats have been beat, haven't they?'

'Hev they?' Joyce said vaguely. She had just seen Steve going into The Jolly Brewers. He was in uniform and she wondered why. He had become a familiar sight about the village, but was usually in a thick pullover with his corduroys tucked into Wellington boots, helping with the farm work when he wasn't up at the Hall.

'Anyway, I'm here now and Ollie is going to try and find out where Wayne is before he reports for duty. Wouldn't it be grand if he could get some leave while we're here?'

They let themselves into the pub, carefully shutting the outer door before opening the inner one, a habit the patrons of the establishment had acquired because of the blackout. The bar was warm and smoky. The regulars were in their usual places, playing dominoes or darts or shove ha'penny, a half pint of beer at their elbows. Steve had just taken his beer to a seat in the corner.

'All alone, Steve?' Joyce asked. 'Mind if we join you?'

'Help yourself.'

'This is my sister, Valerie, and her husband Oliver. And this is Steve Wainright, Kathy's son.'

Steve rose and shook hands with them, but his mind registered that these must be Wayne Donovan's parents.

'I remember Kathy,' Valerie said, trying not to notice his face. 'And William. I suppose he's running the farm now?'

'Yes, my Wainright grandparents died some years ago.'

'You'll be taking over yourself one day, won't you?'

'Yes, but not yet. Dad's in splendid health and I've got a war to fight.'

'I thought you'd finished with all that,' Joyce said. 'Surely they don't expect you to go back?'

'Why not? I can still fly. The country can't afford to leave experienced pilots kicking their heels.'

She turned to her sister. 'Steve and Ken were flying together when they were hit. Ken bailed out, but Steve tried to land the aircraft and got burnt. The medics have done a grand job on you, haven't they, Steve? He was sent to Beckbridge Hall to be looked after between ops, so Kathy was able to see a lot of him. And Laura nursed him.'

'Laura?' Oliver said. 'Isn't that the girl Wayne says he's crazy about?'

'That's the one,' Valerie confirmed.

'I should like to meet her. Is she still there?'

Steve didn't hear Joyce's answer. He didn't want to listen to the rest of the conversation but he couldn't get out without pushing past them, and so he was obliged to sit there, sipping his beer and listening to them going on about Laura and Wayne until he wanted to yell out in frustration. But in a self-flagellating way he also wanted to know the worst; he wanted to be sure there was no hope for him.

'Are you going up to the Hall?' Lily asked Oliver, looking at him with her head on one side.

'Is there any reason why I should not?' It was said defensively.

'No, I suppose not. It's a convalescent hospital now, not the stately home it once was. It's full of airmen like Steve here, and doctors and nurses and orderlies.'

'I know that. Wayne told us.'

'The Earl and Countess are long dead.' She gave him another searching look. 'So is Captain Barstairs. He never came back from France.'

If Barstairs hadn't come back from France, then the Earl had lied to him. It set Oliver wondering, all over again, why Helen had never answered his letters. 'What about Lady Helen?'

'She's still there. What d'yew want to see her for?'

Steve detected undercurrents to the conversation that had not been there before. Mrs Wilson seemed to be advising Major

337

Donovan against visiting the Hall and he wondered why. Both Valerie and Joyce were looking at her in a bemused kind of way.

'I didn't say I did. I said I wanted to meet Laura.'

'She's always very busy, isn't she, Steve? Works funny hours.'

'Yes,' he said.

Oliver suddenly became aware of a conspiracy and wondered at it. 'What's wrong with her?' he demanded.

'Nothing,' Joyce said. 'You go if you want to. If she's on duty, she'll be able to tell you when she's off. We'll invite her to a meal. Christmas dinner if she can make it.'

'Oh, wouldn't it be wonderful if Wayne came for Christmas,' Valerie cried. 'And Ken and Ian and Stella; a really family Christmas.'

'In the middle of a war?' Lily put in. 'Some hopes of that.'

'I must be going,' Steve said. 'I only popped in for a quick one.' He got up and pushed his way past them. 'Nice to have met you, Mrs Donovan. Major.' He shook hands with them and made his escape.

It was a cold night – freezing, he decided. The sky was clear and the road and hedges were illuminated in an ethereal kind of light. He looked up. The moon and stars hung there as they always had; there were no aircraft, friend or foe. The Luftwaffe were as good as beaten, the British Navy once more controlled the seas, and he did not doubt the second front that everyone had been talking about for months would not be long in coming. He would be there. He had been in at the beginning and he wanted to be in at the end. He would try not to think of Laura. Or Wayne Donovan. Or anything except getting the job done.

He was due back at the Hall but had promised his mother he would go in and tell her what Mr McIndoe had said, so he turned in at the farm gate. Meg and Daphne were crossing the yard to go to their quarters and he stopped to bid them goodnight.

'How did you get on?' Meg asked.

'Fine,' he said. 'They don't want to see me any more. Apparently I'm cured.'

'So you've got your discharge?'

'No, I have to go before a medical board and it's up to them to decide if I'm fit for duty.' He said it almost regretfully, having decided not to let his mother know that he was going to do his damnedest to convince them he was, and that meant deceiving anyone who could tell her. 'But not until the New Year.'

'Good, you'll be here for Christmas,' Meg said. 'That will please your mother. She's waiting for you.'

'Right. I'll go and give her the good news. Goodnight, girls.'

He left them and went into the kitchen. His mother and Gran had been doing some Christmas baking and the room struck warm after the cold outside. He shed his cap and overcoat, leaving them on the back of the leather sofa as he went to kiss them both. 'I'm back, safe and sound.'

'How did you get on?'

'OK. I've been given leave until I go before a medical board.'

'And they'll decide you have done your bit and can spend the rest of the war at home, helping on the farm, I hope.'

'I don't know. Maybe.' He sat at the table and picked up one of the mince pies cooling on a rack.

'Be careful, that's very hot,' his mother said. 'Which train did you catch?'

'I got to Attlesham about seven and caught a bus.'

'Why didn't you ring from the station? Someone would have fetched you.'

'It was too cold to hang around. Anyway, when I got off the bus I nipped into The Jolly Brewers for a quick one. You'll never guess who was there.'

'No, so tell us.'

'Joyce's sister, Valerie, and her husband. All the way from Canada.'

'No? How did they manage that?'

'Came over on a troopship, apparently. He was in uniform. According to Joyce, Oliver's been given a hush-hush job to do with the second front and Valerie managed to get a berth on the ship bringing him over.'

'How long are they here for?' his grandmother asked.

'Don't know. Over Christmas, they said.'

'That'll put the cat among the pigeons.'

'Why?'

'That's all over and done with,' Kathy put in quickly, addressing her mother. 'No point in bringing it up again now.'

'What's over and done with?' he demanded.

'The past,' she said.

'It always catches up with you in the end,' Alice said. 'Helen is going to learn that, I reckon.'

'Whatever are you talking about?' Steve looked from one to the other.

'It was a long time ago,' his mother said wearily. 'During the last war Uncle Henry kept open house for servicemen and one of them was Oliver Donovan. He was rather sweet on Helen at one time.'

'So?' He was grinning. It seemed Aunt Helen had hidden depths, but he couldn't see it was anything to get worked up about. 'Was she sweet on him?'

'I doubt she'd even remember him,' his mother put in sharply. 'Let's drop the subject. Have you had anything to eat?'

'I had a sandwich at Liverpool Street. Horrible grey bread, margarine and dried-up cheese. These mince pies are great.'

'Yes, well, don't eat any more of them, they're for Christmas and I only had one jar of mincemeat. Will an egg do?'

'Yes, fine.'

Kathy busied herself boiling an egg and cutting bread and butter, and the subject of Oliver Donovan was dropped, but Steve was curious and wondered if Laura knew anything about it. Having devoured the egg, he said goodnight to them and went back to the Hall. It would be his last night there. Tomorrow he would be discharged and would move back home until his appointment with the medical board. He wasn't sure how he felt about that.

Living at the Hall with so many in the same boat had given him a kind of security; it had been a cocoon protecting him from the outside world. On the other hand, he was fit and well, thanks to Mr McIndoe and Laura, and if he was going back to flying, the sooner he climbed out of that cocoon and tested his wings the better. He certainly did not want to be a witness to Laura's meeting with Wayne's parents. But he couldn't help being curious about what had happened in the past. Had Aunt Helen had an affair with Oliver Donovan? Upright, starchy Lady Helen Barstairs having an affair? No, he couldn't believe it. But if it were true, his grandmother was right; it would put the cat among the pigeons.

Oliver stopped when he reached the bend in the drive and stood looking at the old house. From the outside it looked no different. The creeper-clad walls and rows of windows looked exactly the same. Smoke still drifted from its chimneys, its huge oak door still shut out the unwelcome caller. You had to ring the bell, he remembered, and stand on the step until a butler in a tail suit let you in as far as the hall and then went to announce your presence. Then Lady Hardingham, or even the Earl himself, would come forward and greet you, telling you to make yourself at home and would you like some tea, or a bath. And you would go into the drawing room where a crowd of other servicemen would be sitting around drinking tea and talking, waiting for their turn in the bathroom.

That was in the beginning, before he fell in love with Helen and they started to meet clandestinely. Helen did not want anyone to know about their affair until she had told Richard. She wanted to tell her husband to his face, she had said. He had gone along with that and went off to France, leaving her in tears and wondering if he would live to see her again. He had written to her as often as his duties allowed. He had had one reply and that was before he left England. After that, nothing. His letters pleading for an explanation for her silence had never been answered. He hadn't wanted to believe the love they had for each other could not survive the parting and he blamed the vagaries of the post.

He had come back to England in the January of 1918, and then it was on a stretcher. The first thing he did on being declared fit and being given leave was to make for Beckbridge and the Hall. It was once again simply a stately home; there were no servicemen drinking tea and taking baths. He had stopped halfway up the drive to look up at the house, as he was doing now, wondering if she could see him, imagining her at one of the windows looking back at him, trying to gauge how she would feel on seeing him again. But there had been no sign of her, no one came out of the house while he was there, and he had taken a deep breath and continued to the front door. He had been admitted by the same butler, who said pompously that he would see if his lordship was at home. It wasn't the Earl he had come to see but Helen, but the butler ignored that.

His lordship's greeting should have warned him. 'What are you doing here?'

'I came to see Lady Helen.'

'She isn't here and you would oblige me by taking yourself off.' It didn't need a clairvoyant to see he was angry and only his innate breeding stopped him raising his voice. 'You abused my hospitality, made a nuisance of yourself to my daughter, knowing she was married, and now you have the effrontery to turn up again like a bad penny.'

'You do not understand. It wasn't like that.'

'Oh, I understand all right. It is you who are under a misapprehension. My daughter wishes never to see you again.'

'I do not believe that. Let me see her. I want to hear it from her own lips.'

'Helen is not here. She has gone to join her husband. No doubt they will be looking for a home of their own when the war is over. Please leave now, or I shall have you thrown out.'

He had gone to The Jolly Brewers and got very drunk. It was from Valerie he learnt that Helen had indeed gone away. Valerie was not a complete stranger; he had seen her up at the hall working as a servant, but now she was a barmaid. 'Better pay and more fun,' she had told him, laughing. The bar wasn't busy and they had talked a lot, although he had been far too drunk to be coherent and could not remember anything they said. He had woken up the next morning in the hayloft of a barn and she was beside him, both as naked as the day they were born. He could not remember how he got there or anything about the night before, but it was obvious what had happened.

Standing in the drive, looking up at the house, in another uniform, in the middle of another war, Oliver wondered why he had come. Did he really want to open up old wounds? But had the wounds ever healed? Surely she could have answered his letters, even if it was only to confirm what her father had told him: that she didn't want to see him again. It was water under the bridge in any case. He had married Valerie because she told him she was pregnant, and since then he had done everything in his power to make the marriage a success. And he supposed it had been. He should not even be thinking of Helen. It had been a wartime romance that was bound to end in tears for someone. It was one of the reasons he wanted to meet Laura, to convince himself it couldn't happen to his son. He didn't want Wayne hurt, but that last letter had made him wonder. It had arrived months ago and since then there had been nothing. If she had sent Wayne packing as he had been sent packing, it would not have put the boy in the right frame of mind to go into battle. Was that why they hadn't heard from him? His son was all in all to him.

He threw away the stub of the cigarette he had been smoking and strode up the drive to the house.

Helen put the toy dog inside the box and stuffed crumpled tissue round it before closing the lid and covering it in crêpe paper, smiling as she imagined Robby opening it on Christmas morning.

So much had happened since Anne died, and yet nothing at all had changed. Life had gone on and Laura had become a source of great joy, though the revelation about her birth had strained the relationship almost to breaking point and made them both unhappy. Things were getting better and she hoped that perhaps over Christmas they could get back to the quiet contentment with each other they had built up before Wayne arrived. Robby had helped because they both idolised him. He was not yet old enough to be told of their true relationship; it would be up to Laura to decide when, or even if, he was told. He could never be the Earl but he was her heir, and later, when this dreadful war was over and Robby had grown up, Helen would involve him in whatever decisions she took. If he decided he wanted to keep the Hall, it behoved her to hang onto it, though how it could be done, given the expense of upkeep and lack of servants, she had no idea.

She sighed, wondering how different things would have been if she had not met and married Richard, or if Laura had been his daughter and not Oliver's; if her parents had lived longer or Anne had not died when she did; if Oliver had known she was pregnant before he left. If only he had answered her letters; she could imagine one going astray, but not all of them. She had often wondered what they would say to each other if they ever met again, and in the early years after the war she would imagine them falling into each other's arms and reaffirming their love. She would daydream about it, filling the void in her life with imagined laughter and joy. But the years had blotted everything out – their passion, their ease with each other, the jokes they shared, the love they bore each other. So much love. Twenty-five years on and she couldn't leave well alone, she had to give the past a little stir now and again, twiddle the knobs on the set to see if any of the music was still there. And all she got was atmospherics.

She was laughing at her own foolishness when the front doorbell rang. Knowing someone else would answer it, she continued packing her parcel. She had posted all her cards; dreadful things they were because of the shortage of paper and half the factories making other things, while printers were busy with government posters and leaflets about this or that regulation. They were lucky there were any cards being made at all. Laura, who had a talent for drawing, had made all hers and very good they were too. It was the same with gifts. The choice was limited, but Helen intended to make sure Robby had a good Christmas and had bought a few toys and resurrected a few more from the attic, which some of the patients who needed therapy had mended and painted. She had knitted a pullover, some mittens and a scarf from a hardly worn pullover of her father's she had unpicked. It was what you had to do nowadays: find a second use for everything.

There was a knock on the door which was opened by the young WAAF who acted as a receptionist. 'Someone to see you, my lady.' She stood aside to allow the officer to enter.

Helen didn't hear the click of the door as it was shut behind the WAAF, she didn't move, couldn't move. She was dreaming. It was all part of that nostalgic trip she had been making into the past. He wasn't real.

'Helen.' The voice was real and sounded loud in her ears, an intrusion on her silent tumbling thoughts.

The tumult inside her set every nerve end jangling. He was here, slightly older, slightly thicker about the waist, but still the Oliver she had known and loved. But had that love survived the years, the whole generation it spanned? And the fact that he had married someone else? With a visible effort she pulled herself together. 'Oliver Donovan, well I never.' Her voice was brittle with the effort of controlling it. 'And still in uniform, I see.'

'The opportunity came to do my bit for the war and I took it.' She was thin as a rake, her hair quite grey, yet she was hardly older than Valerie. But in spite of that, she was still a remarkably attractive woman.

'Please sit down. I was just wrapping a few Christmas presents.'

He sat down on the edge of the sofa and looked about him. A thick carpet covered the floor on which stood two sofas and a couple of armchairs. *The Times* and the local *Gazette* lay neatly folded on a coffee table, along with a couple of magazines. A flower arrangement stood on a side table and on a shelf in the alcove of the fireplace were ornaments he guessed were valuable; an ornate clock on the marble mantelshelf ticked loudly and there were several interesting paintings on the walls and some photographs in frames on the mantelpiece. It was exactly as it had been when he last entered it, except for the wrapping paper and the toys. There was a child in the house; no one had told him about a child.

'Well?' she said when he did not speak. 'What can I do for you?'

'I came hoping to speak with Laura,' he said, detecting the coolness in her voice.

'Laura?' She sat down heavily on the sofa opposite him, her mind in a whirl. Had he known about his daughter all along? Had he come to lay claim to her?

'Yes. Wayne wrote so much about her, I thought I'd like to meet her.'

'Oh.' He hadn't come to see her after all, but neither did he seem to know he was Laura's father. 'I'm afraid she is out. She has taken Robby into Attlesham to buy him some new shoes. He is growing so quickly, all his clothing coupons seem to go on shoes.'

'Who is Robby?'

'Laura's little boy.' She was tempted to add, 'and your grandson,' but decided not to make matters more difficult than they already were. 'I thought while he was out of the house I'd wrap up his presents. Didn't Wayne tell you she had a son?'

'You mean she's married? Good God! It's surely not happening again.'

'What do you mean "happening again"? Has Wayne—?'

'No, not Wayne.' He stood up to face her. 'You know what I mean. Is she like you, playing fast and loose until her husband comes back and then it's goodbye and thanks for the memory?'

She was angry. 'You've no right to say that, no right at all. My husband never came back and Laura is a widow. Her husband was a Spitfire pilot. He was shot down and killed.'

He stopped to look down at her. She would have liked to have stood, so as to be on level terms, but she did not think her legs would support her. As it was, she was shaking so much she was afraid he would see it. 'I'm sorry,' he said. 'I should not have tarred her with the same brush. But why didn't you answer my letters?'

'What letters? I received no letters from you, not a single one. I wrote, I don't know how many times… I told you…' She stopped, unwilling to tell him about Laura, though she supposed he would have to know sometime. 'I needed you. After my parents found out… Well, life became a little difficult.' An understatement if ever there was one.

'You wrote and I wrote,' he said bitterly, sitting down heavily. 'They must have intercepted the letters.'

'They?'

'Your parents. Did you never think of that?'

'No, I didn't. I assumed you didn't want to know. My aunt said you had had your fun and that was all you were after.'

'Your aunt?'

'Yes, I went to stay with her for a time.'

'And you believed her?'

'Not at first, but when I didn't hear from you…' She shrugged her shoulders. 'But it doesn't matter now, does it? Water under the bridge. You didn't lose any time in marrying someone else, did you?'

'Can you blame me? I came back. The very first chance I had I came back to you. Your father said you never wanted to see me again, that you had gone to be with your husband and would be looking for a home with him when the war ended. I was gutted. I couldn't believe it.'

'But you did believe it.'

'Yes, I had to. Everyone I spoke to confirmed it. I'm ashamed to say I married Valerie on the rebound.'

'Liar! Wayne was born only six months after—' She stopped suddenly, realising where her words were taking her. 'Papa lied,' she added quietly. 'I never saw my husband again after he went to

France. He was taken prisoner and died in captivity.'

'I didn't know that until yesterday. Joyce told me. And for your information, Wayne was a seven-month baby.'

'Oh.'

'Yes. A mess all round. Don't misunderstand, though; Valerie has been a good wife to me, taken the rough with the smooth, and we both love our son. That's why I don't want him hurt.'

'Is there any reason why he should be?'

'No, but I detected something was wrong in his last letter and that was months ago. We haven't heard from him since and we are both worried. We thought Laura might shed some light on it.'

'As I said, she isn't here.'

'When do you expect her back?'

She shrugged. 'I don't know. It depends on the buses. But she's on duty again this evening.'

'I'll come back, shall I?'

'If you like.' It was said in a monotone. She was exhausted and all she wanted was to be left alone to grieve for what might have been, for broken dreams, for a daughter who was going to be upset all over again before the day was out.

She stood up and went with him to the front door, half afraid that Laura would be coming up the drive. But she wasn't. He didn't touch her, didn't attempt to shake her hand, and she watched from the steps as he strode off down the drive. It was beginning to snow and some of the flakes landed on his shoulders before disappearing. She turned slowly and went back to wrapping her parcels, too numb even to weep.

Steve had gone into Attlesham with Laura and Robby. He wanted her to help him buy presents for the family and the boys, as well as Meg and Daphne. There wasn't much choice but he had managed to find something for everyone. Some of the shop assistants had looked a little sideways at him, but he was learning not to mind. The shopping finished, they had a pot of tea and a bun in the British

Restaurant before going to catch the bus home. Their conversation had been impersonal, mostly about the shopping and their plans for Christmas; Laura was arranging a party on Boxing Day for those patients fit enough to enjoy one and intended to invite any unattached young ladies to join the men. I've asked Meg and Jenny to come – and Daphne, of course, even though she's no longer unattached,' she told him, pouring tea. 'I think it will cheer my boys up.' The patients were always her 'boys'. 'You'll come too, won't you?'

He laughed. 'I'm not an unattached young lady.'

'No, but until this morning you were a patient. Besides, I want you there.'

Steve wondered if she knew Major Donovan and his wife were staying in the village. He had a strange feeling their arrival would be significant. 'Then of course I'll come.'

'I mean to ask your parents too. And there's Joyce, of course.'

She definitely didn't know. He wondered whether to tell her but decided not to spoil the outing, which it most certainly would. 'You'll end up asking half the village.'

'Why not? Food and drink might be a problem, but we'll manage. I'm sure everyone will muck in.'

When the bus arrived, Steve took charge of the string bags of shopping while Laura folded Robby's pushchair and left it under the stairs before moving down the gangway to find seats. The bus was crowded with shoppers, some grumbling about the queues, which seemed to get longer and longer; some making jokes, laughing cheerfully, convinced the tide had turned and the long-wished-for second front was just around the corner. Others talked of relatives and friends who would spend their Christmas a long way from home; some sat silently looking out of the steamed-up window at the winter countryside.

'Another year gone,' Laura said as she settled Robby on her knee. 'I can't believe how quickly it's flown.'

'In one way, perhaps, but in another it has crawled past in a sort of nightmare,' Steve said. 'Are we any further forward?'

'Of course we are. You are well and strong again and that's the most important thing. And, please God, the war is being won.'

'I'm going back, you know,' he said quietly.

'I know. If that's what you want…' She stopped, longing to tell him not to go, that she loved him and needed him, but it wouldn't be fair to put that burden on him. There was so much about her he didn't know and might not like. 'You must do what you think is right, Steve.'

They fell silent. He wanted to ask if she could bear to overlook his scars and marry him, but he could not. It wasn't so much the scars that held him back, not any more, but the knowledge that perhaps next time he wouldn't be so lucky; no woman deserved to be widowed twice by war. Neither could he ignore the fact that Wayne Donovan hovered in the background. She never spoke of him, but that didn't mean she didn't think of him. Where was he? If he was in England, he'd be bound to come to Beckbridge as soon as he could, especially if he knew his parents were here.

It was snowing as the bus drew up outside The Jolly Brewers. They gathered up their bags and the pushchair and started to walk the rest of the way. They had only gone a few yards when the twins caught them up. The school had broken up for the holiday and they were bored. They walked either side of Steve and Laura, effectively ending any chance of private conversation. At the end of the lane leading to the farm, they left Laura to continue alone.

Pushing Robby, she turned into the drive of the Hall to see a tall man in a Canadian uniform walking towards her. Her first thought was that he had brought news of Wayne and her heart thumped uncomfortably, wondering if he had been wounded or worse. 'Good afternoon,' she said. He had stopped walking and was staring at her as if he could not believe his eyes. 'Were you looking for someone?'

He pulled himself together. 'You must be Laura.'

'Yes. What can I do for you? Have you brought news of Wayne?'

'No, that's the problem. Look, is there somewhere we can talk?'

'Come back to the house.'

'I'd rather not. Not at the moment.'

'How very mysterious. We can't stand here, we'll freeze. Let's go to the summer house.' She did not wait for an answer but set off across the grass. He hesitated, but when she did not look back, he followed.

The short walk was accomplished in silence. His head was buzzing over his encounter with Helen, which had not been what he expected – but then he didn't know what he had expected. Over the years he had always imagined her with her husband, living a life in which memories of him hardly impinged. To see this young lady walking towards him when his head was full of events of a quarter of a century before had given him a severe jolt. Here was Helen as she had been, the beautiful Helen of his fondest memories, the Helen he had loved, the one who had professed to love him. Here was the shining dark hair, the widow's peak, the firm chin and expressive eyes. He tried telling himself his eyes were deceiving him but that didn't work; she was real. He wanted to reach out and touch her, just to make sure. And here was the summer house where he and Helen had met and made love, where they had parted in tears. 'Oh, Helen,' he murmured.

If she heard him she gave no indication of it as she opened the door and pushed Robby inside. He followed. 'It's not very warm in here,' she said, shutting the door and bending to let Robby out of his chair to run about.

'I won't keep you long.' He sat down on the bench and looked up at her. 'You are so like Helen, it's uncanny.'

'You know her?'

'Oh yes, from way back.'

She sat down suddenly. 'You're Oliver Donovan.' This was her father, the man who had given her birth, the man Helen had loved, the man who had deserted her and never acknowledged his child. She wasn't sure what she felt, but it wasn't daughterly love. It was more a kind of detachment.

'Yes.'

'Have you seen Helen?'

'Yes.'

What had they talked about? Had he told Helen why he had deserted her in her hour of need and turned to Joyce's sister? Had Helen explained about her? It might account for the strange looks he was giving her. 'What did she tell you?' Robby was clambering on the bench beside her to look out of the window at the lake and she put out a hand to steady him.

'That you were out shopping and to come back later if I wanted to talk to you. You see, we are worried about Wayne, his mother and I. We haven't heard from him for months and we thought you might know where he is.'

'I'm sorry, I don't.'

'Surely he's written to you? He might not be able to say where he is, but he could have told you he was well.'

'He hasn't written since he went back from leave last time.' He didn't know she was his daughter; she could tell by the way he was questioning her. It wasn't up to her to tell him. If Helen had wanted him to know she would have told him herself.

'Did you quarrel? His early letters were so full of you and his hope that you would agree to marry him. His only concern seemed to be that you might not want to live in Canada. We would not stand in his way if he wanted to stay in the UK, but it would make his mother and me very unhappy. He is our only child; we live for him. I wanted to ask you if that was the trouble, and if it was, to persuade you to change your mind and consent to live near us. We would make you very welcome. Life in Canada is good; Valerie will tell you that.'

'Is Mrs Donovan here with you?'

'Yes, she's gone to Norwich with Joyce, visiting old friends, seeing how it's changed. I took the opportunity to come and make your acquaintance; if the news was bad, I wanted to be the one to break it to her.'

'If Wayne had been a casualty, surely you would have been told?

As for my living in Canada; the subject never came up. Wayne and I are not thinking of marrying.'

'You turned him down?'

'Yes.'

'That explains it.'

'Explains what?'

'Why his last letter was so strange. He didn't mention you once. I think you have made him one very unhappy young man.'

'I'm sorry for that, Major Donovan, but it simply could not be.'

'Has he accepted that?'

'I am sure he has. We have agreed to be good friends.'

He stood up. 'Then there's no more to be said. I'm sorry I troubled you.'

'And I'm sorry too, more than I can tell you.' She scooped Robby up and strapped him in his pushchair. 'I must be going. I'm on duty this evening and I have to give Robby his tea.'

He held the door open for her to manoeuvre the pushchair outside. 'If you don't mind, I'll sit here for a while.'

'Of course. Take all the time you want.' She left him and hurried back to the house. The snow had turned to sleet, which stung her face.

Oliver returned to the bench and sat down again. How often had he dreamt of this place, of meeting Helen, of talking of everything under the sun, of their love for each other and plans for the future? It had not been Helen who had wrecked those but her father. All through that terrifying battle at Passchendale, the only thing that had kept him going was the prospect of coming back to Helen. It was that which had kept him alive after he had been wounded. He remembered that acrimonious interview with the Earl as if it were yesterday. Why had he believed him, why had he not had more faith? Why, in heaven's name, had he got so drunk that he had fallen into the arms of the first sympathetic woman he met and made her pregnant? At first he had looked on that as a kind of punishment and marrying her was something he had to do for his conscience's sake, but as the years passed and the memory gradually dimmed, they had been happy, he and Val, working hard, making a success of their lives and adoring Wayne. Anything that hurt his son, hurt him. It was as if he had been rejected all over again.

He rose and went outside to stand looking at the lake. At this time of the year it was cold and uninviting. The reeds were brown and drooping, but there were still ducks bobbing up and down on it. And the old boathouse was still there, more dilapidated than ever. Strange that the boathouse should be falling apart but not the summer house. He looked back at it and realised it had been moved; it was a few yards further from the water. Where it had been was a bumpy square of yellowing grass; the tree that had once overhung it was a blackened stump. The whole thing had been destroyed and rebuilt. Who had done that and why? And who exactly was Laura? She was so like Helen, it had given him a tremendous shock, seeing her coming towards him. Were the two related? He knew very little about Helen's relatives apart from the Earl and the Countess, and her cousin Kathy. That was the one who had married the farmer, the mother of the burnt airman. Their lives had moved on. All their lives.

'Oh, what the hell,' he said aloud and trudged back to the drive and out onto the road.

'I met my father,' Laura said bluntly. Robby had been given his tea and put to bed and now she and Helen were laying the table for their own meal.

'Oh.' Helen paused, a bundle of cutlery in her hand, and looked up at Laura. 'What did he say?'

'He wanted to know if I knew where Wayne was and if I married him, would I consider living in Canada. I told him I did not know where his son was, and that I would not be marrying him. It made me feel – oh, I don't know – mean, I suppose. He obviously thinks the world of Wayne.'

'You didn't tell him—'

'No. I didn't see the point. If you want him to know, you tell him.'

'It's not what I want, Laura, it's what you want. How do you feel about it, bearing in mind it won't make any difference to the way we live our lives? On the other hand, it might be nice for you to have someone besides me.'

'Nice for me! I had a father once, one I adored, I don't want another. And as you say, it won't make any difference to us. I think I'll just content myself with my two mothers.' She smiled as she said it and saw the relief on Helen's face. 'Of course, he might find out. He did comment on how much I looked like you.'

'Plenty of people have done that. We'll just have to brazen it out as we've always done.'

'Wayne might tell him.'

'He's not here, is he? And perhaps he won't, if he thinks it will upset his mother.'

'Let's hope so. There is one thing, though…' Laura paused. Meeting her father had not been the earth-shattering experience she had expected it to be. He did not arouse any feelings of affection in her, but she had been surprised to see a little of him in Robby. Robby's hair had been dark, like Bob's, at birth, but as he was growing out of babyhood now, in certain lights there was a slight auburn tinge to it which she had always thought he had inherited from her. She must have got it from her father, because she had noticed the same shade in Major Donovan's hair. 'There's Robby.'

'Yes, there's Robby, but he's too young to understand. It's up to you what you tell him when he's old enough.'

'I feel like a conspirator. Was that how you and Mum felt when you were ordering my life for me?'

'It wasn't the way I wanted it, but what's the good of going over it? We can't change it. What we have to do is deal with the present and look to the future.'

Laura pulled herself together and tried to be practical. 'Yes, lets talk about Christmas and what we're going to do. I've got a little something for all the patients and staff...' She stopped speaking to go to the kitchen to fetch a casserole; it contained very little meat but the onion gravy was tasty. Helen followed to bring in the tureens of vegetables. Mrs Ward and two dailies from the village were busy washing up after the patients' evening meal.

'The boys have spent most of the day making paper chains with pictures cut from old magazines and flour paste,' Helen said as they returned and sat down to their meal. 'They are quite colourful. And Mr Ward brought the tree in.'

'Yes, I saw it in the hall. I promised Robby he could help us trim it.'

'What about the party?'

'It's mostly in hand. I'll need a couple of strong men to help move the carpet out of the ballroom if we are going to have dancing, and we'll need more chairs.' The ballroom had been converted into a day room, with a carpet at one end with easy chairs, a radio and a bookcase. At the other was a table tennis table and a dartboard. 'I'll put Flying Officer Bowyer and Sergeant Pilot Newnes in the little room at the back of the west wing. They won't feel up to partying and they'll be quiet in there.'

'It used to be the sewing room. In the days when I was a little girl, my mother employed a dressmaker and a general sewing woman to do the household mending. They were always busy.' She laughed. 'There was also a laundrywoman, and dairy maids and scullions, not to mention cooks, kitchen maids, chambermaids, parlourmaids, a butler and footmen. Most of those disappeared during the last war and what was left went one at a time afterwards. Except Mr and Mrs Ward. Apart from when the bomb dropped on the summer house, I can't remember a time when they were not here, ministering to our needs. They could tell a tale or two.'

'About you and me?'

'I don't know. They always pretended to believe the story my father told everyone, and as Richard never came back...' Helen paused. 'Enough of nostalgia. You were telling me about the party. Who've you invited?'

'Just about everyone. All those at Bridge Farm, of course, the parson and his wife and daughters, the doctor and his wife, the teachers at the school, and Joyce. I suggested if any of her family managed to get home for Christmas they would be welcome too. At the time I didn't know Major Donovan and his wife were going to be there. Now I'm in a bit of a quandary. How can we leave them out?'

'We can't.'

'I don't want you upset by them.'

'I won't be.'

'Are you sure?'

'Positive. I'll pretend to be glad to see someone from long ago, and I'll be friendly towards them in the condescending kind of way my mother used for servants and underlings; after all, Valerie was a chambermaid at one time. And if anyone says you look like me, I'll just say I've heard it all before and we might have the same great-great-grandmother, or something of that sort.'

'It will be an awful strain for you, and I did so want everyone to be relaxed and to enjoy themselves.'

'I'm a good actress, Laura, and I've spent years perfecting a stiff upper lip – twenty-five years, as a matter of fact. Don't worry about me. Look to yourself.'

'I'll be too busy to worry about them. Besides, when I met Oliver, I looked at him and I thought, "This is my father, his blood runs in my veins," but I felt nothing at all.'

'Then here's to Christmas.' Helen raised her glass of water. 'And may it be the last one of the war.'

'Amen to that.'

'Happy Christmas everyone!' Steve was the last to come down for his breakfast. His mother and the twins had been up for hours; his mother to get the turkey they had been fattening into the oven, the twins because they were too excited to stay in bed. Long before dawn they had discovered the paintboxes, the jigsaws, the new socks, which they suspected Aunty Kathy had knitted, and the Cox's apples, which had been in store since October – but what excited them more than anything was that their father had arrived just as they were going to bed the night before.

'You are not to go and disturb him,' Kathy said as soon as they appeared in the kitchen. 'If you can't stay in bed, find something quiet to do until they get up.' She smiled as she said it, remembering Daphne's exuberant greeting when she saw her husband on the doormat. She had flung herself at him, winding her legs about his waist and kissing him over and over again. 'Hold on, old girl,' he had said, grinning all over his face. 'Let me get in the door.'

She had dragged him in and Alec kissed or shook hands with everyone. Christmas seemed to start from there. Homemade beer appeared, along with homemade elderberry wine and a bottle of whisky William had been hoarding. Steve was home and needing his bed, so Alec and Daphne had gone over to the stable flat. Meg had gone home for a few days' leave.

Gradually, one by one, they appeared in the kitchen for breakfast. William followed the twins because he had to see to the animals and do the milking before he could sit down to enjoy his breakfast. Daphne and Alec came next, glowing from their loving and anxious not to neglect the twins; then Jenny came to help her mother make breakfast while Alice set about laying the table and, when that was done, poked about among the presents under the tree, as curious as a child to feel the parcels and guess who had given what. And finally Steve arrived, washed, dressed and shaved.

'Happy Christmas, son,' Kathy said, putting fried eggs on one large dish and bacon on another. 'Now we're all here.'

'I met Ken Moreton at Liverpool Street last night,' Alec said as they all sat around the table. 'We travelled down together.'

'Oh, how nice for Joyce,' Kathy said. 'She'll be pleased as punch.'

'I might go to the pub after church,' Steve said. 'Have a natter with him, see what he's been up to in my absence. He's bound to be there.'

The church was already filling up when Kathy and William herded their brood into their usual pew. As the organist played softly, the congregation looked about them and smiled at each other, mouthing 'Happy Christmas'. Steve was surprised to see the Moretons occupying the pew across the aisle; they were not usually churchgoers, but he supposed Christmas was an exception, particularly as they had guests – guests, moreover, they would want to show off. There was Joyce and her mother, and another woman in a fur coat and a hat which reminded him of pictures of Robin Hood. Stella was there, looking very grown-up, and Ken, in uniform. And then there was Major Donovan and beside him another man in uniform. 'Wayne,' Jenny whispered beside him. 'The only one who's missing is Ian.'

Steve turned immediately to look for Laura. She was sitting right at the front in the Hardingham pew next to Helen, Robby on her lap, and had her back to the congregation. Unless she already knew Wayne was there, she would not see him until the service ended. The parson, followed by the choir, which included the reluctant twins, made their way up the aisle and the service began. Steve kept his eyes on the back of Laura's dark head the whole time. They sang the traditional hymns lustily, prayed earnestly for the end of the bloodshed, for forgiveness and tolerance, remembered those who had given their lives, the wounded, and others unable to be with their families, and were reminded in a lengthy sermon of what they were fighting for. Laura did not turn round once.

When the service ended, it was Helen and Laura, carrying Robby, who left the church first, following the parson and choir down the aisle. Steve studied Laura's face as they walked slowly to the back of the church, greeting people and saying 'Happy Christmas' as she went.

Laura saw Oliver first and then Wayne, and for a moment the whole congregation seemed to revolve. She felt Helen's hand on her arm and her quiet murmur, 'Steady,' before she took a deep breath and continued down the aisle, passing Kathy and Steve as she went. Bless him, he did not know the half of it, but he was there, her rock, as always. Out in the churchyard, in spite of the cold wind that threatened more sleet, if not snow, everyone was milling, stamping their feet and blowing on their hands, being introduced and exchanging good wishes. Laura went round them all, before stopping in front of Wayne and reaching up to kiss his cheek. 'Good to see you, Wayne. On leave, are you?'

'Just a week. Are you well?'

'Very well, thank you. You must have been surprised to find your parents here?'

'Too true, I was. A smashing Christmas present. Have you met Mom and Pop?' He turned to Oliver and Valerie. 'This is Laura.'

Oliver smiled at her. 'We have met. Happy Christmas, Laura.'

'So this is the famous Laura,' Valerie said, eyeing her up and down. 'I can see why Wayne fell for you.'

'We are good friends,' Laura said. Then to Wayne, 'I'll catch up with you later. You're all coming up to the Hall tomorrow, aren't you?'

'Wouldn't miss it for the world,' Valerie put in. 'Hallo, my lady. Remember me? I worked at the Hall during the last war. It'll be fun to see how it's changed.'

'Of course I remember you. You will notice a great many changes, I expect.' To Laura, Helen said, 'It's too cold to stand about; Robby is shivering. Let's get home to the fire.' And with that she made her way down the path and onto the road, where the Humber was parked. Laura followed.

'She always was a stuck-up bitch,' Valerie said when they were out of earshot. 'Who's coming to the pub for a quick one before dinner?'

The crowd spilt up into those hurrying home to the cooking and those with time to spare for drinking. 'How's it going?' Steve asked Ken as they walked.

'Same as ever. Dodging flak, dropping flares and high-tailing it home. I miss you.'

'Well, you're not going to miss me much longer. I'm off to Central

Medical in the New Year to be passed fit to return to duty.'

'Sure that's what you want?'

'I'm sure.'

'Wayne's been in Italy. There was a bit of a lull in the fighting and they decided to send some men home on Christmas leave. He's not sure if he'll have to go back or stay here to train for the invasion.'

So that's where he'd been. 'When d'you reckon that will be?'

Ken shrugged. 'No idea. Wayne, you got any idea when we're going to start the second front?'

'None at all,' Wayne answered.

'Do you know, Uncle Ollie?' Ken asked.

'No, why would they tell me?'

'I thought you came over specially to help with it.'

'I didn't say that, did I?'

Ken laughed. 'OK, keep your hair on. I won't ask again, though nobody seems to be talking about anything else.'

'Are you going to Mrs Drummond's party?' This was Stella, who had caught them up to walk beside her handsome Canadian cousin.

'Seems we all are.'

'It's not exactly Laura's party,' Steve put in. 'It's for the patients, to try and get them used to being in the community, and for the community to get used to seeing them about.'

'Sister Drummond always did that,' she said. 'They used to come down to the pub and drink with Dad and then she would have to come and fetch them.'

Wayne laughed. 'I remember once she hauled me over the carpet for encouraging them. They didn't need encouraging, I can tell you. It must have been good for you to be looked after so near to home, Steve.'

'It was.'

'Rotten luck, being brought down like that.'

'Yes, rotten luck. That's why they called me "Lucky Wainright", I suppose.' It was said without a hint of a smile, though he had meant it as a joke. Making jokes when you were feeling down in the

361

mouth never worked. He had heard so much about Wayne – how handsome he was, and how charming – and he wanted it not to be true, but unfortunately it was. He caught sight of himself and Wayne in the mirror behind the bar and wished he hadn't. The comparison was odious. And what made him feel worse was the fact that the Canadians were obviously loaded and didn't have to rely on their service pay to survive. Oliver insisted on buying drinks for everyone and Valerie was soon in deep conversation with Joe, who remembered her from years back. Steve spent most of his time talking to Ken but after his second glass of beer, he said he had to be going and went to fetch his coat and cap from the peg. 'I'll see you all tomorrow.'

'Yes, see you tomorrow,' they chorused. He left them to their drinking and walked home alone.

Chapter Thirteen

EVERYTHING WAS READY. The room, with the help of those patients who were convalescing and mobile, had been cleared, the carpet taken up and chairs arranged around the circumference. A platform in one corner held a gramophone and a pile of records; one of the non-dancers was going to man that. There were paper chains hung everywhere and crêpe paper bells Helen had found in a box in the attic. The tree had been dressed with homemade ginger men, little 'pretend' parcels and candles, also salvaged from the box in the attic. It was dressed over all with 'window' – long streamers of tinfoil dropped by the air force to deceive the enemy's radar. The twins had found it draped on bushes on the common, though how it got there, no one knew. The long table in the main dining room was loaded with food, much of it sent in advance by the guests themselves. There was a bar in one corner with a motley collection of bottles: hoarded whisky and gin, port and sherry, and homemade elderberry and apple wine. There was a small barrel of beer provided by Joe, who said he might wander up after the pub closed. Steve brought the farm's contribution and stopped to help.

'That's it,' Laura said, looking round the room. 'Come and have a drink before you go.'

He followed her to the sitting room at the back of the east wing, handy for the kitchen and family dining room, and flopped down into an armchair. She handed him a glass of sherry. 'Did you have a good Christmas?' she asked.

'Yes, very good. How Mum managed it in wartime I don't know, but we had a feast. And Alec being there made it special for the twins and Daphne. What about you?'

'Robby made it for us. He's not quite old enough to understand what it's all about, but he got very excited unwrapping his presents.'

'Did Wayne come up?'

She smiled, understanding him. 'No, why should he? Christmas is for families.'

'Still—'

'Still nothing.' She sat on the arm of his chair. 'Let's get this straight, Steve Wainright. I am not contemplating marriage to Wayne Donovan. Nor ever will.'

His relief was tempered by a little disbelief. 'I watched your face when you saw him in church; you were shocked to see him.'

'Surprised perhaps, not shocked.'

'What did you think of his parents?'

Careful, her inner voice warned her. 'They seem very nice.'

'Pots of money, judging by the way the Major was throwing it about in the pub yesterday.'

'No doubt he is pleased to have his son with him for Christmas, especially as he's been worried about him.'

They were silent for a minute and then Steve said, 'You remember when I was in hospital at Hammersmith? You said you needed your rock and you've said it again since, though you've never explained why.'

'Does there have to be a reason?'

'Yes. You would not have said it for nothing. Now I am fit and well, thanks to you—'

'Not only me.'

'Don't interrupt. I am fit and well and before long I'll be off back to my unit, so tell me what's on your mind while you've got the chance.'

'Nothing now.'

'But there was.'

'Maybe, but I've dealt with it. Everything's fine.'

364

He would have pressed her but Helen appeared at that moment and the conversation turned to the arrangements for the party, and speculation about how many would turn up and if the food would last out. After half an hour Laura gently sent him on his way. 'I have to supervise the men's dressings, give them their medication and make sure those who aren't well enough to come to the party are comfortable away from the noise, and then give Robby his tea and put him to bed. Then I've promised myself a leisurely bath before I dress. I'll see you later.'

She watched him go, wondering why she had not taken the opportunity to unburden herself to him. She had become so used to her role as nurse and comforter, it had become ingrained in her, part of her character, a mask of coolness she had assumed to enable her to carry on. Once she let it fall, she was done for. Steve was doing the same thing to help him to cope with his scars. To him they were prominent, the first thing you saw on looking at him, but she hardly noticed them. His candid blue eyes and firm jaw were his outstanding features and, once you got to know him, his gentle, caring character easily made you forget any slight disfigurement. Why couldn't she let him know how much she loved him? Perhaps she would tonight, if all went well and the opportunity arose.

She set about her tasks with a will. Helen had volunteered to put Robby to bed, so Laura had more time to dress. She knew all the ladies would be trying their best to look glamorous and dresses not worn for years had been made over for the occasion. Helen had given Laura a green silk dress she had found in a wardrobe which no longer fitted her. 'I've put on a bit of weight,' she said. 'I'm sure it will suit you.' It was cut on the bias and fitted closely at the bust and hips and flared out at the hem. Its sleeves were tight to the elbow and then flared to the wrist. Its V-shaped neckline was filled with an imitation emerald necklace she had bought on her recent shopping trip to Attlesham. 'You look lovely,' Helen said, when she twirled to show her. 'I'm very proud of you.'

Impulsively, Laura kissed her. 'And I of you.'

'Go on with you, you'll have me in tears.' Helen hurried off get ready herself, before the tears became reality.

By the time the villagers began to arrive, the patients had set the gramophone going and were enticing the nurses into dancing. There was a lull as new people arrived and made their way into the room, some a little diffidently, until the men, made bold by a little drink and the company of others in like circumstances, dragged them onto the floor. Everyone from Bridge Farm turned up. William and Alec were soon in debate with the recuperating patients about when they thought the second front would begin and where it would be. Someone said he was making a book on it. The choice seemed to be between northern France, probably the Pas de Calais as it was nearest, the south of France, Belgium or Holland, or if they fancied a long shot, Norway.

'Too far by sea,' Alec said. 'They'd never keep it quiet. Same with the south of France. My money's on Calais.'

Laura, standing in the doorway surveying the scene, was relieved that everything seemed to be going so well. She turned to find Wayne behind her. She took a deep breath and adjusted her invisible mask. 'Wayne, I'm glad you managed to come.'

'I very nearly didn't.' He looked around to make sure his parents had gone into the ballroom ahead of him. 'I felt sure you did not intend I should.'

'Of course I did. Why would I not?'

'You met Pop?'

'Yes.'

'Did you say anything about you know what?'

'No.'

'Why not? You want to know the truth, don't you?'

'Wayne, I do know the truth. You have to accept that. And please don't upset your mother over it.'

'How you can be so calm about it, I don't know.'

'No point in getting worked up, is there? It won't change anything.'

'You're a callous, cold-hearted bitch, you know that, don't you?' He had hardly got the words out when someone grabbed his shoulder and hurled him across the floor. Furious, he got up and came forward again, fists raised. Laura put herself between them. 'Please, don't fight. Steve, you misunderstood.'

'Oh no I didn't. I heard what he called you.'

'He's upset. It was nothing. I'll deal with it.'

Valerie, overdressed in a long satin dress in a shade of pink which clashed horribly with her ginger hair, came dashing across to them, followed by Oliver. 'What's going on?'

'Nothing, Mom, a slight disagreement, that's all. Go back to your dance.'

She stood her ground. 'What are you disagreeing about? Has she been two-timing you with this low-down apology for a man?'

Steve, who had been feeling quite cheerful and optimistic up to then, felt himself deflate like a pricked balloon. For a whole year he had lived with the possibility that someone might say something of the sort and wondered how he would deal with it. Now it had happened all he wanted to do was go away and hide, but he couldn't leave Laura when she needed him.

'That's a dreadful, dreadful thing to say,' Laura said, putting a hand on Steve's arm, more worried about the effect on him than the slur on her reputation. 'Take no notice of her, Steve.'

'Val, you say you're sorry for that.' This was Oliver. He turned to Steve, who was standing staring straight ahead, his jaw working. 'She didn't mean that, son.'

By now, Helen had joined them. 'What are you all in a huddle about?'

'This, this—' Valerie spluttered.

'Careful, my dear,' Oliver warned, reaching out to take her arm.

She shook him off and pointed at Laura. 'This bitch has been leading my son on, making him think she cared for him, when all the time she was two-timing him with…' Her bejewelled hand moved round until she was pointing at Steve. '…him.' The music played on.

'Laura has never led him on,' Helen said quietly. 'She wouldn't.' She sounded calm but inside she was seething and worried. 'If you wish to continue enjoying our hospitality, then I suggest you take back those words and rejoin the party.'

Valerie rocked with laughter. 'My God! She sounds just like her father. He was always throwing his orders about. He sacked me, do you know that?'

'No, I did not, but no doubt he had his reasons and it has nothing to do with Laura or your son.'

'No, Mom, it hasn't,' Wayne put in, pulling on her arm. 'Come away. I'll take you home.'

She snatched her arm from his hand. 'I don't want to go home. I'm going to say my piece...' She looked from Helen to Laura and suddenly saw what everyone else had seen for years. 'My God, she's your daughter!' And her raucous laughter filled the room.

Steve simply stared from one to the other, saw how shaken Laura was and reached out to squeeze her hand. Oliver looked from Valerie to Laura, and then to Helen. 'Is this true?'

She faced him defiantly. 'Yes.'

'When? How? Who?'

'I can tell you when,' his wife told him. 'When she was supposed to be with her husband at the end of the last war. I often wondered about that. He was supposed to be in France and then all of a sudden he had leave, but he didn't come here where he belonged, she had to go and join him. That's what we were told. And then she came home alone. Where did you hide the baby, my lady?'

'I was never hidden,' Laura put in. 'And if we are going to discuss this, we had better go somewhere else to do it.'

'I think you should drop the subject,' Wayne said. 'We should not have come. It was bound to end in tears.'

'Whose tears?' his mother demanded.

'Yours, if you are not careful.'

Steve, still holding Laura's hand, remembered his grandmother using those words. He felt a frisson of anxiety on Laura's account.

'Do you want me to ask them to leave?'

'No. Let's have it out.' She looked at Helen. 'Yes?'

'Not here, in front of half the village.'

'No, I should think you would want to hide your shame,' Valerie continued.

Helen did not answer, but walked away in the direction of their sitting room, followed by Steve and Laura. If the others wanted to follow, they could.

Valerie marched after her, which meant that Oliver and Wayne felt obliged to follow. They all stood awkwardly in the room, too uncomfortable to sit down.

Laura turned to them, her face drained of colour, but there was a determined angle to her jaw and a glint in her eyes which could have been steel, but could equally have been caused by tears. 'Well, who's going to start?'

Oliver, who was standing beside his wife, looked worried and confused, his brain ticking over, juggling facts and dates, mulling over things said. Helen's absence when he returned from France; gone to her husband was the story, but she had told him herself only days ago that she had stayed with an aunt and had not seen Richard since he left for France. Richard could not be Laura's father, so who was? And what had it to do with Wayne? The cogs slowly slid into place and the picture became clear. He had to get his wife out of there. And fast. 'Val, my dear, don't you think this has gone far enough?'

'No, I don't. Lady, she calls herself, but she's no better than she should be. She was always looking down her nose at me, when she bothered to look at all; most of the time I was invisible. I was only a chambermaid, fit only to make her bed and empty her slops and when her old man gave me the push I vowed to get even.'

'But, my dear, was that Helen's fault?' He was doing his level best to speak calmly, to be logical and affectionate, and it made him sound as if he were talking to a child. Val hated him for it, when she felt like screaming and shouting and hitting out because her darling son, the child for whom she had sacrificed everything, had been hurt.

'If she had managed to keep her knickers on the Earl would not have decided to get rid of me and anyone else who could point the finger. I guessed she was pregnant even before she did—'

Helen gasped. 'You are making it up—'

'Mom, it doesn't matter,' Wayne said, anxious on her behalf. 'It's not important.'

She ignored him. 'So, where has your precious daughter been all her life?'

'I was adopted,' Laura said. 'By two lovely people who are sadly both dead. Helen and I became reunited and as far as I am concerned that is the end of the story.'

'No, because you got your claws into my son. He's in love with you, God knows why, but I suppose he found out you were a bastard—'

'Love child,' Helen murmured, risking a glance at Oliver. He was looking at her in a strange kind of way, sorrowful, worried and bright at the same time, a sort of 'I'll talk to you later' kind of look. She wasn't sure if she wanted to talk to him.

'Is that so?' Valerie seemed completely oblivious of her husband; her concern was purely for her son. 'Then do Wayne the courtesy of naming your daughter's father.'

'Mom, I know. Leave it, please.'

'You know?' She looked from him to Helen, and then to Laura and finally her husband, who seemed to have been struck dumb. 'Aren't you going to say anything?'

'No.'

'No?' She suddenly realised she had fallen into a pit of her own making and put a hand to her mouth. 'Oh my God, what have I done?' She collapsed into one of the armchairs. 'Why didn't I put two and two together?'

'Pity you didn't,' Helen said coldly. 'Then you might have left well alone.'

'Oh, Wayne,' Valerie wailed, hugging her arms about herself and rocking backwards and forwards, while her tears washed her mascara down her cheeks. 'Me and my big mouth. I am so sorry, son.'

'It's not your fault, Mom, and Laura told me ages ago she was my half-sister.'

Steve stood with his hand in Laura's, unable to believe his ears. It was hard enough to credit that Laura was Helen's daughter, but that she was also Oliver Donovan's took some believing. No wonder she had said she would not marry Wayne. No wonder she needed her rock. His own emotions were in total disarray. His main rival had been ousted, but did it make any difference to the situation between him and Laura? He was still only an apology for a man. Mrs Donovan had only said what was in everyone's mind, but this was no time to speculate on that. Laura needed him. Already tired from the harrowing work she did with burnt airmen like himself and with getting the party ready, the last half hour had exhausted her. He bent his head towards her. 'You've had enough. Let's get out of here.'

'Not yet.' Valerie seemed to have recovered from her bout of weeping and had wiped the mascara from her eyes. 'Wayne, do you still love Laura? Would you marry her if you could?'

'I can't, she's my sister.'

She stood up suddenly. 'No, she isn't. If you want to marry Laura, you can.' She heard Oliver gasp but ignored it. 'This is a night for letting out secrets, so here's another—'

'No!' Oliver shouted. 'I forbid you to say it.'

'How d'you know what I'm going to say?'

'Don't, please, Val. For the love we bear each other, for the love we have for our son, I beg you not to say it.'

'Our son?'

'Yes.' He spoke firmly.

'You would sacrifice Wayne's happiness for your own? Fine father that makes you. I would rather go to hell than let him suffer a single minute of unhappiness. And if he wants Laura—'

'No one has asked me what I want,' Laura put in suddenly because, like everyone else, she had realised where the exchange was leading. 'Brother or not, I have no wish to marry Wayne and I never told him I would. I am not in love with him.'

'You might have come to it,' he said. His face was chalk white, his lips pale and his eyes sunk deep in their sockets. He was hanging on to his hopes and dreams by a thread, but the thread was so fragile it could not support them. He sank into another chair, putting his hands over his face.

'No, Wayne, you have been deluding yourself, and if anything I said or did contributed to that, then I'm sorry.'

He got up suddenly, grabbed his mother by the arm and hauled her to her feet. 'We're going home and you're going to tell me the rest of it, the whole truth. If Pop wants to hear it too, that's up to him.' He dragged her, protesting, towards the door. As he opened it they could hear the sound of music and laughter in the distance.

Oliver opened his arms and let them drop. 'Helen, saying I'm sorry is entirely inadequate, I know, but there it is. If I had known… What can I say? What can I do?'

Helen felt extraordinarily calm. The tensions of the last few days had drained from her. The past had been confronted and overcome. 'To me, nothing,' she said. 'Go to your wife. She needs you. And when she is ready to listen, you might tell her I never looked down on her; she imagined that.'

He turned to Laura. 'You are my daughter. I need to say something about that.'

'Not now,' she said. 'Enough has been said tonight. Another time perhaps, when everyone has calmed down.'

'Yes, you are right. Goodnight. I am sorry your party has been spoilt.'

'I don't know that it has,' Laura said. 'It sounds as if everyone is enjoying themselves.'

Oliver left, shutting the door behind him.

Laura's knees buckled and she leant into Steve, burying her head in his shoulder. He put his arms about her and held her silently, rock steady.

He heard Helen go to the sideboard and the clink of a bottle and glasses. 'Here, give her this.'

Laura lifted her head and looked at Helen. 'You've been through the hoop yourself tonight, more than me. I kept saying to myself "If my mother can stay calm, then so can I," but it was a terrible effort.' She allowed Steve to settle her into a chair and give her the large tot of whisky Helen had poured. She sipped it and coughed. 'It's neat!'

'Do you good.'

She looked up at Steve. 'Thank you.'

'What for?'

'Standing by me.'

He sat on the arm of her chair. 'I'll always do that, you know that.'

She smiled. 'My rock.'

'If you like.'

They were silent for several minutes, each going over the events of the last hour, trying to come to terms with the situation. The secrets were all out now. Helen did not care for herself, but she worried about Laura. 'What do you want to do now?' she asked. 'About the party. Can it go on without us?'

'Hardly,' Laura said, heaving herself to her feet. 'Steve, will you dance with me? If anyone asks where we've been, we can be all mysterious and let them draw their own conclusions.'

He laughed and held out his hand. 'It will be a pleasure and a privilege.' Later he would talk to her, for the moment he would simply enjoy her company.

'I think I'll stay here for a bit,' Helen said. 'You go.'

'You're sure?' Laura asked.

'Yes. I need to gather my wits.'

Steve led Laura back to the ballroom. The music had stopped between dances and as they entered the room everyone turned to face them. Someone started to sing 'For she's a jolly good fellow', and the refrain was taken up by the whole company. Laura had been dry-eyed throughout the encounter with the Donovans but this was enough to make the tears flow. She wiped them away and thanked everyone. 'Go on enjoying yourselves,' she said. 'Make it an evening to remember.'

'It's certainly that,' Steve murmured, taking her into the dance as the strains of *I'll be seeing you in all the old familiar places...* came over the gramophone. He stuck close by her side for the rest of the evening and after they had danced the last waltz together, he remained in the background while she stood at the door and said goodbye to everyone. When the last guest had gone, she turned and kissed him on his scarred cheek. 'Thanks, Steve, thanks for everything. Go home now. I'll see you tomorrow.'

'You'll be all right?'

'Yes, I must do my rounds, making sure this lot are safely tucked in.' She nodded her head towards her patients, who were dispersing to their own rooms. 'Then I'm off to bed. I'm shattered.'

'It's hardly surprising. Goodnight then.' He kissed her gently on her forehead and set off down the drive, wondering what the repercussions of the night's events might be.

Laura wondered too as she went from room to room, from bed to bed, taking the congratulations on a great evening and the teasing about Steve with gentle good humour. She checked that Robby was fast asleep, clutching his new toy dog, and then went downstairs again to make herself a cup of cocoa. Helen was in the kitchen doing the same thing.

'Have they all gone?'

'Yes, and the men are all tucked up.'

With the cocoa made they sat at the table to drink it. 'What a night!' Helen said.

'You can say that again.'

'It's all out now. I suppose it will be all over the village tomorrow.'

'Maybe, maybe not.'

'Do you mind?'

Laura considered. 'Not any more. But what about you?'

'In a way I'm glad it's out. Now there are no more secrets.' She paused. 'Does it mean you'll be leaving here?'

'Oh, Helen, of course not. We decided to brazen it out, remember?' She put a hand out and covered Helen's. 'I loved Mum and I hold her memory dear, but you are my mother and I love you too.'

'Oh, my child.' Helen's eyes were bright with tears. 'How I've longed for you to say that.'

'I think we should go to bed,' Laura said. 'I have a feeling we are going to need our sleep. I don't think it's the end of it by a long chalk.'

Oliver rose the next morning bleary-eyed. He had spent the night on the scratchy horsehair sofa in the living room. It seemed as though his life had been shattered into a thousand little pieces and could never be put together again. Wayne, whom he adored, whom he had brought up as every loving father should, was not his son. Valerie had used him; he had been in the wrong place at the wrong time, an easy target for her. He felt sick. And he felt worse when he realised he did have a child of his own: Laura. Helen had not rejected him; she had waited for him and needed him. If only he had known at the time, he would have beaten down the door of Beckbridge Hall and demanded to be told where she was. He would never have gone to the pub and got drunk, never slept with Valerie, never married her. At that moment he hated her. She had known Helen was pregnant and she hadn't said a word. He had taxed her with it on returning to Beck Cottage the night before.

'Why should I even think of it?' she retorted. She looked a mess; make-up streaked all over her face, eyes red and swollen, ginger hair all awry. 'I had no idea you were her lover. Though I should have guessed, I suppose. You spent enough time with her.'

'That's not why you were sacked, was it?'

'No, stupid, it was because they found out I was pregnant.

Couldn't have someone like me corrupting the morals of the rest of the staff, could they?'

'Who's Wayne's father?'

'What d'you want to know that for?'

'Because I do. Perhaps Wayne does too.'

'No, I don't,' Wayne said. 'I don't want to know anything about the sordid past of either of you. I wish I'd never come to Beckbridge. And I'm leaving at first light.'

'Where are you going?' Valerie wailed, grabbing his arm.

'Back to my unit. I only had a forty-eight hour pass. The war must go on. And if I die in combat, then you won't have to worry about me any more, will you?'

'No, don't say that, Wayne, don't ever say that,' Valerie implored him. 'You are my whole life. I did it for you, to give you a good home. If I'd stayed in England we'd have had a terrible life, scrimping and saving to make ends meet and everyone looking down on us, calling us names. We couldn't have stayed in Beckbridge, so where would we have gone?'

'I don't know. I can't think about it. I'm going to bed.' He had slammed out of the cottage to go to his grandmother's, where he had been sleeping since Ken had returned, leaving Oliver and Valerie facing each other.

'I suppose first chance you get you'll be off to the Hall, making it up with her ladyship,' she said bitterly.

'I don't know what I'm going to do. Now, if you don't mind, I'm going to kip down on the sofa. I'll make up my mind tomorrow.'

Tomorrow had arrived and he got up from his uncomfortable bed and pulled on his clothes. Then he went out to the back scullery, had a quick wash and shave and returned to the kitchen. Joyce was up and cooking breakfast. 'What happened to you last night?' she asked him. 'One minute you were there and the next you had disappeared.'

'Valerie wasn't well.'

'What was the matter with her? She was all right when we set out.'

'Better ask her.'

'You had a row?'

He gave a wry smile. 'And some.'

'Make it up. Life's too short for rows. Go and see if Wayne is up. I'll put an egg in the pan for him.'

He was glad to go. Lily was in her dressing gown clearing out her grate, raking the clinker and ashes onto a sheet of newspaper. 'Wayne up?' he asked.

'He's gone. Said he had to catch the early train. Didn't you know?'

'I knew he was going today, but I didn't realise he'd be off so early. How was he getting to the station?'

'He said he'd walk. He was in a funny mood.'

'He was tired, I expect. We had a late night.'

Oliver went back to Beck Cottage. Joyce and Valerie were sitting at the kitchen table drinking tea. Joyce poured another cup and pushed it silently towards him. He drank it standing up, then reached for his coat and cap. 'When are you coming back?' Valerie called out as he reached the door.

'Don't know. Expect me when you see me.'

'Where did you and Laura get to last night?' Kathy asked Steve. She was in the kitchen cooking breakfast. He had come down as soon as he heard his parents moving about. His father was outside looking after the animals, Alice was the only other person in the room.

'We had some talking to do.'

'Oh, does that mean you and she—'

'No, Mum, it doesn't.' He was weary beyond imagining and he didn't feel like a cross-examination.

'If you're not careful, you'll lose her.'

'I never had her, Mum.'

'It's that Wayne, isn't it?'

'No, it's not.'

'The cat's out of the bag,' Alice said suddenly. 'I knew it as soon

377

as I heard the Donovans had come over.'

He turned sharply towards her. 'What do you know of it, Gran?'

'You tell me.'

'Yes, what's it all about?' his mother asked.

'Laura is Aunt Helen's daughter,' Steve said.

'That doesn't surprise me. When she went away at the end of the last war, she never wrote. I guessed something of the sort.'

'Did you guess who the man was?'

'I put two and two together.' Kathy paused. 'I know it's shocking, Steve, but it was all a long time ago and none of it is Laura's fault. Did she know about it?'

'Aunt Helen told her some time ago. She didn't tell me though.'

'And you think she should have?'

'It would have been nice to know.'

'Don't blame her, Steve, we all have our secrets. You can forgive her for it, can't you?'

'There is nothing to forgive. She's been a brick, an angel. Without her I don't think I could have survived.'

'There you are then. When are you going to propose?'

'Propose? Don't be daft! I can't ask her to marry me. I am an apology for a man.'

Startled by his vehemence, Kathy stopped what she was doing and came to put her hand on his arm. 'Steven, how can you say that? I never heard anything so ridiculous.'

'You would have heard it if you had been standing next to me last night.'

'I don't believe Laura would ever say that.'

'Not Laura, she's far too nice to hurt my feelings; it was someone else, but it doesn't make any difference who said it, it's the truth.'

'It is nothing of the sort. Snap out of it, Steve. There were at least a dozen men at the party last night who look ten times worse than you do.'

'I know. But I have to prove myself to myself, and until I've done that I can't ask anyone to marry me, least of all Laura. And you'll do me a favour by not mentioning it again.'

'Very well, I won't.' And because there was nothing else on the minds of either of them, they let Alice have the last word.

'I knew it would end in tears.'

Laura was kept busy the next morning, clearing up the ballroom after the party and supervising the replacement of the carpet and furniture, and she did not hear Oliver arrive. Helen took him to the sitting room and sat him down. Overnight she had had time to think. What she most wanted, had wanted all through the years, had come to pass: Laura had called her 'mother' and said she loved her. She could not ask for anything more. Expecting anything else would be greedy. And to be honest, whatever she had felt for Oliver had slipped away. She had nurtured it for so long, she hadn't noticed its going. But the revelations last night had left her feeling free, free of its burden, free of secrecy and lies, and it was a wonderful feeling. 'It's a little early, but would you like a drink?' she asked, indicating the bottles on the sideboard, which had been brought there from the party. Most of them were nearly empty.

'No, thank you.'

She sat opposite him. She was, he decided, still a very attractive woman. She was neatly and quietly dressed in a tweed skirt and a twin-set; her hair, which had been so lustrous, was still heavy, though it was grey now. If things had turned out differently she could have been his wife. 'You know,' he said suddenly, 'we might have been celebrating our silver wedding this year.'

'Whatever is the good of talking about what might have been?'

'None, I suppose. I just wanted to say I'm sorry. If I had known about Laura, nothing on earth would have kept me from you.'

'And if I had known you still loved me, I might have tried harder to keep her, though it would be difficult to say how I could have done that. I fought tooth and nail as it was. She was literally dragged out of my arms.'

'Oh, my dear... I don't know what to say.'

'There is nothing you can say. Laura was given a good home and she had a happy childhood, and for that we must both be thankful. I have my daughter and my grandson now. We are a family. And you have your family. Whatever the rights and wrongs of what your wife did, she is still your wife and Wayne is a fine boy. You should be proud of him.'

'I don't think I can ever forgive her. She used me.'

'And as I understand it, you used her too, so go back to her, Oliver, make it up. There's a war on, we might all be called to account before it's done.'

He rose. 'Where is Laura. I'd like to say goodbye to her.'

'She's about somewhere. I'll go and fetch her.' She paused with her hand on the doorknob. 'But please don't go asking for or making promises. Promises have a way of being broken and only lead to heartache.'

He followed as she made her way to the ballroom, where Laura was gathering up paper chains that had come down during the jollity the previous evening. Robby was supposed to be helping her, but he was rolling about in them, laughing. 'Laura, Oliver has come to say goodbye.'

'Oh.' Laura looked at them both. They were both pale and a little tense, but appeared calm. She held out her hand to shake Oliver's, but he took it in both of his and held onto it. 'I'm sorry I wasn't around to see you growing up, Laura, but your mother tells me you had a happy childhood.'

'Yes, I did.'

'I'm glad I met you at last. And young Robby here.' He smiled down at the child and murmured, 'My grandson.'

'You will have others. Wayne—'

'Wayne is not my son.'

'Oh, but he is. I always thought Anne was my mum, and even when I discovered she hadn't given me birth, she was still my mum. I am sure that to Wayne you are still his pop. Don't let anything change that.'

'You aren't going to change your mind about him?'

'No, I won't change my mind. I have been thinking of him as my brother for over a year now and that's how it will stay.'

'Then I wish you all the happiness in the world.' He lifted her hand to his lips and kissed it. 'Goodbye, my child. And when this war is over and we are all back in our proper places, I'll write to you. Will you write back?'

'If you like.' She leant forward and kissed his cheek. 'Good luck.'

He turned and strode away, leaving Helen and Laura facing each other. 'All right?' Laura asked.

'Yes, and you?'

'Fine. Let's get this mess cleared up. And then I must do my rounds.'

It was Ken who told Steve that the Donovans had all left the village. They were enjoying a pint in The Jolly Brewers before Ken returned to the squadron and had been talking about Steve getting back there himself and flying together again. The subject of the Donovans came up when Ken said his mother would feel strange having the house all to herself again; Wayne had gone back to his unit, the Major and Valerie had gone to London, where he had to report for duty, and Stella had gone back to Northampton. He would be the last one to go.

Steve smiled. 'I'll be joining you in no time. Then we'll show old Hitler a thing or two. Have you heard any whispers about the second front?'

'Lord, no! But I reckon it won't be long. When do you go for your medical?'

'Day after tomorrow. I had notification yesterday. I'm going to travel up to London this afternoon and find a hotel for the night.'

'Good luck, then.' They shook hands and parted.

Steve walked home, thinking of the squadron and the men he had known. How many were still there? He had been out of it over a year, but he thought going back would be a piece of cake after the events of the last few days. Momentous didn't cover it. He wondered if Laura and Wayne had seen each other before the Canadian left. Laura had assured him she would not marry Wayne but that was before she knew she could. He thought about going to see her, but decided not to. Everything depended on the verdict of the doctors.

The Central Medical Establishment was situated close to the Middlesex Hospital, and though Steve arrived early, it was already filling up with men waiting their turn and thumbing through the magazines which did nothing to take their minds off the coming interview. Steve joined them and sat in a brown study, wondering if he truly wanted to put himself back in the firing line. He didn't need to; he could ask for his discharge and work on the farm, and even if he stayed in the service there were desk jobs he could do. But the thought of sitting at a desk or in the ops room while Ken and others like him set off on bombing missions without him was enough to stiffen his resolve. How could he prove to himself or anyone else that he wasn't an apology for a man doing that? Valerie Donovan's words had bitten deep, deeper than the scars which he was convinced disfigured his face.

His name was called at last and he was shown into an office where an adjutant looked at his file and asked him if he wanted his discharge. 'No, sir,' he said firmly. 'I want to go back to flying.'

The man looked at him as if he had taken leave of his senses but sent him along the line to be assessed. They were very thorough, taking his blood pressure and a urine sample, testing his lung capacity and his reflexes, examining his ears, nose and throat, testing his eyes, making him grip things with his hands and walk up and down. The Air Commodore at the final interview, which didn't take place until after he had been sent out to find himself some lunch, sat and read his notes and the results of the various tests, then looked up at him cheerfully. 'Want to get back to flying do you, Squadron Leader?' Steve assured him that was all he lived for.

'Then I'll pass you for non-operational flying. You'll have to convince your wing commander you're up to it before you go fully operational.'

It was as much as Steve could hope for, and he knew the big test would come when he climbed into the cockpit and took off for the first time. If he didn't do anything stupid, the fact that they would need all the experienced pilots they could find for the invasion meant he would soon be flying with Ken again. He left to catch the train home with mixed emotions, but predominant among them was the feeling he was being given the opportunity to prove his worth and he would not have to apologise to anyone. The Luftwaffe were bombing London again. The Underground stations were once again filled with people kipping down for the night, huddled in blankets and eiderdowns; suitcases, holding their precious possessions, being used as tables for Thermos flasks and cups. If anything were needed to convince him he was doing the right thing, these stoic Londoners provided it.

Laura met him at Attlesham Station. She was in uniform, holding her cape close around her against the bitter cold. The sight of her bright face set his heart racing.

'What are you doing here?' he asked. 'How did you know which train I'd be on?'

'I called at the farm.' She had not seen him since the dreadful night of the party and had wondered if he was deliberately avoiding her. 'Your mother told me where you'd gone and I guessed which train it would be.' She led the way to the Humber parked in the station yard. 'And before you ask, I did have a legitimate journey to make, so I'm not breaking any rules.'

'Thanks.' He settled himself in the passenger seat.

'How did it go?' she asked, when they were on their way.

'OK. I'm fit to fly non-operational.'

'Thank goodness for that.'

'Oh, you want to get rid of me, do you?'

'No, don't be silly. If I had my way you wouldn't be going at all. I meant thank goodness it's non-operational.'

'Oh, that's only until I've had a little practice and convinced the wingco I'm up to going on ops. That won't take long.'

'When do you go?'

'The day after tomorrow.'

They did not speak again until they were out of the town. 'Steve,' Laura said slowly. 'I want to thank you for the other night and to say how sorry I am you got caught up in it.'

'I did nothing, except lose my temper and precipitate the whole thing. I should be apologising to you.'

'It was coming anyway. As soon as we knew Major Donovan was in the village, we knew something might happen.'

'How you managed to keep quiet about it all this time, I don't know. You could have told me.'

'I was going to, but then you were shot down and it seemed more important to get you well again. I decided I'd tell you the night of the party, if we had a quiet moment together, and then everything happened at once.'

'What happened afterwards? Between you and Wayne, I mean. He was pretty cut up.'

'Nothing. I didn't see him again.'

'Oh.'

'Steve, it makes no difference. I told you I had no intention of marrying him. I meant it when I said it and I mean it now.' She drew up in a field gateway and stopped the car, so that she could turn towards him and concentrate on what she wanted to say. She could not let him go without saying it. 'There is only one man in the whole world I would consider marrying and he doesn't seem inclined to ask me.' She laughed as his face suddenly cleared and his eyes widened. She put her hand up and cupped it round his cheek. 'Steve Wainright, do I have to beg?'

He grabbed her hand from his face and held it with both his own. 'Are you sure?'

'I'm sure of myself, but I'm not so sure about you.'

'But you know why I've been hanging fire. I'm a mess.'

'Oh, you're a mess all right,' she said cheerfully. 'But the mess is in your head. You don't seem to understand that it's the man I love, and if he has a few battle scars, that's part of the man he has become, part of the man that's always been there. I don't even see them, all I see is my rock.'

'Oh, Laura, bless you for that.' He still had hold of her hand and he put it to his lips. 'You know I'm crazy about you, so if I ask you again to marry me, will you say yes?'

'At last,' she said, laughing.

He laughed too. 'Is that yes or no?'

'It's yes, silly.'

'Oh, my darling.' He leant over to take her in his arms and kiss her but it was awkward with the gear lever and the steering wheel getting in the way. They giggled like a couple of schoolchildren, and then, without a word being said, got out of the car and in again – in the back seat. Here, they snuggled up together and Steve kissed her properly for the first time. His previous kisses had been brotherly pecks or a tentative meeting of lips, without pressure and over in a moment, but now all his misery and frustration was kissed away in their first real lover-like embrace. It was some time later they raised their heads to discover the steam on the car windows had frozen. 'We'll freeze to death if we stay here much longer,' she said. 'They'll find two mummified bodies—'

'And wonder why we got in the back instead of driving home to a warm fire.'

'I don't think they'll wonder at all, but it might be a good idea to get going, don't you think?'

'Yes. Let's go and tell the family the good news.'

They spent several minutes scraping ice off the windscreen. 'Do you remember,' he said, his breath coming out in clouds of steam, 'I said I'd take you boating on the Cam when I asked you that question again.'

'I remember, but it's hardly the weather for boating, is it?'

'No, nor for sitting in freezing cars either. Let's get going.'

They finished the journey singing 'Keep the Home Fires Burning' at the tops of their voices. He led her by the hand into the warm kitchen of Bridge Farm where everyone had just finished an evening meal. 'We've got some news for you,' he announced. 'We're going to be married.'

'That's not news,' Daphne said. 'Tell us something we didn't know.'

'You couldn't possibly have known,' he said. 'I've only just asked.'

'Is it our fault you're slow off the mark? We've known which way the wind was blowing for months.'

'Take no notice of her teasing,' Kathy said, coming to kiss them both. 'I'm very happy for you.'

They moved forward to warm themselves at the kitchen range as everyone crowded round with congratulations. 'Does that mean you won't be going back?' Kathy asked when there was a lull in the conversation.

'No, I'm going back. The day after tomorrow. But don't worry, I'm not going to be operational, not for a bit anyway.' He felt a heel saying it, but once she became used to the idea of him being away, she might find it easier to accept he was back in the front line. Besides, there was always the chance that he wouldn't be passed to go on ops; there was no point in worrying her for nothing. He looked over at Laura and saw her slowly nod her head and knew she understood. They had always understood each other. For a moment he was sad thinking of Bob, but Bob had wanted him to look after Laura and he must have known what the outcome would be. Steve felt, somewhere in the ether, his friend was looking down and smiling in satisfaction.

'When's the big day?' Alice asked.

'We haven't decided. We might not—'

'Oh yes we will,' Laura said. 'It'll be the next leave you have. I'm not letting you off the hook.'

'My next leave,' he confirmed. 'Shall I come with you to tell Helen?'

'No, you stay here in the warm. Come up to the Hall tomorrow.' He went with her back to the car, kissed her again and watched the car disappear up the lane before going back indoors. Life was good after all.

In spite of the bitter weather, which seemed as though it would never end, there was a feeling of optimism in the air that spring. You could sense it in the way people went about their business; in the conversation on trains, which seemed to be crowded with troops; in the chatter in pubs, where everyone had something to add to the guessing game. When and where would the second front come? No one knew for sure; the top brass were playing it close to their chests. 'Careless talk costs lives', had been the maxim drummed into them since the outbreak of war. Even Stella, whose factory had switched from making barrage balloons to making rubber inflatable lorries, did not even tell her parents. She and her co-workers had been sworn to secrecy. Not that she could have told anyone what they were intended for; some giant hoax, she supposed.

Oliver, at the Canadian Embassy, pretended he knew nothing; Wayne, down in Hampshire, practised storming beaches – something he had already learnt in Sicily; Ken was bombing the hell out of strategic targets in France and Belgium; the Americans were making daylight bombing missions over German cities. As for Steve, he took to the skies at every opportunity, ferrying aircraft from one airfield to another and delivering top officials to locations for meetings. There was no doubt something was building up and he didn't intend to be a taxi driver for the rest of the war.

'I'm ready to go operational,' he told his wing commander the day he discovered his replacement leading the squadron had finished his tour of duty. 'I'll do anything, just give me a chance.'

'Right. You'll take over the squadron tonight. Briefing at six o'clock.'

The task they were given, he discovered that evening, was to drop arms and ammunition to the Resistance in France. The dropping zones would be marked briefly and they would need to be accurate, so it would be in low and quick, and then out again.

'It makes a change from dropping bombs,' Ken said, as they made their way to their aircraft.

'Looks like they're being readied to join in the party. It can't be long now.'

Two weeks later, after he had been backwards and forwards almost every night, with a different destination each time, he was given forty-eight hours' leave. 'Make the most of it,' he was told. 'You might not have any more for some time.'

He almost ran to the mess and put a call through to Beckbridge Hall. 'Get a special licence, sweetheart,' he told Laura. 'I'm coming home next weekend.'

In the weeks since Steve had left, Laura had made what arrangements she could in advance. She had chosen her dress – not a white one this time, but pale blue. It was made from a ball gown of Helen's. Helen never threw anything away and, as there was ample room in the huge house to store things she no longer needed, Laura had several to choose from. Jenny, Meg and Daphne had agreed to be bridesmaids and Robby would be a page boy. Kathy had made her a cake; Laura suspected Joyce had let her have more than her ration of dried fruit.

There were last-minute things to arrange, of course, like the buffet reception and the flowers. Having organised it all, there was nothing for Laura to do but wait for the weekend and meet Steve's train. It was then she worked herself into a panic. The other wedding day, the one she had schooled herself not to think about, kept coming back into her mind. At first she felt as if she were betraying Bob, but then she remembered his loving letter, telling her to be happy, and hadn't Steve said Bob had asked him to look after her? He would approve. It was not that which worried her, but the terrible thought that something might happen to Steve at the last minute. She was never more relieved than when she saw him step from the train.

'Steve!' She ran all the way along the platform and hurled herself into his arms. 'Thank God!'

He rocked against the onslaught. 'What's the matter?'

'Nothing now.'

He understood. 'I'm here, darling. It's all right. I don't have to go back until Monday morning. And by then...' He stopped to kiss her, in front of everyone scurrying off and on trains, who smiled indulgently. '...you will be Mrs Wainright. That's if you haven't changed your mind.'

She punched his arm. 'No chance of that, you're well and truly hooked, Squadron Leader.'

The whole village had learnt about the wedding, and if they were not to be invited to the reception, they certainly intended to be at the church; it was packed to the doors. Lenny and Donny were kept busy acting as ushers, grown-up now in long trousers, grammar school blazers and their hair slicked down; butter wouldn't have melted in their mouths. Robby was over-excited and not at all sure of his role, so Helen, who was giving the bride away, held tight onto his hand. Steve, in uniform, with Ken beside him, turned as Laura came down the aisle towards him, and he didn't think she had ever looked lovelier. If he had had any doubts about people staring at him and wondering how a beautiful girl like Laura could fancy a man like him, his mother had nagged them out of him. 'You are as handsome as the next man, so just be yourself. And you won't be the only one who's been in the wars, Laura tells me that every patient who's fit enough to dress and get to the church, will be in the congregation. You will give them hope, don't you see?'

He did see; they were looking at him now, and every one of them was smiling. Several gave him a thumbs up sign. As Laura reached his side, he felt for her hand and the service began.

Afterwards, they stood outside the church in the first really balmy day of the year and received the good wishes and congratulations of everyone, and then it was back to the Hall for the wedding breakfast. In the middle of it, someone asked her where they were going for their honeymoon.

'I think that will have to wait,' she said.

'Oh no,' Steve put in. 'We're off in the Humber tonight, and don't ask where the petrol is coming from.'

'Where are we going?'

'That's a secret too.'

He had booked a room at the University Arms in Cambridge. They had stayed so long at the reception, they didn't arrive until late, but that didn't matter. They went straight to their room, drank champagne, made love, slept a little, made love again, had breakfast in bed and then made love a third time. It was better than either had dared to hope for.

'We can't stay here all day,' Laura said dreamily.

'Don't see why we can't, but if you think we should show ourselves to the world, then I've got something else planned.'

She sat up. 'What? Where are we going?'

Steve tapped the side of his nose and got out of bed. He tied on a robe and went into the bathroom. When he came back he was tempted to begin making love to Laura all over again, but he was exhausted and sated and he didn't think he could manage it, not before lunchtime anyway. 'Go and get dressed, sweetheart. Wear something casual. Slacks and a jumper, it might be a bit cool.'

She guessed they were going on the river and her guess proved correct. He rowed them up to the spot where they had picnicked before. They didn't talk much, there was no need to, but they looked at each other a lot and smiled and kissed. It was blissful. They returned to the hotel in time for tea and then drove back to Beckbridge. She saw him off on the train that evening.

He had hardly got back to his station when all leave was cancelled and travelling was restricted. Steve, who flew over them regularly, was aware that all roads leading south were clogged with military traffic. From The Wash to Land's End, everything was on the move; weapons, ammunition, stores, medical equipment and men. Troops practised what they were expected to do without knowing where they were going to do it; paratroopers and gliders were prepared and ships were gathering in their thousands all along the Channel coasts. But still no one knew their final destination.

On Sunday the fourth of June, the United States troops entered Rome, and on the fifth, the twins were woken by the sound of aeroplanes going over. They droned on and on and Donny scrambled out of bed to draw the curtains and look at them. 'Lenny! Come and see. There's hundreds of them. Thousands.'

Lenny joined him at the window. The sky was black with aircraft. No sooner had one lot gone over than another appeared. 'Cor! It's the invasion.'

They were not the only ones to come to that conclusion. William and Kathy were also awake and at their bedroom window. 'Please God, look after them all,' Kathy murmured. 'And especially our boy.' She turned to William and laid her head on his shoulder.

He put his arm about her. 'He'll be all right, love.'

'Yes, I know he will. He's already done as much as anyone could ask of him and been through so much, God won't ask more of him.'

He hugged her against him, wishing he could have her simple faith. 'Let's go back to bed.'

She turned towards him. 'William, I do love you. I know I don't say it as often as I should, but I've never regretted marrying you.'

He kissed her fondly. 'I know. And I love you.'

They climbed back into bed and lay in each other's arms, listening to the drone of the aircraft until they fell asleep.

Laura and Helen and just about every patient who could get to his feet were at the windows of the Hall. The men were cheering as wave after wave of aircraft went over them. Robby had been woken by the noise and Laura held him in her arms as she watched. Steve was up there somewhere. She worried about him, of course, but she could not help being thrilled by it all. He would come through, she knew it. Robby, his face uplifted to the heavens, pointed a finger. 'Daddy.'

'Yes,' she said. 'Daddy's up there.' Bob would look after Steve for her and one day, when Robby was able to distinguish one daddy from the other, she would explain everything to him. He would never be kept in ignorance. Keeping secrets could lead to so much unhappiness. But it was over now, her own personal battles had been won, and when the war was over she and Steve would decide where they would live, but for now Beckbridge Hall was home. 'Come on, little one,' she said. 'Back to bed with you. No doubt we'll hear all about it on the news in the morning.'

Daphne was up before anyone to do the early milking. There had been a lot of activity in the sky during the night and she wondered if the second front had started. If it had, ten to one Alec would be involved. She prayed for his safety, as she prayed for the safety of everyone involved in this war. She couldn't wait for it to be over so she and Alec and the twins could settle down as a family. They had made such plans, and it was the prospect of these coming to fruition that kept her going.

Alec, a few miles off the Normandy coast, had never seen so many ships together at one time. There were thousands of them, of every shape and size: battleships; cruisers; destroyers; command ships; troopships loaded with men; landing craft, so low in the water they were swamped with every wave. The seas were mountainous. The assault had already been put off by a day because of bad weather, but now, in the hours before dawn on the sixth, it was going ahead. He felt sorry for the men in the little flat-bottomed boats who would be the first ashore; they were probably wondering if they would even get that far. And the troops on the larger ships were hardly better off; they would have to scramble down nets into boats for landing, or be lowered on davits. To men not used to it, that would be hazardous in itself, even before they reached the beach with its mines and deadly obstacles. At any rate, he and his gunners would give them as much covering fire as they could. Already the guns were red hot and their crews were hosing them down with sea water to keep them cool.

Wayne watched the shore of Normandy coming closer and looked round at the men beside him. Nearly all of them had been seasick and were longing to get off that craft onto dry land, even if it was bristling with Germans. He should have gone back to Italy after his leave, but somehow had found himself drafted with the invasion force. No ship or aircraft to take him, he supposed; they were all here, the greatest invasion fleet ever assembled. There would be five separate assaults on five stretches of beach; two American to the west, and one Canadian sandwiched between two British on the east, each with their own objectives, the most important of which was to fight their way off the beaches where they were vulnerable and get inland. Paratroopers and gliders had dropped behind the lines the night before to secure certain roads and bridges for them, though he did not know how successful they had been. Ahead of him on the beach, a whole armada of strange tanks cleared a path. There were tanks that could swim, which were being offloaded before they even reached the beach; there were tanks with chain flails that beat the ground in front of them and detonated mines, there were tanks that rolled out a carpet of lathes, which made a firm base on which others could follow. He had been involved in getting those ready and now he would see how effective they were.

To take his mind off his queasy stomach and the noise of battle ahead of him, Wayne thought of his parents. He had done a lot of that lately. Mom had done what she had for his sake, so that he could have a happy childhood, free of want and one where he would not be stigmatised for being illegitimate. He should not have been so angry with her. As for Pop, he had been the best father a boy could wish for. He had met him in London just before all leave had been cancelled and they had had a long talk. Pop had said he had forgiven Mom and they were going to stay together, and that was the best news Wayne could have had. He didn't want to know who his real father was. All he had wanted to know was if the man had been married and would he inadvertently find himself with another sister. 'No, son,' Mom had told him. 'He was single and he died in the war.'

While the battle raged on the beach and he stood waiting to take his turn to go, Wayne thought of home and Canada, and the life he had led before the war and would, please God, one day lead again. He thought of his friends, his school and his co-workers at the garage, of Jean Carlton, the girl he had been dating before enlisting. He hadn't thought of her for ages, but an image of her came unbidden into his head. Dressed in a plain cotton frock, her hair blowing all over the place, her piquant face was looking up into his, laughing because he had kissed her. Now, what he wanted most in all the world was to go back to her and do it again.

The craft suddenly lurched as it hit the shore; the ramp was put down and the whole boatload of men, weighed down by their equipment, surged ashore, urged on by the sound of a bugle. This was it; this was the beginning of the end and he was going to survive to go back home.

Steve, returning from a bombing mission in support of the troops, flew over the invasion force and could not help gasping at the size of it. From the air it looked like another Dunkirk, except everything was going in the opposite direction and there was a lot more of it. And, thankfully, the only enemy aircraft he had seen were two lone fighter planes. The pilots were either crazy or very brave because they zoomed down towards the men on the beaches and emptied their magazines, and though everything from ships' guns to Sten guns were aimed at them, they had managed to reach the safety of the clouds and had disappeared. Steve flew back to base and touched down, his day's work done, though he knew he would be up again the next day and probably the one after that. His first thought was for Laura, but before he could let her know he was safe, he had to go for debriefing.

'This is the news, and this is John Snagge reading it.' The voice, in its usual authoritative, unemotional tone, came over the airwaves at nine-thirty that morning. Almost everyone in Britain must have had their ears glued to a set somewhere. It was certainly true of those in the south, who had woken up that morning to find the army camps which had sprouted up all over their woods and fields in the last few months were empty and deserted. It was also true of the inhabitants of East Anglia, surrounded as they were by air force stations, whose aircraft had almost blotted out the moon the night before last. 'D-Day has come. Early this morning, the Allies began the assault on the north-western face of Hitler's European fortress.' The bulletin went on with a report of the first landings, the organisation and preparation involved in the undertaking, and added that the weather had not been favourable: cold and cloudy with rough seas. Nothing was said of casualties, though every one of John Snagge's listeners must have known they would be considerable.

Joyce heard it in the post office, just before she set out to deliver the mail on her bicycle. By the time she had finished her round, no one was in any doubt that the second front had begun. Many were already out on the streets, waving flags. They knew it was not the end, that there would be more setbacks and casualties before the war was over, but it was what they had been waiting to hear for so long. When the church bells began ringing, they were not a bit surprised and left off doing whatever it was they had been working at and made their way down to the church, where the minister conducted a short service of thanksgiving and prayer.

Steve had a job getting through to Beckbridge on the telephone but he persevered and was rewarded with the sound of Laura's voice at the other end of the line. 'Sweetheart, I'm OK. How are you?'

'I'm fine, absolutely fine.'

'Have you heard the news?'

'Yes. It's wonderful, isn't it? I've got some for you too.' She paused. 'I'm going to have a baby.' She heard his joyful shout at the other end and smiled.

'Look after yourself,' he said. 'I'll get home to you just as soon as I can and we'll celebrate.'

Laura chuckled to herself as she put the phone down and set off for church with Robby in his pushchair. She had more than most to give thanks for.

Epilogue

8th May 1945

It was over. The dreadful carnage in Europe had come to an end and the whole country had gone wild. People crowded onto the streets in great multitudes, cheering, dancing and singing, waving flags, climbing lamp posts, piling onto whatever vehicles were trying to make their way through the throngs that spilled onto the roads. The sound of church bells, whistles and hooters added to the noise. Flags were brought out from wherever they had been stored and were hung on public buildings and draped over the upper window sills of private houses. Half the people on the streets had a small Union Jack in their hands and others sported red, white and blue ribbons in their hair.

The people of Beckbridge rejoiced with everyone else and gave thanks that so many of its inhabitants had come through alive, if not exactly unscathed. Steve and Ken, Wayne and Ian were all safe. There were those who mourned the loss of dear ones, and for them the day was tinged with sadness, and Laura, in thankfulness, uttered a prayer for Bob and all those who had lost their lives on both sides.

The last year had not been plain sailing. Hitler had taken longer to defeat than anyone had expected. After the D-Day landings the previous June, many had predicted the war would be over by Christmas, but it had dragged on. Hitler still had one or two surprises up his sleeve. The pilotless flying bombs, or doodlebugs as many called them, had terrified the population of the south-east, if only because of their unpredictability and the damage they caused, and these had been followed by the even more unpredictable V2 rockets. It was like the Blitz all over again, made worse in a way because the missiles had no specific targets. And just before Christmas the Germans had counter-attacked and held up the advance. Steve was in the air constantly bombing German cities and strategic targets; Laura had lived on a knife-edge until she knew he had landed safely on home soil.

How he had managed to get leave, today of all days, she did not know, but here he was, home safe and sound, sitting beside her on the sofa listening to Winston Churchill on the wireless, telling them they could allow themselves a brief period of rejoicing before getting on with the task of beating Japan. Helen sat knitting on a chair on the other side of the hearth, while four-year-old Robby played with his wooden bricks on the floor at her feet, unaware of the tumultuous events that were taking place around him. Thomas, three months old, lay contentedly in his father's arms. Steve kept looking down at him, a silly grin on his face. He could not help it; he just could not stop smiling. This child of his was so perfect, so adorable, with his mop of fair hair, rosy cheeks and bright blue eyes, shut now in sleep.

'I pray he will never have to live through what we have lived through,' he said, putting his arm about Laura's shoulders and drawing her to him. 'It must never happen again.'

'Amen to that,' she said. 'We must see that it doesn't.'

'What will you do?' Helen asked. It was a question that had been bothering her for some time. Would they leave her? Would she be left as she was after the Great War to struggle alone with the upkeep of the Hall? For the moment, it was still needed as a convalescent home and would be for many months, but after the airmen had all gone and the Air Ministry handed it back to her, what then? Its role as a private residence was long gone.

Laura, who knew perfectly well what was in Helen's mind,

hastened to reassure her they would stay at the Hall until Helen, herself, decided what she wanted to do.

'And I would like to go on flying,' Steve said. 'Civilian pilots will be needed in peacetime. I have a feeling aeroplanes will be the transport of the future.'

'We thought that about the motor car after the last war,' Helen said with a laugh. 'But what about you, Laura? Will you mind that?'

'No. At least he won't risk being shot out of the sky, will he? And I want him to do what makes him happy.' She smiled and put her hand over Steve's as it cradled their son. Robby, seeing that, ran over and pushed his way up between them, so that all four were closely entwined. Helen ran and fetched her camera. 'This must be recorded for posterity,' she said. 'The day the war ended and the family is all together again.'

'Then put the delay on it and join us,' Steve said.

And so it was that in pride of place in the family album was a snapshot of Helen with her daughter and son-in-law and two grandchildren – something she had not even dared to dream of on that long ago day when her daughter had been taken from her. The future might be fraught with difficulties – a country did not get over a gruelling war without problems – but while she had her family, she would never cease to give thanks.